Penguin Books
As If By Magic

Angus Wilson was born in England in 1913. A South African
childhood was followed by education at Westminster School and three
years at Oxford. He joined the staff of the British Museum Library
in 1936. During the Second World War he worked in the Foreign
Office, but after the war he returned to the British Museum and became
Deputy Superintendent of the Reading Room. In 1955 he resigned
from the Museum, and since 1963 he has been associated with the
new University of East Anglia, where he is now Professor of English
Literature. He lives in the country but has travelled in the past ten years
to most parts of the world.

His first volume of short stories, *The Wrong Set*, was published when
he was thirty-five; this met with immense critical acclaim, and was
followed a year later by a second collection, *Such Darling Dodos*.
In 1952 his short critical study, *Emile Zola*, was published, and this was
followed in 1952 by his first novel, *Hemlock and After*. In 1953 he
published *For Whom the Cloche Tolls*, *A Scrapbook of the Twenties*,
and his play, *The Mulberry Bush*, was first produced in 1955.
A Bit Off the Map, short stories, was published in 1957; *Anglo-Saxon
Attitudes*, a novel (1956); *The Middle Age of Mrs. Eliot*, a novel (1958);
The Old Men at the Zoo, a novel (1961); *The Wild Garden*, a critical
autobiographical study (1963); *Late Call*, a novel (1964); *No Laughing
Matter*, a novel (1967); *The World of Charles Dicken*s (1970), and
As If By Magic (1973), his latest novel. Many of his books are
published in Penguins.

Angus Wilson

As If By Magic

Penguin Books

Penguin Books Ltd,
Harmondsworth, Middlesex, England
Penguin Books, 625 Madison Avenue,
New York, New York 10022, U.S.A.
Penguin Books Australia Ltd, Ringwood,
Victoria, Australia
Penguin Books Canada Ltd, 41 Steelcase Road West,
Markham, Ontario, Canada
Penguin Books (N.Z.) Ltd, 182–190 Wairau Road,
Auckland 10, New Zealand

First published by Martin Secker & Warburg 1973

Published in Penguin Books 1976
Reprinted 1976

Copyright © Angus Wilson, 1973

Made and printed in Great Britain by
Hazell Watson & Viney Ltd,
Aylesbury, Bucks
Set in Linotype Granjon

For Nicholas and Pamela Brooke

Book One

Departure from Home

Wisps of fog had collected high up against the ceiling of the hall. You could see them interweaving, swirling like smoke rings, grey and brown, around the electric light bulbs that hung so nakedly over the heads, the something too few heads of the audience.

The vicar had placed himself in a corner at the end of a row, obscurely as he hoped, so that the audience should not seek to measure its appreciation of the performances by his facial expression; though he would, of course, lead in laughter if required (unlikely? the Absurd? who could say these days? But not the Cruel. He must draw the line at bearbaiting. Where the refined met the primitive was the Devil's land). He gazed upward, with folded arms, and saw some mysterious fitness in the floats of fog.

Gas-lighting, he found himself thinking, would have been more appropriate. The Church Hall. The Institute. Good Faces seeking earnestly as the Wonders of the Great World Around Us, God's Purpose clear whether in desert or jungle, flickered for a moment and then clicked into place on the white-sheet screen. Hands, rough with honest labour, groped after knowledge. Lips formed the letters silently that they had learned so laboriously, yet so lovingly, by oil lamp, after the long day's work was done. Coming in from a thick pea-souper, a London partickler, with what eager ...

He cut the image very short, unfolded his arms and sat up straight. That a few wisps of fog should so carry him away to sentimentalize over a Victorian world of gas-lit institutes and self-improvement, dead and gone long before he had been born! To sentimentalize about fog when the one thing, above all, that the Church today was doing, leading indeed, was in the dispersal of fog in racial questions, in the fight against poverty and hunger and bad housing!

Magic-lantern Wonders of the World when today everyone saw for him or herself: parishioners who talked of the Seychelles and not Seaford; who delayed him with accounts of hearing their first muezzin; and even he, the poor parish priest, by the invitation of old friends, with a winter fortnight in the Algarve to look forward to! Yet there are few thoughts that do not have some foundation, fulfil some useful purpose in our minds. So, leaving aside any momentary nostalgia for Victorian days – 'and ordered their estate', not to speak of the Singhalese labelled as vile! – perhaps the attraction of the fog did have some meaning.

These young people, for example, who had just given them all those wild disordered lights – beautiful up to a point, but going on, he was afraid, far too long for this audience – now about to present this mime; wasn't it a healing, soothing fog or, at least, mist, that they were after? With all this craving for ecstasy, and sheer experience – if the coloured lights had lasted longer perhaps, well just as well not, such of the audience as he knew, the few regular churchgoers, would have made embarrassing dervishes! Perhaps the bright light of reason, no, he wouldn't admit of reason, but, say, of science had shone with too hard clarity for too long. Science that should have been a handmaid. A robot world! Encased in their hideous steel he saw the monsters stumbling blindly forwards. Could it be the age of the Daleks again? 'Dr Who!', the young Scots voice familiar from the screen sounded in his ear. And then – 'THE HUMAN RACE MUST BE DESTROYED. THE HUMAN RACE MUST BE DESTROYED.' He shuddered involuntarily for a world devoid of Christian humanism.

The Daleks indeed! Nevertheless, the young people had something in their Luddism. How easily one fell into using these modish words! – he who had but the vaguest idea of where or when the Luddites. Without mystery, our faith is nothing. Not by works alone. But *true* mystery, the *great* mysteries were never obscurantist, never foggy. The words of Saint John of the Cross burned through the soul with the clear Light of Love. A light that I have never been quite able to face. He flushed at this thought, forcing it with a struggle back into its cage where only at long intervals was its desolate whimper heard to render life waste. He closed his eyes, summoning Keeper Humour and

Keeper Self-Mockery to his aid. And as always they exorcised the lean last hungry thought. He laughed at the posh Sunday-paper image he was making of himself: the clergyman wondering whether he could bring the young people in if he donned a loin-cloth. His well-being restored, he opened his eyes as loud thumpings announced the start of the mime.

It was just as well that the whiskered young chap had insisted on removing the platform stage, tiresome though the whole business had proved and upset though Mr Carter had been at what he seemed to feel an insult to his caretaking. At this rate they would have gone through the boards. What a thumping! But then, as one of the young women had told him, the last thing they aimed at was professionalism. There they were – twelve indistinguishable young people in grey cotton tights. One could see now what unisex meant. But perhaps that was part of the point too. 'Batteries'. Caponed broilers, no doubt. Well if it was parables they were offering, a parson ought not to miss their meaning. But then his eye caught sight of something grotesque peering in at him through the frost-patterned fog-shrouded windows – three? four? five? eyes and some white blobs. Visitors from another world they must be, coming out of the yellow horror. Then all but two eyes were gone, and one of those slowly winked. But, against the white blob, the deliberate wink seemed not to mock but to ask for pity. And then all were gone. Children, of course, poor children out there in the bitter cold and fog. Waifs and carols, Barnardo boys, Tiny Tim, collecting-tins – and he with no cast-offs or steaming turkey – 'fails my step I know not how, I can go no longer'. But what nonsense! Just well-fed, well-educated boys from the Cooper estate drawn by the mystery of these thumping antics offered by their hippie elders; but not betters, for in ten years' time the same urchins might be grant-aided students offering whatever the young might offer in ten years' time. But laughing now no doubt at the loonies much as healthy ten-year-olds had laughed at anything odd or unintelligible in the days of Dickens or of General Booth.

And, indeed, Paul Latter, Hosein Fawzi and Charlie Webster, pressing their noses flat against the steamy window-panes of the hall, had watched the assemblage of mummers with silent wonder; but had greeted the first movement of the mime with loud, delighted cries – guffaws of pleasure and ridicule, until Mr Sarson, late arrival and founder member of the Over-Sixties Club, had driven them off with a shout of 'Get out of it, you little buggers!' Only Charlie Webster had realized that the mime meant something, that the loonies were poultry. In his delight at this surprising unknown power of interpretation in himself, he winked through the window at the vicar, then ran off triumphantly shouting, 'Chicken! Chicken!'

Five years before, Leslie, driven beyond his endurance, had written on their lavatory wall – 'Hamo Langmuir likes chicken.' They had had an almighty row, for Hamo was well aware how Leslie knew that he did not like chicken in the age of that word as used by the world at large (or rather by the relevant part of it). The injustice of the charge, its echo of common and detestable prejudice, goaded him to fury. 'Chicken-loving is a monstrosity,' he had cried. And, 'Youth-loving, of course, is honourable and Spartan and so on,' Leslie had mocked. But he had kissed him. Reconciled momentarily, they spent half an hour of loving and shared laughter, scrubbing, not wholly successfully, the indelible purple scrawl on the white wall. Yet only a fortnight later they had finally split up and had left the Islington house for good.

All around London, from the Church Hall in the south-east to the Rapson Institute in the north-west, damp white mist clung to the great stretches of clayey soil where houses lay crumbling or crumbled, where gardens lay wasted, and allotments turned to wilderness in order that great office blocks and throughways and car parks might take their places. Large floating clouds and swirls and wisps of this mist danced and dodged about among the motor-cars of those for whom the changes were intended – making it hard to distinguish the way to work from the way to home.

But the white mist lay thick, too, upon the old allotments and fields as yet untouched, thicker, some thought, than upon things to come. It lay heavy even upon the Institute's trial fields, so that it would have taken any visitor who had come by the outer door into the glass houses (but no visitor could) some minutes to observe that the boxes upon boxes of cauliflowers before him were not just visual distortions due to the mist. Some had white heads, pinlike, scarcely to be seen in the jungle luxuriance of the gross, fatty leaves; others were vast powdered wigs beneath which only a magnifying glass could have revealed two stubby leaves like little crippled thumbs. And on, into another great glassed house, where box after box of antirrhinums offered now huge lips that threw proportion into limbo as do the artificially extended lips of some negresses in Central Africa; and then, as perhaps only among Venusians or the inhabitants of Andromeda, showed only the overhanging petal and no lips at all, mouthless velvet creatures. In an ever-changing range of colour from deepest red to deathliest white, through apoplexy, blood, blush, pallor and anaemia, *pentstemon agate* showed her controlled rage, with here and there, specially ticketed, a flower that had exactly divided its petals into deepest red and clearest white. But now, it grew warmer, and in the temperate air bougainvillaea tumbled its magenta streams as in any respectable Edwardian greenhouse, but the admired, showy, colourful bracts were vestigial, and the modest, usually unnoticed cruciform, cream-coloured flower petals were monstrous and bold – modest housewife and flaunting mistress swopping roles. At last, in a final room, the air was nearly as misty as outside, but lacking the graveyard cold of London's winter clay – hot and steamy. Here, overhead, nodded great scarlet and apricot hibiscus blooms, as in the Singapore or Peradeniya Botanic Gardens, but their leaves were chequered mosaic from chessboard green and yellow through harlequin and back once more to the boldest jade and the lightest lemon. An endless riotous, profligate chimera world; a Paradise garden of controlled monsters.

Beyond the glasshouses, but framed in hibiscus vine, stood two men, the very tall one in well-tailored tweeds, the shorter wearing a laboratory white coat. They stood in front of the gleaming white of a super-speed preparative ultracentrifuge of precise temperature control. But their conversation seemed disagreeably overheated.

'This is ridiculous, Hamo,' Nelson Hart said. He looked up from his stocky sturdiness to the small moustached head at the top of the long, absurdly swaying stalk. 'I can well understand your aversion to meeting all these admin people, but to dismiss the value of field observation entirely to fit in with your distaste isn't good enough. You've only to take classic cases. You yourself in your original paper on the photosynthetic properties of "Magic" wrote of the value of those field observations from Java on the relative respiratory activities of Jhona 20 and Jhona 227 during hours of illumination. You called it a moment of breakthrough.'

'Hardly.'

'No, those *words* were Sir Alec's in his annual report. I apologise. But take Wilkinson's work on the carbohydrate properties of small tillers. It was a field report of the effect of a chance preservation of what had been thought parasitic waste ... Or again, it was only in complex populations that analysis of yield and quantitative traits revealed how additive gene-action predominated. If we'd stuck to hybrids we could only have observed epistatic-type gene-action.'

'Please spare me any more classic cases, Nelson. I have already told you that I accept the Director's decision that I am holding up our work on *pennisetum typhoides*. I think it is allowed that, in the restructuring, I have contributed to a high-fertility crop and an increase in protein content. The poor resistance to fungus disease is, as you rightly say, in the main your concern, as the team's physiologist. You have felt my presence an increasing hindrance. If I dispute this, I only hinder you further. The Board has been good enough to send me on a world inspection tour both of plant genetic centres and of selected agricultural schemes. A well-intentioned alibi for the failure of a reasonably eminent plant breeder. I am grateful for their courtesy. And I shall, of course, carry out their instructions carefully. But I had thought that our long association, even despite its recent souring, might have allowed me, in talking with you, to dispense with any pretence at liking for this V.I.P. world inspection. And now, may I come to the point for which I sought you out? I had forgotten to give you these tables of variability of protein and lysine content. They appear to be somewhat relevant to mutational manipulation. I should particularly draw your attention to 9066, 9078, 9079, and D.118 – the figures for lysine per 100 gram flour against lysine per 100 gram protein. I think them relevant. But that, of course, is your affair.'

'It is really. But thank you. When do you leave?'

'I should be gone now.'

'Well, good-bye, Hamo. And, perhaps, you'll return to take over from Sir Alec.'

'I don't find that funny. I'm not being kicked upstairs, you know. When I have basked in the glories of what I have done for the world of rice, I shall survey the sorghum field and return with propositions for restructuring, over which we shall no doubt again quarrel.'

'A bloody cheerful cyclical view of history.'

'I have never pretended to optimism. That's why your fears that I shall be shocked by the social conditions of Asia seemed to me so peculiarly unpenetrating.'

'I was giving you credit for humanity.'

'Oh, I shouldn't do that. However, I am optimistic enough to hope that I may return to find Sir Alec retired, though not to take his place.'

'If that famous "soccer knee" plays him up any further, we may be lucky enough ...'

'Ah, Langmuir. There you are.' The hearty Scots accents of their Director startled them both. Nelson Hart looked grimly social; Hamo Lagmuir coldly polite. 'I'm interrupting a fond farewell.'

'We were talking of your old "soccer knee",' said Nelson with only a pretence of commiseration.

'Oh, really?' You're neither of you great games players, I believe,' Sir Alec commented.

And Hamo said, 'I think not.'

'You forgot these letters, Langmuir. For Professor Hakadura at the Tokyo Institute. There's a strange little chap for you, but a brilliant man. Oh, you'll like the sheer cleverness of the Japanese. For the rice people at Los Baños, you'll get the letters in San Francisco. It'll be, in the main, Americans there. I believe Fuggersheim's working now on a derivative of 188. Give him my regards. Intellectually an American's impressive, and a Jew's outstanding, but an American Jew's the salt of the earth. Here's your letter for Darwin. I envy you your visit there. It's a wide-open space and an outdoor life. And all the chances in the world open to you. If I had a young man with a real turn of genius, say you Hart, as you seemed when you first came to us, I'd give him the chance of Australia. Now here's a letter for Doctor Fung in K.L. His best work's done, but it was fine work. He'll talk a lot against his Malayan colleagues to you, but don't take too much notice. Of course the Chinese are ahead intellectually – a wonderful race – but the Malays are coming along, coming along. Two letters for Ceylon: Subramanian's a Tamil, a fine, courteous, accomplished cytogeneticist of the old school; Abbegurewadena's a young chap, and like all Singhalese a bit happy-go-lucky, but with a streak of real brilliance. They'll talk agin each other, but it's more talk than do, you'll find in these countries. Your Indian contacts, of course, you have, but don't be too ready to believe all these stories about the educated Indian mind. You know the babu stories.'

'I'm afraid I don't.'

'No? Oh, well, they're told. But it's a canard as the French say. The best Indian mind, for all its generalizing, has a remarkable grasp of detail. For Karachi ... but that's the second leg of your journey, your sorghum research begins there. I'll send all the letters for Pakistan and Africa to reach you in Delhi. You'll be a seasoned traveller by then. I hope what I say appeals to you?'

'You have a rosy view of foreign parts certainly.'

'Oh, you'll like the red carpets they lay out for you well enough when the time comes.'

'You mustn't forget my humble position. You speak from your experience as Director of the Institute, a Fellow of the Royal Society and so on.'

'What? Langmuir, the leader of the team who gave the wheatlands "Glorious". Langmuir, who modified the Mendel–Osborne method. Langmuir, who produced the fractination that led directly to the great rice breakthrough. Langmuir, the "Magic" man. Good God, man, you're a hero in every zone. You've let this year's little setback get you down. You've given millet a high fertility, you've increased its protein content. That's enough for one man. Let Hart here and the biochemists solve these fungus problems. It'll do you good to get away. Have a look at bigger things. The I.W.P. for example. You specialists despise these world plans. But the little anecdote here, the sudden glimpse of things on the spot there, will throw it all into perspective for you. And then you'll prepare us for the biggest revolution of all. The restructuring of sorghum. It's the rice of Africa as you'll see when you get there.'

'I doubt if I have such a generalizing capacity, Sir Alec, as you have reason to know. "In general, the new handbook under Sir Alec Jardine's editorship can be highly recommended. It is unfortunate that an earlier chapter (Langmuir) should be well below the level of the others."'

'Good Lord, man. You haven't let that worry you? I've never given it a thought again. Passmore wrote it, you know, and he wanted to dig at me, not you. You're too thin-skinned. This dive into the way the world's run will do you a power of good. I know I'll be called an enemy of research freedom, but concentration on the pressing problems is the best way to solve them and the best way to use public money.'

He came to an abrupt stop, and seemed surprised at the nature of his audience.

'Well, I'm keeping you.'

Both Hart and Langmuir said together: 'A little, yes.' But Hamo said it with cold courtesy, Nelson with a warm rudeness. The telephone rang. Hamo answered it: 'Oh God! Mm. At once. That,' he told his colleagues, 'was Watton to tell me I'm already late.'

'You've helped that young chap on greatly,' Sir Alec said. 'It was a sad pity the regulations didn't allow the institute to give even a wee farthing to the cost of his travel.'

'Yes,' said Hamo, 'it was.' And he was gone.

'A brilliant man. A perfectionist in everything. That's why he resents the smallest mistake,' Sir Alec commented, sighing deeply. 'He's tired though. It's a long body to carry around with you.'

'Ah, so you think the Lodger is at last about to lodge.'

But Sir Alec preferred not to acknowledge this long-treasured technical joke against Hamo Langmuir's height. He merely said, 'You'll be glad of a free hand, I dare say.'

And this time Nelson Hart preferred not to comment. They

appeared unable to go their proper ways. Which would have budged first remained unknown, for once more the telephone rang and a very loud bantering Cockney voice said: 'Look, you're gonna miss the moon, Chief, if you don't get crackin'.'

'This is the Director.'

'Oh, sorry, Sir. I thought it was Mr Langmuir. I don't want him to be late for countdown.'

'Quite right, Watton. Well, happy landing, and don't forget to bring us back some rock samples.'

'I don't suppose you'll know the Institute, Sir, this time next year – it'll be so thick with genu-ine moon dust.'

'Right you are. Good-bye.' Sir Alec was chuckling when he put down the receiver. 'Not much danger of Langmuir getting lost with that chap to look after him. And he'll be a cheery companion for a world voyage as well. Always the comic side of things. These Cockneys have a way with them. And he's a good worker, too.'

'Yes. He should be after ten years at lab work. Still Hamo would be lost without him. He must make a tidy sum from his photographs for *Nature*. I believe he has ambitions to become a film director. Makes home movies and so on.'

Nelson laughed with some scorn, but Sir Alec had heard a word he approved.

'Ah, ambition. That's always good. He reminds he of a batman I had at Mersa Matruh.'

'He reminds Langmuir of that, too, I think.'

'Langmuir is far too young for the war.'

'I meant if he hadn't been. If I had been in the war, you see, I shouldn't have had a batman.'

Sir Alec's dentures came together loudly as he removed his smile.

'Well, the lassies here will miss him. I thought there was something between him and little Heather White.'

'So did she. But Watton saw more opening in a world tour.' Nelson Hart laughed coarsely. 'Why not? He knows which side his bread is buttered.'

Sir Alec looked into the distance.

'What extraordinary expressions we do use. It's hard to imagine that any man can have failed to know which side a piece of bread is buttered. I respect the chap for keeping his Cockney. I've always found my plain Scotch speech a great help to me in the world.'

Nelson Hart liked to think the same of his Midland accent, so he merely said, 'Ah.'

Hamo Langmuir, with the longest of Scots ancestry, would have been surprised to learn that anyone should seek purposely to maintain a Scots accent like Sir Alec; it was something one expected of the villagers and tenants he had known as a boy on his grandfather's estate at Loughaugh. Had he thought about it, he would have explained Erroll's Cockney as, given all the circumstances, very fitting. But his mind, as he edged his way towards London against the outcoming commuting traffic bowling up out of sudden banks of yellow fog, was on visual objects, of what he hoped to see abroad. Slender, shapely figures, brown, amber, olive, almost black, danced round and round and round in the swirling mists like some vapours in a centrifuge. But for one moment, it is true, they seemed the more delectable because he realized suddenly that, for the most part, he would understand but few words they said, have little or no insight into their minds; not as here, for example, where a Northern voice too fully conveyed all the clogging, deadening contents of an empty Northern mind. Even so, as he neared London, Northern or not, he felt a pressure against his flies that seemed to promise an end to these wretched barren months.

Alexandra, in line, let her left leg shoot forward, knee bent, foot inclined towards the floor, every muscle loose as she had practised during the whole of the preceding fortnight. Now they were all conditioned in reflex – peck, peck, scratch, scratch. To feed, to lay, to feed, to lay, to feed, to lay. Not even necessary to mate.

No, that was the wrong way to think of it. Meaning was secondary, must come to the audience by conviction of sensation. Ned had convinced them. Further down the line, three away from her, he was there, as she knew, and he would not be *thinking* – feed, lay – *he* would be *feeling*, feeling the sharpness of his claws scratch, scratch, feeling the dust fly up from this bare

19

earth yard that would not for him be wooden boards; he would sense the scaliness of his feet and legs, would itch in his feathers, shake and spruce them, flick his comb, and, later (as he had made them ache with funny sadness at each rehearsal), stretch his neck to give that once-virile crow that was no longer there. She could feel Ned's warm loving body against hers and for a moment the attendant pressure of Rodrigo's lips upon hers, his tongue slithering into her mouth. But she forced her thoughts away from that – that, later it must be. But now, in thought, pressing her body to Ned's body she merged into it, until she felt herself to be Ned.

And so feeling, she began to sense her own feathers, her own wings, her own long scaly yellow legs, her own sharp out-stretched claws. And peck, peck, scratch, scratch; here there was a small corn seed, there a minute grain of wheat. Conscious, however, of Rodrigo somewhere in the audience, mocking. What right had he to mock? He could move so elegantly out there in the world of getting and spending. Out there, if he said, come, she would gladly follow; as, out there, if she called to owlish, whiskered Ned, *he* would come ambling up at her command. But here in the world of release play, where Ned was her leader, she would compel Rodrigo with all the others out there in the hall to need what her play had to tell them. The old, scarey, longed-for, triple knot pressed upon her again; she *was* that knot, taking the strain of their tug of war. She sagged as she felt the wrench. Night after night, as Rodrigo had quoted 'talking and fucking we lay waste our powers'. To counter the exhaustion she made an urgent act of self-dissolution. She was a hen.

And now to enforce this feathery, scaly, beaky feeling came 'hens to the centre'. Six of them, feeling nothing but this; and she feeling just herself and yet part of the battery, clucking and fussing and brooding, and straining to lay her egg, until she feared that the grey cotton crotch of her grey cotton tights might split. And around them circled Ned and five other capons. She could sense them stretching, and stretching their necks in a chanteclair that would never sound. Six here, six there, useful to man. . . .

Later, Hamo lay back on the bed, legs neatly together, hands cupped under his neck – in no sense sprawling. The ruffled pillow next to him fussed him, a dark pubic hair on the slightly crumpled sheet at his side irked him. He would be glad for the youth to be dressed and gone so that the bed could be stripped to the neat bare skeleton it would remain during his own months of absence.

Meanwhile it appeared less wasteful to watch Brian splashing about in the bath, through the half-open door. After all, with last week's failure added, ten pounds would have been spent in fruitless play. He tried to express the thought brutally, sadistically. But money, as he knew from experience, was as dangerous a road where sex was involved as social class or accent or any other diversion that took one's thoughts away from the body. And, of course, that he should try to equate the boy with money was only an expression of bitterness, unfair to Brian, and as pointless as it was detestable in himself. He concentrated on what he saw.

It seemed, taking every feature into account, impossible that the stimulus should have failed for a fifth or sixth time. Straight black hair, small ears, high cheekbones rose-coloured at the pommets, for the rest a whey-white skin, wide mouth, small teeth, slender neck, chest 30 inches, waist 24 inches, hips 35 inches, length of leg 28 inches (he had taken the most exact measurements), plump but firm buttocks, a curly pubic bush not too thick, slender smooth thighs; above all, well within the age-span, eighteen years and ten months next week, it seemed. A perfection among the few optimum varieties.

Indeed the arrangement had worked with regularity every Thursday for some months, but ever less well as familiarity had led to talk, to human exchange – Langmuir's inexcusable law of diminishing returns.

But at its peak it had been ideal. At the memory, stimulation returned. Brian looked round, smiling.

'So the old magic can still work. Do you want to see the picture through a second time then? You don't want to go round the world on a plane, when you can go round it now with your tongue. For old time's sake with your laughing lad.'

Instantly stimulus had gone.

Embarrassed, the boy who had found his confidence, so disastrously for Hamo over the months, turned to nervous chatter, said, his accent thickening, 'So it's New York. And after that, San Francisco. They say that's really good. Will you be growing a beard then like the hippies? And Hollywood it'll be in the end. An M.G.M. star. Fabulous! Anyway, you'll find plenty of chicken over there. What about taking a poor orphan boy with you then?'

Hamo closed his eyes; wearily he could only blame himself, and the boy's bantering tone didn't lack a certain desperation at seeing Hamo go out of his life. Not only had he put the youth's whining between himself and sexual satisfaction, but he had mined a whole seam of self-pity and misery in Brian himself, which had been happily buried beneath the hardness of his everyday life. More than two months ago, over-greedy for information for his coming travels, for news of the Promised Paradise he – who knew too well that the satisfaction count was always of random origin – had asked Brian for contacts. He had got in return one dubiously attractive Tyneside youth, now a Sydney barman, address almost certainly garbled. But he had also let loose all Brian's self-justifying reminiscences over the following weeks. His voice, once just a stimulating accent, as much just a part as a nipple or bum, now sang at each meeting for Hamo's praise of his orphan-boy courage.

As it was singing now to Hamo who was desperately seeking not to hear it. Sensing this desperation he applied the curative sedation method. Indeed, miraculously (or rather, as with all discovery, by some suppressed step of logic), going over the figures for lysine content in recent sorghum returns from Karachi laboratories, he suddenly saw an important connection between these mutations and certain others, occurring it seemed naturally, in Uganda. Getting off the bed and putting on first his white towelling robe, and then his cork sandals, he went from the room to his study, noted the figures and added a reminder to inquire as to the Uganda soil analysis.

Then, relaxed, he took out Brian's envelope from a pigeonhole in the desk, reflected that, on his return, the boy would be too old, or, if not, irrevocably lacking in anonymity; perhaps mercifully returned to the mysterious North. With decency, not sentimentality, remembering the relief the youth had given him during their first months in which he had still been doing some of his best research work, he unlocked the desk's central drawer, in which as a routine precaution he had put his wallet, extracted from it a ten-pound note, and, opening the envelope with a paper-knife, added it to the five-pound note already there.

Then he sensed that Brian was standing, dressed, behind him. He handed the envelope over his shoulder, not turning. In thanks the boy said, 'Travel'll get the old banger working again before you're air-bound. Just think of all those Indian boys. The Fathers never taught us any of those positions at Sunday School.'

Hamo guided the boy, his overcoat not yet fully pulled on to his left shoulder, to the front door. Then to modify this appearance of haste, he held out his hand in a good-bye gesture. So little was this part of any usual order that Brian stared at the hand for a moment, then ignoring it, leaned forward and kissed Hamo chastely but firmly on the lips.

'You'll do all right,' he said, soothingly.

Hamo was startled into speech.

'That's a question I've never allowed myself to consider since my twenty-fourth birthday.' And he gave little pats with his index finger in turn to each side of his small moustache. Opening the front door, gently and firmly he pushed the youth out on to the landing; then, closing the door again, shut Brian and all the satisfaction he had once provided out of his life.

Zoe, pounding the ducks' livers, the garlic cloves, and the bay leaf, tried to make no conscious effort to bring Concepcion into the conversation. She had long ago decided that to find special speech for these household conversations – other, that was, than the interlarding of her normal English with Spanish words and phrases – would be condescension. Besides, considering the limitations of her peasant upbringing and the debilitating poverty of those monstrous childbearing early married years, Concepcion, as Zoe had soon found out, had an extraordinary sensitive hold on life, a real feeling for people.

As now, when holding up into the air a leg of the pheasant she was jointing, this stout, merry black-eyed woman made with her lips and teeth comic grimaces of greedy devouring (she had a splendidly natural lack of concern for appearing a clown and so never lost her native dignity).

'Mister eat,' she said, 'Mister write.'

And she imitated with her other hand typewriting movements. The two gestures taken together were so reminiscent of Perry, when, his absurd schoolboy appetite for food satisfied, he sat down blissfully to write, that Zoe burst into delighted laughter.

'Carlos, too, eat big and working all day singing,' Concepcion added, miming her husband's busy life of hammering and planing.

Zoe, thinking of all the many jobs in the house that Perry frequently said he would have to carry out himself because Carlos had neglected or performed them in a slovenly fashion, returned to the pâté, measuring the half glass of armagnac required. Carlos who had forced all the children on his wife, Carlos – his lean, vain, handsome looks turning to pampered fat – stood for so much which held up decency's progress that she preferred to return to her own husband.

'You won't tell Mr Grant that you are sad you do not go down to the cottage these winter months, *mes do invernado*, will you, Concepcion? I know little Miguel's disappointed. But I'm honestly not sure that it's good for him to be in the country in these wet months anyway. You *have* kept him in *today*, haven't you?'

At Concepcion's looking down, Zoe assumed great sternness, for the terrible thing about peasant simplicity, with all its compensating insights, was the sheer failure to grasp the smallest basic principles of reasoned hygiene.

'That's very bad. *Muy malo*. You remember what Dr Powlett told you about any suspicion of fog. You *must* do what he says. Otherwise you'll lose Miguel, you know, like you did the other two.'

But, as so often, Concepcion rebuked became Concepcion tearful, so that Zoe decided to return to happier things.

'You see, I just want these next week-ends to be a sort of relaxed honeymoon for Mr Grant. That's why I'm taking down all this rather grand picnic food with us. And for me, of course, Marriage needs these renewals. *Renova buena por matrimonio*. Not that we've ever lost each other. But we've changed and we've got to find those changed selves. Mister grow older. I grow older. Must find what he is, what I am. I'm sure that's the way Perry will start writing seriously again. Mr Grant writing new book. Very funny. *Mucho comico*. And sad, of course,' she added.

Concepcion said, 'New book good.'

'Very. And that's why I don't want Mister upset at all. Not tell him you are sad not to be at cottage. Mister is very kind, you know. He will be sad; think little Miguel want to come to cottage, little Miguel must come. Then he will not write book. Anyway, Concepcion, you're going to have the cottage just for yourselves for the whole of May. That's the best month in the garden. Heaven knows *we* wouldn't go abroad then if that awful controller hadn't practically *made* Perry take his holidays in the spring. Of course, he'll be able to write in Sicily, but we're going to miss the lilacs terribly. You'll have to write and tell me how the garden's getting on.'

'Miss Alexandra make garden when you no here.'

'Alexandra! I hope not; she'd pull up all my best plants. She's not interested in gardens. And I shouldn't want her to be. The young don't need that sort of sense of continuity. We didn't either. On the other hand, we didn't make such a conscious revolt against it. But I didn't *really* care for anything but the present when I was at Cambridge. There was so much to do all the time. And so there is for Alexandra. It's the most marvellous time of her life. And thank goodness for it! Just at the moment when Perry most needs to have me on his own.'

'Miss Alexandra no sleep enough. So beautiful, but very thin. No sleep enough. No ...' and in want of words, Concepcion sketched out the shape of Zoe's ample breasts in the air.

'Yes, she is lovely looking, our Ally, isn't she? And as to all this,' Zoe copied Concepcion's gesture, 'I've got more than enough for two. Anyway the young men don't like it. But sleep! Dear Concepcion, I really truly am grateful to you for loving Alexandra. But I'm not a careless mother. Honestly, truly. Sleep! That's the last thing you want at that age. With all the reading to do for her finals. And she has to fit that into travelling with this mime show. And talking! All the talking that we did at Cambridge! Sleep! Did *you* sleep at that age? Yes, well, of course you did. With all that back-breaking work in the fields and getting up at five. But I'm sure Manuela doesn't want to sleep much. *Manuela no quiere dormire*. What do they tell you about Manuela in the dancing class?'

'Lady teacher say very good, but afraid Manuela grow so big, too big to dance.'

Now this really was serious; not the sort of undergraduate nonsense of Alexandra's mimes. Here was a girl, a possible Fonteyn – the school had committed itself, when she had agreed to pay the fees – and growing in the extraordinary way that talent did out of such utterly dusty soil. It was a classic case and neglect would be criminal. She paused in her dripping of the oil into the mayonnaise. She frowned. To stop growth. It was such a hideously ironic need in this stock stunted by centuries of bad feeding. Nor was it easy to see what could be done. Yet medical science these days ...

'Look, you're not to worry, Concepcion. I'll talk to Dr Powlett. There must be something they can do with hormones. Oh, Lord, who would have children?'

But thinking of how few she had had and how many Concepcion, she turned to more general things.

'I think your church soon agree with birth control. Very good. We have two Catholics on the Clinic committee. They really do seem hopeful.' And, as Concepcion did not respond, she explained, 'Pope agree you use pill.'

Concepcion said, 'No,' and added, 'Priest tell.'

But Zoe, thinking now of something more important for a woman of Concepcion's age, went briskly from the room and returned with a small pink card.

'There,' she said, 'you put name here. I arrange you go to Clinic this month.'

'What for card?'

'They give you test. Not worry. All women our age must have test.'

She saw no way of easily and quickly explaining cervical smears.

Concepcion said, 'I ask Carlos.'

To forestall this, Zoe opened a dresser door, and put the card on a shelf with some seldom-used liqueur glasses.

'We talk next week.' But she feared for the survival of the card, since Concepcion, to whom the order of her kitchen was paramount, was eyeing its place among the glasses with much disapproval.

Zoe finished off the mayonnaise.

'Will you pack everything, please, Concepcion. Oh, and put the pieces of pheasant on the top where Mister can get easily. I drive. Mister eat in car.'

She smiled as she foresaw Perry's greedy, greasy, bone-picking.

'Now I must go pack suitcases. Alexandra's godfather's coming. Mr Langmuir,' she explained.

'Ah! Mr Langmuir! Good man.'

Concepcion had been told once of Hamo's work on cereals for the developing countries.

'Yes,' said Zoe, submitting to a certain Topsy Eva tone to sustain this valuable ethical point, 'Mr Langmuir make rice in Concepcion's home very big.'

'No rice in Galicia.'

The agronomic lesson was delivered firmly but kindly.

'Well, whatever crop you do have. Mr Langmuir go now all round world, making bigger crops.'

She stored up the image to tease Hamo out of his usual devout silence.

'Mr Langmuir no wife?' asked Concepcion.

Zoe stood for a moment by the door in silence, before saying, 'Mr Langmuir not like women.'

Concepcion laughed loudly at the absurdity. But Zoe was determined.

'Mr Langmuir like making love men.'

For a moment Concepcion looked at Zoe with affronted horror, then, when she saw the resolutely happy look on Zoe's face, she began to laugh, and, slowly, with one hand on her hip and the other arm held delicately in the air, she swayed her large figure from side to side in a mincing walk.

'*Marica*,' she announced.

Zoe frowned. She didn't feel happy with this response. She took down the Spanish dictionary she kept handy on the dresser shelf – Marica,' she read, 'A magpie. A thin head of asparagus. A mollycoddle.' The first, although elegant enough for Hamo, suggested thieving. The second, if not completely zany, sounded faintly obscene. The third, though clearly the origin of the trouble, very ill described Hamo's stoicism. She decided to refute the first.

'Mr Langmuir not *marica*,' she said firmly, 'very honest man.'

Concepcion was clearly pleased that she had been mistaken.

'Mr Langmuir no *marica*,' she repeated, 'good man.'

Zoe went out of the kitchen quoting to herself one of her grandfather's mumbles, 'So much to do, so little done.' She had no clear memory of Cecil Rhodes as having been a force for good, but she sympathized with his dying feelings. No wonder the young, like Alexandra, refused to be bothered with the past. There was so much to do in the present.

Perry said, putting down the receiver, 'God, I'd like to buy the ghastly Whizz Kit at *his* price and sell him at my own.'

And while his new secretary nodded her meaningless, moronic miniskirted affirmation, he reflected bitterly that, in fact, Zoe and he had money enough and more to pay even Kit Coates's high estimation of himself; or, what was equivalent, he had no monetary need to do this exhausting, demanding, trivial job where he must listen to the arrogant demands of ludicrous star interviewers like the Whizz Kit, even try to meet their nonsensical needs.

'It isn't as if he didn't know,' he said, noticing the vulgar stupid prettiness more closely – where did they find them? 'Kit Coates has been working for the Corporation for at least six years. He knows perfectly well the expenses allowed to camera crews, and the accommodation agreed when they're on location. And if the B.B.C. wasn't as mean as hell over such matters, if it really was the maternal employer it claims to be, there would still be Union regulations. Regulations which, of course, are too lowly for Mr Coates, who has taken the mickey out of every Trade Union leader in England, to bother about. And "can I be sure that the Erawan of Bangkok has 'tub baths' as well as showers? His secretary is very English." Just so that we shall know the great Whizz Kit himself is as phonily mid-Atlantic as his accent. And he's heard that "the only place with proper sea bathing at Colombo is the Mount Lavinia", so will I see that his camera crew are quartered there? "His crew" and "quartered"! This is a happy ship, I'm glad to say, Lord Hill.'

'Faraway places,' said the secretary – she had rather a fetching grin when she relaxed. 'We can't all be stars and millionaires, can we?'

It occurred to Perry to explain that he and Zoe had thought of going to Ceylon for his annual leave two years ago, but he had decided that the Seychelles would be less tourist-ridden. However, if pride would not let him use Zoe's money to buy his liberty to write, he was not going to let vanity betray him into enjoying vicarious income prestige. All the same, the suppression made him more cross than before.

This Susan Nebble (or was it Nipple?) didn't improve matters by looking at her watch, and saying, 'Well, he'll have to wait until Monday, won't he?'

He disregarded the remark. 'Get on to Mr Forbes's secretary and arrange an interview with him for me first thing on Monday. I'd better see him personally. I might just be able to fiddle something with him about the rooms at the Mount Lavinia. And then get on to Travel and ask them (a) does the Erawan Hotel in Bangkok – it's in Thailand in case you didn't know – have baths repeat baths, and not only showers, with the bedrooms; and (b) don't let them palm you off with half answers. They're inclined to.'

She looked so surprised that he said, 'Getting things done for people, however bloody silly they are – that's what administration means.'

Her expression told him that he might just as well have said, 'You see, I'm a sort of superior office boy.' The conceit of these half-educated girls with nice suburban backgrounds! If he had had no creative powers, then the most valuable occupation he could imagine would be exactly this one – to see that things were done well and quickly. Far better than all the pseudo-creativity that went on the box – the degrading clowning that passed for creation in the so-called new media.

As it was, he intended to be both. He had a whole chapter planned for writing this week-end and he knew it was going to be good. But he dared not think of it until he was quite free of the building. Just let that bloody phone ring again.

After she had telephoned to Forbes's grim woman – she did it, he had to say, most efficiently – she said in a slightly too casual

29

voice (but the girl was, after all, a secretary not an actress): 'I wonder they've never made a teleplay out of *Above His Station*. A serial, I mean. It's got such super dialogue.'

There were a hundred reasons why not, applying to his novel and to most others, and she must know them; but that didn't matter beside her saying it. The sudden pleasure made him catch his breath, but he did not look up.

'Do you? Flattery has the opposite effect in this office.'

'I just hoped it might make you a little less cross. Anyway, it wasn't flattery. *Above His Station* was the best of the ang –'

'Say it. Let's have the whole thing. Better than Amis or Wain or Braine or Osborne. "Why didn't it sell, Mr Grant?" '

'Didn't it? I suppose it couldn't have done or . . .'

'Or I wouldn't be here. You're a great half-giver of offence, aren't you?'

'I wish I'd never mentioned the bloody novel.'

She was very pretty and on the verge of tears.

'Oh, don't take on. I'm very grateful to you. Most people have forgotten the book. It didn't sell because it didn't flatter the middle-class book buyers by sufficiently distancing them from real working people – in the Midlands, or in the North, or in some other region of absurd accents, or among freak out-of-work actors with sweet stalls. In fact, among anybody they could patronize. It was just about working people in the South – right where they live.'

'I know. It was about Seaside Road, Eastbourne. "The wrong end of the town." "Where we get our maids from." That's why I found it so real. My grandmother lived there, when she wasn't out in service.'

'But my grand –'

'I supposed so from the book.'

'But I never . . . I mean . . . Of course, you'd be much younger.'

'I doubt it. But I only visited Grandma there as a kid, so we wouldn't have seen each other. My mother moved to Brighton. Kemptown. She served at the Co-op. Now we've gone right up. She's got her own café.'

'Café! My mum's are licensed premises. She started as a barmaid.'

'Oh, really. Quite a coincidence, as they say.'

Yes, you *have* gone right up, you snooty little bitch; she had delivered her comments with her back to him, busy with a filing cabinet. But this had its compensations. Miniskirts were a good thing.

'Why haven't you followed it up?'

For a moment he could hardly believe his ears, but then he found relief from disappointment in explanation.

'Oh, I have. I'm writing now. That's why doing a job is so important. If I'd made the royalties the angries made, I'd be writing about commuting adultery among the sailing set, or ghosts, or the sex lives of film directors. As it is, I can still feel what the real world is like.'

'Has it a name?'

'Yes. I'm calling it *Seasmell Terrace*.'

The very slight puckering of the flesh around her eyes as she turned to him was exactly Zoe's reaction; and he knew Zoe too well to mistake distaste when he saw it. As with Zoe, he pushed on into defensive explanation.

'It's purposely crude. Like the old seaside dirty postcards.'

She asked, as Zoe had stated, 'Do you mean the kind that intellectuals send to each other on holiday?'

All his fury against Zoe welled up in him and, mingled with it, a delicious vision of this girl's (for he still must call her so) thighs and buttocks stripped naked. Very deliberately he cleared his desk of some papers, locking them in a drawer; then pointing to those that remained, 'Get rid of these, will you? And don't forget to ring Travel. Don't take no or any vagueness for an answer. Good night. You know about locking up.'

If the little bitch's body should come between him and a weekend's solid writing, he'd have her fired the following week. He registered his thought with a swaggering gesture, and so was able to accept it.

Brian gone, Hamo turned on his bath and while he waited checked his packed suitcases, one, two. Then he looked over his notes for Mrs E. How good to feel that he had the perfect technical assistant to go with him and the perfect housekeeper to leave behind. The thought occupied him pleasurably as he put into his pigskin dressing-case first his ivory monogrammed hair

31

brushes, then his silver shoe-horn (paternal heritages), only to realize with acute annoyance that he would need them *after* he had bathed. He took them out and irritably replaced them on the dressing-table.

He left the case with its silver hasps and hinges open, only taking the precaution of seeing that the new reports on the IR.8 rices from Manila were available for reading during the flight. He also, with a certain delight, carefully fitted among the folds of his Paisley dressing-gown the two pages of amino acid records of *pennisetum typhoides* that Erroll had failed to reclaim from him for filing.

He could not but look forward to rebuking his perfect assistant for such an unusual forgetfulness – perhaps, the result of another triumph with what he called 'a chick'. He found himself wondering why he always hoped that Erroll's affairs with girls should end as male victories – it was not, he was sure, anti-feminism, rather that Erroll's successes added to his own hoped-for sexual masteries. To the weak, the wall.

He plunged into his bath with a gurgling and splashing that he had maintained since boyhood, as he had the huge lemon-coloured natural sponge which he now soaked and squeezed out over his thick curly hair.

But, as if a complete déménagement was not enough upset, the telephone rang. Ordinarily he would have ignored it, but it might be Sir Alec with some last-minute wishes. Depressingly out of touch with the realities of their work though the old man had shown himself during their recent interviews, instructions from seniors were after all, as all matters of order, a necessary obligation. He put on his bathrobe, slipped his wet feet into his sandals and made for his study.

"Yes. I have. And you *had*. Well, let's hope there are no other important papers missing from the files. And at what time are you proposing to be at Heathrow? No, that will *not* do. I do not intend to board every plane – and that means, on my computation, during the coming months, between fifty and sixty, leaving out routine changes – with my peace of mind and capacity to think agitated, if not wrecked, by your hair's-breadth arrivals. I am going to visit some friends to say good-bye. In point of fact my goddaughter and her parents. I shall have a hired car waiting to pick me up from there to take me to the airport. I suggest that you come by taxi to my friend's home. Number 8 Dames Road. It's between St John's Wood and Swiss Cottage. Arrive at no later than 7 o'clock. That's exactly why I am making it so early. If by some chance, you *do* arrive on time, the Grants will give you a drink. You will like each other, I believe. Then I'm afraid you will have to make those good-byes shorter than you intended.'

It seemed, as he let out the now tepid bath-water, in keeping with this wretched anarchic afternoon that he should have arranged for one part of his life to meet with another. All these Sir Alec-type introductions! 'You will like each other' – who could possibly predict human likings, and, if the prediction were true, what purpose would it serve? Travel, it was clear, disordered the mind, even when, as in this case, months of careful preparation had been made to ensure that the enterprise ran smoothly.

He dried vigorously, then put on newly laundered pants and vest, a clean shirt with links inserted for him and fresh socks with toes pushed in ready for his feet. All had been prepared by Mrs E. His only task was to unscrew the trouser press inherited from his grandfather, which sentiment, he had to admit, had made him use up to this last minute, for he would not have it with him in the many months to come when these lofty rooms made for gentlemen used to spacious privacy, would, no doubt, be exchanged for air-conditioned, strip-lighted boxes. He took out the shoe-trees. With the aid of the shoe-horn, he eased his feet into the highly polished brogues. A puff of spray on his moustache and he was ready for air travel.

But, before leaving the flat, he made sure of the few locked drawers that he was leaving behind. Valuables he had left at the bank; but there were private things he preferred to leave locked up here – a few mementoes of his parents, some school photographs, some college dining-club menus, Leslie's few letters. He had not been unaware of the highly increased risk of death that the months of air travel held for him; he had deposited a duplicate set of keys at his lawyers where Perry, as his executor, would find it, in order to act on behalf of Alexandra, his sole heir.

If the eventuality should occur, Perry would be discreet. Or would he? He would not, of course, be directly indiscreet. But – he had been forced to notice it – both Perry and Zoe, so wonderfully taken up with each other, were not of course negligent of Alexandra, but inclined surely a little to give her responsibilities beyond what should be asked of a young girl. He was willing to accept this whole family world into which he had been miraculously admitted (the miracle, of course, being that Perry was Leslie's brother) as a mystery, or rather a skill to which he had no key. Many parents, no doubt, were more skilful than Perry and Zoe, as some few plant geneticists were more skilful than he was. He had no means of judging. He must simply thankfully accept their acceptance.

Still, in this one case, he felt a sudden alarm. He had a horrible vision of untouched Alexandra opening that third drawer of the desk, of her finding and reading, or, even if she did not understand, seeing ... He unlocked the drawer, took out the magazines (they were so few, just some favourite ones he had kept over the years), but Alexandra, so distant, providing him incredibly with a responsiblity he could not remotely meet, demanded the sacrifice of anything, however long cherished. Mrs E., wise woman, sceptical of public services, had insisted on a supply of candles; two of which he now lit – a non-smoker, he had no other means of steady flame; and tearing the pages into small pieces he burnt them one by one, catching sight, even with his averted eyes, of a thigh here, a nipple there as they turned to ash. There remained only an inserted single sheet – an advertisement for some magazine he had never subscribed to – which had slipped to the floor. The difficulty of seeing the tiny photographs or of reading the minute prints so teased him that he went back to his study for the magnifying glass. The photographs revealed, even in enlargement, no more than three slender naked or near naked bodies crowned by cowboy hats; but the print he could read: 'Mack and Rod were pretty surprised to find themselves at the dude ranch of the wealthy stranger, but it was not too long before those loose-limbed, well-built kids found plenty to occupy them. A day out duck shootin' or learnin' to break in young steers, was usually followed by a session in the showers. Here Mack seems reluctant to take that evenin' shower, and Rod wrestles with him to get him under. But, hey, who's this? Well, this ain't fair. Two up against one. Pete – the blond stud who acts as hired boy around the place – is a hefty young giant too. They don't seem to be having too much difficulty in forcin' the rangy, curly-headed youngster under that stream of water. Uh huh, looks as though Mack's gonna lose his trunks ...' Hamo mopped *his* trunks as best he could with a handkerchief. There would be no time to change them until he reached the United States, land of dude ranches.

The two bearded young men from York were doing their thing with empty packing-cases. Alexandra had seen it many times before at rehearsals, even so she would have liked to wait for the great comic sequence when each made a funeral pyre and burned himself under the false impression that he was the last human left on earth.

Unfortunately she had suddenly remembered, as she had been scratching and pecking her way out of 'Batteries', that she had forgotten to pack either her Yeats notes or *Women in Love*, both of which she absolutely had to revise during these days' touring in Corby or Luton or Boston or whatever these places were – a whole list of names like those in the fifties novels that for some reason He was so proud not to have written – but Him she quickly put from her mind.

Ned would have Yeats – if only, like Tolkien, because of its magic properties for him; and Rodrigo might have the Lawrence, because if Ned began Birkining too much, he liked to look up bits of Gerald and produce them unexpectedly to make Ned explode. But what she wanted was her own copies with her own notes; and that, if she told it to either of them, would make them gang up against her – it would be an 'Ally for victim' time and she was so tired that she'd get frightened and cry, or worse.

Thinking of this, of the faces, of how she couldn't get away from Ned and Rodrigo yet must not let 'that' happen again before she had thought of what it was leading them into, she saw Ned on the other side of the hall arguing with the anaemic troublesome girl from Warwick and he gave her the look. Immediately the blood drummed in her ears, excitement and longing, and, stronger, an engulfing panic desire to run; yes, even home to Them rather than enjoy it again before she could measure its hold upon her. And then she thought, this panic, this running away, isn't it just to get Ned and Rodrigo to come after me? Isn't all this hysteria just a squalid kind of flirtation? The whole thing was absurd. The magic was entirely a game, as Rodrigo knew, even if Ned sometimes let his thoughts out of control. She must go to him and quite simply say, 'I've left some important things at home' – no need to particularize, it wasn't his business – 'please bring my suitcase in the van and pick me up at Number 8 in about an hour.'

When she reached Ned, he was saying, or rather mumbling into his beard, as he did at his fiercest, 'Look, y'know, those movements, they've got to go.'

'But they're the logical expression of the hens' collective hostility to the system.'

The Warwick girl felt it all so deeply that she was wiping the sweat from her hands on her tights.

But Ned said, 'This is a magical structure. Half-baked materialist ideologies only ...'

Very calmly Alexandra said, 'I'm awfully sorry to interrupt, Ned, but it's just that I *have* to fetch something at home. So could you pick me up there in about an hour. You know – Number 8.'

He gave her the special controlling look that he reserved for her panics.

'No,' he said. And, as she was about to speak again, more fiercely, 'No. And that goes for those steps, y'know. They're out,' he told Warwick, who began to argue.

Alexandra saw that she must wait until he was alone. So to gain time she shrugged herself into her white lamb fur coat with the red fox fur collar and sleeves – the most wonderful second-hand buy – and then she had to search for her hat. It seemed nowhere. Other hats there were, some felt, some straws, two Russian fur hats, and military overcoats with froggings to equip a movie regiment, and even a bright cerise feather boa; but not *her* hat. She began on hands and knees to look for it beneath the forms, and, at once, of course, at contact with the wood floor, her bloody knee began to bleed again, where she had cut it slightly in the sequence when the rest of the hens pecked her. At last, there the beige felt hat was – for a moment in her dizziness, she had thought it a horrible crouching sandy cat – now crushed into quite a bad shape, despite all those wettings and thumpings and stretchings it had received over the weeks to get it into a good one. It lay behind an old coke stove, under the silver-painted chimney duct, its beige felt looking not beautiful now but nothing, and as for the long mauve chiffon streamer which hung from it, that was all covered in sooty cobweb, and, when she went to pick the hat up, this streamer caught on some bolt and tore.

And there, of course, behind her, in his large-lapelled grey suede suit and his beautiful lemon chiffon cravat, was Rodrigo, offering his dandy elegance to be ravished by her sluttish disorder. His hands came from behind her, stroking her breasts. She would have responded, but feeling his body tremble, she knew suddenly a desire to take advantage of her power. Turning her head, she kissed his ear.

'Look, Rodrigo, do something. I can't talk to Ned now. But I must go home to fetch some books. Will you please ask him to come for me in the van?'

Let them fight over her, it would diminish their dangerous energies.

'But I'll take you home in the M.G., Ally, and then on to blissful Luton where you should have a super audience of wealthy motor workers on permanent strike.'

She hadn't time for all that.

'No, my luggage is in Ned's van.'

He came to her side and put his arm round her waist, and said in a 'seducer's voice', 'No need for luggage. Anyway, why not travel in comfort to perform in squalor?'

She longed to respond to the feel of his hand, but . . .

'No.'

A sense that she was lost if she did not prove her will stronger than theirs constricted her throat. She broke from him. Tears of anger came into her eyes; and he, seeing them, was suddenly, as he could be, marvellously wily-understanding and, kissing her lips, told her to go off home and she would be fetched in an hour.

When she opened the door of the hall to leave, there, in the still and freezing foggy air that caught her breath, stood a dark-haided young man. 'Excuse me, but you were in that last piece, I think, weren't you?'

He pushed back his black locks as though he were standing, not in the still fog, but on the clearest-aired, breeziest cliff of Albion's shores, so that Alexandra, used to regional television news from childhood, looked in turn for a microphone and cameras, but none was there.

'You were in the last thing, weren't you?'

He was shouting now, for fear, presumably, that the non-existent gales might carry his voice away.

'Oh, I know roughly what was meant. Well the name tells you really – "Batteries". And, of course, there's a lot in it. You ought to see life round here. Eat, sleep, make love, die. Or variations. But what I didn't quite get ... Your knee's bleeding.'

She said, 'Oh, yes, yes,' impatiently, and then, 'thank you,' as though he'd done something to stop the bleeding.

'Well, what I didn't know was when you went off on your own – that bit – and the others fell on you. What was that? Was that sex? Or was that the flock or clutch thing pecking the loner? It's for the local rag. Not that they'll give much space as I expect you realize.'

As this very point had been under discussion with no final solution at every rehearsal, Alexandra felt at bay. She opened the door – and, although you never called people's names out, it seemed an occasion for pardonable exception, so she shouted: 'Ned, Ned. I think you'd better see Ned Phillips, our producer.'

Ned, in an agony of horror at his name proclaimed aloud, shook his head to show that he was too busy. She said, mumbling for lack of certainty:

'It could be either really. Or given the way the system works, probably both, I expect.'

He looked alarmed rather than puzzled, so she felt compelled to add:

'We're not Marxists, you know. Or Women's Lib. I mean if I seemed to *imply* anything like that. It's a question of structures.'

Rodrigo appeared again. He removed her hand from the door knob and closed the door.

'Just because you were the only one with any real idea of how a hen moves, you're not entitled to kill all the rest with pneumonia,' and to emphasize the point he fastened the silver clip that held together the high neck of his bottle-green felt cape.

'He's a reporter,' she explained. 'Ned ought to see him.'

But Rodrigo ignored the young man. He kissed Alexandra again but more passionately this time.

'Killing people with your draughts of honesty. Old Ma Failing.'

As this was a joke from the Forster seminar, where they'd first met by quarrelling publicly, she felt all her tiredness flow out of her in his embrace. Assured, he said, in rebuke, 'You'd better get home since the show *must* go on.'

He dismissed her and turned to the reporter.

'In bringing together arts conventionally impoverished by the isolation of self-styled professionalism, this group, drawn from a number of the universities, and produced by Ned Philips, is seeking, despite lack of money and inadequate equipment, to suggest a restructuring ...'

If Ned were to hear, there'd ... And now there *was* Ned, come to fetch her in. Rodrigo had reached a splendid climax.

'We do not ask to be judged professionally, still less intellectually, we make our appeal to the initiated ...'

He was clearly finding it difficult not to laugh, when Ned lunged out and hit him hard on the face. In seconds they were locked, struggling on the pavement, in one of their fiercest wrestles. Alexandra felt triumphant, but she knew that her victory could lie only in flight, so, gathering her coat in her left hand, she began to run towards the lights of the main road. They were not so absorbed in their intimate fight that they did not sense her movements.

Rodrifio called out, 'All right, you bloody little bitch, you're to blame for this.'

Ned shouted, in his special menacing voice, 'We shall come after you and we shall get you.'

The young reporter ran after her.

'Silly fools. And speaking to you like that. Structures! They ought to think more of manners like ordinary people.'

Alexandra turned on him, tears streaming down her cheeks.

'Please, please, go. It isn't fine to be ordinary, you know; it's stupid and beastly.'

Perry, driving his E-type home through the fog, was exultant to find that despite all his determination to have no thoughts but for the road, *Seasmell Terrace* had taken over. It worked, this dual life; and, with the long week-end in the country, he would bring his man Jack through his comic-sentimental return to the Terrace in his Cambridge vacations. There'd be the girls to pick up with again from the County Grammar, but first, to get into the mood, a visit to his first (pre-pubertal) window into the Wonder of Woman's Body – the good old pennyworth on the pier: What the Butler Saw. Turning off Maida Vale, the kerbs giving a white frost warning of their presence through the mist, he strove to go back to those flickering hazily seen girls (to recapture the vision and then find the words – that was the method). Surely they had been shingled or even Eton cropped. They must have been twenty-year-old flash cards even *then*: sort of Berlin twenties whores, and they'd worn something incredible, probably called cami-knicks, what the Little Mam might have worn if she'd been a tart instead of an honest barmaid; but he'd got a tremendous kick from it. He tried to hold the flickering picture firmly in his vision. He saw – Susan Nebble slipping out of her tights.

Punishing the neat little body pleasurably for having got in the way of his creative activity, he drove very slowly towards Primrose Hill. Remembering that Blake had here repelled the devil in archangel guise, he sought to drive Susan's desirable form from his vision. He tried to reach his hero Jack another way. How would he feel now, who, too young to vote for Utopia in '45, had yet kept faith and put his party in power again, and now was watching them turn Blake's Jerusalem brown and sourtasting? Poor Jack! His pity somehow followed Jack away from Labour's failure, to the failure of his marriage. Poor Jack, sterilely married in his gilded, gelded cage, seeking (who will cast a pebble?) his little bit of fun away from her high-mindedness, and clinics, and uplift, and money guilt. One of the oldest jokes in the pack, but none the less pathetic for that. But he must play it for laughs and let the pathos come of its own accord. And the wife's name – something stuck-up – Celia, Viola – no, crude and easy – Honey, the bitch with the money. The name came to him as a triumph as he entered Number 8.

In the hall, he heard voices from the first-floor sitting-room – hers and, Oh Lord! Hamo's. He'd forgotten that farewell call. Hamo, moustached and elegant, like some prize Sandhurst prodigy, seated primly upon the edge of one of her Louis Seize chairs, his primness parodied above him by the stiff Zoffany family, by the geometrical lines and vanishing-points of the Pannini pillared church interior. Death to *Seasmell Terrace* lay there. Not, anyway, that old Hamo would resent his creeping upstairs, as he began to do. For all his narrow specialism, perhaps because of it, Hamo had always been appreciative of his writing, had even read and remembered for quoting *Above His Station*, probably the only novel he'd ever read in his life and with a social setting that must have been unintelligible to him. But then they were both craftsmen and could speak to one another in respect. He could clout Leslie for not marrying Hamo. That was how life treated one. Broadminded as hell about having a queer brother. Trying to get him settled. And Zoe, to do her justice, being wonderfully helpful about it. And then Leslie ups and offs with this ghastly rag-trade queen. Sold himself for money, for that was what the little bastard had done, and into just that sort of impossible screaming world that was too much to stomach. Leaving poor old presentable repressed Hamo probably too frightened to have even the odd wank.

Nevertheless it was curious that Hamo had continued to see them for all these years, nine or ten; sitting there, saying nothing. Zoe seemed to like it, encouraged it. Maternal feelings, no doubt, or ... Feeling at last that he was getting somewhere, he threw his overcoat over the chairback, poured out a whisky and sat relaxed in the quiet of his study to let a new shape compose itself. 'Sitting in *her* drawing-room, surrounded by *her* taste, Jack felt stifled. Bugger them, why couldn't they keep their flabby camp for their country cottages and garden paths? ... By the very smell of the house, he was sunk in a dismal torpor from which Honey's high, smart voice awakened him, "Darling, do you *have* to sit about like a manic-depressive? I mean it's not exactly what one wants to find at home after a fascinating evening." ' Yes, that was the right tone for Honey – hard, moneyed, and a bit socially uncertain. And Jack always a trier – ' "Sorry, darling. Where was the wonderful evening spent?" "Oh, with Freddy Roe and his new boy friend. He's rather enchanting ..." It was the tone; Jack knew it so well – the over-emphasis on the boy-friend. Suddenly everything snapped into place; watch the birdie, it's cuckoo; and, hey presto, Ladies and Gentlemen, you have your picture. And a very dirty picture too – what the modern butler saw.'

Perry glowed with creative self-satisfaction, you could call it nothing else, for here it was – Seasmell Terrace, but it now took in the sort of view of the sea that the reader of today was looking for. A nasty dead fish pong it gave off, too. Their Fellini unisex decadent world. Sterility. Yes. That could be the dénouement of the scene, when Jack cleared out, telling Honey where she could stuff it, all her worldly goods, including her poove lover. A very unjokey Jack would face her with it, one that she would hardly recognize as the poor old fireside Tom she'd castrated with her cash. ' "It doesn't shock me. It just depresses me. It's so anti-life and so boring. You take a thing that's about as good as anything that exists – the pleasure that a man and a woman can give each other with their bodies." ' Steady on here – no Lawrence crap; avoid bodies. ' "A man and woman making love, and you play nursery games with it. Pansy petting, for that's all it'll be. A lot of titillating, tit-touching is as far as it can go. *You* dressed up as mummy or nursie ..." ' And then, surely reasonably, or so the reader must be made to see, all Jack's bitterness would well up, thinking of where he had come to in his long climb up the hill above his station. He would break out, ' "Well, one thing, good old Freddy'll never plough deep enough to find he's bought sterile land." ' And Jack'd leave Honey's flat, glad at last to have shed all the fake gentlemanliness he'd acquired in these years since Seasmell Terrace, glad he could kick a woman in the cunt again when she deserved it, throwing their childless marriage right back at her barren belly where it belonged.

Perry, carried away by the scene, got up and began *his* determined stride out of the room, out of Zoe's house. As he came to the door, it opened before him. There stood a creature, flat-breasted, thin-lipped, with enormous eyes staring from purple-tinged, translucent-skinned sockets set in a pinched, grubby, greasy white face, hair streaming negligently around the shoulders, the whole dressed in a filthy, dusty, blood-stained grey prison uniform. He stoked up these epithets of disgust to banish the chill he felt at seeing Jack's ultimate grievance bound back in his own face, the deeper chill at being reminded of what he had creatively denied – the ultimate tie and the ultimate barrier in his marriage – Alexandra!

Alexandra did not look at Him; she seldom did. She sensed His feelings always too strongly and too immediately to need to see His expressions.

She said, 'You have to be interrupted because Hamo's here and he's going on that world thing. Mama says to come down.'

With weary fury he answered, 'The new prose when given verbal utterance makes once more its tediously reiterated conviction of the value of sloppy nothingness.'

He could have kicked the dusty-seated, over-narrow little boy's bum as it moved down the stairs ahead of him for making him once more speak forth in such usherish, prissy words instead of his own usual plain and vigorous prose.

All the time Alexandra could hear Him braying behind her, could imagine the red clownish face split open at the wide sloppy mouth in a Francis Bacon cardinal's shriek, but, in fact, for one of His most effusive welcomes. Arms outspread, eyes all liquid and alive-o with insincerity.

'*My* dear Hamo!' All on a *decrescendo*. '*My* dear Hamo! Every apology, my dear fellow. I was "brooding" – you know how we writers "brood" – I suppose you chaps daren't brood for fear of breaking a beaker. I've been brooding over the old by now rather high-smelling masterpiece.'

Swallow, swallow, puff and blow like a bullfrog.

'What is that horrible concoction like iced nail-varnish? Darling, why ever not champers?'

Fuss and clink, clink and strain, and pop of cork and braying laughter.

'A million things to tell you, old man, and now you're going half round the world.'

The low contralto murmur. 'He's going *all* round the world, Perry.'

And twisting the sapphire in Her left ear round and round so that one still watched after all these years since childhood, to see the blood that never came, and now wringing the bit of chewed lace handkerchief with Her beautiful, plump blue-veined white hands. And all this handwringing because He bullfrogged as He always did, and sounded blah, blah, blah in false friendship. And her wonderful breasts, soft, white, swelling away from the cleavage like two snowy hills (oh to have those breasts !) blushing or flushing or whatever pointless spoiling, all because corks popped vulgarly and His laughter echoed round the room making it empty, making all Her squirrel's hoard of beautiful nuts (the pictures, the porcelain, the mirrors, the tables) seem nothing, seem no protection against His hollow laughing. His laughter of unhappiness. She hated Their unhappiness. His blah, blah, blah, and Her twisting torment.

Drawing away from Them, she sought (with no gorgeous, sinister Rodrigo there, no loving, frightening Ned) to snuggle into the luxurious warmth of her fur coat, but her thinly fleshed shoulder blades found only the painful pressure of the rococo twisted strut of the chairback. Her hand went to stroke behind her and found no soft fur that she had flung there with negligent ease as she went to summon Him. (Oh to trail down Embassy stairs with Roddy or to sit back in opera-house boxes letting furs fall from one's shoulders.) Looking down at the rug (Bokhara, botherer), she saw beside her chair no beautiful shading hat, trailing its garden-party loveliness, where she had let it fall in gracious disorder. Both, she first sensed, then saw, had been tidied away on (as He in His awful, careful send-up of Her culture called it) the gilded Ompierre Chayz Long.

Miles away it seemed to her exhausted body, every muscle tightened to withstand the impact of Their unhappiness, of Their rebukes (His hurt look and bray, Her silent tidying away) – miles of sliding bokhara botherer on which to prove herself the ungainly gawk. They always denounced, to call for all the *wrong* attentions.

Let the Hamster's mumble soothe her tensed body, flow through her torn, exhausted head. Mumble, mumble, mumble, and sitting up, oh such a tall hamster, little pink nose quivering, little paw cleaning his little whiskers. 'Lysine content, amino acid content, protein content.' But Mama not content with all his contents.

'No, no, don't try to make it all detached and scientific and *small*, Hamo. You can't look *small* however hard you try. Anyway, I won't let you belittle yourself, it is the *most* important work *anyone* can be doing. And, of course, no one else can do it.'

And all a low contralto moaning for the world's ills, and twisting Her handkerchief, wringing Her hands, and with Her guilt for all her Ompierre, in fact because of it, murdering sleep, since Her contralto declaiming broke again and again on the shore of one's head, battering and bruising, just as sleep was coming down, a comforting shrouding fog blanket that could replace the banished warmth of the fox and lamb, her treasured liberation while she waited for the dreaded delights of Rodrigo and Ned, in whose fox and lamb battle for her she could abandon her weary body and exhausted mind.

'But, of *course*, without full stomachs, everything one is trying to do – contraception, literacy – makes nonsense. A full stomach is the prerequisite to self-respect. Surely, Hamo, surely.'

And mumble, mumble, rolling in his little paws his own little nut.

Must work without pressures, objectivity, check and check again, no falsifying claims of human urgency.

'Oh, certainly! But they're not going to put such things on to you, surely. *You* must be free of all that. Policies, administration, those are things for non-creative minds. For people like me who can't . . .'

And then stopped, rigid, like a circled hare, or like a beautiful statue, Venus or somebody with those rounded arms and shapely breasts and all the high colour draining from Her cheeks, for the thousandth time that twisting, twisting handkerchief had tied itself tight into *that* particular knot. Help! Help! She signalled to the world as She turned the sapphire's beam now here, now there – I'm strangling him, I'm strangling the man I love.

And, all unwittingly, the Hamster's mumble, mumble came to Her aid – a hamster a day keeps the psychiatrist away. And to

His aid, for as She had whitened so had He reddened until His bloodhound dewlaps became turkey wattles. But now He could gobble again.

'Absolutely sure you should take no notice of her, old boy. Creation and administration are natural twins. The one feeds the other. Sounds improbable, I know. But it's the truth. Not as to the physical twins, of course. That would be a disgusting operation, I imagine.'

And now the wattle had so swelled and the gobbling so filled the room, that He felt big enough again to strike with His curved sharp turkey beak.

'Mind you, *I* can't say. Because *we've* never had two of a kind. Or two of different kinds for that matter. Whether the one we've got would share her brown rice with her twin is a macrobiotic question that I can't answer with my flesh-eating prejudices.'

Mama, who had suffered as by rote the pain of Her own anguish, half rose as though to come towards Her bleeding daughter's aid, but, as so often, He forestalled. Came over, put His hand on her grey cotton arm.

'No. Don't believe it, Ally, *I* don't. You'd give all your brown rice and the contents of your begging-bowl to the first who asked. It's the disease of women – giving. You inherit from Zoe. And I – I'm just a great big, ungenerous, small-souled Hector.'

Looking at Her with His large, hurt bloodhound's eyes. It *was* like. And Mama, laughing and explaining.

'Perry *is* that dog Hector. Aren't you, darling? But it won't do for Hamo who never watches the box *and* hates dogs. Don't you remember when we had poor Mariette?'

'I hope I never *showed* my dislike.'

'Of course you did. Your impassive scientist's mask's just like the sizzlegraph that tells where earthquakes are happening abroad – at least, thank God, it *is* always abroad.'

'Seismograph, I think. But I must *admit* I don't care for pets. I doubt if animals are intended for that sort of exploitation.'

'Exploitation! What about you and your hamsters. Wretched things! Fed entirely on sorghum! Whatever that may be.'

'Oh! That's necessary verification. But to use creatures to satisfy *emotional* needs seems to me unnatural.'

And now Mama, almost girlish, as always when She and He

found themselves for a moment publicly on the same side, shaking Her head, not controlling Her ridiculous giggling.

'*Don't* "do" Hector, darling. Pet dogs are *unnatural* and that will never do. Really, Hamo, you *do* want it all ways.'

But His hurt eyes were still levelled at her; His hand was still fondly upon her shoulder. She saw no hope of let-up unless she, too, played along. She said, in a mistress-to-dog voice: 'Go away, Hector. You're muddying my tights with your great paws.'

As she had hoped, a buzz was at once released that hovered over her for only a sentence or two – 'Forgiven, tail-wagging, grovelling old Hector.' Then, happy, released, braying, as the generous uncle at the Christmas party who has saved the best games to the last. Just as at every children's party she could remember from her early years, he had saved his story-telling to break up whatever spontaneity had taken over.

'Well, we've talked enough about others. Let's talk about me.'

And now she *could* let the grey, soothing fog envelop her, for it was The Novel.

'Everyone sees the seaside landlady from the Cockney's or Wakes Week point of view . . .'

'*I* don't, darling. I think of poor old drunk Winifred turning a dishonest penny with those foreign students at Brighton.'

'Middle-class bohemia. I'm talking about the real thing. In the childhood section of the new novel I shall be giving or trying to give the horrible sense of being a national, pilloried, comic figure, the unwilling companion of stout lady and bare bum and the spinster praying for a man – the comic postcard set. Her house invaded, inspected, found wanting; children piddling on the parlour carpet; that nice Mr Snooks in hardware bringing back a nasty tart; six months hard labour and six months solitary confinement; trying to change from the Hoggart sacred hotpot to the trendy sacred spaghetti bolognese, and getting a fart in the eye for both; the backbreaking work, the bills, the bilking, the . . . well, you'll see. Mrs Reynolds, as I've called the landlady, the hero's mother, comes wonderfully out of the Little Mam, the same incredible courage when it comes to the crunch, the same absurd "gin and it" jollity to get through the ordinary . . .'

Through the gradually settling soothing fog, through a determined revision of the school inspection scene – Birkin's angry rejection of the true blood values as served up to him through Hermione's ego-conscious, mind-dominated voice, a supreme blasphemy – she could sense the sapphire turning, turning, the crumpled lace handkerchief, probably now, too, the involuntary twitching and screwing up of the eyes. Oh God! It's *His* mother, let Him do what He likes with her, what does it matter what goes into His silly book that, probably, luckily, will never be written? Hermione saying children shouldn't know about the way flowers function, and Birkin saying they were bound to know, so let them know rightly. But that didn't sound like Lawrence, and Birkin was Lawrence's voice. Only six months to go and she couldn't remember exactly who said what! And the text was everything. The trouble was that Birkin's voice had become so lost in Ned's version of Birkin redeemed in loving. And Mama had rounded that corner, choosing something else, something less deep to attack.

'Darling, nobody has Wakes Weeks now. I'm sure they don't.'

'Don't be tedious, Zoe, it's *just* a simple verbal shorthand. Now, Hamo, the Little Mam has this extraordinary resilience, because she always has a sense of reality, of the concrete things, never lets illusion take over.'

The Hamster primly mumbled.

'I've only met your mother briefly once or twice.'

'Well, she *has*. And this means I've got to be extraordinarily careful that the language is exact, every word meaning what it should, no bloody fake poetic prose. Mrs Reynolds is too real for that, like the Little Mam . . .'

'Oh Perry! Don't sentimentalize! Your mother lives in a dream world of gay pluck and golden hearts that has never allowed her to face anything, and when anything faces *her*, she cries. And why not, poor darling? She's done her best for life, keeping everyone laughing, looking beautiful. "Gin and it" indeed.'

And Birkin said: Humanity is a dead letter, let humanity disappear as soon as possible. Or be restructured with love, Ned said.

'Darling, of *course* you have to synthesize and invent. And if it helps to attach your inventions to your mother, it's not for me, Heaven knows . . .'

'No, it's not . . .'

And the Hamster, tactful hamster, ering and ahring, and pulling out a hamster auburn whisker or two with his paws in agitation, poor nervous hamster.

'Er. And yes, there's that. And er . . . how is the boat?'

Oh God! The Boat! Worse than The Novel.

'It still makes a wonderful escape from all this . . .'

But The Boat was so awful that it really *did* bring down the comforting fog in automatic self-protection, softer fog to lie back in, fox furs and feather boas in which to bury one's tired body, feathers and fur, fur and feathers, Rodrigo's stroking hands, Ned's lap to take one's head, feathers and fur. A staring face, eyes hard and mad, a green-white, cheesy epileptic face, and a fat lower lip drooping like a pale blood pudding, bubbles of foam at the mouth corners – no one I know! no one I know! Yet someone, she was sure, who with others equally horrible, was always in wait. And his fingers! Her head clicked open as she woke. She'd woken herself. She must have screamed. But far away, Mama, kind, but embarrassed (Oh, keep your shame for Him).

'Ally, darling, no one blames you for going to sleep. At least, I don't *think* Hamo does. With finals next year and a choice of young men, and mimes, anyone sensitive would go to sleep. But you really ought to learn not to snore.'

And He giving her a large whisky, which she drank at a gulp. Oh, how super the burning warmth in the tummy. And Mama.

'Gracious! And *we*'re always being told that booze is fit only for geriatrics.'

And now the Hamster, so curiously short-paced and mincing for such a tall hamster, rises and gets her fur coat, places it round her shoulders.

'You're shivering. You mustn't work so hard, Alexandra.'

But mumbling, as always when speaking to her, and trying, what could he be doing? to take something out of his well-cut hunting-jacket pocket at the same time as he firmed the fur coat to her shoulders. And suddenly, rip, the lovely fox collar was half torn from the lamb. Hamster stutterings, and fumblings in his pocket, now pulling out an envelope, now stuffing it back again. And Mama.

'Please *don't* worry, Hamo. It was half disintegrating already. That's the whole *point* of it, isn't it, darling?'

And bray, bray Ha ! ha ! ha !

'Haven't you got a decent miniskirt? I thought the young lived only in the present. But it seems with you that when you're not dressed as a S.F. robot, you're got up like Isadora Duncan in her cups.'

'Take no notice, Ally darling. Papa has an Edwardian dirty mind. That's why miniskirts are such a joy to him.'

'Miniskirts are the antithesis of smut, Zoe.'

'All right, sweet. I hate them just because they make me look like a senior girl guide. It was a *beautiful* coat, Ally, and I'm quite determined now to give you a new one. We can have it infested with moths and so forth first, if you must feel that it's moulting.'

And now the Hamster looking straight at her, actually looking.

'*I* like the *tights*.'

'Yes. Well, Hamo dear, I suppose you *would*. But let's not talk about *that*. I do think, Ally, miniskirts aside, that you should put on something warmer. And I *am* worried about the knee. Even Fonteyn would have had no artistic scruples about using Dettol.'

'Yes, rag bag, off with you.'

And, heaven-sent bliss, after enduring Hector's old paw on her shoulder for a moment again, she was released.

Looking at the deep cool green bath, she longed to soak her weary body for hours with all sorts of magic scents to cloud the brain and drown the reason. A drowsy numbness wouldn't pain *her* sense. It would be delicious. But Rodrigo or Ned or both would soon be here. And how awful if they were to be confronted with Them and the Hamster. So she stripped off her tights, thought to wash her knee under the tap, but, seeing it already scabbed, decided better to leave it, put on the glorious swishy pink satin petticoat she had bought at the High Street Mart and over it her other wonderful buy – a blue-green sequined evening dress with shoulder straps and waist almost at the knee. The skirt just reached the top of her leather boots. To it all she added the double row of wooden beads that fell below the knee. Threading a large needle, she cobbled the lovely fox to the lamb – your generation live in the present, He had said, all right this would do for the present. But it didn't, it fell apart as she put it on; she she was forced to make do with her black patent-leather coat. Before going down, she looked at herself in her dressing-room mirror, and enjoyed watching the reflection as its eyelids shone a brighter and brighter silver and green with the make-up she was applying.

As she reached the drawing-room door, He was braying again.

'My dear fellow, they're obviously kicking you upstairs. A very good thing, too. The more *creative* men make the policy . . .'

But Mama did one of those things. She came over and kissed the forehead.

'It looks quite lovely, darling. Oh dear! Why was my generation so unenterprising? Doesn't she look enchanting, Hamo?'

And Hamo, looking anywhere but at her:

'Very with it.'

'Dear Hamo! What words from the past! No one says that now, do they, darling? I appeal to *you*. But never mind, even if he doesn't look at your sequins, he approves the *tights*.'

All this fuss and innuendo, and now the Hamster making a coy little smile, as though to say to Mama, 'Thank you for accepting. But not before the children,' and burrowing into his arm-chair (insofar as Ompierre could be burrowed into), making Her drawing-room his nest. As if it mattered. And when Rodrigo had lain on the rug at the party kissing Douglas White, she had been pleased not jealous, because it had only been for effect, and as Douglas was so pretty the effect had been good. And between Ned and Rodrigo, too, there was mutual physical feeling, but what it was and how, and, no, she would not think of that; if they lived as they felt, it would come out right. But an old whiskered hamster would surely do better to keep his flirta-tious looks for the privacy of that vast desolate swimming-bath flat of his. And whoever with anyway? Perhaps another whiskered hamster, the two of them together there, like some wonderful nineteen-hundred ad for gymnastic belts or trusses or whatever, probably in those long woollen things like tights that came down to the ankles. Marvellous for collage.

Yet this sort of jokey thought she must banish, for bitching about sex was unforgivable – worse even than all this nasty suggestiveness and coyness. Though it drove the blood to her head, made her ears sing, she tried to form in her mind some sentence to meet him, hamster or no hamster. But what? – as for example quite boldly, 'I hope you have a nice lover'; but then, suppose he hadn't – certainly the lover wouldn't be nice to her view, for he'd have to be pretty old, and probably there wasn't anyone at all, and then one would have been kind only to be cruel. Anyway from all Leslie had said, the Hamster had been pining away ever since Leslie and Martin had been together. 'Cheer up' would seem to be the friendliest thing, but even that seemed hardly worth saying when somebody's been determined to pine away for what must be years and years.

Remembering all his expensive, embarrassing presents, and his more than embarrassing devotion, she tried to think worldly Ottoline Morrell sort of thoughts about slaves at one's feet and so on. Playing with the long string of beads, even tossing them to and fro a little, one still could not forget that handing it down in love was a beastly uptight sort of woman's fake and, anyway, far too close to 'how to comfort Ned' and even 'how not to let Rodrigo hurt'. Nevertheless, as the Hamster was going half or all round the world, she must make some contact, show some feeling (sincerity, after all, can be a heartless luxury), as though he (nicer to say Wilfred Owen than that awful Rupert Brooke person) were going to that blood-soaked front. And, of course, although it was only air flights, there must be hundreds who never return. 'No, I'm afraid they're not in. I'm their daughter. Of course. He's my godfather. Oh no! No!'

No survivors, and probably he'd leave everything to her, and she'd find porn pictures, moustachioed sergeants facing each other with dumb-bells for some obscene use, wearing long woollen – she remembered the word now – combinations. Well, at least she'd never let Them see.

But she'd got nowhere in such circular thoughts and now it was too late, for His blaring had filled the room again, brushing aside beads and bugles and innuendoes.

'They'll try to run you, of course. Keep half the evidence concealed. Feed you only the facts they choose. All the same, not to worry, you know. They can be beaten if you're dogged enough. I've found that out at the Corporation. And if *I* can do it, you certainly can with all that scientific persistence.'

With much whisker-touching and an air of distaste for his food offered him, the Hamster refused it. Research scientist. Own field work in India, Ceylon. Visits to plant genetic centres; additional work undertaken for F.A.O. Reported observations, not policy. Contacts I.R.R.I. And, no doubt, O.A.C.D. And purring now, not mumbling. Just those groups of letters making him into a sleek, proud pussycat. But then that was the scientist's life – letters, letters and numbers – look at Alan Grayson's room with all those chemical equations or Nickie Culmer's desk covered in weird-looking economists' graphs –

$$A = 2q + \frac{\sigma v (AL)^2}{2} B = \frac{\sigma v}{2}$$

or whatever it all meant. So to throw letters at them, even these awful organizational letters, no doubt, brought him out of his hamster cage, or rather brought them in so that there they were – humanist Him and Her – thinking they'd gone on a charming visit to a pet hamster's cage, but, in fact, faced with a purring tiger.

And really that was what he seemed now, for he'd left those organizational letters for formulae and his purr must be audible to his caged brother tigers a quarter of a mile away at the Zoo. Anxious to discuss A.2 P.5 with a chap in Tokyo, and B.3 L.7 with another chap in ... Roaring he was now, despite the prim Cheshire grin – a smile on the face of the Tiger, so that She could only bleat.

'But surely, Hamo, you care about what *happens* to your work?'

And He: 'You'll find yourself caught up in it all. The admin men will get you.'

No good, the great striped Hamster drove all before him.

But not herself, for she knew exactly where she stood about letters, letters and numbers, graphs and equations, figures and fractions, that threatened the humanity of words. Everything worthwhile would fall, if the letters and numbers conquered instead of words and visions and sounds. Of that they were all sure – Ned above all, of course, but even Rodrigo who, after all, cared so intensely about style in living, dandy rebellion. Oh God! let the roaring striped Hamster have shrunk to his mumble again before Ned arrived, otherwise Ned would sense him at once as an enemy of magic, of its glory and its terror.

But now they had shifted on to numbers of a different kind – pounds and pence, but especially pounds – the old bourgeois standby numbers; hence He and She felt once more at ease (a guilty ease).

'It's the *one* part of taxation that I feel really happy about paying. Well, that, and schools of course, and health.'

'Yes. But I doubt if much of Hamo's dwarf wheat and hybrid rice came out of our pockets. Mostly American dollars, wasn't it, Hamo?'

'Oh, Hamo, do say not, because that would mean ...'

'In point of fact the major programmes are financed by the countries themselves, I believe.'

'What, Zambia, Gambia and Anyoldambia? You're joking.'

'Perry, don't be so vulgar.'

'Sorry. Penitent old Hector. All the same, they surely just *don't have* that sort of money. Or else they've been telling the story very smartly.'

And the Hamster, now amused, an on-looking sort of hamster.

'Good heavens, I had no idea that Number 8 was such a fund-raising centre. I must put James Kepple and Sir Alec Jardine in touch with you. The financing of world projects is the refuge they've taken in their inability to keep up with the new projects themselves. Myself, as long as I get my adequate thousands for my own work, the millions may be left to you fund-raisers. However, if the honesty of the under-developed countries' claims to be under-developed troubles you, Perry, I can assure you that that much is done by *international* funds. In my own case, for example, by the Rapson.'

'The Rapson. Good God! That means your villainous great-uncle James.'

'*Hamo!* Your work surely doesn't get money from him. The

54

monster uncle! He must be draining millions away from the starving.'

And now the Hamster preening himself in a new way, a hamster modestly connected with prize hamsters.

'Among the innumerable and world-wide financial enterprises with which I am concerned, the Rapson Fund is, I assure you, only a drop in the ocean.'

And, oh Lord! could it be? the Hamster was now imitating another hamster; yet, apart from blowing out his cheeks, he was, voice, look and all, exactly the same as if he had never tried to imitate.

Seeking a reflection of her embarrassment in Mama and Him, she found none. It was obviously some old joke of their long-ago youth, for there was laughter and filling-up of glasses.

'I do wish that just for once I could *actually meet* the wicked uncle. Not to speak to, of course, because I'm no good with tycoon monsters.'

'I *have,* Zoe. I passed him in a corridor at Television Centre. He's a monster B.B.C. Trustee, you know, as well, only, thank God, too busy to do much harm.'

'Exactly, as I said, my interests are world-wide and innumerable. Four hundred and eight in all.'

And Mama glancing now as if to say, listen, see the Hamster doing his tricks; and even He had a little smile, that said, it takes time to unfreeze hamsters, but we do know how to do it. A great longing for Rodrigo to put them down, to break up their superior talk with his real ease and worldliness came over her; or, if not that, for Ned with his integrity to batter through their satisfied glow of memory, as they invited her to come into the circle by the warm fireside of past jokes even though, of course, being still a child, she could hardly have a proper adult palate for the roast chestnuts (that was good – she would remember that for Rodrigo) and mulled claret.

'I'm afraid his arithmetic will become worse now, for his new occult interests include Atlantean mathematics. My poor aunt is supposed to be revealing the significance of Stonehenge measurements through some medium. Although as far as I remember her computing interests never went any further than a very proper control of the household accounts in her lifetime.'

They were sparkling now – this was how it used to be, those were the days, my friends, and we're going to see they never end. Mama's ear-rings a-glitter, and His liquid eyes aglow, and even the Hamster's little nose twinkling. Twinkle, twinkle, little wits, you'll never send me into fits. To tell to Ned, for there was always Lewis Carroll to fall back on.

'Has he still got that tame medium, Hamo? I always remember your description of her – the fat one with mauve hair that put him in touch with Piero della Francesca or was it Leonardo? You made us laugh *so* much.'

And, looking up at the Moroni portrait as though to ask for post-grave news at a rather cheaper rate, and then twisting her handkerchief again because could one, should one in view of everything and all that was suffered everywhere, hoard away nuts even so comparatively modest as the Moroni? As if life could be measured by the modesty of one's store of nuts.

But the Hamster was almost chattering now. So this was what the mysterious words meant that she had heard all her life. 'Hamo *can* still be wonderfully funny. If only Leslie ...'

'I'm afraid the extra-terrestrial voices have moved on from art where their nonsense was not wholly out of keeping. He's launched into so-called science now. But of this very special kind. Apart from my poor aunt, he's in touch with one of the initiates from Avebury, some refugee from Atlantis who's trying to teach him the mathematical foundations of the esoteric wisdom. But for all his great financial powers, it seems that Uncle James isn't quite up to occult addition and subtraction yet.'

And laughter and sparkle and more champagne.

But if this did mean that the Hamster had put aside his pining, his life-long widow's weeds or whatever men wore for the men they'd lost, she ought (because human beings *do* count and gratitude *is* a good) to try to reach him. And at this point, anyway, thinking of Yeats and all that Ned had said of the Golden Order, she thought perhaps she could. So breaking through their bubbling, she heard her own voice, rather shrill and serious and little-girl-in-class, but commonsense and rational not to offend his prejudices.

'How well authenticated are the mathematical surveys of

Avebury and Glastonbury and the other neolithic places? Do serious scientists find any conviction in it, Hamo?'

And the Hamster stopped dead, as though God had asked him the time.

'Well, to begin with, of course, Alexandra, I'm only a fair mathematician. And then I haven't familiarized myself with any of the evidence offered. Aerial survey, isn't it? It's really an engineer's problem.'

Imploring her with his eyes not to break contact, but also telling her that he couldn't find the wavelength. But now He wheeled round with delight not to the metres and cubes of the ancient solar wisdoms but to dear old pounds and pence.

'What do you think the old boy'll leave?'

And Mama, fearing for the loss of the Hamster's recovered virgin sparkle, cried, 'Avebury! So that's why he bought that estate in Wiltshire. Great-grandfather's letters are full of it. You know how he thinks anyone from London and especially tycoons come to the country solely to shoot the last badger and cut down the last wych elm. But it's vast apparently. Do you think he might leave it to you, Hamo? If he left you his money *and* his estate you could set up your own research centre there without all these awful admin people.'

'Yes, old boy, how would Wiltshire be for the sorghum revolution?'

But the Hamster had suddenly gone all prim again.

'I imagine Uncle James will leave the major part of his fortune to charity. I may get some memento. Though I hardly deserve it, offering feeble mimicry of what is no doubt a necessary manner for a man so eminent in that financial world. You must always remember that he was the second son. As my father always pointed out, with Grandfather inheriting Loughaugh, there was little Uncle James could turn to but the City. He wasn't, thank goodness, born to the Victorian tradition of the Church for the younger son. My father respected him greatly, although I think he found his manner a little ostentatious at times as I do. And he always showed the most laudable and genuine admiration for Father's distinguished military career. No, you really mustn't encourage me to mock him.'

But She would not be repressed. 'You mark my words, Hamo. You'll inherit. And I am sure that his will'll be one of the enormous ones in *The Times* that are so fascinating to read. They're always Baronets in Wiltshire or Caithness.'

'Or widows and old maids in Eastbourne.'

'Oh, do stop about Eastbourne, Perry. It's getting as irritating as the *Guardian* misprints. Anyway, those poor old Eastbourne women aren't *really* rich. They just live in those hotels because they can't afford servants. But people like Hamo's great-uncle – company-director squires – you can see how clever they are to be both at once ! – *they* leave millions.'

And, happy with the millions because they reflected no guilt on large Hampstead incomes, He and She were off now on a whimsy about wills, should they or should they not be one's favourite *Times* reading, and was it widows or squires, and in the U.S.A. certainly widows in Florida, and, if in the U.S.A., why not in England? With the Hamster rather feebly following in the wake.

And their voices cut off all thought, all connection, all meaning, all love. Her limbs ached, now her arms, then her thighs; her head throbbed, and her cheeks burned; and, how, with such aching limbs, to scratch, peck, scratch, peck in any hall, after the van jolting and brown rice cooked in the van on a primus? And how to respond to Ned's arms round her and his beard so deliciously, clumsily scraping her lips, and Rodrigo's cool, practised hands, stroking, exploring among the beads and satin petticoat? And Birkin where had he fled? And Ursula? But now the room spun round and the Hamster was upside-down like the dormouse in the teapot, and for a moment everything was black and she shut her eyes, for Rodrigo's bare thigh was taut against Gerald's naked back, and his arm was forcing Ned's head backwards, no, Birkin's. And suddenly, but not in sleep, for she could see Them and the Hamster and hear Their willy, willy, wetlegs talk, a woman's thin face, every wrinkle, even blackheads clear, old white skin grubby, mouth pursed, blackish hairs spread loosely on the upper lip, pince-nez but behind them the eyes bleeding (*Potemkin?*) but none the less hating, hating. She held to the sides of the chair, rigid, in order not to scream, she told herself it was no woman, just Loerke, she'd called up

Loerke. In Lawrence at least she would get a first from empathy. Here was a joke to tell Ned. Oh where *was* Ned? Where *was* he? And then the doorbell.

She was up at once.

'I'll go. It's them in the van, the mime van. I'll be back next week. Have a good world trip, Hamo. And Mama's wrong. Don't fuss about the starving. From now on everyone must do their own thing.'

But it was no good.

'Alexandra, darling, you might at least bring your friends in for a glass of champagne. We haven't got bubonic in the house.'

And He, old Hector, 'Unclean! Unclean!'

'Stop it, Perry, they'll think we're mad. Have you got food, Ally? I can give you some rather good pâté sandwiches. Wouldn't that be a good idea? Who is it anyway? Someone we know?'

'It's only Rodrigo and Ned and we've got to get to Luton or somewhere for a rehearsal, so there isn't time.'

'Ah,' He all friendly and bubbling, 'Jekyll and Hyde.'

And Mama shushing Him with one look, and another to the Hamster – 'These are the Alexandra problems I was telling you about.' How to explain the awful confluence that threatened to drown her?

'I mean about wills. They wouldn't be any good about that. You see we don't know about wills. Ned won't say anything. But he'll hate it. And if Rodrigo does say anything, it will be an awful show-off, because his parents are really quite ordinary and they don't have any large property or anything . . .'

But Mama's arm was around her waist; even a light kiss on the lips to silence her.

'Wills! You make us sound like the Forsyte Saga. You seem to think that we're critical of you for having two boys after you at once, darling. We're just jealous, aren't we, Hamo? And, anyway, they're both tremendous charmers in their different ways.'

And He, 'Splendid specimens of the Hungry Generation's Tread,' but giving her a special smile to admit that He was only human, fallible, might have misjudged the worth of her followers.

And, Mama, unfolding, did one of her rare hostess sweeps, and in a minute her voice could be heard distinctly.

'But, Rodrigo! Ned! How nice! Come in!'

'She stood at the door welcoming them in,' but no chestnut tongue-twisters could make her heart beat slower, her thighs run less with anxiety's sweat.

An open door, but no escape. Some hope perhaps through sensory evasion. Feeling the creases, the orderly, exact creases of the solid, expensive, correct tweed of his trousers, pinching that razor edge, tightening his finger's hold upon such sober substantiality, might blur if not blot out the cracked, self-pitying note of Perry's voice, Zoe's anxious, unassured sounds heralding further unexplored confusion. Useless to deny that this apparently perfect family fusion had suffered some powerful fission, but he could not, would not be drawn into testing, evaluating the causes. But, far worse, the ragged-boy misery of Alexandra's pinched, large-eyed face and wan figure – how could he help her, he of all men asked to meet boyish despair? How much he longed that he were young enough to share her misery – two ragged street urchins shut out from the chattering family feast – mudlarks! he thought, that was what he would wish to be with her, pinched-cheeked ragged mudlarks, but for all the mud and squalor up to all sorts of boyish larks. Physical pressure surely, if firm enough, would save him from letting in such chaos. Chaos and guilt. Through the good rich tweed, he gripped his own thigh to banish in sensation his utter impotence to re-order a demolished structure, to offer any sieve through which to restore the fruitful selectivity of Number 8 as he had always graded that cherished group. He to re-order, to restore! A sterile mutant had no place in this warm granary. And now something of the unknown confusion had been announced by Zoe.

'Ned. It's so awful, I never *can* remember your other name.'

And a bearded mumble.

'Phillips! That's it. But you're one of those essentially one-name people, and I mean it as a compliment. A young man from the mysterious North.'

Hamo felt his heart jump; but here was no second Brian. Rather a beard covering young flesh – something he had rigorously trained himself never to see, for this blasphemy against the ideal human form was one of the disgusting aspects of modern life, one that, if not insulated, could make obscene one's daily conference with one's fellow men. So to Ned, with formal bow and automatic smile, *nyet*. Smiling would do, it seemed, for the beard, whose swallowed remarks were audible to no one, nor clearly expected to be. If silence or mumbling was the youthful fashion, he could replicate to order. He sat back, relieved and, with the beard, let five minutes of Grant chatter flow over him.

Then ... suddenly, his bowels heaved, his scrotum tightened, the room, the beard, Zoe, the gilt, the porcelain, Pannini's church, the goldfoil corks, the beaded dress all whirled and grew dim. Surely, even the agonies buried so deep within him for fifteen years could not have such force to tear him apart, as they wrenched themselves free from their tightly bound grave-linen! There, in the doorway, where he had stood many millions (it seemed) of times that made up, in fact, just one era of happiness, was Leslie, aged twenty, yes, surely not yet twenty-one.

'Rodrigo Knight,' Zoe announced.

Straight chrome-yellow hair, small ears, large blue-green eyes, high cheekbones, rose-flushed, down-powdered golden skin tight to the skull, small teeth, wide mouth, slender neck, chest 30 surely, waist within a fraction of 24, and tapered hips that sloped back and away to give promise of firm full buttocks. Not to choke was all the problem. And then, quite involuntarily he caught the youth's eye and his glance was returned, seemingly conscious, provocative.

Alexandra's admirer! Leslie returned again and still willing in Alexandra's admirer – or, perhaps, for by elevating women he too often, he knew, denied them physical humanity, perhaps her lover. Escape he must, from *that*. He could leave – but not, due to his own old-maidish fears of lost planes, missed trains, until Erroll came. He would go to his lifelong refuge, to the lavatory, but the thought of the seat warm still from these slender thighs (for that was where the late entering young beast must have been) made such retreat too pleasant to be right. But, in fact, surely that glance *must* be the acquiescence of good manners – indeed the now voluble speech with its carefully worldly, elaborate (mannered? good-mannered?) drawl suggested the sort of deference that too often deceived one into imagining compliance.

'I think your loo-lady is very special, Mrs Grant. Isn't it Queen Mary? I've seen her picture somewhere before. That primeval hat and all that "trespassers keep out" wire or net round her neck and bosom. And what a welcome change from Lord Kitchener. I am really *against* loos with Lord K.'

Turning to *him* as though he knew anything of what such nonsense was about. Challenge or politeness, the look must be met by a frown, even by a softened look towards the unspeakable beard to underline the contrasting receptions. But to no effect, or, rather, for a moment the easy torrent was turned on to the others.

'Some friends of ours in Sussex have the most terrific loo. With an absolutely genuine early box-seat in real mahogany. You know, that wonderful kind that looks like polished chestnuts. And a pull-up chain! I mean it was *always* there. They didn't collect it or anything awful like that.'

'Mama collects all the time.'

'Ally means I'm talking too much, Mrs Grant.'

'Oh, no, Rodrigo, it's much more direct than that. She just disapproves of my collecting.'

'I could have meant both, couldn't I? Anyway, it isn't me that disapproves of your buying pictures and china like that. It's you. You wouldn't want to do it if you didn't disapprove of it.'

'Do you all invent characters for older people like she does for us, Rodrigo?'

'Well, I think it's only "doing the novel". We get into the habit of making convenient mock-ups.'

'But I thought "character" in the novel had been dissolved.'

'Oh, Mama, please!'

'Yes, I know, darling, not in neo-trad and all that. After all, we have a living exponent of solid character creation here with us now.'

Perry, refilling glasses, offering pâté and hunks of French bread, placed his hand for a second on Zoe's plump shoulder so what she had said must have been loving, and not, as it sounded, jeering.

Rejoicing that the structure – at least the Perry-Zoe section – was not quite so destroyed as he had feared, he yet felt only the more isolated, in so obviously understanding nothing of the mysterious links that threaded the whole. Looking at the beard – hunks of bread and pâté and gulps of champagne disguising its anti-social silence – he hoped that around that corner of the room the cold wind of isolation blew a little also, as around his own. But now Perry widening another breach.

'Nevertheless, for a writer of the English language to have a daughter studying the English language who yet says "pictures and china *and that*".'

'It's what Grandmother says. I thought we mustn't lose our roots.'

'Roots! All this loose romanticism! What the Little Mam sweated herself sick for in all that "how's things tonight, Mabel?" and smoke was to give me a formal control over the language I speak and write. To allow her son and granddaughter to celebrate their roots *coherently*.'

'Gracious, darling!'

But Zoe stroked his arm. Alexandra's beads glittered aimlessly with her body's trembling. The beard's hand had found hers.

'Words ... celebration ... like, y'know, shit.'

Such as he could hear had a snarling sound to its flat Northern vowels.

Only slightly shaking from a sobbing gulped down, Alexandra said, 'In that case why don't we say "toilet" and not "loo"?'

And Zoe, hands to ears as though genuinely shattered by noise, 'Oh, no, no! Not all that, darling. We had the whole of that ten years ago at least.'

But Elegance was ready with social tact, and really, the golden brown fair skin cried out to be stroked.

'Aren't such changes in vocabulary only what there should be in a mobile society? I mean my parents always say "lavatory". But I'd hardly like to remember all the efforts I've made to change to "loo".'

The appeal of the youthful mockery of himself, of such an innocent young self-confessed thruster, was presented straight, oh God! at *him*; the blue-green eyes rounded in mock innocence stared at *him* demanding *his* delighted amusement at this naïve self-accusation.

'And what do *you* say, Mr Langmuir?'

He could have sworn that the youth had, as Leslie long ago,

swelled his cheek out with his tongue and slightly winked, so that, from all those years away, he found a coquetterie he thought for ever gone. He could feel himself fluttering his eyelashes.

'Oh, I? I say "gun room".'

And, as though miraculously ten years had never sped, the mock retired-colonel primness brought laughter from them all, Elegance leading with: 'You're the immovable object then in our irresistibly fluid society.'

But snap, something of the lovely, sloppy sensuous mouth closed tight with self-congratulation at the repartee and, so closing, brought little lines at the corners of the lips into sight; and suddenly, there was a faint hair recession to be seen at the right top of the brow, a roughness everywhere upon the golden skin, the pale rose of the cheeks revealed in closer view small patches of redness, perhaps little broken veins – twenty-four years old, surely, or at the very least, twenty-three. At any rate, beyond the pale. Relief at a danger vanished, a sudden trap that had threatened most indecorous capture happily sprung, made him smile so spontaneously at this young elegant, now no threat, now indeed nothing, that he could sense at his side Zoe's disquietude, her body tautening with conjecture.

He wondered a little sadly that, after all these years of friendship, she could have any fears of his looks at Alexandra's admirer, lover; but then had young Elegance been, indeed, eighteen or twenty, what guarantee would he have cared to give for the quality of his glances? Certainly her alarm at what she thought she saw was enough for her to forget the unspoken ban of six years or more, a ban she had herself imposed. Was it to punish or distract that she now said the never-uttered names?

'Did you know, Hamo, that Leslie and Martin have bought a house on Corfu? For retirement, if you please. Leslie's thirty-four and I doubt if Martin's fifty yet. The way people prepare for death nowadays. I call it obscene.'

He had by good fortune no need to reply, for Perry's indignant voice now invaded the whole room.

'You *don't* admire Bloom in the toilet, the intimate portrait of the saint in the shithouse! My God! I'm not asking you to accept all Joyce's verbal fireworks, but the basic common humanity of Bloom!'

And the beard scattering saliva in his excitement.

'I sho'dn' have thought that just 'cos you can't accept that synthetic icing-sugar of so called poetry and stuff, y'know, you ness'rily have to swallow, I mean, all that indigestible journalistic realist dough.'

And the din burst.

But for him it could only be a distant noise of battle, bawling about books, and jangling generational noises, for at the moment of Perry's provocative remark that let loose the noise, looking at Rodrigo, he saw quite clearly the creases in Leslie's neck as he had seen them in that same room ten years ago. And the sight let loose visual waves that bombarded the identity he had so carefully constructed over the last years and fractionated it far more completely than any audio waves of literary chatter could ever do.

They had arrived too early for Sunday dinner (Perry and Zoe not yet returned from the cottage). Leslie, as usual, had sixth-form essays to correct. In his own head an equation; and, thinking it through, he had been gazing unseeingly ahead, when a last splash of the dying summer sun lit up, almost bloodied a surface that banished all figures and left him only with unease, turning to disgust. What were those folds and lines, that coarse grain, those pits? Then he knew that they announced to him a *man*'s flesh – how any man, not to say woman, could touch or get pleasure from such texture, as though one were to stroke and fondle a macadamized road surface, or, since it was 'living', rather, perhaps, an elephant's, a rhino's hide. Better really the pink and white softness, the disgusting marshmallow gooeyness that women brought to mind. And then Leslie had turned his head, the folds of his neck had straightened out, the flesh had become once again taut yet smooth, soft yet firm. All the same one of the few lines of Shakespeare that he remembered from the dreary wastes of school English lessons stuck in his mind during the following months and would not budge – 'What's done cannot be undone.'

Not that he had not tried. Now, as Alexandra's elegant young man's neck revealed itself in its turn as simply the maturing neck of Alexandra's young man, those hours, days, months, that whole desperate year returned to him in a series of fast blows of memory, like the series of stars enclosed in the balloons that come from punched heads in strip cartoons – Owooch? To meet the impact of such a knockout, to find his feet again, before he was counted out, he knew that he must be alone, with his back to the wall, only so could he sieve the sterile experience from the fruit-ful, go back over all the painful, often absurd testings by which he had at last reassembled the fragments of his life into its present reduced, yet verifiable formula.

He got up from his chair and walked from the room, un-noticed in the insane babel of voices clashing in subjective argu-ment. Opening the lavatory door, he caught only a flash of soft powder-blue that denoted her late gracious majesty (the Garter?). He could only think it a blue that might distract. Pictures in the lavatory! It showed how undesirable were all departures from strict convention. But there in its proper place was the wooden seat, the proper good place from schooldays onward for reflec-tion. Here he could review watchfully but shortly the orderly system by which he had arrived here, a system now under the threat of rout from chance words, impressions, lights and sounds. One thing he noted, with approval, his back was up against the wall. It was a salutary reminder of his solitary defensive position in life, a rebuke for fostering illusions of fellowship in the very house where he had sentimentally indulged them for so many years.

How good if Mrs E. or Erroll were here to arrange these thronging, jostling memories, under his direction, into an ab-solving pattern. But to the comfort of his hidden sexual life Mrs E. lent only the aid of an unseeing eye, and Erroll a friendly smile. How Erroll, though, with his tedious talk of cutting and montage, would have loved the job of cutting up these memories to make a tale to show – 'the art of the cinema', the only pre-tentious phrase that ever came to his assistant's lips. But he had to do the job for himself, as far as he could, for, in great part, the memories, too headlong for producer's discipline, rushed in and showed themselves. All he could do was to separate them out into scenes: the Ludicrous Love Life of Hamo Langmuir; and then to let each scene, wobbling a little in memory's uncertain blur, a little hazy, click into place, not that of time's simple sequence. To start with his own defence. That he *could* choose.

He remembered exactly when he had presented it to Leslie, and a worse time and place he could hardly have selected.

He had chosen Sunday evening, 6.30 p.m., seven years ago. He had come into the large, splendidly equipped kitchen (the furnishing had cost more than that of all the other rooms put together) of their Islington house – 'Leslie's laboratory' had been one of their ironically offered whimsicalities – Leslie had been cooking for a small dinner-party, one of the dinners he was so rightly proud of. He had come, it could hardly have been worse, at one of those crucial moments when a sauce must be kept stirring (all Leslie's sauces demanded perpetual motion), an oven door opened, a roasting bird revealed to be basted in its own juices – a balancing trick requiring, as Leslie frequently remarked, full concentration. Sitting down, he had said, in what no doubt had been a ponderous tone: 'The trouble is that your chickens have come home to roost.' He writhed on the wooden seat as he remembered.

To keep his temper, Leslie had answered, 'Could you leave whatever it is until later, lovey. Anyway this is not a chicken, it's a duck.'

'Yes, of course. Only I've been thinking it all through and I do just want to plead for myself that we wouldn't be in this ghastly mess if you hadn't made me see things straight when we were at Cambridge.'

Leslie had shut the oven door, carefully, not banging it. 'Yes? I can deal now with what you want to say, if it's not too long. It was only while I was doing the sauce *and* the bird. Don't take any notice of my stirring, just go on.'

'We've been through such ghastly months trying to pretend this hasn't happened when it has. Or trying to make it work when it doesn't. It's just humiliating us both.'

'*I've* not been humiliated. I've offered the same goods as per order. If you can't come for them, that's your fault, not mine. No, sorry, rub that out. But if we're going to discuss this, and I do think your sense of occasion is a bit at fault, I'm bound to say bitter things, so you must expect it.'

'All right. We can leave it until after they've all gone and discuss it then. Only you've told me to work it out for myself and I do believe I have arrived somewhere.'

'For God's sake, out with it then. Better a ruined dinner for the Easons and Perry and Zoe, than us sitting there bursting with suppressed emotion and Zoe looking all womanly concern. Better, too, than another session until the early hours. We've had a solid three weeks of those. That ghastly youth Jackson said yesterday, "Do you know, Sir, you've said Thomas Cromwell three times this afternoon when you meant Oliver. Isn't that a psychological thing?" I longed to tell the little beast that it was only what happened to you when your boy-friend keeps you up night after night to tell you that he sees you have to shave and that makes him vomit. No, I'm sorry, lovey. If you knew – what worries me most is that all these ghastly long arguments and failures in bed and all-night soul searchings must take their toll on *your* work. And that's what's important. Anyone can teach a lot of kids, who don't want to know, exactly who the gentry were who joined King Charles's standard, but only you and Jesus Christ can feed the hungry millions. So go ahead. Zoe's the only one who knows a bigarade sauce when she tastes it, anyway.'

'Well, it's this. I don't believe I can ever free myself now from the importance of pure physical sex, even with someone I love as much as you, because *you* taught me that importance at such an absolutely vital moment of my life. If you hadn't done so, I should have gone on to be a dried-up, repressed old bachelor, but as it is, I can't . . .'

'You can't have it off with someone of twenty-five. I think I can take that part as read now.'

'All right. Make it difficult for me to say. Anyway, with anyone else but you, it would be twenty-two. Only you look so young.'

Leslie had reached for one of the many little bottles, and said, 'Sage. Now chop an onion . . . Perhaps *I* should be going to witch doctors, not you. "Oh Mr Doctor, whatever shall I do? My boy-friend won't fuck me, 'cos I don't look twenty-two."' And he had added, 'I saved you from spending your life masturbating – oh, mentally, if you prefer – on your father's photograph. All right, so he got killed at Arnhem. That doesn't make him the ideal lover for an intelligent handsome son. Mental necrophilia, ugh! And as for that bloody housemaster horror, who told you that love between men was a fine ideal so long as it remained ideal ... All public schools ought to be netted then gassed like vermin. And I save you from all that filth and now you throw my five-o'clock shadow in my face. All right, yes. So I am bitter. Go and see all these precious doctors. It's the sort of goofy idea that Zoe *would* recommend.'

As he remembered the little domestic melodrama, he felt a sudden surge of anger. Perhaps, as his pick-ups sometimes said, he asked to be conned. All Leslie's talk about the free sex life of the working class. Wasn't it like Perry on his Mother's pluck, just a confidence trick that the Grants put over the more guilty middle class, over himself and Zoe? For a moment, the thought that the whole of his happy years with Leslie had been only a superior confidence trick, in which he had been left holding the forged five-pound note, made him tremble with anger. He pushed his long legs against the wall opposite to relieve the tension. Only the costive sweet expression upon her majesty's face broke through his sense of murderous anger with all life – with Truefitt, his housemaster, with Leslie, with Perry, with Zoe, with Sir Alec, with Nelson Hart, with Alexandra, with the witch doctors, with Erroll, even with Mrs E. – scene by scene they had acted out their parts with him as stooge, turning him into a sterile mutant. But there was something about the very iciness of Queen Mary's gracious smile, the ramrod discipline of her carriage that said to him 'and what do you think they made of me? and did I complain?' Drawing in his legs, relaxing his muscles and his anger, he said aloud, 'All right. As one queen to another. No self-pity.' It was the sort of joke that Leslie had taught him to make, but he did not laugh, for he never found that he made jokes from a sense of pleasure.

And then he cupped his face in his hands with an access of self-disgust: to start to blame Leslie who had given him his happiest, most fruitful years, had done everything that he could to prolong the union (massages, casual clothes, hair remover), and, then, when it was clear that nothing could make it work, had so reasonably gone off with Martin and taken all the blame. Leslie who had been so unfairly blamed by everyone, by Zoe, even, Zoe, the guardian angel of their homosexual marriage. For although it was absurd to talk as Leslie had of Zoe being the cause of his consulting doctors, she had been the occasion for his final decision. He remembered St James's Park, five years ago, a summer afternoon, before them the lake and the island. What he and Zoe were watching on this warm summer afternoon amid the throng of foreign tourists, were the wildfowl, jostling and swarming for the visitors' offerings of bread.

He must have been boring her to death. No, others would have been bored. But the wonderful thing he had found with Zoe was that he could talk ramblingly without its seeming foolish.

'And so, you see, the control of genetic diversity in cultivated species is only a human ordering parallel to the less strictly controlled, more wasteful selection occurring in wild species,' he had told her.

And she had come back, as always, fiercely. But all their talk was a half-accepted parody which only his years with Leslie could have allowed him to accept as intellectually respectable.

'Only! But that's *just* what we're arguing about. You put in that "only" to annoy. In fact, all your kindly explanations of your work are just done to help while the afternoon away. Dear Hamo! So they should be. And so are my explanations of what we do at the clinic and all the rest of it. Frivolous use of the serious. To me it's the essence of any real friendship. You can't live on separate diets of serious emotions and jokes all the time like Perry and Leslie do. Oh, look at those mandarin drakes' wing feathers, they go through the water like, what do you call those things? Portuguese men-of-war. Or shark's fins.'

'How do you know they're called mandarin?'

'Oh, I've always known. Idle rentier women are like magpies. They collect any random fact in sight. Anyway you couldn't do without names for the plants you work on. I've got nothing but idle vision, but at least I must name what I see. Especially if it's beautiful like the mandarin duck. But, as I was saying, idle interchange *is* the only foundation for a civilized friendship. Seriousness I like to leave for action – like your work. Oh, look at the barnacle geese honking away to make a passage through the ducks to get at the bread. The whole thing's just like I imagine some great naval base – Portsmouth, perhaps. Like you'd see it from the air. Ships steaming off in all directions and then stopping for no reason whatsoever. The tufted ducks popping up like submarines just for the hell of it. But then I can't imagine any armed forces having any sense in their activities …'

'Not a very happy parallel for the pacifist's case. All the activities of these birds can be explained, no doubt, on the basis of territoriality, pecking order and other well-observed phenomena.'

'Oh, evolution! Well, all I can say is just look at that pelican. Why on earth does a bird like that need a beak like an excavator?'

'I think you're confusing the beak with the pouch.'

'Yes, of course I am. I shall confuse everything while we go on talking just to avoid speaking of what's in our minds. What *is* happening between you and Leslie? Going off like that to Cannes or some terrible place with that tat man, and down every week-end at his gracious Thames-side residence. Has he gone mad? You two were a kind of advertisement to show how it could be made to work. To treat *you* like that, Hamo. I *can't* forgive it. Why don't *you do* something about it? Make him jealous. You're handsome enough, Heaven knows.'

'You shouldn't blame Leslie. *I* am to blame.'

'What do you mean, *you're* to blame? Oh, you mean something physical. Well what a pair of babes you are. You must go and see your doctor. They can get these things right in a second these days. Anyway that doesn't excuse Leslie.' And, of course, he thought, savouring a little the hardness of the wooden seat against his thighs as a well-merited punishment, he'd never had the courage to tell her – perhaps if she hadn't been, for all her goodness and kindness, a rentier woman, perhaps if their conversation had not been only a frivolous civilized passing of time, perhaps if she had not been a woman … But then what man would have had time to listen? There it was, anyway, he'd left Leslie to carry the can.

But he *had* gone to the doctors – an endless series of them – although not with the question she had supposed him to be asking. Leslie had been very unwilling: 'Spending valuable time and a fortune of money just to learn that you once saw your father's hairy thighs straddling your mother's smooth belly, and heard her call out, "No, Algernon, no, no, no," and then to be told that's why you can't take my hoary old legs. I'd rather spend

71

the money on an electric waste disposer.' And he had made him promise, whatever else, not to engage in a long analysis, whether Jungian, Freudian (orthodox or unorthodox) or any other. He'd agreed, because, like Leslie, in his deep convictions he thought the problem insoluble. But it was no less than his life; he was a scientist committed to rational examination of phenomena; as a specialist, he knew how all too often the layman, in his woeful ignorance, underestimated what the sciences could perform. He owed it to Leslie, and God knew to himself, not to avoid sheer embarrassment. So he *had* gone to the doctor. But now, when he thought of all the trials by witchcraft he had undergone, his cheeks burned with shame.

First, at least, he had kept some scientific respectability. He had seen in turn a biochemical physiologist, then an endocrinologist. But, correctly, they had mocked him. 'Is it possible, Mr Langmuir, by a series of injections to raise the age of the object of your desires to thirty years? The answer is no. We don't have that kind of possibility. Progress endocrinology offers to our suffering age, magic it does not.' The man had been an American.

Then the withcraft had grown more intense. Sitting before desks, plugged into electric circuits, reclining on couches, gazing at points of light (Mr Langmuir, you are getting sleepy. Oh so sleepy. Soon you will be asleep, cared for, all your troubles smoothed away. You are in strong arms, Mr Langmuir, how peaceful you feel with those strong muscles to crush you, what strength in the black hair on those arms, you are sleeping now as happy as a little child, sleeping with a grown man ...). It was Leslie who had brought it all to an end. He could look back now and tell the exact moment when Leslie had felt that they had both suffered enough humiliation.

It was the day when he had returned with that ridiculous pile of books to verify Dr Laibach-Troppau's 'helpful quotations'. All the lines of Leslie's face, as he had looked the titles over, had been drooping with misery to read this vague humanistic muddle – translations of the poems of Goethe and of August von Platen, the Loeb translation of the Greek Anthology, Gide's *Corydon*, Mann's *Death in Venice*. And on top of the pile of books, a membership card for the Y.M.C.A. Leslie tore up the card and threw the pieces into the wastepaper basket. He took the books from the room, and, from the window, Hamo saw him descend into the basement area and stuff them into the dustbin. Then he came back up into the room and, approaching Hamo from behind, he bent over and kissed him on the forehead. 'Hamo Langmuir *doesn't* like chicken,' he said. A week later he had left permanently for Martin Abdy's.

The cost to himself had, in the first months, been an almost unbearable loneliness, and had assumed, above all, the form of unassuageable lust. Knowing nothing of 'picking-up', he had soon been the lighter of a good deal of cash, of clothes and a valuable microscope. But once again, when Leslie knew of this, he had come to his assistance. It was Martin, in fact, who, having an interest in some clubs (he had interests everywhere), knew of the chain of desirable young men which had ended in Brian – and all of high physical excellence, for as Leslie said, 'At least you can pay me the compliment of keeping up your standards.' And not one, until Brian, more than anonymous, wishing to be more. They left no trace upon him, and, to the relief of his conscience, he left no trace upon them.

'No, y'know, I don't notice like. I mean it was quite a bit of a giggle once. I went back with this guy ... I didn't even remember the house, let alone the guy himself. And then he had this sort of mole. It was on his left leg. And it all came back to me. I don't think he knew. Well, it's natural, isn't it? I mean, you know ... like you've got other things to think about.'

'Well, my friend makes very good money, you see. And as soon as I've finished the apprenticeship, I shall start in at Yvette's too. The tips alone are fab. Well, I mean with these rich bitches. I shall give up the game then. But we're very extravagant really. Entertain a lot, you know, people in for drinks. And my friend likes everything just so. And it doesn't seem fair if I don't contribute. But I try not to notice the clients. Well, they're not of interest to me anyway. I mean what you do and that wouldn't appeal to me really, would it?'

'I've got this chick I go out with. And I was talking with her one night and I started on about this pop-group guy I'd been with. She properly let me have it. "I don't mind you going with them," she said, "especially if they pay good, but I don't think you ought to let it be personal." I got thinking about what she said, and well, you know, I saw what she meant. So I never give any thought to them. It's just a business deal. Though, mind you, I always do my part as well as I can. But I mean when we was coming across the street here, if you was to have been knocked down by a lorry, that wouldn't have concerned me, would it?'

As a result, until Brian, some of his best scientific work had been carried through. Catching a glimpse of his sad expression reflected in the glass of Queen Mary's portrait, he felt that a little self-mockery might not come amiss. Preening his moustache, he said aloud, with an attempt at self-caricature, 'Yes, I can safely say that my working hypothesis, which seemed so shaky, has stood up to such evidential testing as, given the imprecise data of personal relationships, it proved possible to set up.' Splendidly, in fact, until Brian thought he'd got clap; then followed the youth's real terror of seeing the doctor, of how to explain, of whether such an explanation would inevitably mean trouble with the police, and so on. Leslie, on the telephone, had soon allayed these alarms. Martin knew exactly the right specialist. And so, still shamefacedly, he had accompanied the frightened Brian; only to learn that it was a false alarm. But there was no escaping now the flood of welled-up gratitude and sentiment, thickening to syrupy self-pity, that had been released from Brian's loneliness. The emergence, in short, of a personality, and the beginning consequently of his own impotence.

Feeling a sharp cramp in his left thigh he stretched his leg only to sense a muscle in his calf seizing up. In this position, however he moved, he would be more closely knotted. The seat, this room, this house, this country, all were a box too small in which to set things right. He rose and left the box. The trial was over. The charged man was released, but placed on probation for the rest of his life. As always, taking to the lavatory barricades, which he had done from boyhood whenever hostile forces seemed to be closing in, had helped to renew his strength. As always, too, at the end of this detailed review of his reasoned defence, it was the seemingly irrelevant thought which proved the most valuable: personal relationships such as those with Perry and Zoe (last hangovers from the heady spree of his days with Leslie) were incompatible with his regime; as to Alexandra, it would be more fitting for him (who had neither advice to give nor base to offer it from) to send her his paltry cheques by post with an expression of good wishes, and thus to leave her free.

He urinated, then pulled the chain. Reminded of a joke of Leslie's, he laughed aloud, as very seldom even in company. 'The sound of Hamo's think-tank emptying,' Leslie had explained once to friends. As his laugh echoed away in the small room, the joke seemed a desolate whimsy. It needed, as people said, the proper setting. As for the awful Dr Laibach-Troppau (awful? intellectually disreputable – well, what can be more awful?), *he* had said, 'Go East'; and now he was about to do just that, although by the roundabout Western route through time's barrier. Who knew what unknown, what fruitful cultivars he migh find there in that primitive peasant economy? Beauty, at any rate, the perfect form, where religion, diet, climate, language were all impenetrably alien, would stand alone, anonymous, unspoiled by muddying claims of human intimacy.

He had promised Leslie, too, that he would take every opportunity, follow every clue that might lead to perfect enjoyment on this trip. 'You're too choosey,' Leslie had said, 'all this anti-gay thing of yours.' 'Well, I don't like homosexual company.' 'Stop being so stuffy. Even the most depressing old queen may lead to something.' 'Nonsense. These worlds are entirely separate.' 'Not outside Europe. At least I don't think so. Hold on a minute. Yes, Martin says it's quite different outside Europe. Any contact may lead anywhere. Even a sailor's hornpipe – and we know that's your low point thing – may point the way to a college opening. So promise you'll go up every avenue.' And he *had* promised. Doctor Laibach-Troppau and Leslie!

He closed the lavatory door with a firmness that came from a sudden elation – memory's arts were left behind, now he would walk through the doorway of Eden into a world to feast the senses without troubling the sense – what could not be understood could be enjoyed unspoiled. Perhaps it was what that gnomic German charlatan had meant when he urged him to be bold. Meanwhile, as he grasped the knob of the drawing-room door, he faced this short interval of an already rejected human contact as an irrelevancy.

Hamo Langmuir's departure from the drawing-room had

passed unnoticed. Five people, feeling their way into the future, manoeuvring for love, for lust, for mastery, for pity, for simple recognition as human, had little time to hear the scratchings of the past that troubled Hamo's mind. Indeed as each went into attack under the pretext of that most all-embracing human cause, the worth of Leopold Bloom (involving, of course, also that of his wife Molly, *née* Tweedie), their battle-cries of assault had been far too loud for anyone to hear any sound but his or her own voice. Hamo made his return, however, to a battle fully engaged, to strengths tested and probed, to alliances formed and broken, and now they could see him enough to register his irrelevance. Perry, with a gesture of his glass, referred him to an empty chair; Zoe put a finger to her lips to enjoin silence; Rodrigo drew a fold of his grey suede coat aside to let him pass, as one would for a stranger coming down the aisle of a cinema; Ned put out one hobnailed mountain-crossed-with-bovver-boot as another kind of person might claim his living-space at the same cinema; Alexandra paused in her rapid, tense speech until he was seated. Zoe held her left arm back over her shoulder and then released it in a short, sharp gesture of command, 'Go on, darling,' she said, as though she were starting a hurdle race. Alexandra, indeed, took up her course with the breathless panting of one at the end of her tether.

'Well, I've *said* about *them*. They're horrible, awful. And they aren't anyone I've ever known, or for that matter seen in dreams. At least I don't think so. I mean about the dreams. Because, of course, you can't remember all dreams, can you? And they just come without my expecting it, or willing it. No, no, *not* just when I'm tired. All sorts of times, quite suddenly in the morning when I'm alone and remembering wonderful things that happened – you know like all those holidays at Beynac, or when I'm enjoying myself tremendously at a party – but not just sort of pretending to so that you're in a state – but *really* enjoying, and, most incredible, when I'm reading something I care about terrifically and always have, like *Wuthering Heights*. It just happens, that's all. And it's horrid. And of course it's hard not to think one's going mad. I mean not that being mad is necessarily bad or even awful, only *this* would be. And then I get frightened about could it be the incurable kind like Joyce's daughter?'

'I don't thing you should think of "mad" like that, darling. You're obviously not schizophrenic which I think is what you mean. I believe it's probably just one of these horrid things that happen with overstrain and can be dealt with easily. Even if it's a more deep-seated neurosis, it's bound to yield to treatment these days. But you should have told us earlier. What are we here for, Perry and I, but to hear that sort of thing? And as for you,' Zoe turned on Ned as though she would spank him, 'if it wasn't that you're obviously filled up with half-digested, idiotic so-called ideas, I should call you a criminal. To tell her that these faces were a sort of punishment. It's like a lot of Calvinists. Where can your generation have got to?'

'Didn't say punishment. But if you try to live, y'know, like this, as though, what you say, everything can be just "dealt with", like Ally's been taught, then evil faces *are* a good sign. They're, y'know, some real in all this,' and he levelled his beard accusingly, first at the Pannini church and then at the small School of Bellotto view of Dresden.

'All this! You speak as though just because we own a few pictures that we like, we have the social values of Bernard Berenson!'

'Oh for God's sake, don't let's have all that again, Zoe. Will you all, please, not get steamed up. It can hardly be a help to Ally's hysteric condition. And anyway, darling, you know nothing about Bernard Berenson's social views. That's the trouble with the sort of world we live in. Now if we'd had a full-scale slanging match like this when I was a kid, we'd have said our say and done with it. The Little Mam used to tell us to bugger off sometimes, but she didn't feel it necessary to use Oscar Wilde's name to give it backing. No. The main thing is: sorry and all that, but no more mimes for Ally.'

'Yes, now, about *that*, I *do* feel we must apologize to you, Ned, abominable influence though I think you've been. The mime is your creation. I don't know whether it's any good or not, but anything anybody creates as a work of art matters to them. And obviously it matters to you if part of the shape as you see it is lost, especially Alexandra who must look absolutely enchanting. We apologize to you for withdrawing her, but, under the circumstances, we must.'

Rodrigo twisted the lemon foam around his neck until it flew out and twisted around Zoe's firm breasts making a unisex bubble bath advertisement.

'I think you must be what's called "a woman with a mind of her own", Mrs Grant. I'd no idea I'd like anyone like that, but I do like you. If that matters. But even if you have a mind of your own, Ally's over eighteen and it's really her mind that counts, isn't it? It happens to be a very good one, nasty faces or no nasty faces. Surely *she* must decide. Also it can be awfully bad for people – I mean emotionally – letting other people down. I know 'cos I'm always doing it.'

'You are disgusting, y'know, you don't think Ally's mind's good at all.'

Ned kicked out towards Rodrigo, only succeeding in giving a glancing blow to Hamo's shin. Zoe or Perry might have protested, but to their evident surprise, Rodrigo got up, walked the few paces to where Ned sat and pulled at his beard.

'Shut up, guru-face. You're not bloody Gandalf, so don't think it.'

'Oh, he is,' cried Alexandra, 'and you're the wicked Sauron. At least you'd like to think yourself that, as much as he likes to think he's wise Gandalf. But, Ned, when he said I had a good mind, I think he meant it. As soon as he looks at my body, he likes to think I'm perfect, because he wants me. Well, you *are* conceited, Rodrigo, that's how your mind works. In fact you're both horribly conceited, but I can channel all that. That's why I *ought* really to be with the mime.'

Ned was chuckling now, and Rodrigo began to giggle. 'She's the Lady of Lorien handing it out. Well we don't need your amulets, lady, thank you. We Hobbits can look after ourselves, can't we, Sam?'

'That makes you Frodo, I suppose,' Ned said, 'Frodo the beautiful.' He seemed pleased, not angry.

'Well, he *is* Frodo,' Alexandra said, 'stupid and brave. He's got the Precious. The nice Hobbit's got the beautiful ring. Beastly Hobbit!' She copied Gollum's voice.

Rodrigo's giggles increased, as did Ned's deeper laughter. 'Would you say it's true, Sam? That I've got the beautiful ring?'

'Yes, my lord Frodo, I think I would.' Ned took Rodrigo's hand and kissed it.

'Well, it was *she* who said it,' cried Rodrigo. And they both laughed spitefully.

Alexandra also began to laugh, but not wildly, rather more it appeared as polite accompaniment to her friends. Then large tears ran down her cheeks.

'There you are,' said Zoe, 'I'm afraid you really must all go ... Anyway, all this Tolkien. It's unhealthy for mature people to take a fairy story so seriously. It's like Peter Pan.'

Ned said, 'But that's the whole point of *The Lord of the Rings*. It's a kind of play on a grand scale. You don't take it seriously. Least *we* don't. We're not *science* students or engineers and that, are we, Roddy?'

But Rodrigo was kneeling at Alexandra's side, his arm round her shoulders. He kissed her mouth.

'Don't worry about all *that*, Ally, sweet. It's only a sort of game, a bit of camping up like your dress spangles.'

'I know. I know. But I don't think I can do it. You have to be very strong for games, stamina and lasting power and all that. I don't know how to do things like games, I'm not *serious* enough.'

'You are, Ally,' Ned called to her, 'you're very serious. That's why you're worth playing games with – Gandalf and that. You know they're the only thing that's left. *He* doesn't,' he turned savagely towards Rodrigo. 'He thinks he can play seriously and keep all sorts of disgusting options open.'

'Oh, of course. I simply see it as wild oats, didn't you know?'

But if there were likelihood of a fight between the two men, the woman put paid to it.

'Oh, shut up about yourselves,' she cried. 'This is about *me* and what on earth can be done with *me*. At the moment I'm pretty sure that I must do what They say. Even at the cost of the structure you've made. I'm sorry, Ned."

Ned stretched across Perry and took her hand. He held it for some while, saying nothing. It was Rodrigo who acted as showman.

'Your absence would be a sort of ruin in itself. It would be an absence of beauty. Isn't she lovely? I appeal to you, Mr Langmuir.'

Hamo was far away from them all. He stared.

'Well, come on, Hamo,' Perry cried. 'They're letting us into the conversation at last. Don't sell the pass.'

'No,' said Hamo. He stared ahead of him, hearing nothing, feeling only for a moment an intense horror of this poor little waif Alexandra fallen among delinquents. Something in Beard and Elegance alike was dangerous. But he let the thought drop – it was none of his affair, he must go East where he could do no harm.

'What?' cried Zoe.

'No, you don't appeal to me,' said Hamo to Rodrigo, 'not at all.'

Although Rodrigo blushed up to the roots of his pale gold hair, he joined with all the others in laughing. But Hamo was unaware of their laughter, far away from them. He looked at his watch.

'I do hope Watton isn't going to let me down. That hired car will be here at any moment. We shall be late.'

'For the duchesses' ball,' Alexandra said, but Perry motioned her not to laugh.

'Your young chap rang up while you were in the toilet. He said he'd been held up. He said he might be a minute or two late.'

'Oh! How tiresome!'

'I don't think he's Hamo's young chap, Perry. He's his assistant, isn't he, Hamo?'

But Hamo didn't answer and now it was Ned's turn to take the floor. He rose to his feet with a great nailed clatter and a large fall of crumbs of bread from his oil-smothered fleece-lined khaki anorak. He made a little German student's bow to Zoe.

'I've been considering. Actually you couldn't understand "Batteries" because its structure isn't part of the way your generation comprehends, but I do promise you it *has* a real structure. It isn't just because we *can't* be professional that we refuse that name, y'know. I mean it really is its own thing. So in giving up Ally, I *am* making a sacrifice. I don't think you really understood when you said what you did, but in case you did, because

◀	⋮―	02.95 NO TX
◀	⋮―	04.75 NO TX
◀	⋮:	00.00 TX
◀	⋮:	07.70 SB TL
◀	AT:	07.70 :
◀	⋮:	00.00 BL DU

THANK YOU

002   46 7   : - 1

I don't believe in class determinism and all that materialist fraud, thank you. And we ought to go.'

Rodrigo said, 'I am sure Mrs Grant *did* understand. And what's more I think she'd comprehend the mime completely and enjoy it.'

Alexandra got up and smacked Rodrigo's face, but if she hoped to get away with it, she was wrong; he twisted her wrist viciously.

She said, 'You think you can be clever about everyone. Your stupid, pretty face smiling so self-satisfiedly.'

But she was not crying when she sat down.

'Could you not say any more complimentary things to anyone, please?' Perry asked Rodrigo. 'We value the objects in this room rather.' His banter was icily hostile.

Ned, who now appeared to have assumed a permanently youthful suppliant rôle to Zoe's statuesque manorial lady, said, 'But about India and all that, and perhaps North Africa, Ally *could* come *then*, couldn't she? I mean I don't suppose we shall, but there's this festival . . .'

Rodrigo said, 'What, that thing of that Elinor's? I don't believe too much in her, do you, Ally?'

'No, I *don't*, Ned. I've only spoken to her once, because I don't usually have anything to say to Americans, but it was after that lecture on dandyism. The Elinor person said how she looked on Firbank as the poetry of Freud, which was so awful. No, I don't think she'd be very good in anything important. But that doesn't rule out the festival, does it?'

'Of course it doesn't,' Ned told them. 'Anyway it's called the Malabar Festival. And it might be in Cochin or it might be in Goa. According to how the communities work out. Both would be super, wouldn't they? And you promised to come,' he told Rodrigo and Alexandra. To Zoe he said, 'It wouldn't be for months yet. After finals. We'd probably go via North Africa. By Land Rover or something on wheels.'

'Machinery and macrobiotics,' said Rodrigo and giggled.

But Zoe didn't laugh. She got up and gave everyone some more champagne; then she sat down, took a large gulp from her glass and said, 'Look here. Is this drugs? I'm sensible you know. I'm a magistrate.'

'The non-sequitur of the year,' Rodrigo said, but quietly so that she could only just hear, then more loudly he told her, 'yes, if you mean pot.' And to the frowns of Ned and Alexandra, 'No, when people of Mrs Grant's generation are really prepared to talk about this, they have to be answered. I have worked that out as a basic moral proposition. I don't remember the arguments now though, but it *is* basic. Mrs Grant, pot means different things to different people. But to everyone it means peace. Well, except to oddities like Ally. But for Ned it gives a whole new dimension of sensation and an entire structural revelation. I'm frivolous, as you can see, me it just gives a fillip – isn't that an odd word? remember it to use, Ally – to all my colour values. But Ally, it just makes vomit and be gloomy, so she never does. Anyway, if you're a magistrate, you'll know all that. And we're not habituated,' he added.

'I'm not sure,' said Perry, 'since my wife *is* a magistrate, whether you should have said any of that.'

But Zoe frowned. 'I should never have introduced the subject, as this boy,' she touched Rodrigo's shoulder, 'reminded me with the greatest tact. He's a delightful boy. And with the most beautiful hair.' She stroked the long straight half-ripened green-gold corn absentmindedly. '*Hamo's* going to Asia,' she said. 'Aren't you? Will *you* be at Goa? I expect you will. I ought to have said before, he's a very famous cytologist. Is that right, Hamo?'

'Plant breeder will do.'

'My dear, I never knew it was correct to use only the Anglo-Saxon words in science as well as in other things.'

'Do you know Dermott Harvey, he's a biochemist?' asked Ned.

'No.' Hamo still spoke from far away, but urging himself to join them. 'Naturally I do know a number of biochemists, but no one of that name.'

'He revolutionized light filtering. We owe everything that's good in psychedelic lighting to him. With his machine you have precise control over the amount of fluid and the point at which it enters the slide. It means that every movement is unpredictable and can never be recaptured. Random science. That's something worth having. I should think he's about the only scientist who isn't anti-life. I mean the only scientist who allows for magic. Except for Laing.' He looked slyly at Hamo. Then he roared with laughter.

'Any scientist of standing knows that he works within an unpredictable framework, but that's hardly the formal beauty of his work,' Hamo could not avoid sounding severe. He turned his head away from Ned's laughter.

Ned said, 'Formal beauties laid up in people's heads, imposed on others, each a little box hoping for eternal fame. It hasn't got us very far, has it?'

'It rather sounds, surely,' said Zoe, 'as though the mime came from a little box and was imposed.'

'Oh God! Mama, don't be coy with Ned. Kick him or kiss him. But, anyway, I expect Hamo's work is what they call teamwork, isn't it?'

'Some people call it that,' Hamo smiled, but he could not gauge the intention of her words.

Something obviously impelled Alexandra to respond. She said to Ned and Rodrigo, 'His uncle Sir James something is learned in Atlantean science.'

'Sir James Langmuir that's going to, like, finance a college of occult science. He's a Superman. It's because of men like that having money that you have to be on the side of capitalism. Sort of. I wish he'd grant *me* a grant.'

But Rodrigo's excitement was greater so that Ned's was drowned. 'Sir James Langmuir! He's the most fabulous dandy ever. He dresses – well, for an old man – simply fantastically, doesn't he?'

Hamo was pleased at this praise of his great-uncle. It atoned. But he said, 'He has a good tailor and valet, I expect.'

'Well, he would. All dandies do. Brummell did. He lives in our county. And he's terrifically rich, and marvellously arrogant. Of course my mother was mad to know him. And she set Father on to him. He snubbed them both superbly. And then he's got this interest in groups. He asked me all about pop festivals.'

'But you don't know about them,' Alexandra objected.

'Well, I said all that about classless dandyism. And he was really impressed, which made my bitchy mother much angrier.'

Hamo didn't care for the tone of this. 'I really think I shall have to leave without my assistant.'

But Zoe motioned him to stay put. 'We'll get these two young men off first. Then we can say a proper long good-bye to you, darling Hamo. Ally, I'm going to give *you* dinner in bed. And then Perry and I will have our delicious picnic. I can phone to Mrs Mather at the cottage tomorrow to explain. And after that he's going to be shut up in every comfort to write his book. There's a limit to what your states are going to do to this household, Alexandra darling, and getting in the way of Perry's novel is the chief one.'

Alexandra uncurled her legs, fastened the wide belt of her black leather coat with a decisive gesture.

'Yes,' she declared, 'we must be off.' And into the silence, she said, 'You didn't really think I was going to stay here, did you? That would have suited your books nicely. At least Mama and Him were trying to feel for the size of wearing parents' shoes. But *you* two, you were just suiting your own books. Well, they don't suit mine.'

'We haven't any books,' Rodrigo cried, 'any of us, Ally darling. So don't you think it.'

'*You* may not have, but I have. Let the selfish little bitch go. As her father, I am pleased you want her. As a man, I am amazed. I'm trying to write a novel that's something to do with *real* life and *real* people ...'

'Yer. I heard about your books once from the guy that taught us English at school. He read us a bit out of one once. Was it some seaside place? Sort of social realist crap to do with who's got a level on whom in dear old England. And your hero had, y'know, the right heart and all that. The guy said it was all more real than the Angries. And we said we wouldn't know.'

' "More real than the angries".' Rodrigo took it up, 'I expect Ned's making it up. But it does sound wonderfully like a quote doesn't it? If I have to do copywriting to make lots of lovely money, as I expect I shall, I shan't go for publishing. I'd much rather get people to stop having smelly armpits than persuade them to buy books that no one wants to read.'

'That's where you're entirely wrong. A great number of

people enjoy and respect my husband's work. I really think you'd better go, both of you, before you say anything more that's thoughtless and heartless.'

'She's right. We must go. And you are *both*. Oh! not Ned perhaps. He's self-centred. But you, Rodrigo, what you said to Him was awful. You don't know anything about his books, but (*a*) you wanted to show you're of a superior class, especially to Mama, because you think she's the right class too. Oh yes, and because you can see she and he quarrel and so you thought it would please, as though she didn't love him quite as much because of it. But how could *you* know about that sort of thing? And anyway (*b*) you spoke against the books because they aren't in fashion. All you care about is being trendy and the right class, only even you can see that they don't go together and that's why your life's so awful for you.'

'Oh, my darling Alexandra, if this is how you talk to one another. Such hurtful things! No wonder you're ill. Now both you men must go at once. I'm not blaming anybody. But we can't have our daughter in this state. It's all the fault of these finals. I remember myself at Girton. Exams! Why, they're medieval. They ought to have gone long ago. When they're over, you can all meet again. And the whole of this will be forgotten.'

'Forgotten?' said Ned. 'If you're *dead*, it's *forgotten*.'

'And you,' Alexandra cried, 'you think that being sly is being strong. We'll see who's stronger . . .'

'Hysteria isn't strength.'

'Who says? There was an hysteric woman once and she brought a paper-weight down on a man's head, as you well know. Or nearly.'

'Nearly.' Ned spoke sneeringly.

'Anyway hysterics get what they want mostly. Oh, yes,' she told her parents, 'didn't you realize that's what I am? That's why I staged all that demonstration for love from you all. Only *they* were sneering. But now I've had the demonstration and we're leaving. You see I live all the time with a little game inside myself. That's how hysterics are. Didn't you know? – You ought to, sitting on benches and writing novels. Well they are. You'll find out if you look in *real* books, good ones.'

'Too many books,' Zoe cried. But Alexandra had collapsed into sobbing. Suddenly Hamo got up from his chair and came over to her. He took her hand.

'You mustn't do it, if it seems frightening and secret,' he said. 'Please believe me. I know too much of that and how it destroys one.'

She stifled her crying and looked up at him in surprise, but with a tamed, gentle look. 'I must,' she said, 'it makes everything have some sense. I can't bear things without it.'

'I know. That's why you mustn't do it, whatever it is. Look,' and he fumbled in his pocket and produced an envelope, 'I meant to give you this. Perhaps it may help. Open it later.'

But she tore it open at once and took out ten ten-pound notes. She burst out laughing.

'How disgusting,' she cried, 'dirty filthy hamster-fodder. Oh yes, didn't you know you were called the Hamster? It's because they're so stuck away and sexless and dirty and smelly in their cages like you.'

Zoe cried, 'Alexandra!' and Perry, coming up, took her by the shoulders and began to shake her; but still she continued to tear up the notes and scatter the pieces in the air.

Hamo had, at first, retreated, his face scarlet with shame, but now, at Perry's action, he felt his way forward again.

'No, no, it's my fault. I should have seen. The young don't care about money.' 'As long as they have it,' Perry added.

But Hamo had caught his foot in the long folds of Alexandra's coat that swept the ground, he tottered, fell full-length, and clutching at a small Louis Quinze table, brought it to the ground with him and, with it, Zoe's Nymphenburg Harlequin. He lay sprawling on the floor, his forehead bleeding, while Zoe cried out, 'Oh no! I loved that piece so much'; and then very bitterly, 'Never mind. We destroyed the Zwinger in the name of freedom, I suppose the poor Harlequin can go in the name of science. Oh, I know, Hamo, it was just bad luck. But your instruments, my dear! How *do* you work?'

The heavily-built young man with the knowing boxer's face who came in at the door, took in a great deal at once. He went up to Alexandra who was screaming, 'Smelly dirty Hamster', at

Hamo as he struggled to rise, smacked her face sharply, then kissed her. He helped Hamo to his feet.

'Sorry, love, you're wrong there. I've worked for Mr Langmuir for ten years and there's never been a pong out of him that wasn't the finest Jermyn Street after-shave. Sorry to come in unannounced, but the door was ajar. And I'm sorry to be late,' he added politely to Zoe.

'Surely you're not. You rang.'

'Yes, but I said two minutes late and I'm four past the time. It's put the chief in one of his King Kong moods and I'm not surprised. China broken, eh? Well, I must tell you you're lucky to have a stick left in this room. Now, when he's really roused ... Ah! That's better. I've got you all laughing.'

'Well, you haven't really,' Zoe decided, 'but somehow you've made us all feel we ought to be.'

'Yes. And you'll all be glad to know the fog's clearing. Icy patches though. The Harrods' driver out there is bellyaching about it. I think,' and he surveyed the room and its occupants as he spoke very deliberately to Hamo, 'that we ought to be getting along, you know, Mr Langmuir. I looked at that old bloke who's driving us and made my will. If there's one thing that's certain murder on the roads, it's careful driving. And that man out there's got death from caution written all over his face.'

Hamo, correct and on his toes, presented Erroll Watton, his assistant, to his host and hostess, and to 'my goddaughter'. He left the introductions to Alexandra's admirers to Zoe and when she didn't make them, he said, 'This lateness is most unforgivable, Watton.'

'I know. I was afraid it might be worse than that.'

'Well, what excuse have you got?'

'None that you haven't heard and rejected.'

Hamo smiled. 'I was afraid of that. Well, as you say, we must go.'

'Not before you've had a farewell glass of champers,' Perry spoke with bonhomie, but he didn't move to carry out his invitation.

Alexandra took her father's arm in her own. '*I* shan't have any,

Pa. In fact we *must* go. I don't think drink's my thing any more than pot. I promise I'll rest, Mama, I promise – *after* this; only I can't not go on now. And hysteria isn't important. And as to the faces they'll just have to look after themselves. And don't give any drink to *them*, Pa. The chief point of my going is that you and Mama should be alone as soon as possible. I don't believe you mean to open another bottle anyway.'

Perry didn't answer, but he put his tongue out at his daughter playfully, and, going up to his wife, encircled her waist and squeezed her.

Zoe laughed. 'She knows us too well. That means we haven't altogether failed. But Ally, darling, I *am* worried about you.'

'I don't think *that's* going to help her, Zoe. All the same, just because Zoe and I have got the lustful itch doesn't mean that we mustn't think about *you*. Are you sure you're all right, Ally? For all your disgusting appearance, I trust you know what you are doing.'

'Yes, I am, Pa. Besides, apart from you and Mama, you know how important these week-ends are to your writing.'

'Well, they are rather, but . . .'

'You're frightened the week-end's not going to work. That's it, isn't it? Well, you're not going to make parenthood the excuse.'

Zoe corrected her daughter, 'I don't think you really *do* know about Perry and me. We never have failures. And I insist on the right to a maternal conscience. For example, icy roads, darling. You *will* be careful whoever's driving, won't you? And sleeping in that van in this cold.'

'Look, Mama, if the road seems too bad we'll all three come back and sleep here. Will that satisfy you?'

'Yes, that would be better. I'll tell Concepcion.'

'Yes, but we don't want her fussing if we do come.'

'No, no, just to make up the beds.'

'I promise you I'll see that we don't take risks, Mrs Grant,' Rodrigo said.

And, then, lots of handshaking and kissing and they were gone; but in a moment Alexandra returned.

'A very good journey, Hamo. I was awful just now. But that's how I seem to be these days. Anyway, here's a present for *you*. I bought them last week and then with all this I almost forgot.' She gave him a handsome pair of binoculars in a leather case with a shoulder strap. 'Frodo had the ring on his journey, but Hamo's eyes aren't quite up to that. Magic glasses will have to do. So that you'll be able to see things more clearly wherever you go. And I expect there'll be lots to see.'

Hamo looked very confused, but she kissed him so warmly that he straightened up with an unwonted look of content.

'Bird-watching,' Erroll said.

Alexandra put out her hand. 'And *you'll* be able to keep him amused, Mr Watton.' He shook her hand, but he clearly did not know where to put her remark. She turned to Zoe, 'Of course I wasn't talking about you and Him when I said that about the week-end's not working properly. I'm not disgusting. I was just trying to pretend to take some interest in the famous novel.'

Then she was gone.

Zoe sighed and asked, 'And what will *you* be doing in those foreign parts, Mr Watton?'

'Oh, without him,' Hamo said, 'I should be lost. Just now when I broke your beautiful figure, for which there's no forgiveness, you asked why any of our lab instruments remain intact. This is the man who protects me from my clumsiness. I don't trust other technicians, and then, if it were not for his evaluation of their application of techniques, I should be estimating from uncontrolled norms.'

'Oh dear! Well that would never do, I can see. Take some of this pâté, Mr Watton. American food's so awful you must eat as much as you can now, you know.'

'Like the camel,' he said. 'Well, I won't say no.'

'I personally shan't be sorry to have done with North of England hot-pot for a while,' announced Hamo.

'Hot-pot! Wherever do you get *that*? I haven't seen it since Bedales. No, I think, the nursery.'

'He doesn't get it in the canteen, that's for sure. They do a very nice line in fish and chips there. And something they call risotto to raise the tone of the place.'

'And, of course,' Hamo went back to the point, 'Erroll is a

very professional photographer. He has commissions for work on this voyage from the *American Scientist* and from some of those Sunday coloured things. That is so, isn't it?'

'Well. Bites from the *Sunday Times*, yes. Mind you, what I'd like is to be doing a bit of real movie work. You know, the Away with Whicker sort of thing.'

'My dear, don't we all say that,' Zoe put it.

But Perry told him, 'I've worked with Whicker.'

'What! Are you camera then?'

'No, I'm just a backroom boy. Arrange their luxurious quarters when they're on location, see they take the right wage-packet home, iron out the inter-union squabbles.'

Perhaps it was the joviality of Perry's tone that made Zoe say, 'My husband's really a novelist.'

'None of my books has been filmed though.'

'No?' Erroll sounded surprised. 'Not that I'd want to be a cameraman. A mug's game. No. I want to produce. That's my dreamo.'

'Every man his own Walter Mitty,' said Perry generously.

'I don't know anything about that. No, in fact, of course, I want to stay with the Chief's outfit. Are you really interested in the cinema?'

'No, Erroll, we must go.'

'The Chief can't stand it.'

'Well, I have to be really. Working with the B.B.C.'

'I don't see that, but still ... I'll tell you what I think. With the proper backing, and it means big money, you could break the movie world wide open today. And I'll tell you what I mean. You know the Keystone Cops? Fresh today as they ever were. But they want an extra dimension for the modern audiences. I mean I'm only an ordinary bloke, but I've had that much education like all my generation and we want a bit of philosophy to our pratfalls. Theatre of Cruelty. Theatre of the Absurd. But all quick-moving, funny stuff.'

'Crazy shows?' Zoe asked.

'The Laugh-In?' Perry queried.

'Nah! Rowan and Martin! That's all cackle. Purely visual's what's needed. One minute up, next flat on his fancy lace. Like the Chief here when I came in. Charlie Chaplin – the typical, comical history of the ordinary bloke.'

'I shouldn't have thought Charlie Chaplin was very ordinary,' Zoe said, 'and I'm sure darling Hamo isn't.'

'Well, that's my opinion.'

But now the doorbell rang and the Harrods' man told them that they must leave.

'Well, Erroll had the last word,' Hamo said. As he kissed Zoe good-bye, he seemed pleased about this.

They appeared to have been travelling for hours. The endless drinks and snacks which should have distracted Hamo's mind from the time only distracted him from the Los Baños reports he sought to read. There was too little room for his long legs; how fortunate, he thought, that I took the aisle seat. He put out his right leg to stop what he believed was the beginning of cramp. Long though his leg was, the handsome Steward did not see it. He tripped, and the orange juice with ice that he was carrying, though not the glass, shot forward, struck the Stewardess who was coming the other way, and poured neatly down between her breasts; the Steward fell full-length. Hamo leapt up with profuse apologies to help the man to his feet. Sudden turbulence shook his balance and he fell full-length on top of the Steward. When the entanglement was sorted out and Hamo was back in his seat, the Stewardess gave him a very cold look and went off to retrieve the ice. The Steward, who was unhurt, said, with a wink to Hamo, before reprimanding him, 'You're not very good with the girls.'

Later, Erroll said, 'Well, you're a fast worker – got them rolling in the aisles already. Wrong side up, but never mind, it'll work out on land.' He went back to reading *Sight and Sound*.

Through a thousand miles of darkness, to the sound of Erroll's snoring, Hamo lay awake, dwelling on the enormity of these words, coming on top of the absurdity of all that falling-about. Never had Erroll Watton made such an overt allusion. But still, that was forgivable. They were about to be close companions for many months. Champagne, perhaps, had gone to his head. Yet the implications were revolting to Hamo. If people knew and said nothing, which was very proper, then one always assumed that they knew rightly. And now Erroll had supposed that this Steward, well over thirty, muscular and hairy, could have been some object of desire. And if his words were really precise, something far worse; that he, Hamo, was a pathic. Nothing appalled him more than elderly pathics. And if Erroll, who was under thirty, thought this, one could never know what expectations he had of misconduct. He fell asleep at last with sheer weariness at the ramifications of it all.

But when, with dawn, he took his sponge bag to beat the other passengers to it, he found Erroll busy in laughing, intimate conversation with the Stewardness. Chatting her up, no doubt, was what it was.

And so it was confirmed to be by Erroll himself, when they were both back in their seats.

'She's all right. Two-day stopover in New York. Maybe the New York chicks won't fancy me. If so, I can always call her up.' He pulled out a card on which a telephone number had been scribbled, and read, 'Miss May Latimer. In foreign parts where you don't know the form, never let a chance go by.'

So there it was, Leslie and Erroll, his twin mentors, both gave the same advice. All the same when Miss Latimer appeared with glasses of refreshing iced orange juice, Hamo caught her embarrassed eye and had a sudden panic that the whole of this year abroad might prove to be an unending succession of humiliating farces.

Ned's head had slipped from the pillow and lolled over the side of the bed. Against the mustard and white stripes of Zoe's linen the mass of his ginger-flecked dark hair and his gingery bristles appeared like a pet animal asleep where it should not be. Only the round dark hole of his mouth, from which dog-like snorings filled the faintly scented air of Zoe's bedroom, gave clear sign that here was a human face in sleep and not Rags curled up on his mistress's pillow; the mouth and a slow trickle of saliva that ran from it down his beard on to the striped linen. Ned, for whose visual excitement so much of these triplings were devised, had, as so often, come too soon and slept. Yet Rodrigo's excited shaking of the great parental bed as he drove into Alexandra brought a tremor even to Ned's youthful deep slumber – he mumbled and threw out a freckled arm over the sheet top and for a moment his extraordinarily white, shapely, so-often washed hands smoothed in automatic delight Alexandra's now satisfied body. His shoulders, white, thin-fleshed and bony, showed above the Spanish jet counterpane. Against those hands, so delicate, so fastidiously clean, the room's baroquerie was as dusty, cobwebby, neglected as a drab's dressing-room. Against them, too, the ivory Bernini entanglement of Rodrigo and Alexandra bore a suspiciously grubby patina. Ned, such fresh-cut marble, was indeed a Canova but incongruously bearded.

For minutes Rodrigo and Alexandra lay in normal supine exhausted satisfaction, smiling and now gentle Rodrigo, appeased and smoothed Alexandra. But she, the first to return to life, slid across the bed, over Rodrigo's firm buttocks, to paddle her feet into slippers, drape her black leather coat over her shoulders, and, fingers to her lips to say 'let sleeping Neddies nod', beckoned her partner out of the room.

'I think we'll just rumple the other beds. At least, I shall. I don't feel at all like sleep. We'll have to wake Ned before five. It seems that's when Spanish peasants rise. Or, at any rate, Concepcion. And I don't think she should know we've used *Their* bed. Oh! I *am* hungry. I'll just rumple and then I'll fry eggs and bacon.'

'Do I look nicer naked or in my grey suede?'

'Both. But I do wish you'd asked *me* that question first. Oh, I know there aren't special questions for girls and for men. I didn't really mean all *that*. I meant just a special question for *me*.'

Rodrigo kissed her all over her breasts and her belly and down her arms. 'I'll dress,' he said.

It was while she was breaking the eggs into cups and singing tunelessly 'Green Apples' that Rodrigo put his painted face round the door and made a Japanese warrior's grimace, all teeth bared Noh-play style. He had put on Zoe's kimono and painted his eyelids and cheeks with her silver eyeshade. He advanced towards Alexandra with great bounds, hissing, with his arms held stiffly curved above his head. She retreated from him and, pressing her back to the sink, she began to scream. This time Rodrigo did not kiss her, he shook her.

'Oh, shut up, for God's sake! You're not in the bloody mime now.' Then, taking her by the arms, gently, he asked contritely, 'Was it the faces? I'm sorry.'

'No, no. Not that. Just all these theatricals. It was phoney, suddenly. The kick I got, we got, out of doing it in *Their* bed.'

'Proust gave his beloved mother's chairs to a brothel.'

'Proust was an asthmatic old homosexual with cork legs. And I'm not.'

'Not legs. Walls.'

'Cork balls! Poor thing! The blessing you don't have those. But I should think *Ned*'ll end with them. Shall I do fried bread?'

They were eating greedily, when Alexandra said, 'It didn't feel any different. Of course, it wouldn't. But somehow it does seem extraordinary, when it's said by everyone to be so important, that it shouldn't. I shall tell Ned what absolute nonsense all his stuff about natural union is. At least for the woman.'

Rodrigo dropped his knife on to the Delft tiled floor. When he climbed back on to his high stool, his hand was shaking.

'Alexandra, you didn't take all that nonsense we talked last week seriously?'

'Oh, don't worry, I shan't bother *you* with it, if it goes wrong. I meant it for Ned anyway, but of course ... Chiefly it was, I thought we oughtn't to *talk* so much and never *do* any of the things. I mean if play's as serious as that, and if the pill is really a false chemical interference with the way things should be, as Ned said ... And *you* agreed, you know. Or pretty well ...'

'Oh, Alexandra, you're going to be such a terrible self-punisher. Hugging all this innocence. I'm sure of it, now I've seen your mother in full action,'

'Mama! Then *she*'s put it over you. She's indulgence itself. You realize I'm *the* only little unwanted one just because she found having me so hard and so she wouldn't do it again. At least I might have had a little unwanted sister. Or even better, two, then we could have made a group like the Supremes.'

Rodrigo licked the last of the egg off his knife. He got up. He was shivering slightly.

'I'll go and dress. It'll be all right, of course. But you should have been honest with me.'

Alexandra was on the point of weeping. 'But you *enjoyed* it.

We both did. And *you* were lucky. I have told you it was meant for Ned.'

When he came back he was more than usual his svelte self. 'I'll take a taxi to Wilton Crescent and get the M.G. out of the garage. No one will be up yet. We can drive by way of the van. I know exactly where we left it – not half a mile from the café where we picked up the lorry. We can arrange to have it towed away later and pick up the essential props Ned wants now. It was so awful for him skidding. That's why he came too soon. Poor Ned! We mustn't be late for his rehearsal, whatever happens.'

'Stop patronizing. He *always* comes too soon and goes to sleep like that. And you know it. Birkin indeed! He's more like the dormouse. He ought to be between us, if that made sense. Then we could put him in a teapot. That would complete our happy, whimsical, little Mad Hatter's breakfast in bed.'

'Oh shut up, for God's sake. I don't know whether to quote adulterous Aunt Rosemary to you – "Inquests are terribly bad form," or my mother, "It never does to be bitter." '

'And don't *you* be so grand and worldly. You don't have to be *frightened*. I've told you I shouldn't dream of worrying you if anything went wrong.'

'Oh that isn't it. It won't, I'm sure. And if it did, we could work out the answer. And I should do my part as well as I must, I suppose. No, it's Sauron thoughts.'

'Well then, you must tell. That's part of the bargain. If we do this and we feel it's a game of significance, then all Sauron's dark thoughts *must* be declared. Otherwise we Hobbits are done for.'

'All right. When you told me, I got a hard just thinking how defenceless you were. And I suppose also because it had been in my power. I am beginning to wonder whether the game-playing doesn't lead to thinking too nastily. Nastiness is always second-rate.'

She climbed off her stool, went up to him, and re-tied the lemon tulle. She kissed his nose.

'Don't talk so much. It's bad. Just look pretty.'

'I know. Like I said my aunt says, "Inquests are bad form." And she ought to know. She was the guilty party in four divorces.'

But now came Ned, an honest, travel-stained, hobnailed old Hobbit dressed for the road. 'Where's my egg?'

'You've got your own brown rice stuff. You must have *some* relation to your preaching.'

'Yes,' said Rodrigo, 'devouring pounded goose livers last night like Moloch! Now I think of it, I expect Moloch was covered in red coconut fibre round his lustful brass mouth. A randy orang-outang.'

Ned pulled Rodrigo from the high stool and began to force him towards the floor, but Rodrigo was fully awake and reacted too quickly for Ned. He freed himself sharply and got back on the stool, smoothing his ruffled clothes, saying, 'After your premature performance last night, you lack Birkin's magic.'

Immediately Alexandra sprang to the attack. 'He's only talking like that, Ned, because he thinks he used me like a machine. Well let me tell you, Gerald Crich, it was a fluke. The machine was intended for Ned. Let's do the mime, Ned.' And they quickly excluded Rodrigo from their practice steps.

He left petulantly to fetch the M.G. But his pleasure on his return was considerable.

'I've borrowed Father's Bentley which will get Chauffy into trouble. But he's such a servile man. The M.G. would have done just as well. I do think that makes my action genuinely wilful.'

'Baudelaire balls,' Ned said; and Alexandra, 'Elekhamin, Sabaoth and all your brood, come to me.' And they continued their exclusive steps, keeping Rodrigo waiting.

Yet, as they drove up the A.1 in search of the skidded van, it was Rodrigo and Ned who, in animated exchange about Nashe's hero Jack Wilton, kept Alexandra out, for she hadn't taken 'the genesis of the novel'.

Book Two

The Journeys

Alexandra in search of a hero;
Hamo in search of a Dream-youth

Elinor put her shapely arms out from the fringe of her kaftan across the table towards Ned, her bangles clashing on the deal table. 'But Ned, I'm not suggesting that Lawrence wasn't making the right *search. You* know that. Nobody, I should think, saw through the *false* values more completely. But this thing he put on top of it all, this so-called answer, this shared maleness that Birkin seeks of Gerald, this hardness of will beneath Birkin's so-called love. It terrifies me. Not like he thought it would, when he gets a kick out of bullying poor neurotics like Hermione, but because of its insufficiency, its awful capitulation to a doing, making, power civilization. Oh, I know the power was to be his, to use from "the true dark centre of life" and all that, but to preserve this hardness of will and this *being*! How could he hope to get there? All this male blood brothership and so on, like some Bedouin, like the other poor Lawrence, B.E. and C.G. or whatever. And yet *this* Lawrence had real sensitivity, real empathy; we *know* it. Look at his animal poems. And he clung to the *will*! It's unbelievable. And *he* talked of founding a community! Can you imagine a vihare or an ashram with that lust for will let loose in it? It's all this pride he pleads for. It destroys all his intuitive love. As if Dostoevsky hadn't created Myshkin around half a century before.'

'Birkin fails, y'know.' Ned was on the defensive.

Alexandra felt as though she must spring at him and kill him, or, more likely, dissolve into the hopeless crying that was so near anyway nowadays. To boast of Birkin's failure to make a real relationship with Gerald, to excuse Lawrence because of it, when the whole of their tripling, the whole of their secret 363 – Rodrigo-herself-Ned – was to show that Birkin need not have failed, that Lawrence was wrong, that the old hard lines of man/woman could be dissolved into man/woman/man or into every combination of love you could think of. And Ned was denying it just for this awful pretentious, false, spiritual Elinor person!

'Oh! if it's *failure* that is the sign of sanctity,' the awful Elinor person said, raising her well-structured head on its long pre-Raphaelite neck, 'Dostoevsky's divine idiot wins every time – a rare Chinese porcelain smashed to fragments, Aglaya married lovelessly to a *Pole*! – think of what *that* meant for Dostoevsky! – a prostitute murdered in her own blood with a fly buzzing round her head, and Myshkin himself at the end, a babbling idiot. Oh yes, if *failure* was the answer, Myshkin has it over Birkin every time. *Failure's* no good, Ned, it's just as concrete and material and choking as success. Myshkin's divine idiocy has something more than that, a surrender, a comic dissolution of the self that at least looks *on* towards non-being.'

The awful sweetness of Elinor's high-class American accent brought Alexandra near to screaming point. She looked desperately towards Ned for a refutation, she hoped a fierce, overwhelming refutation, but, at any rate a refutation. He looked quizzically at Elinor for a moment. 'If she's got a paper-weight, take it away from her, somebody,' he said. Burying his head in his arms, he appeared to go to sleep.

'Oh, no!' Elinor cried. 'Not British humour!'

Alexandra kept her eye on Elinor's plump arm, and, stubbing her half-smoked cigarette out in one of the many boot-polish tin lids on the seminar table, she felt it burn deep into that too smooth flesh.

Rodrigo, sensing her anguish, said in his most drawling voice, 'Elinor's right. The divine idiot as hero *is* rather important. It's an English invention, of course. Mr Pickwick and Sam Weller! Bertie Wooster and Jeeves! A *class* function where the servants do the thinking, and the aristocratic idiots offer the sainthood of elegance. Dostoevsky didn't understand any of *that*, of course. But then, foreigners wouldn't.'

'And Don Quixote?' Elinor asked, trying not to be aware of the laughter Rodrigo's English clown act had aroused among the seminar.

'Oh, a sentimental primitivism that the English later put right! We English gave the knight's sanctity a polished finish, and the clown's knowingness a hardness of wit that make the ethical whole something uniquely our own.'

But his last words were drowned by the voices and the clatter of feet outside, as seminars in rooms along the corridor came to their end. Their tutor, who had detected some note of private purpose in these last minutes of her students' interchange, led the way out, for she disliked above all any involvement with her students' private lives.

As the dying sun cast for a few minutes a muddy pinkish light on the debris-strewn table, there was a gathering of coats and baskets and scarves. Alexandra lit a fresh cigarette, but otherwise she remained seated at the table, oblivious of all the movement around her. Ned lifted his head from his arms, and seeing her expression buried it again. Rodrigo hovered behind her. Elinor stood by the open door.

'I've had a letter from the Community, Ned,' she told him, 'they say that they surely want the mime. We could meet up with them in Morocco around July. Or go straight to Goa in August.'

Alexandra turned towards the door.

'Will you let us know your agent's fee,' she asked, 'then we can consider the offer. We have a lot of other possible bookings.' Her tone made it impossible to take her remark as a joke.

'Oh, God !' Elinor cried in protest.

Ned raised his face from the table. 'Please go, Elinor, will you?'

Rodrigo added very politely, 'I really think it would be better, if you please. After all you have your thesis. Crashaw, isn't it? Or one of the metaphysicals. Anyway far too spiritual brideish to be bothered with us.'

But Elinor had something still to say before she left them.

'If you would let me, I think I could help you,' she said to Alexandra, 'but I can't until you've relaxed that hard, self-torturing will of yours.' Then she was gone.

Alexandra began to cry until she was hiccoughing with sobs. The absurd sound made her giggle. A laughing gleam came into her eyes. The men saw it through the large tear drops that fell from her long lashes. It seemed to them like sunshine through rain; it gave them a conventional, sentimental sense that all was better, that she was happier, that the disagreeable black clouds of her misery and their own consequent sense of guilt were rolling away. They visibly relaxed. Ned sat up and began to clean his nails; Rodrigo lit a cigarette and sat down.

'Ally's right. She really *is* a most awful bitch, Ned.'

'No she's not. She has a thing of her own that's quite, you know, something. And, too, she really knows all the stuff that she's rejected. She's not just a half-baked flower child.'

'Well, my little dandy piece made her furious. And I'm very pleased. Anyway, fuck her!' Putting all else aside, he came and crouched on his haunches at Alexandra's side, looking up at her with a half-pleading, half-sharing smile. 'It'll be quite all right, Ally, you're not to worry. It'll be easy enough to arrange. Although, of course, we know it all ought to be much easier. And it won't be sordid like in books. Not nowadays. Anyway you don't have to decide about it yet. I know at least three contacts . . .'

But Ned, who was stroking Alexandra's hand, said, 'Shut up, Rodrigo. You know, either of us, we'll be happy to be father, if that's what you want. There won't be any, like, awful tests or doctors interfering. It's part of you. And the way we've been, you're part of us. So you choose.'

'You mustn't listen to anybody but yourself,' Rodrigo followed up, and he touched Alexandra's waist in a special sign they had of loving Ned but not telling him things.

'Or if you don't want a father, well . . . Think what an advantage, y'know, like it'll grow up in the new world, in a community. It could be one of the first never to have been fussed with all the usual bourgeois crap.'

Ned was growing lyrical, when Alexandra withdrew her hand.

'Yes,' she said, 'I shall do exactly what I decide. Stupid, weak girls who let themselves be used have that advantage. After all they've been done wrong. And you did, you know, take advantage of my weakness, of my being silly and randy and sentimental. You took advantage – you, Ned, with your big invasive ideas, and you, Rodrigo, with your big invasive prick.'

The two young men looked away from her. In all their triplings, she had used the basic words only tenderly; and *they* had used them in this brutal way, on occasion, in a little side game they had of speaking of her body coarsely to one another as she lay naked between them. The game was spoiled. Rodrigo voiced it.

'Then the Fellowship of the Ring is at an end,' he said, trying with mockery to lighten the atmosphere.

'Oh, no,' Alexandra told them, 'just because you've been weak and silly and let yourself be used, doesn't mean that you cease to want your users. At least I don't think so. I don't feel any different towards either of you. Why should I? I mean you aren't different because Ned urged me not to take the pill and Rodrigo fucked me when I hadn't. It's just that we aren't protected by magic. And, of course, I knew we weren't, but our game seemed so important that it made me feel we were different. And I think I want to go on playing it. What else is there to do? But now I can't tell, because now I'm different from what I was. So there's only one thing that's definite: *I* shall decide now. If I want your help I shall tell you. If I don't have the baby that is. But I expect I shall. And *then* I may not want you at all. Which would be the better father? I don't know. I must think about it. Ned the putative, Rodrigo the real. I don't know.'

Rodrigo said, 'All right, Ally. But you never warned me, you know.'

'No, *you* were used. I think we all were. But I'm the user now.'

'If it's not to be a bourgeois thing, if we could live in a community, I should, y'know, like it. Being a father, I mean.'

'Yes, Ned, perhaps you would. But we shall see. *I*'ll decide and I'll let you know.'

She thought she saw that they were frightened and she had expected to be pleased, but their fright only seemed a further evidence that the game time was probably over. It made her sad. She had to grip the sides of her hard wooden slatted chair to prevent herself feeling for them both. Then she saw a sullen look forming in Ned's eyes, and Rodrigo's jaw setting in a hard line, and her softness went from her.

'I could take you both to that Singhalese place in Market Street,' Rodrigo suggested. 'You could have those hopper things with a fried egg that you like, Ally.'

'Or,' Ned took over, 'if you don't want the fuss of people, we could cook a tin of spaghetti on my ring. I've got some rosé.'

She said, 'Treating me now won't undo the way I've *been* treated. Anyway I won't be with you much until I've decided. Loving people and admiring what they say, or liking their bodies, makes me too weak to find out if I've got a mind. So you'd better leave me alone until the term's over.'

She let Rodrigo kiss her, Ned squeeze her hand before they left her. Ned came back into the room and showed her what he had written on a pad during the seminar : 'When Myshkin met Birkin, He was eating a gherkin. But when Birkin met Myshkin, He talked about Pushkin.' 'Notice the "but",' he said.

She answered, 'Yes. It makes me laugh. Now go away, Ned dear.'

She stayed in the room after they'd gone. The light almost died away. She stared above the chipped primrose paint and the vast grubby window space through which the shadow of the angle of another block of buildings loomed obscurely towards her. She must have dozed off, for she came to, shivering slightly, to a bright electric light and a young man chalking on the blackboard – equations or something, probably some awful language lab thing for tomorrow. Getting up stiffly from her chair, she put on her dirty old fur coat, thinking how nice to live in a world of figures instead of a world of words, so empty it must be and easy, and – she giggled with real pleasure that broke through her numbed misery – so 'non-being'.

She had 'run away'. She was 'on the run'. She was 'in hiding'. The phrases and the images that accompanied them had pursued her all the way in the train going North. As she sat calmly and sedately reading *Portrait of a Lady* in the spring sunshine almost hot through the window, her leather coat shining clean, its brass buttons burnished, her boots a miracle of good polishing and professional lacing, she felt as though those in the carriage – the pearl ear-ringed lady in the astrakhan coat going home after a dinner-and-show-night with friends in London, the two men who checked specifications and exchanged thrusts of office politics in the guise of bonhomie – were covertly noting her dishevelled hair, her torn mudstained trousers, her one bare foot, her victim's anorak, so that when at last, traced by the police, or, at worst, by police dogs, identification should be required, they could identify Alexandra Grant, aged twenty-one, last seen by a lorry driver on the A.1 going out of London wearing, etc.

And now, in this box-like bedroom, with the bamboo design wallpaper, the orange glass bed-lamp, the travel-poster oil painting of a Mediterranean harbour, the two taps that always ran at the same time either burning hot or freezing cold, she anticipated the clatter of feet coming up the stairs. There would be loud whispers and the landlady's voice shrilly demanding entry (but at this hotel she had found only an elderly porter and a young waiter). There would be the policeman with his 'Miss, this' and 'Miss, that'! No doubt the welfare officer too, a bright, trained, belittling enemy of a woman; or maybe, for the worst must always be feared for the missing, the pathologist (deep incisions on the inner thighs suggesting the attack of a maniac), with an overcoat, a black homburg hat and, of course, the small professional doctor's bag. She sat on the unmade hard little bed, with its rumpled, stained, pleated orange satin eiderdown, around her the debris of breakfast in bed, and she made it all as funny as she could, for she was so frightened.

Frightened of being alone, frightened of past, present and future, frightened of the faces that came to her now, she felt sure, quite involuntarily. She had put herself on her honour that it was not, as so often in the past, a half truth, that she had not at all this time, as often previously, closed her eyes and thought of how horrible it could be and then let it happen. She was frightened, too, yes, genuinely frightened that at any moment, in these strange surroundings, down in the dreary dining-room that rose to shrimp cocktail and fell to O.K. Sauce on every table (how Mama would go on about it, as if it mattered!), there would turn a back at the table in front of hers, or suddenly in the corridor on the way to the loo, or, worst of all, a little scratching tap on her bedroom door (ominously gentle, yet gently imperative) and there one of them – the man with the huge bristled purple growth on his lip, the white wrinkled woman with the yellow-toothed smile, the little man whose head bobbed and whose cheek ticked and whose left eye ran a blood flecked rheum of glaucous egg white – would be 'come to find her'. 'I've come to find you, my dear.' She tried to make the voice creepy-funny. But, in this menacing world where every time she walked on a crack it meant the baby would be born dead, or every time she counted the damp stains on the ceiling and they made thirteen it meant the baby would be born blind, the threat that one of those haunters, those faces, would come alive was absolutely real. It would be to punish her for her half-self-deceptions about running away.

She *had* run away. She had done so in a moment of determination not to let Them have any say about the baby, in a moment of alarm that Their anxieties and shames (His shame, Her anxiety) about an illegitimate grandchild might, in fact, persuade her to the abortion she knew it would be wrong to accept – the abortion She so humanely and so sensibly, He so conveniently and comfortably, urged upon her, Their beastly conventional bourgeois abortion.

She had chosen at random a Northern town to hide in (the North that she knew not, so warm and un-N.W.3, un-New University, the North where Heathcliff and Cathy had known the passion that was missing, that indeed she'd sought to eliminate, from her life). She had dressed, carried downstairs quietly a good-sized suitcase, already packed for Sicily with Them, and had come by train to the chance town.

All this *was* a true flight, and she a *true* missing person. But then, in choosing the town, she had consulted an A.A. map, and doodled on a piece of paper, writing on it again and again the name of the place she had chosen, and then she *had* meant to destroy that tell-tale sheet (yes, she *had* meant it, *must* have done, for it would be ridiculous to advertise one's *secret* destination); indeed it was only in the taxi a quarter of the way to King's Cross that she had remembered her failure to destroy it, and she had thought of going back, but Mama would almost certainly have returned from the chemist's (*His* airsick pills, *His* prescription for tummy upsets abroad) and so it seemed necessary to chance it and to go on. But in deciding not to turn back, she *had* told the taxi-driver something of her story, not, of course, all, but that she was running away from home, for, truth to tell, she was rather hysterical. An elderly man he was, and he appeared (she couldn't much like him for it) not much interested, not even when, worked up by his indifference, she had said that if They got her abroad, God knew, They might force the abortion on her. So he probably wouldn't have returned to inform.

Information laid against one Alexandra Grant that on the same morning she did knowingly and maliciously act under false pretences, namely to mislead her parents and other authorities to suppose that she was running away from home, when that, in fact ... For really it *did* look peculiar. So many things : for example, that in giving the taxi-driver her short, garbled hysterical outline of her plans, she had let fall the secret name of the place she had chosen at random ... but then, on arrival at King's Cross, she could so easily have chosen somewhere else, except that when, with closed eyes, her finger had descended on that name on the map she had known that now it would be all right, she was *not* mad, the baby would *not* be born an idiot or destined, after a short brilliant erratic youth, to twenty years' confined schizophrenic oblivion. You do not lightly change a destination which insures you against such horrors as those.

She tried to laugh at superstitions that could reach such lengths, but it seemed too likely that this very absurdity of belief that now controlled so many of her actions revealed, if not congenital madness, then some grave temporary mental disorder which needed proper care before her confinement. And who knew, They might, in their fuss to get in time to the airport, not see the doodled tell-tale name. The inward-looking, uptight old taxi-driver (she saw him now as senile, criminally unfit to be in charge of a motor vehicle) might *not* return to Number 8 with a 'was you worried about the young lady in the leather coat, Sir?' And They (He in his intense self-concern, His wretched old novel, She in her concern for Him) might just take off to Palermo, offering the final proof that she, the peculiar, the abnormal, the unattractive daughter, was unloved. What *should* she do if her call for love was unanswered? What could she do save start, with her twenty-one years, with a good sum from Mama in the bank, her own native wits, and a baby coming, to plan and run her own life? And that was what she wanted to do, intended to do, but she needed a sign of Their love first to give some promise of a light in the window should her erring steps ever retrace their way homeward. Some sense of a path not cut off behind her.

And, of course, she knew really that she would get that sign. He would grumble, She would be coldly silent, but They would come after her, if They hadn't missed that clue, or, even if They had, eventually They would come. Their voices would sound below in the dusty plastic-flowered gloom of the bar entrance hall, and then ... she suddenly knew that then she would have to run again from sheer shame. To have lost Him a part of His precious few weeks' holiday from the B.B.C., His few weeks' devotion to His book; to have made Her put Him second to something else, perhaps to have cost the money of three cancelled passages to Palermo (although this, with her mother's money, meant nothing; but one mustn't ever say so). Their cold hurtness, or, perhaps, Their genuine warm love, if it came, would be too painful. She tried to feel her action as something of which she should be ashamed, as something she had cruelly done to Them, but she could only feel it as a weapon of hurtness – in Their battle to make her do as They thought right. They would accuse her of hysterical pretence, as she was now accusing herself, and the genuine fear, the real wish to run away, the true longing for some recognition from Them which lay beneath all this game would never now be believed. She could not face Their cold, kind hurtness. Before They arrived here she must pay her bill and go on elsewhere, pursue in earnest the flight that she had begun half in trickful enticement.

Putting her satchel bag (providentially twenty-five pounds in notes and £250 in travellers' cheques) over her shoulder, she opened the door. Something in the smell that came up the stairs – dust, beer, scented disinfectant and horse manure – made her feel sick. Not the morning sickness, she felt sure. But she had been kept awake so much of the night by the loud clashes of the shunting yard, the sudden deafening crescendos of passing trains.

And yet as she accounted for the symptoms, they vanished. Perhaps they had only been her own creations, physical cries for help, since her alarms and fears had not been allayed. God, if this was to be life, the body as well as the mind a factory turning out real that seemed fake, and fake that could be taken for real, it would be exhausting indeed!

And then, facing suddenly a monstrous tall art-nouveauish pot filled with crimson-dyed teasels on the first floor landing, she realized that this was it, she had arrived – at the first stage anyway, appropriately as the embryo was growing in her womb. She was shedding the three centuries of blind rationalism, of empty humanism, she was experiencing a new way of feeling. Welcome confusion! She was beginning a new life on every level and she would need all her animal senses to see what was what. She could not be weakened by fighting Them or fighting her way out of all the tangle of shame and guilt her relations with Them brought to her. She would pay and go to where the simple tranquility of her childhood holidays could help her to live anew, to sit by the Lot or the Dordogne, watching the blue flash of the kingfishers as they streaked into their nests in the banks, deciding where best to introduce the baby to the new good world that was coming, whether with wily, cool Rodrigo, or with wise, muddled Ned, or with both, or with herself alone.

She got ready to say in the awful bourgeois voice that was a still-needed disguise in this society, 'May I have my bill, please?' when she heard from the bar Their voices – 'No, we must collect ourselves for a quarter of an hour over a sherry, otherwise we shall scare her into some silly step of panic defiance.' 'For God's sake, Zoe, a sherry! If ever there's a "situation" to face, you behave as though it was 1911. A strong dry martini and a pint of draught bitter, please.'

Smiling wildly at the cashier in excuse, Alexandra ran upstairs again to the third floor. The very familiar sound of Their interchange made her soft with unaccustomed love for Them. That They should come to her aid and, above all, that They should come so hopelessly unchanged, so entirely unaware of all that had altered in and for her; and this, after all the hours, exhausting hours, she had spent in the last few days explaining to Them the full meaning of the new world she was entering, made her feel tender towards Them, almost as much as she did towards her coming baby. And she could not afford that tenderness, could not be sure where it would take her.

She went back to her room, repacked the few things that she had taken out for the night, and, suitcase in hand, pulled open the heavy emergency exit door at the end of the corridor and stepped out on to the iron fire-escape. It was an action familiarly appropriate. And the scene before her, as she looked down from the iron stairway, was surely the right surrealist industrial setting: to the left were many railway sidings and beyond them a sort of Victorian-castle kind of station; and to the right, stretching on and on, miles of factory – some blackened red brick and old, some glass equally, more filthily, blackened with soot, but new.

All the time she could hear the swishing of the endless stream of cars on the new nearby by-pass road. It seemed to her that here – ugly, contradictory and utilitarian – was the grim reality on which Pannini and Meissen at Number 8 and the Hepworths at her University depended, it was right that she should dig down to these painful, raw roots before extracting the decaying tooth for ever.

Then she began rather gingerly to descend the iron escape stairs, only to see below in the little garden of the hotel, now part car park, part patio, two people staring up at her. They were shouting something – a fat, blonde-dyed haired woman in what seemed a white silk shift, and a straight-backed, pouter-chested man with handlebar moustaches ... Of course, they must think she was leaving without paying her bill – and suddenly, it occurred to her that, of course, she was doing exactly that. She took the suitcase inside and left it in the corridor – there would be more than enough in it to cover what she owed for one night. Now, indeed, she thought, I'm a missing person, as she stepped out once more on to the iron stairway, suitcaseless, and intent upon her next move, to thumb a lift on the by-pass.

The man shouted in his Yorkshire voice, 'Don't come down there. It's not safe.' The fat, baby-faced woman called shrilly, 'No, stay where you are, love. It'd kill more than any fire, that staircase would. They ought to have something done about it, they really ought,' she told the man. The heat was intense for April. The woman sat down in a hammock that was slung between two budding lilacs above a very small rockery; she fanned her fat, pink flesh that wobbled over her décolleté white dress like melting jelly over a mould; from a paper bag she was eating some sort of sweets which she stuck each in turn on her thumb before she gobbled them. The man bent over the rockery. He was planting out bedding annuals.

Alexandra's increased fear of the anyway alarming giddy-making stairs kept her rigid, gripping the rail. The man stopped working again, went up to the woman, swung her fat legs up into the hammock, tucked her into it, kissed her on the mouth, she held him tightly, then he went back to his planting. They were in a world on their own, creating a ludicrous love scene in this English Northern industrial setting. For a moment, despite their physical ugliness, Alexandra felt like saluting them as fellow dropouts. But then she thought that they were after all no more than an inefficient, indulgent bourgeois pair of elders. Failure of this kind, as Elinor, for once rightly, had said, was only the reverse side of the bourgeois gold medal. She turned into the hotel, determined finally and calmly to deal with her parents.

She walked straight down to the bar. She chose a quotation that she knew would enrage Him. He hated *Alice* as whimsical upper-middle-class reading or some silly thing like that, when anyone could painly see that it was a marvellous and funny book. There had been rows with Mama when She had introduced them into the nursery.

'I am not,' she announced, startling Them both, and indeed the barman, by speaking loudly before They had seen her, 'part of your dream any more than Alice was part of the Red King's. "If that there king was to wake up, do you know where you'd be?" Well, I know where I'd be, if you two woke up from your dream which is not very likely. I'd be exactly where I am, living my own life. Do you hear? Living my own life. And now, go away.'

She screamed this last command, but her scream died away in sobs and tears.

Perry, not moving from his bar stool, said loudly, 'Oh, Christ! Fuck!'

Zoe, in a low voice, murmured wearily, 'Oh, dear God.' She added, and she obviously tried but failed not to shake her head a little sagely, 'Oh, Ally, all these grand experiments in tenderness. How can they be right, if they make you so unhappy?' But Perry banged his hand on the bar top.

'Oh, for Christ's sake! As if she wasn't hung-up enough already on this absurd idea of happiness. Happiness!'

Zoe slid herself off her stool, but so slippery was the scarlet rexine that she lost her balance and, kicking out, knocked over a small table, scattering wrinkled stuffed olives and dusty chips, breaking the glass dishes that contained them.

'Oh! this bloody hotel!' she shouted. 'This bloody hotel!'

There and then, in this shiny platinum saloon bar in that cheap little hotel, with a sprinkling of regulars trying to resume their regular talk to disguise their shocked curiosity, mother pulled daughter to her and, stroking and kissing, she eased Alexandra into hugging her tight. Each tried to find her heart for the other by sobbing it out. But each knew this was an interlude, not a solution.

And now the Sunday drinks guests were gone. Martin came back from seeing them off. He had one leg slightly stiff, otherwise he might have been a young man who had swelled and thickened rather than someone who'd grown old.

'Leslie will serve us something delicious out here in a moment.'

She began to get up to go to Leslie's help, but Martin, horrified, motioned her to lie down again.

'For God's sake don't fuss him when he's serving. You talk to me. Shall we finish this bottle?'

'I'd like a towel,' she said, shaking her head to refuse more drink. And he handed her one. She didn't want to be either sweaty or lightheaded for the coming conference. He poured the rest of the champagne into his glass and gobbled down the two remaining stuffed eggs with satisfaction. He smiled at her. Immediately honest terrier turned to many-toothed shark – 'inviting little fishes in'. He patted her hand.

'They all liked you.'

'They didn't *notice* me.'

'I said. They liked you.'

He was clearly pleased with her. When the male troop of regular week-end visitors had descended, unexpectedly to her, she had almost run for it, and then had hoped that the sun might shrivel her up; but oiling her back had saved the day. They had felt occupied with her, and, so occupied, she had become machinery for them, part of the scene, an aid rather than a hindrance to the Sunday morning great relax. As she felt Martin's satisfaction, she stretched out her legs and wriggled her toes with relief. Not only that this ally was in a good mood, she told herself, for truly self wasn't her only thought, but since she seemed fated to bring division wherever she went, to Martin and Leslie as well as to Them, it was nice to know that she had done a little comforting as well.

'It's what I told Leslie last night, you're a sensible grown-up sort of girl. Not the sort to bitch or act coy or offended when you find yourself with a gay group. That ought to show him that you're old enough to know your own mind. But I don't suppose it will. Not to worry. We'll fix it our way. Only don't go into all the *reasons* with him, Ally. It only sends him up the wall. And anyway it doesn't sound to me as if *you've* understood yourself what it's all about *or* those boys of yours. Well, don't tell *me*, duck, because I never went in for education and ideas and all that, so I shouldn't understand anyway. But it makes Leslie feel his age not being with it, or whatever you say. So don't fuss with it. Just stick to your point and I'll back you. All this about how you *got* the baby! I can't understand your parents, they're supposed to be swinging. What's it matter who the baby's father is if it isn't going to have one? And if it is, well so much the better, but it doesn't matter either. Anyway I didn't give Leslie that villa in Corfu to leave it empty. All those servants doing nothing! If he hasn't the head or the energy to make himself a bit of money by letting, then the least he can do is to lend it to his niece when she's in trouble. I built a house for my old mother, you know. And I keep my auntie and her son too – he's simple . . .'

As Leslie came out with the laden tray, Martin's tone to Alexandra became more gossipy, casual and yet heart to heart.

'There's a very good English doctor lives on the island which is just as well since it's your first. And Elena, Leslie's housekeeper, will take midwifery in her stride, I'm sure. She can do anything, that woman. And then when it's all over and you're rested and you know how you're placed, we can think again. One thing I do agree with Leslie is that all this University hasn't helped. What do you want a degree for anyway? It won't bring you men or money. Take warning by Leslie. No! I should have thought a boutique would be the right thing. I know there's a lot of money lost that way lately but that's their fault, they don't work hard enough. Finding the right site's the great thing. And, of course, *never* rent. But if your mother won't help, I could always find the capital for you. As a loan. Who knows, people might think the child was mine. *That* would give them something to talk about . . .'

Leslie said, 'There's lobster salad in there, chicken salad there.

Help yourself to mayonnaise. I hope you're not fussy about garlic. The other day I had to make a separate salad for some silly model bitch Martin brought back here. "Anyone can tell you don't cook for women, Mr Grant." Silly cow!'

Alexandra could not bear to see her loved uncle's pretty face looking so cross. She tried to reach him on their usual wavelength.

'She might have been a witch. Garlic's one of their banes.'

But he merely said to Martin, 'Do I open a Niersteiner? Or have you drunk enough? You sound as though you have. The great understander of the young! Jesus God, as if I don't suffer from the effects of that sort of self-indulgent wish-wash from the parents of all the dribbling horrors in C stream who make my life hell.'

'Do make up your mind, Leslie. Either teaching school is hell or it's the one thing important in the whole of your life. You scream rape every time I try to find ways for you to give it up.'

'I'm not discussing *our* affairs now, Martin. They've been on ice a long time and they can cool a bit longer. But I am *not* having Ally going to Corfu to have this baby which never ought to be born. You gave me the house. I never wanted it. But now I've got it, it shall be used as *I* choose.'

'Oh, Madam *is* upset. But Madam's very silly. She's too grand to read her terms of settlement. I gave you that house, Leslie, as you well know so that you could get a rent out of it as well as a holiday home. To help you get away from teaching snotty-nosed little bastards who tire you out and make you look old before time. But you should know me better, love. I tied it all up with Hugh when he drew up the settlement. It's only yours, dear, if you use it for an income. But Madam's too grand to be a landlady. So *I* do the inviting for you. And I invite your niece to go there. As *you* would, if you had any proper sense of what's due to your family . . .'

'I couldn't, you know, Martin . . .'

'Shut up. And you too, Martin. Listen, Ally! When you told Perry and Zoe that you chose me to advise with while they went abroad, you thought I'd be flattered like Martin here and say just what you wanted to hear. That's typical of the basic soppiness of your generation – "If I show you love, give me what I want." And, on top of that, that soft discipline – Eng. Lit. If you'd studied history you'd have known that the world's changed by changing the power groups. Fucking in threes is quite irrelevant. Only somebody who'd been fed on Rousseau or Shelley could believe such bourgeois crap. I'm fond enough of Zoe but that's where it comes from, Lytton Strachey–Bloomsbury group nonsense! And as for you, Martin, if you'd had a bit more education and a little less so-called horse sense you'd know that if these ideas of Ally's ever did catch on, you and all you care for would be shot to pieces far quicker than any guerrillas could do it. It's lucky for you it's all moonshine.'

'Now, Leslie Grant – three things: One: Ally came to you, when her parents made her choose someone to talk to, not because she thought you'd give her what she wanted, but because she's in trouble and needs help. And if blood doesn't count for that, I don't know what it *does* count for. And in any case, she only agreed so as to get them to go abroad for Perry's novel's sake. I think that was the best mark you earned with me, Ally. It showed you're not half as self-centred as most of us were at your age. Not that I could read more than six pages of his first. But then I never *can* read novels. They're made for people who haven't got lives of their own to live. Anyway she only chose to come to see *you* to get *them* to agree to go away. So let's have no more of this beloved uncle stuff.'

'No, no, Martin. I *did* choose Leslie especially because he's always been someone I can talk to.'

'My dear Ally' – for the first time, Leslie came and sat beside her. He put his arm round her waist and stroked her hip. '*I* want to talk to *you*. You know that anyway. But talking does mean listening to the answers. Oh blast being a schoolmaster! It means I can't say anything without preaching. But just *listen*. You try out a new way of sex – new to you that is – all right, have it your own way, a new way of life. An accident happens and you insist on standing by it – no matter how the poor little bastard's going to suffer . . .'

'Oh, shut up, Leslie. Don't be so hypocritical. We've all tried sex for tricks in different ways. Oh, yes, *you* have as well. And now you speak as though she'd been trying to blow up Parliament. I'm sure I've been the spread in more than one sandwich and I'm as die-hard a conservative as you could find. It isn't as though Ally even took part in one of those sit-ins, did you, love? No, I'll tell you what it is, Leslie. I thought it the other day when you started standing up for that stupid Gay Power thing, you're getting to be a bigoted queer. If Ally had been your nephew, more fun to him, but when it comes to girls, you go all prissy. I hate that.'

Suddenly, it seemed to Alexandra as though the whole discussion of her future was being swallowed up in this mess of Leslie and Martin. She could see them squaring up for a fight. Leslie had pushed his plate of chicken salad away hardly eaten and was swinging his chair on to its back legs, like a sulky schoolboy. Martin had doubled his already voracious intake of lobster and hardly bothered to push in the long strands of lettuce thickly coated with mayonnaise that hung from the corners of his mouth. She was forgotten. It didn't seem sensible, right or fair.

She said in a high, tense voice, 'Very well, I've heard *you*, Leslie. But why don't *They* want me to have the baby? Why would *They* stop at nothing to prevent its being born? Even to taking me off to Sicily against my will.'

Leslie took his arm from her waist. He got up and sat at the other end of the wrought iron and marble table.

'Oh, don't be a silly little fool. Where *do* you get hold of all this romantic rubbish? I suppose you think poor old Perry had hired the Mafia to hold you down. A hideous, cackling old crone, a Harley Street man who once held his head high now struck off and shaking with D.T.s, the lonely maquis, the polluted instruments, and what about an unfrocked priest to bury you? Really! No, Ally, come.' He came over again to her, took both her hands in his and began to chafe them. 'We all love you. And we understand. But you *must* stop play-acting.'

She drew her hands away. 'I know,' she said, in a far-away voice, the words very exactly enunciated – she wanted to produce it as casually as possible, to take him by surprise, 'I know exactly what you're all trying to keep from me. There's a taint of madness, isn't there? Oh not with you and Him. The Little Mam's sort of almost too sane and straightforward. But with Mama. Why did she have no more after me? It's like Virginia Woolf, isn't it? If people had only been honest. It might be Victorian times, the way it's been kept from me.'

'Rubbish, Ally, and you know it. This hysteria of yours, yes, all right, even those faces, which must be very frightening, are simply exhaustion and being in a mess. When you don't encourage them yourself. What sort of a doctor there must be at Zoe's famous pre-natal clinic not to give you proper sedatives, I don't know. Now if you blamed your mother for *that*! She seems to come out of Peter Simple sometimes, she's such an N.W.3 caricature. But it doesn't mean she's mad. Nor are you.'

'She's much more hysterical than I am. The other day at the hotel she screamed and broke all the glasses in the bar. I *never* lose control in public. Or not yet.'

'No, you're much too canny to risk trying it on with anyone you're not sure of. I'm sorry. I'm sure you're having a hell of a time and it's not your fault. But the poor woman hoped to be in Sunny Syracuse and thanks to you she landed in Smoky Skipton. And then you complain because she didn't act proper in the bar.'

'All right, then, why *didn't* they have another child? Why *didn't* they? Tell me that. And why did my grandparents die so suddenly together like that?'

'A suicide pact in their madness, of course. Didn't they tell you? They cleverly found tainted shellfish in Ceuta and died in agonies.'

'Leslie, really! The poor girl's dizzy with worry. This is *not* the time for campy jokes.'

'Isn't it? It has me howling. But then you can't take Orton, can you, Martin? A nice matinée and a tray of tea at a play with a problem like *The Winslow Boy*, that's you, isn't it? In her present mood my niece can put on a problem play a day for you. Why didn't your parents have another child? All right, I'll try to answer that one. Because Perry thought it would get in the way of his career as an artist and Zoe told him he was right. And maybe she said it all the more strongly because she had had a bad time having you. I don't know. Ask her grandparents, the old Needhams, *and* about the family madness. If you slip the question in in your clever, casual way, you might set the old woman off in maniac laughter. That would prove it, wouldn't it?'

'I insist you talk seriously to Ally if you're going to discuss her life with her.'

'*You* insist! What the hell do you mean? Because you were lucky enough to get me on the rebound, doesn't mean you can tell me how to behave to my own family. You and your bloody money! Oh, God, now *I'm* shaking all over. And saying things to Martin I shall be sorry for. If you wanted to make another household miserable, you've succeeded nicely. And that lost little flower-child face isn't going to help. I'm taking the car and driving straight back to London. This talk's gone on too long.'

'Her Ladyship wants the Daimler – and how am *I* to get back?'

'If you're so stinking rich, you can hire one. But let me say this before I go, Martin, I'm not living with you on a blackmail basis. If Ally has her baby in *my* villa then that's the last you'll see of me.'

'Blackmail!' shouted Martin, 'and what do you think that threat is?' But Leslie had gone.

Alexandra had it all planned, when, after resting on her bed, she came down to make a scratch meal for herself and Martin. And a great success it was. She had never talked with him alone before. Now, rested, anxious no doubt to put the row with Leslie out of his mind, he expanded and chattered for hours over coffee, which she had brewed strong like Rodrigo insisted, and brandy. She had made up her mind that, of course, she could not accept the Corfu villa, sad though it was to dismiss the picture of herself and the other two cartwheeling and handspringing (three wonderfully graceful acrobatic Hobbits) on the sun-baked beach; but, in any case, she would not be graceful then. Oh God! Not to think about that. She couldn't bitch up the relationship of two people she liked, but she must get out of it without wounding Martin's pride.

Now, all the blame could go on her – 'ungrateful little bitch' – so long as he and Leslie were reconciled. She would go away tomorrow and write a letter explaining, perhaps a little curtly, so that, disliking her, he would more quickly be ready to forgive Leslie. But before she made this sacrifice – which of course it wasn't, for she had no one to blame but herself for being in the position – she could see no harm in bathing in his pleased friendliness, in giving him the surely first-time pleasure of expanding with a young woman.

So she let him talk and, indeed, became absorbed in what he said, so strange were the pleasures of life that he revealed to her. There was bribing a cutter for patterns of a rival's new spring models (not a money bribe, but getting him some frightfully difficult-to-procure kinky gear). Then there was knowing the right moment to flood a small man with excess orders when he's holding out against your price. He had wisely remembered nothing of his hint to his long-serviced, too-sure-of-herself overseer to keep a toilet time register for the girls and had taken the credit for forcing a public apology from her to the staff when the toilet time had been slashed to a minimum. He had written a letter to the labour people about the Jap chef's sex record so that his work permit was cancelled when Bob Fanday had learned the sukiyaki and the tempura and could take over. He had made old Mavis, six or seven of the boys, Mrs Newsome, and three of the girls' mums write letters of complaints about the rats at the Splendida Mare to the tourist agencies the year before he opened his own two hotels near Rimini. And there was all the other fun of the fair, including sending sick people on holidays, couples away to repair their marriages, taking old people to the theatre, giving young people a start, even sometimes a shove, and so on, which, as he said, he could never have done, unless he'd been sharper than the next man and made money.

Alexandra felt that she had little to tell from her young life that could vie with all this, but, not wanting him to feel that he was giving his friendship (even though sacrifice, common decency must force her to return it the next day) to someone completely hopeless about life, and encouraged by the brandy, she did give him an account of how she and Ned and Rodrigo had nicked from a London store for three whole weeks without detection. She didn't tell him how Ned had done it as part of undermining the established unloving world of buy and sell, and Rodrigo as a kind of training for toughness and cunning like a peace-time commando, because she thought he was concerned enough most of his time with what boys did, and the special thing *she* was giving to him was to know a girl's mind. So she said quite a lot about the dangers, the quick thinking and the plausibility needed with shop assistants and floor managers in her role as decoy.

'But I mustn't tell you what shop it was,' she ended, 'because it's very well known, and when they settled without the police, partly I'm sure because both Mama and Rodrigo's aunt are such very good account customers, we swore on our honour not to tell, because they were frightened letting us off would encourage others.'

He looked restless as she spoke, but he then said that he must go to the toilet and should they call it a day? So she supposed it must have been that which had set him twitching, and she made her own bemused way to bed, happy that she'd given him an unusual evening in return for his understanding.

The next morning when she came downstairs late with a head-ache, she found only a countrywoman washing up at the sink.

'Miss Grant? Ah, he left that for you, Miss, there,' and she indicated a letter on the kitchen table. It was quite a short note:

Dear Alexandra,

I've lain awake a good deal of the night thinking over all our conversations of yesterday. I think you will not be altogether sur-prised when I write you I have made the decision of not going ahead with out little schemes. What you saw between Leslie and I in yesterday's little 'Scene' was not representative of our life together. We are very much in love. But marriage has its 'danger-ous corners' as you will already have seen with your parents and yesterday gave a red light which as a good driver I cannot afford to ignore to my peril and what is more important, for he has nothing of his own, Leslie's. So good-bye and good luck and bless you for standing up for yourself in a world where too many lean on others. I enclose a small cheque which may come in handy when there are two mouths to provide for and I sign myself, seeing your encour-agement and affection yesterday.

Uncle Martin.

Alexandra *was* very surprised. Of course, it saved her the misery of surprising him. But where to go next? And this bloody cheque for £100. Always bloody cheques! And there was no one, no one to go to, no one to talk to about all her plans for the baby and how she would care for it and how it would grow up (as she had hoped to do with Leslie). She took the cheque. She tore it into pieces. She lifted a big majolica pot and, out on the sun-baked terrace, she threw it on to the porcelain tiles and smashed it. It did those handmade tiles no good either. The woman came out at the noise.

'Whoever done that?' she asked.

'Who the hell do you think?' and Alexandra ran indoors and up the stairs to pack her bag. All the same, for some reason – panic no doubt – she persisted in feeling that if her elders couldn't help her, who could?

'I'm afraid this is a terrible bore for you,' the nice Embassy man said, as they were removing their shoes in the entrance way.

Hamo made a small gesture to convey that, after three weeks' experience, the custom gave him little annoyance.

'Oh, no, I don't mean that. Although you would be better off with slipper shoes.' And indeed Hamo's lengthy unlacing did mean that they were five minutes or so behind their hosts and the other foreign guests. It seemed to make them the target of a whole bevy of the smiling, bowing young women who were Hamo's chief cause of distress in a Japan he otherwise found so decorous and agreeable. 'I meant this business dinner. Professor Hakadura's tremendously excited about your conversations of the last three days.'

'He's a remarkably interesting man. Although I don't understand all his English easily . . .'

'Oh, one always guesses a good deal.'

'His findings on protein-lysine synthesis are first-rate work. In particular . . .'

'Oh, indeed, yes. He strikes one as very able. And a complete charmer, too.'

The Embassy man was very nice but perhaps a trifle smooth.

'But the trouble is that you simply won't have a chance of talking with him at this dinner, I'm afraid. It's absurd, I know, because after all what you've come here to do is to talk shop. But our host Kobayashi Shigeru – Mr Kobayashi – well you know all that name business now – is one of the principal financial backers of rice research in this country. It's only a fraction of his interests, of course. He's a tremendous tycoon. And as you're the guest of honour . . . But you'll find him a splendid host. Immensely shrewd, of course. Also a great deal more generally cultivated than his silences suggest. But my fear is that the other big gun – this American senator – will blaze away the whole evening and that could be a most colossal bore. Our Japanese hosts will know it at once, of course. But seniority's so deeply revered in this country that they'll listen as if to ... I just deaden my senses as I suspect they do. Look grave and smile at alternate moments, preferably the right ones. Ready? Then we'll go in. The other American, the younger one, looks so Brooks Brothers as not to be true, doesn't he? All the same I very much doubt his being the genuine Ivy League article. Toothpaste advertisement really, I suspect. Some representative of commerce, I dare say. Name Endell. Willard Endell. Too perfect, isn't it? I was so glad, by the way, to hear you say you'd liked America. It's a never-ending fascination to me, in small doses. Don't feel that *you're* bound by this Japanese thing about seniority. If you get too bored, just shout the senator down. After all, you're the bigger gun.'

Hamo said, 'As a matter of fact, it's a sentiment that I totally share. Social respect for age and authority surely must always take precedence before any personal gratification. That's been one of the most pleasant aspects of Japan.'

The Embassy man looked up from under his shaggy eyebrows with surprise. Then, adept, Hamo could see, at sweeping snubs under the table, he said loudly, 'Aren't these little gardens enchanting? It seems impossible to think we're in the heart of Tokyo.'

Hamo looked at the minute dusty courtyard in which some sad bamboo too evenly balanced some small cobwebbed and apparently artificial lava rocks from which a little water sadly trickled. He had praised Japan enough for the moment, he thought. He said nothing.

'You can tell we're in a four-star place by the tatami alone. A superb finish.' The Embassy man's compliments grew louder as they approached their host. Hamo felt it vulgar; also he didn't wish to be told all the names for Japanese household objects for the fifth or sixth time.

He said with a sarcastically sharp edge, 'And the niche as I recall hearing is called the tokonoma.'

A young Japanese man said, 'So Mr Langmuir knows all about

Japan already. Takahashi Isamu,' he bowed, 'Mr Kobayashi's private secretary.'

'Ah!' said the Embassy man, as the Secretary led Hamo away. 'As I thought. The place of honour opposite the senator. Well, remember what I said, my dear fellow.' And he gave Hamo a look intended to tease him out of his dignity.

Half an hour later, Hamo was retaining his dignity with difficulty. His head was a tank of swilling saké fit for an aquarium. The little meaningless, glittering questions of the moon-faced hostess darted in and out of his brain, little fish among the curious shaped monsters of syntax of what Mr Willard Endell called obligated courtesy, while overall loomed the vast whale of Senator Tarbett's continuous rhetorical boom, well-informed, sage, educative, highly ethical yet dryly humorous. Looking at his host's heavy impressive Roman mask, at Professor Hakadura's gravely distant smile, even at young Mr Takahashi's spectacle-disguised smooth equanimity, Hamo envied them the gift of totally courteous abstraction. That his crossed calves were an agonizing knot of cramped muscles at least prevented the dizzying swim of these contesting fishes from lulling him into sleep. But to fight sleep, endure cramp, and give attention, with due courtesy to everyone yet with proper regard for the Senator's precedence, all at the same time, was a balancing feat which was only made possible by the shock of the surprising variety of tastes which touched his palate rapidly one after another as more and more little dishes were served – some utterly delicious, some so remote as to need chasing for definition, some to him quite repellent.

He gave the *most* distant attention to the claimant most close to him. He had endured enough friendly girlish giggling about his clumsiness with chopsticks at previous banquets, so that, instead of all that pantomime, he had asked straight away for the fork to which he would inevitably come anyway. This had not prevented the moon-faced young lady, whose plump thighs against his he could, thank goodness, no longer feel because pins and needles had now given way to total insensibility, from constantly placing delicacies in his mouth with his discarded chopsticks and even, when on one occasion he had failed to take in

123

a sheath of beanshoots with one gulp, poking the extruding ends between his lips with a sharply painful dig. It was she, too, who made him conscious that his expression of close attention to the Senator's flow must betray some admixture of his dismay, for she said, 'I think you are missing your wife. Where is her photograph?' 'I'm a bachelor.' 'How many children?' Ashamed to have perplexed with a difficult word a young woman who was, after all, only doing her paid job – oh Lord, what could that job eventually entail, what might it not demand of him? – he said, with what he intended to be a smile, 'I'm not married.' 'Oh, I see.' Then she added, 'So you are missing them all. Wife and little ones. It is nice when the little children are running into the room, laughing and shouting: "I want this", "I want that", and we must give it to them.' Hamo had already experienced something of this aspect of Japanese children at Professor Hakadura's home, so he said, 'I don't believe in spoiling children.' 'Oh, I see. You love children very much.'

Hamo wondered, were he to put his arm round the young woman's waist as Willard Endell had done with his hostess, or stroke her leg as the fine old patrician hand of Senator Tarbett was doing with his hostess, whether he might reduce her to the same giggle-punctuated silence. But he couldn't bring himself to do it.

And, through her continuing remarks, came Willard Endell's obligated courtesy. 'I sure wish Mrs Endell and I had had the chance to invite you to our country club. There is a gentleman there I'd like to have you meet. I'm of the opinion that no person has moved faster or further up the agro-business ladder than Holmes Shipley.'

'I'm afraid I have never met him.'

'Well, he's not a man too many people visit socially. If I can use your British understatement, he's an individual who is somewhat competitive in his philosophy. A person in business has to be aggressive, but Shipley's psychological stance has put him in the position of competing with most everyone he meets.'

'Yes, I think I see what you mean. We should call it rather pushing. But I suppose in the business world ... My great-uncle ...'

'I don't know what you'd call it. Let me say I don't think you can easily categorize Holmes Shipley. He's the kind of individual that's very hard to evaluate. Let me illustrate anecdotally. Shipley plays a very good game of golf. But it can be a mean game. Oh boy! Can it be mean! Well ...' But since Mr Endell seemed quite unwilling to let him contribute, Hamo did not see why he should listen; in any case, the Senator was now demanding his direct attention.

'Now, Mr Langmuir, do you think we could remove ourselves for a moment from the elegant austerity of these traditional surroundings and the sumptuous variety of this traditional banquet to a noisier, more brash, more aggressive milieu?'

Hamo thought for a moment that he was suggesting some expedition into the streets of Tokyo. Perhaps it was an invitation to what Leslie called 'cruising'. He would hardly choose such venerable silky-white hair, so patrician a skull-like head for a guide and companion, but still if this were a breakthrough in the total sexual impasse of his world tour up to now ...

'It sounds delightful,' he murmured. But the Senator was sweeping on.

'The gentleman from your Embassy informs me that you didn't wholly disapprove of the United States.'

'It was in many ways the most stimulating experience of my working life. The degree of expertise and the sheer weight of research work ... of course, it makes me inevitably very jealous like any other scientist from abroad. The equipment alone seems to make all one's own efforts and hopes ... I only wish that my faithful technical assistant were here to express some of his envy of what his counterparts in America have to play with.'

'Well, as a guardian of the taxpayers' money, I naturally have two views of the expenditure on scientific equipment in our country. Especially if it's being played with. But I doubt if our scientists are so frivolous as to ...'

'It's a phrase.'

'Oh, I recognize British understatement. And it's praise indeed from a man who has made so fine a contribution to his branch of science. As I get older the delight of words remains one of my increasing pleasures. And I use "fine" here in the aesthetic sense to tributize the beauty, the elegance as you scientists call it, of the details of your work, as well as the great human contribution you have made to the wider problems of our society. But an American-loving Britisher is a rare find, and I should like to have this opportunity to ask how you found our *general* hospitality – a degree overwhelming for your British reserve?'

'Well, of course, I was only in a few places. Those that concerned my work. But the direct and simple friendliness of all my colleagues and their wives was ... In New York, which after all ...'

'So you liked Noo York?' Mr Endell's voice had taken on a new warmth.

'Oh, indeed. And Louisiana. And California. In their different ways. I only regret that I was unable to get to Arkansas.'

'You regret that you couldn't get to Arkansas. Oh boy! wait till they hear that in Little Rock.' Mr Endell's tone was this time remarkably less warm. 'So you liked Noo York, the deep South, *and* California. Well, I'd heard the British didn't have very discriminating palates. You've certainly gotta believe it.'

The Senator reprehended this mildly. 'In this land of goormay feeding and at this rare goormay banquet, it may seem a little perverse to praise British cuisine. And they certainly do have an article of faith that when you boil a vegetable you make sure that it's boiled to a very wet death. But perhaps that derives from some of the old medieval traditional punishments.' He twinkled wryly at Hamo and the Embassy man, 'Nevertheless my good friends at Brown's Hotel or your Savoy Grill have occasionally urged upon me traditional English dishes that proved most agreeable. Simple, calorie-loaded, but agreeable. I believe there are regional specialities in your Northern country. And I don't mean the renowned but inedible haggis.'

The Embassy man answered vaguely, 'Oh, yes, in Yorkshire and in the North generally there are still many dishes. The famous tripe and onions. And blood puddings. And faggots ...'

'Well,' said Mr Endell quietly, 'so the British can talk dirty.'

'How do *you* feel about all our nursery dishes, Langmuir?' the Embassy man asked.

'I confess to a certain weakness for boiled puddings. Cooked by people who know, of course. I've never ceased since my schooldays to enjoy my spotted dick.'

'*Can* the British talk dirty!' said Mr Endell.

This time Hamo *could* hear. Looking at the flushed, sweating faces of the American guests, their increasingly straying hands, he decided that if he was to avoid open conflict with them, he must diminish the level of saké in his head. When, then, Mitsu (for so, with Shizu and Setsu, these three little maids were called. Who could think that a song, favourite he had been told of his grandfather's, could prove so unattractive in reality?) sought for the ninth or tenth time to turn the sort of double egg-cup thing upside-down (could there be an upside-down in this strange looking-glass country?), he firmly said, 'Thank you, no more saké for me. Can I have some more of that refreshing green tea?'

He said it, however, directly to the elderly grey-kimonoed proprietress of the restaurant who hovered in the background, partly to avoid addressing Mitsu, partly to reprehend what he felt to be an impolite Japanese oversight of consideration due to a lady of maternal age and housekeeperly appearance. 'The tea blends so particularly well with these little ...' But what to call the various batter-disguised fishy objects he did not know. There was no need for concern. His words won him instant approval. Mr Kobayashi bowed his brutal Neronic head and spoke to the hostess who then bowed repeatedly. Mitsu, anxious to assert her claims, said, giggling behind her hand, 'I think Mr Langmuir's wife is a very good cook.' While Mr Takahashi wiped his spectacles with delight. 'Mr Langmuir is a gourmet, I think. He knows already Japanese food. To drink green tea not saké with tempura is Japanese way.' And Hamo then saw that the Japanese diners had indeed ceased to drink saké and were drinking tea.

His unintended triumph had also involved unintended snubbing of the American guests – but really they were very tiresome. How travelling always proved true, as he had known it would, dreary clichés such as that Americans were wonderful hosts and terrible tourists. He ventured further. 'This is a particularly succulent creature.'

The host's brutal jaw fell into a delighted smile, revealing gold teeth here and there. 'I think you are epicure, Mr Langmuir. This is kuruma-ebi. Great delicacy. From the Ise peninsula. It is the best tempura dish.'

The Embassy man was beaming. The hostess, apprised, bowed again, very often. The three little maids set up a twittering dawn chorus. Young Mr Takahashi followed up his employer's approval.

'I think you will visit Ise peninsula, Mr Langmuir. It is most beautiful sea coast of Japan.'

'I'm afraid my travelling in Japan is at an end. I have to go on to the Philippines. Los Baños is the real centre ...'

'Oh, I see. I think you will like Ise peninsula.'

Mitsu said, 'Sea coast in Japan means we are happy and we are sad, because we think about our absent family. We are happy to think of them and sad that they are absent.'

But the Senator had had enough of all this.

'I want to ask all you good people to give me your opinion of something that has troubled my mind while I have been sitting here listening to your informative and civilized talk. I opine that right here at this end of the table we have by a curious chance three men – our distinguished host, a universally respected scientist and a humble senator – may the Lord forgive me for that phoney adjective, my mother, a very proud Virginian lady, would not – three men who together embody the deep concern that every thinking person ...'

Hamo, looking at Mr Takahashi's skin, thought how intolerable it was never to be sure : it could be a very young man's skin, even not more more than nineteen or twenty, but then to be secretary to this tycoon person so young; and there were shadows around the horn rims that could just be shadows or yet could cover lines of age ... If Asia were only to prove a fruitless speculation of this kind, a constant tension of uncertain youth ... But this was simply because everything had been so fruitless up to now – the night club near New Orleans airport, for example, with its great broad-shouldered guardsmen of creatures, with padded-out busts, looking nine-foot high in their high-heels. *And* in San Francisco, what could have been real youths, slim, graceful, perhaps the Fairest Youth in the World among them, in vile women's long evening dresses, high wigs and heels, twelve-foot high not nine, mincing into buses for their Ball, like suburban housewives in West End coach parties. No trace of Rod or Pete. All that side of his plans had proved a mistake, a tease he would be better without. Frustrating digressions from the rewarding exchange of ideas he could enjoy with colleagues, as this endless

Senator's talk kept him from asking Hakadura that vital question.

'Together we try to pass on some material decency of living. But into that legacy, even into the very smallest portion of that legacy – and the Lord knows when I think of the little that can still be done in some of the more backward regions, why, I frankly admit that I should be ashamed to name so small a sum as a legacy in my personal testament – three men are putting contributions so enormous in comparison with anything the beneficiary can comprehend that it sometimes appears to me that we've happened on a cock-eyed proportion that just can't make sense. Our host here deals daily in millions – millions of yen, millions of dollars, millions of anything you like – they are a part of his daily life, like taking a shower or massage to any of us. Langhorn there sits down to a feast of complex concepts, formulae and mental ideas as we would to a fine filet mignon and French fries. And I ... well I, after so many years in the House of Representatives, tempered let me admit by a few years of more disciplined oratory in the Senate – though we can talk some in the Senate too, let me inform you good people – let me put it kindly, I make oral use of words beyond the average, as some of the smarter among you will have already noticed. Langhorn thinks what to do, Kobayashi's millions make it possible, and I make it intelligible to those who must live it through. And this we do to make more decent the lives of millions of little guys in Milwaukee and Manchester and Kobé, guys who themselves are not likely to have half a new thought in their lifetime, guys who are pleased to bring home eight hundred dollars at the end of the month, guys whose most expressive words don't go beyond four letters and may not be repeated here before these very charming young ladies.'

Mr Kobayashi nearly spoke but he was too overcome by a laughing yawn which he covered with his hand. And the Senator continued.

'Now those are our countrymen. That is democracy. As we know it. As we believe in it. And as we shall continue to further with our money and our ideas and our language. But the nucleus of our philosophy and practice has gone way on from that point. We're trying to bring a new and, as we see it, decent life to the little guy of Latin America and Africa and South-East Asia and the Indian peninsula, guys whose minds do not work in ideas as we know them, guys whose languages the world does not talk. It is to these little guys that Langhorn here has devoted all his fine mind to give a new and highly nutritious rice. Right?'

Hamo bowed. He found it fitting that the Senator should be unsure of this point, as he himself had not attempted to absorb the purely administrative details of the Overseas Agricultural Development Corporation here in Tokyo. As to his failure to get his name right, the old and the busy ... But Mr Kobayashi clearly felt differently. He said with a curious hiss and an indecipherable grimace.

'Mr *Langmuir* famous lice Magic.'

'I thank you. That's a very precious word you've given me and despite all the visual techniques, all the McLuhanism among which we live today, I am old enough to treasure words. Now I don't want you good people to think that I am talking politics. I *am* a politician. I sat as Democratic Representative for thirty years. I speak in the Senate as a Democrat. But the older I get – and this has nothing to do with any change of administration' – Mr Endell chuckled – 'the more I am concerned not with a man's politics but with his philosophy. A person who is philosophically conservative is a person who thinks as I do. And some of us are beginning to ask the following. If the Asian little guy doesn't want the benefits which we're spending all our money and ideas and persuasion to send to him – and remember that if he doesn't think very deeply like our friend Langham, he has patterns and shapes in his mind which we can call prejudice or superstition, if we so wish, but which many great thinkers even of the West believe to be a very ancient, albeit a very passive wisdom – if this be so, have we the right to force our benefits upon him? He has his own magic. With deep respect, does he need ours? And,' the Senator held up his hand against an imaginary storm of protest, 'I am forced to ask as a legislator of a nation whose ethic has always been individualistic, acquisitive, aggressive and prudential, momentarily, whether we have any right to levy taxes or spend the corporation investor's dollars on these projects, however lofty and humanitarian they may be in conception. And that's pretty well the way that conservative philosophical thinking is running these days in many channels in Washington, and more importantly in the main arteries of the United States – the corn belt, the oil wells, the lumber yards. What's your answer to it, my friends? For I am sure that it has an answer like all questions, and I should certainly like to hear that answer.'

'I think it's your play, Langmuir,' said Embassy, to Hamo's annoyance. That this old man was asking vague or irrelevant questions, remote no doubt from the practical and scientific problems posed by Asian sub-culture, was a matter to be referred, if at all, to demographers and dieticians. Of all people, a diplomat should have known how diplomatically to by-pass on so unsuitable an occasion. To refer it to a plant geneticist!

'I am not at all concerned with the political aspects of my work, I'm afraid, I am posed problems and I try to solve them.'

'Now that's an honest answer. But it's an artist's answer. Or a scientist's. It's the same thing. As was recognized in the days of Leonardo da Vinci and Michelangelo. I know it is the fashion for governments and corporations to purchase the brain-children of Picasso and other modern artists. But I am not too sure how far good conservative philosophy can go along with that fashion.'

He leered triumphantly, first at Hamo, then at the Embassy man. But the latter was not so easily to be trounced.

'With due respect, Sir, I doubt if the supposed conflict between Asian magic and Langmuir's Magic has much to do with it. The problem surely is to assist the very poor nations to increase their productivity so that they can at least feed a very large number of starving people.'

Hamo thought, oh dear, no doubt the man's right to insist on these things, he's paid to emphasize British policy which rightly always tends to be humane; perhaps he himself should say something in support, but really it wasn't his affair. In *scientific* circles in the United States there had never been a murmur of all this political stuff, and now ...

But to his surprise the Senator looked appeased not inflamed.

'That's a very good answer indeed, if only because starving people are a source of ideological infection. The government of the United States has recognized this from way back. For example, we have legislated to prevent the expansion of that very rice industry which Mr Longhorn so admired in California and in the South. In the interests of the poorer Asian producer, we have restricted the natural activities of our own native enterprise. And if that's not un-American, I don't know what is. I believe that deep instincts in our national life will run against such things. But temporarily, and in the hope that we may erase a shameful stain on the world's surface, we have *taken* that very un-American action.'

But now he suddenly turned his venom upon his host. 'I am not aware that Japan has done many things of that kind. Oh, I know all about O.A.D.C.' He waved aside Japan's contribution. 'That's peanuts! Now if a rich Asian nation who shares much of the wisdom of those poorer countries were to make a big-scale gesture of the kind this British gentleman has suggested . . .'

It was hard to say who was the more embarrassed, the British or the Japanese. Mr Kobayashi's shame for his visitor led his giggling to a range of very high notes. His hand was big to cover, but his face was enormous to hide.

'Japan not a rich nation. Poor nation. Little guys of Kobé not bringing home eight hundred dollar in one month. Much, much less.'

Mr Endell supported the American attack. '*That* I can believe.'

'Oh, I see.' Mr Kobayashi's reply was invested with exceptional meaning and menace.

It was all, Hamo saw, about to become intolerably contentious and tedious, but he was instantly deafened as the room was filled with a high musical note emitted by an unseen stringed instrument; this sound was at once drowned by drums banging in what sounded like a competition between loudness and rapidity without concern for note; then many more stringed instruments set up a strange sexless wail into which equally sexless voices mingled, now following the strings' castrated note, then beating it down with a chant that was nearer to shouting than music; once more the drums shook the room; then silence followed; then a single crisp, but distant and foolish high note was plucked on some string and died slowly away into silence again.

Hamo, who had already heard ancient Japanese music, was not surprised, although previously there had always been a ceremonious introduction. A warning would have helped: he could have sought to move his legs – even a little – for what he guessed might be a long artistic session. The effect on the American guests was immediate, startled, then angry. Hamo could see both their mouths open in some attempt to continue the argument, but nothing, nothing, could be heard. And now even their mute protests ceased with the politeness necessary to a lady and their professional hostess. For to Hamo's surprise, the drab, shapeless, grey-kimonoed, grey-haired proprietress of the restaurant had risen and was entertaining them with a dance.

He felt attracted to the near motionless dignity of the perform-ance – an elderly Western danseuse would no doubt have in-dulged in demeaning contortions; yet he had to suppress a sense that, without a key to its meaning, these long rigid postures fol-lowed by random tripping steps were a trifle ludicrous and, as such, a little unbecoming. The Embassy's face was, beneath the shaggy eyebrows, an explorer's paying due courtesy to the rites of a newly discovered tribe. Mr Endell had fallen into a near-sleeping posture, in which Mitsu and Setsu were propping him up with cushions – while the Senator's face was set in rigid skele-ton lines from which his eyes stared wildly as though he had suffered a saké-induced stroke. After what seemed to Hamo quite a quarter of an hour of this, he suddenly had a vision of someone of different age and of different sex dancing with an altogether frenzied abandon. It was while he was feasting on *this* vision that he was suddenly aware that the music and the lady had gone. The performance was over.

Looking to thank his host, he saw that he too had gone.

Embassy said, 'Takahashi Isamu san, please convey to our host ... I'm sure I speak for all of us in saying that this was quite one of the most impressive ...'

Mr Takahashi said, 'Mrs Sato was famous dancer once. Dance is Western Calendar – fifteenth century. The lady stands with umbrella and chrysanthemum blossom.'

'Ah, yes. She holds the umbrella against the rain. One could see that.'

'No. Is not raining.'

'Oh. It's what we call a parasol then. Against the sun.'

'No. No sun. It is beautiful day. No rain, no sun. She holds the flower to warm the air. The umbrella to the *ground*.'

'Fifteenth-century weather conditions seem to have been pretty durable timewise,' Mr Endell remarked, rising with difficulty to his feet. 'I guess we had around a half hour of that particular meteorological sitting.'

Mr Takahashi said, 'Oh. I see.'

They began to move from the table.

'I think there might be the off-chance of a pee, which I should certainly like,' said Embassy.

And sure enough Hamo found himself peeing next to Mr Endell. Since the evening was at an end, he felt quite genial, but only for a moment, for this odious man said casually: 'Get any tail in the States?'

Could it be that the creature was making direct and coarse reference to his tastes? It proved to be worse, for, making a moon face identifiably like Mitsu's, he added: 'Looks like you're gonna get some tonight anyways.'

Hamo sought immediate refuge with Embassy. However, Mr Takahashi intervened.

'Kobayashi Shigeru has sent motor-car for Mr Langmuir. I shall go with him.'

'Oh, that's awfully good of you,' said Embassy, 'I confess I do feel a bit fagged. You'll sleep splendidly after our delicious evening, my dear fellow, I'm sure. And Mr Watton knows all about the arrangements for the car to take you to the airport tomorrow morning. I'm only sorry no one will be there to see you off. I understand you prefer ... Well, it *has* been the most enormous pleasure.'

The drive with Mr Takahashi, despite the extraordinary luxury of the motor-car, was rather less pleasant. Firstly the soupy comfort of the car seat made Hamo inclined to sleep, but this was entirely prevented by Mr Kobayashi's chauffeur who drove at a highly dangerous speed as they raced above the beautiful geometric pyrotechnics of Tokyo's innumerable neon-lighted hiragana signs. Mr Takahashi appeared more relaxed and yet, as Hamo sleepily and irritably registered, somehow increasingly nervous. He talked about the magnificence of Mrs Sato's dancing movements in minute detail, interspersing, perhaps as an excuse, again and again, 'This lady great dancer when I was little child. But I heard of her. Everyone heard of her. The great Sato

Yukiko.' Hamo interrupted once only to express his sadness that so famous an artist should now have to work in such a way for her living. Mr Takahashi was surprised.

'She is proprietor very expensive restaurant. I think she is rich.'

'Well, yes, but at her age, standing about every evening, serving and so on.'

'She is woman.'

After this Hamo tried to focus on the illuminated signs, the sight of which had sent Erroll into such ecstasies and such busy camera-work – 'Christ! Look at those shapes. Picasso on fire.'

But even into Mr Kobayashi's Rolls the acrid, chemical-laden smog with its faint pear-drop scent had seeped. His eyes were beginning to smart so that when Mr Takahashi said, 'Do you like to stop for delicious cool beer, Japanese beer, Tokyo bar?' he didn't say no.

In the large dark bar-room that they entered Hamo saw at first only an old crone with a fierce masculine aquiline face and towering confection of black dyed wig. She bowed to them deeply. His own little bow, however (a recall of grace said at school meals), was arrested in motion, for he saw sitting on high stools at the semi-circular bar Three of the Most Beautiful Youths in the World. The one, perhaps a fraction above the ideal height, a fraction below the ideal weight, was a beautiful willow growing beside the black lake of the bar's formica top – a willow crowned by a high-cheekboned lemon face of such elegance, a smile of such mystery, slanting eyes of such complicity in that mystery that he could have cried out ... had it not been for the boy seated further round the bar, a fraction perhaps below the ideal height, a fraction perhaps above the ideal weight – his frame was of a stocky, sturdy peasant independence that suggested rice fields (what Magic lies in those) in a charming Japanese bucolic idyll print, and above that firm neck and powerful yet youthful shoulders was an open honey-coloured moon that spoke of a week or even a fortnight's sweet dalliance. It was sad to see that they were so drably dressed – T-shirts and, from what he could see of the delicious protrusions on the bar-stool tops, Levi's, and shod, no doubt in sneakers, all those terrible words he knew so well from the adventures of Rod and Pete and the other ranchers where, of course, they were highly appropriate. But sadder still to see the Third Lovely Youth's near black clerk's suit, a row of pens clipped to his breast pocket. For in that dim suit was near perfection – as neat and cool and sleepily comfortable as a cat by the hearth, as his little pink tongue crept out for a moment to lick contentedly his pale coral lips – the perfect boy-wife with the slippers warmed and the fingers supply ready for conjugal massage. Like a Japanese character he was so exact and clear-cut in his black outline. A Japanese calligraphic masterpiece.

All the same he could have wished something more gracefully native for all of them, one of those charming happi coats for example. But nothing exotic, nothing to resemble the alarmingly colourful girl (could she be one of the rare real geishas?) who with high-built lacquered hair, and bustle, her long slit eyes lengthened out with silver paint, sat between him and the lovely youths; a charming enough absurdity, indeed *very* charming Hamo had to admit, as he realized suddenly that this fantastic figure was also a Very Beautiful Youth Indeed – perhaps the most beautiful, for this was a youth of so lovely a face that one must believe that beneath all that exotic feminine absurdity all proportions of height, weight, girth and bone structure would be bound to be perfection. He sat transfixed, his heart beating faster, when this ravishing creature served him with a cold beer, aware only that behind him Mr Takahashi was in animated Japanese conversation with the proprietress (no doubt another famous diva of the past).

Then he was aware, out of the blackness of the bar-room, in the direction of the Lovely Willow Tree, of a sound of sobbing. At once his knight-errant instincts were aroused. But peering ahead, he saw that the crying came from a very ancient, unshaven, toothless, dirty, white-faced old man in a turtle-necked sweater that fell away from his scrawny throat. In his trembling orange-stained fingers he precariously held a burning cigarette with which he feebly stabbed the air as he spoke. Glutinous yellow tears were dribbling down his hollowed cheeks. His voice was both cracked and flutey. Hamo found it hard to understand what he was saying, for he was not only a very ancient American, but with an accent or of a region totally unfamiliar to him.

'That's how it was, son. She was givin' it out to every guy that walked by the house. She who had been so goddamned beautiful.' His words were lost in sobbing. Willow (or was he Bamboo?) took the dirty cigarette end out of the trembling old hand and stubbed it. Putting one slender arm round the old man's shoulder, with his other hand he poured some of the whisky from the old man's glass into the blubbery toothless mouth. The old man's hand found the youth's knee. 'And then I'd look at our kid sleepin' and it'd tear me up sometimes. Tear my guts.' In his emotion he buried his hand deep. 'I'd gotten times so I might have beat the shit out of her. So then I quit. That was the day I signed with the *Mary Lou*, and Cap'n Masterson. A good ship and a good cap'n.'

Beautiful Willow-Bamboo bent down and kissed the slobbering lips amid the bristle. 'Good Papa san,' he said, and led him from the room.

A voice near Hamo woke him from his astonishment.

'And was *that* a bad moment for the White Whale?'

The voice, rasping yet comfortable, made him think at once of the whisky sours, so revolting in name, so delicious in taste, that had been one of his many happy American discoveries. It brought back visual memories of smartly dressed, sophisticated elderly New York ladies at parties he had been taken to, frightening yet friendly, all cigarette smoke and elaborate white hair, young smooth cheeks and old stretched necks. He looked up and there was just one such seating herself at the bar next to the Geisha youth. The long cigarette holder preceded the rasping drawl ... when Hamo, looking at the sexy brown eyes, the snub nose, the wide mouth and long jaw, the little bow tie, was reminded suddenly of a famous cinema star of the thirties, so beloved by Erroll, one whose photographs from magazines so often festooned the lab at infuriating times, that famous star who always danced. Below the white hair was a little boy's face, stretched tight, and, below that, an old, old, old sagging neck, older than time. The very old man, now sitting, his long legs crossed, on the high bar stool, spoke to Hamo with a shrug of one shoulder.

'Don't look at me, dawling. If it's Ahab's curse that's worrying you, forget it. He takes it with him.'

But any further such alarming addresses were cut off by the sound of another voice coming out of the darkness, and another

137

old man, certainly in his seventies, although beside the smart ladylike one he seemed quite young, appeared at the stool by the side of the Rice Youth. He was buttoning up his flies.

'Yeah, like I was tellin' you,' and his voice was near to tears, but not sobbing, 'I guess I was twelve and some. We'd been out cuttin' the corn all day, the old man and me. Some days he'd talk. Pretty wise talk too. 'Course I couldn't every time figure out what he was aimin' at. But mostly I learned. That day he hadn't said nothin'. No sir, nothin'! When right out of the blue he makes an awful sound, kind of a gulp like the end of time it was – somethin' near between the mewin' of a buzzard and the rattle of a sneaky snake. Next thing he was lyin' there, like he was measurin' himself. It was just like he was asleep. Like I said he didn't hardly breathe for the longest, longest time. But there was the blood tricklin' out from his mouth, way down his chin.'

Down the fat, creased, grey, grey, old cheeks and the creased grey, grey double chins the tears ran. Sturdy Little Rice Shoot (no lodger he) stretched over the bar, found a hot towel and wiped the old man's neck and his huge, flabby, dry-skinned face and right up his great creased forehead to the line of his grey crew-cut. This old man was quicker off the mark. His hand went straight and deep.

'Yeah. That was the day I left my boyhood behind. 'Course I stood up and was counted as a man. But I hadn't really figured it out. Couldn't do. Guess I wasn't more than twelve and some. Standin' out there in the corn, with the sun blazing down and the buzzards flyin' way up over my head. The day my old man finally died on me.' He paused, then he added with a sob, 'And I guess I haven't properly figured it out yet.' Rice Shoot patted his cheek.

'Poor Papa san,' he said, and he led the lumbering old bear from the room.

'The fairy Huck Finn and her Japanese Jim,' said the elegant, 'of all the phoneys ... Dear God! no, *not* of all the phonies. Here *she* comes, the phoniest of them all! Lorelei of Little Rock. And is her rock little!'

The petite little old man with a blond dyed quiff of hair and the little old, old baby-pouting face, dressed so neatly in a dove-grey suit with a dove-grey stock, his little plump but blotched white hands glistening with rings, hoisted himself like an arthritic kitten on to the stool next to Calligraphy.

'Shush yo' noise, honey,' he said to Elegance. 'Yo' sure is the most embarrassin' person I've known since I lost my po' cousin to self-destruction a while back. Where you from, honey?' he asked Hamo.

'I am from England.'

'A British gentleman. Why I just love the British. They're *so* refined. What you all doin' here? Well, we know that. But I mean what's yo' business?'

'I am concerned with rice breeding.'

'Rice breeding,' said New York elegant, 'Why you two girls just talk away. Lorelei there's the wild hyacinth itself.' Hamo murmured '*eichornia crassipes*'. 'Is that so? You may well be right. She was born and bred in rice country. She was irrigated before she was knee-high. She's from Arkansas.'

Hamo looked wildly round for Mr Takahashi, then sought desperately to hold the conversation at a tolerable level.

'I can't say how much I regret missing Arkansas.'

'Well now, honey, that's the nicest thing I heard anyone say in a long, long while. British gentlemen always have the finest manners ...'

'Aren't you singing your siren song up the wrong creek, darling?'

But Lorelei was up to all Elegance's jibes. 'Yo' look a mite pale, honey. I hope you're not sufferin' from irregularity. You're such a nice, nice person. My, how these stools crowd one ...'

'But I found Louisiana very rewarding too.'

'Well, honey, don't say that to all Arkansas boys, but it so happens that I know *that* country too. Oh, just talkin' about it makes me so sad.' He took out a small lace-edged handkerchief, and dabbed at the red rims around his faded, surprised, big baby-blue eyes. 'I was rose in rice. That's where my Daddy was at. One time he sent me down to the Bayou country to see what they all was doin' down there to control that beautiful weed Madam there just mentioned. That is one thing we know in the South and one lesson I learned then, honey. If it's beautiful, it's sure gonna up and leave you. Like the beauty of the South. All those miles and miles of just lovely purple swamp. But it had to go, it was killin' the rice.'

Mascaraed tears were running down his cheeks. Calligraphy (the more sombre the dresser the bolder the action) stuck out his little coral tongue and licked the tears away.

'Thank you, chiley,' said Lorelei and his little jewelled claw went quickly round to the back of the stool and dug into Calligraphy's buttocks. 'I sure grew up that time. Just guess what they'd done to keep those lovely flowers down. They'd brought in manatees from way down in the tropics, up from the Gulf. I'm just wondering if you all know what manatees are?'

'Well, yes,' said Hamo, 'they're a sort of vegetarian seal.'

'Vegetarian seal! My, that's kind of nice and zany. You British wear your education with such a lovely humour. I tell you honey, they're the nicest lil' ol' creatures that ever were, just browsin' around, with wide open eyes, eatin' seaweed and hurtin' nobody and nothin'. Sea cows they call them. Well those poor sea cows couldn't eat that lovely purple weed fast enough, so some Yankee scientist came down with his big ideas and chemical spray. And they shot those sea cows and they sprayed all that lovely purple hyacinth right clean away. I sat just right there and told myself "Get off by yourself and play, baby, 'cos that's the way it's always gonna be in the South, no more beauty, just the blues!" And that's when I left for Europe.'

Calligraphy's tongue was having to work so fast to catch the tears that flowed now, that he clearly decided that a climax was coming and, putting his arm around the ancient slender waist, 'Silly Papa san,' he said, and led the little frail old porcelain Southern gentleman from the room.

'Well, there they go, the whole Easter parade! Fairy Huck Finn, and Uncle Ahab and Little Rock Lorelei ...'

'They were rather drunk, I'm afraid. Frankly, I was surprised ... Well I mean they're not awfully cosmopolitan ... I mean I could hardly understand what they were saying, and how those boys ...'

'Oh, they *don't* understand. They're just yen-minded. Anyway all those tears and all those stories! They were just turning on, dawling. They've bummed around, all of them, long, long lives in every gay bar from Sydney to San Diego but they still have to find the Great American Excuse – Broken Marriage, Death of Daddy, The Spring Seed. Shall I tell you the tale of what my Momma did to me? No? Okay, we'll skip it. But don't believe *those* bums. Why, all those accents! Dawling, they haven't been back home in fifty years. Well, who does Fairy Finn *remind* you of, that Roman Imperial frown and hair do? Gertrude Stein, no less. And that's just around when *he* made the Montparnasse gay scene. Two Oakland Girls together they were. With Isadora Duncan, three little maids. But Fairy Finn's too tough to get his scarf caught in an automobile wheel. Well, away idle gossip. What in the hell's a kid like you looking for here?'

Before Hamo could answer there was a loud rustling in the darkest corner of the room and a young man stumbled towards him – a beautifully shaped white youth, with a lovely face but of such intense pallor, eyelids of such translucent violet, and with so pink-rimmed a nose sniffing so vilely and such pale lips twitching so sharply, that Hamo was shocked by this vision of beauty damned. The young man stood by Hamo and stammered something at him incoherently. Elegance reacted with a fierceness that equally shocked Hamo.

'Go on, piss off, you misery faggot, or I'll turn you over to the M.P.s.'

The youth looked vacantly about him and then stumbled from the room.

'Filthy little hustler! An American, too! She's on a trip. Well, I just hope it's a bad one. She's a deserter. I must tell Sunarko to keep her out of here or I shall have to take myself to the Embassy. God! how I hate the young. Not you, darling,' and he patted the Geisha's painted cheek. 'Well,' he said, 'what's it to be? I don't know what you British like. Is it a gang bang? You tear off one wing, I'll tear off the other. Could be fun to hear those little mandarin butterfly cries. No? Well ...' And twisting the youth's arm sharply, he propelled him from the stool. 'Give my love to Piccadilly. Now that's one place you can be really sure of an *un*hygienic hustler. Genuine Victorian crotches. The British like their meat *really* high. Come on.'

The youth, his eyes staring out in a wild way from the riot of silver and red paint, said, 'I come, Grandpappa san.' And they were gone.

Hamo sat a long time, sipping at his warming beer, waiting for Mr Takahashi, for the dawn, for death. The scenes of the last half hour had given him the horrors, but as well – and this was the top horror – the horn. He felt a hand on his shoulder and there was the elderly proprietress who he saw now was in fact an elderly man in Japanese drag.

'Come please.' And the man led Hamo down a corridor and into a room at the end, empty but for a bidet and a pile of mattresses on the floor. On the mattress lay the deserter, naked, on his stomach; with his desolate lovely face hidden in the pillows. Hamo looked, and his mouth became dry as his heart beat fast with randiness.

'American ass,' said the proprietor in a friendly, informative tone, 'English arse, Japanese not have.' Before he went from the room, he said, 'No need to leave yen, please. Kobayashi Shigeru pay all. Very rich. New client.' He was delightedly proud.

The youth hardly stirred, but, at the culmination, a wild stuttering flow of words came from his mouth; or rather, as it seemed to Hamo, one word only – 'yellow', repeated about twenty times.

He washed thoroughly, but the youth lay quite still. Before he went out of the room he tucked a pile of yen under the boy's shoulder. He remembered his father saying (and it seemed that *he* had had it from *his* father) that, in his heart of hearts, every soldier and officer knows that, next to bravery in the front line, it takes most courage of all to desert.

As the Rolls swept smoothly through the now almost empty Tokyo lanes, Mr Takahashi spoke volubly at his delight in meeting the proprietor.

'Sugemoto Sunarko san very interesting man. I remember everyone talk of him when I am little child. Was once great Kabuki actor. Play women parts. All Tokyo. All Japan. This evening he tells me all movements, singing, dance, all traditions. Very interesting. I like traditions.'

Hamo was determined to be casual. 'You've never met him before, then?'

'Oh, no. You are first homosexual gentleman Mr Kobayashi ask me to arrange.'

Hamo made no comment. He said only, 'I saw no Japanese people there.'

'Oh, no, Japanese people like only girls.'

'I can't quite believe that.'

'Oh, yes. Maybe Kabuki actor sometimes like men. Or in Shogun times. Or with Samurai. Now only girls.' Then he added, 'I hear once a very rich man, a banker likes boys. But such rich man will go to hot springs. Japanese people like to make love only with – I don't know what you say – girls who can sing and speak poems and talk beautiful love. Hostesses in hot springs. No foreigners there. Same I think for this rich gentleman who like boys. This kind of bar is for shayo-zoku – what do you say? expenses accounts – for tourists and foreign customers.' He bowed a little to express the inferiority of such a place.

Hamo had nothing to say to this. Mr Takahashi covered his nervous giggle with his hand and plunged on.

'Mr Sugemoto say to me these boys like very old gentlemen, I think. All Japanese people respect greatly old age.'

'Yes. I noticed that.'

Giggling wildly, Mr Takahashi said, 'Mr Kobayashi pays you great compliment. He thinks you very old man, may be. Arrange this bar. But all is good, I think. American boy is very pleased. Poor deserter. No money.'

Hamo wanted to ignore all this, but he found himself replying, 'He didn't *say* anything except "yellow" about one hundred times. I can't think what it meant.'

'He is dreaming of beautiful blonde girl, may be. I also like very much blonde girls.'

'Well, whatever he was dreaming of, when he wakes up, *I* shan't be part of his dream.'

Mr Takahashi was puzzled. 'Oh, I see.'

And now, at last, they had arrived at the hotel.

The next morning as they drove to the airport, Erroll told him of the splendid dinner that his English girl-friend had made for him.

'Proper sukiyaki. Nippon style. But with a spot of brown sauce straight from old Harold at Number Ten to give it a bit of a relish.'

Very old Sir Thomas Needham helped himself, despite his wife's remonstrating frown, to another dollop of Stilton.

'Yes, yes,' he said, 'I know. But this cheese scoop is half the size of a normal one. I don't know where you got the thing.'

Alexandra sat, as it seemed to her, impenetrably shut in by a forest of wine-glasses and finger-bowls and cutlery and jugs of thick-bloomed, heavily scented lilacs, all of which profuse elegance, vestigial and irrelevant though it was to the frugal life the old couple now lived, appeared to make her inelegant problems even more unbroachable.

Sir Thomas perhaps sensed her feeling. He said, 'We haven't forgotten you, my dear. Don't think that. I'm turning your business over in my mind, such as it still is. We had an inkling from Zoe, and we guessed the rest. But I'm only allowed half a glass of claret with my luncheon nowadays. And I keep it to the end. To savour it. Until that's done, I like to steer away from serious topics. Anything that might upset the digestion. Old people are like that. Selfish maybe. Or not having a lot of time to waste. But to put your mind at rest, I'll say that I think you've done very wisely to come and talk it over with *us*. We're old, you know, really old. Too old to have any idea of what's the conventional thing we should think, or to care about knowing it. Not that I was ever *un*conventional. Civil servants can't be. Not if they're going to do their job properly. People think differently, because of men like Eddie Marsh who got into the public eye. Or Humbert Wolfe. But they were never taken seriously in the service. Eddie March suited Winston in the First World War because he did what he was told.'

'My dear, Alexandra hasn't the least idea who Eddie Marsh was.'

'She's not alone in that, Lucy. A most forgettable chap. No, that's not quite fair. He helped a lot of people, poets and painters. But helping people is the last thing to make you remembered. Too embarrassing for them. Forgotten as quickly at possible.'

He gave a short bitter laugh which appeared to conjure an equally bitter wind into the room.

All the windows were open, for, as her great-grandfather had explained, 'I have to have plenty of air, I get such a lot of these hot flushes.' Despite the sunny last days of April, a cold northerly draught blew directly into the carefully sited dining-room. Alexandra felt shivery, but then nerves and body had become so inextricably muddled in their effect upon her that she disregarded all sensations, save for short periods when she thought even a stiff neck a precursor of death. She was far more concerned, if it were possible, to stand away and sort out the nerves from possible real insanity.

Her great-grandmother, so paper-thin, so tiny, huddled herself into her stole. She made a small grimace to Alexandra which might have counselled patience or might have been just a charming intimate signal, for Lady Needham in her hostess prime had depended greatly upon facial gestures for her communication with others, or it might now, as Alexandra realized during only an hour's stay, be involuntary.

This very old lady said in a half whisper, 'Remind me to talk to you about the *label* aspect of it all. I think that's so important. But Tom doesn't want any of it discussed now. Shall I tell Harriet to serve coffee in the library, Tom?'

'Good God, no! I have to remind you, Lucy, that those photostats of Cabinet papers are on loan. She's a splendid housekeeper and hostess and all that, but it's taking a long time to train her as a secretary, Alexandra. She types after a fashion with two fingers and keeps the papers in good order, but she asks all these ghastly people from around here, who keep calling, God knows why, into my library. The results are disastrous: "Oh, Sir Thomas, are those your memoirs? Am I in them?" "Not on your nelly, Madam."'

'Don't be so absurd, Tom, you know no one around here expects to be in your memoirs. Why should they be? This is only the place we've retired to.'

'They may not expect, but they'd give their eyes to be there. County neighbours! I don't know which I dislike more – the rich or the impoverished. Not a person of real distinction between them. All entirely taken up with parish pump affairs. Just because I've given a lead in nature conservation locally, they appear to think that I wish to be involved in every petty affair of the place. I wanted to prevent urban sprawl because I came to live in the country in order to have trees about me instead of buildings. That's why I led *that* campaign. And the animals and birds too.

Keep 'em alive. Even if you never see 'em, you can hear them or find their traces. And that means less people around. Which is also what I came here for. But these fools seem to think I'm giving my last years to altruistic schemes to soothe their nostalgias, like that chap who wanted me to sponsor a ball to redecorate the Assembly Rooms. "What on earth for?" I asked him. "There's acres of second-rate Regency rubbish going to pot in everyone's attics without restoring that white elephant." Build a new palais de danse I told him. And you let *him* into the library, Lucy, where he promptly slopped a perfectly adequate port over Kingsley Wood's letters to Hore Belisha.'

'Oh dear! Well, still the memoirs are coming along. Where will you have coffee then?'

'I should think in the drawing-room. Though *you* should tell us *that*, my dear. The drawing-room belongs to the lady of the house. A woman's room. Or so they said in Victorian times. Lot of rubbish. As though women were to be segregated like Turks or battery hens.'

As they passed through the icy hall on the way to the drawing-room, Lady Needham slipped her arm through Alexandra's.

'There you are, you see, labels! Remind me to discuss that aspect of your problem. It's *so* important.'

The drawing-room, though long and sunlit, was yet a sad desert. Dotted about like so many oases too far apart for human communication, were some faded gilded Empire and Regency couches and chairs, and an early Broadwood. On the walls were portraits of the school of Hoppner. But the room rejuvenated Sir Thomas for he began immediately to return to his first relevant remarks.

'Yes, you were right to come to us. The very old have no time for clichés. Clichés are for people who have to keep their end up. They "disapprove of modern youth", or they think "modern youth much maligned", or some other such rubbish. I don't care twopence about modern youth one way or the other. Nor does Lucy. She sometimes pretends to. But that's my fault. I forced her to be social for the sake of my career. But I *do* care about you. And I shall judge your problem dispassionately in relation to your life which is all that matters.'

The old man gulped down his coffee, although Alexandra had

burned her lips even in attempting to sip hers. While he was wiping his moustache with a large check silk handkerchief, she thought it only right to explain exactly what she had come for.

'I wanted to ask you about my grandparents, and about Mama.'

She spoke very evenly and carefully, for she was determined to approach this problem of family sanity with the greatest deliberation and, if such were not an impossible paradox, nonchalant seriousness, so that they should be neither offended, nor suspicious of her own mental balance.

'Ah,' said her great-grandfather, 'now if you're talking about the past, that's different. I can't be sure of my objectivity there. I've got a very good example of that with Neville Henderson. As you know his very name rouses abuse today. Yet I liked the chap, and within his limits I think he did his best. Not that I was ever a Chamberlainite. No, no, like any good civil servant I had no politics, which meant a sort of washy liberalism that didn't get in the way of competent administration. Of course, Henderson was quite out of his depth with Hitler. But so were all these chaps who criticize him. A decent late-Victorian or Edwardian education didn't prepare any of us very well for an encounter with Caligula or Genghis Khan. But I simply can't tell how objective I've been about the fellow in my chapter on the lead up to Munich. Yes, yes, what is it?'

Their beloved old parlour-maid bent down and whispered in Lady Needham's ear.

'Mrs Hoyland Leach, my lady, about some business or other. Can you spare a few minutes?'

'I'm afraid we *can't* see Mrs Hoyland Leach, Harriet. Say we have visitors. And could she call again.'

'Good God,' cried Sir Thomas, 'you can't send the woman away, Lucy. If you live in the country, you've got to behave decently to your neighbours.' Which, thought Alexandra afterwards, she supposed he had meant to do.

However Mrs Hoyland Leach, a florid, fortyish, go-ahead country lady, did not help by her initial attempts to deal with the old and the eccentric.

'There you are,' she announced when she had been presented to Alexandra and given coffee; this made Sir Thomas snort derisively and even Lady Needham smile a little contemptuously. But their visitor meant more than an observation of the obvious. 'I told Angela Frame that you didn't go in for afternoon naps. I knew I mustn't interfere with the memoirs, so that meant the morning was out. And I do think tea-time calls, unless they really *are* that, are an impossibility. And the same with drink time. That leaves the early afteroon. But they'll be sleeping, Angela insisted. I knew she was wrong. "He'll be writing and she'll be working in the garden," was what I said.'

'Then *you* were wrong too,' Lady Needham told her.

But Mrs Hoyland Leach was not put off. 'I must say Anne Hedges was on my side. She said, "The Needhams are definitely not siesta people." '

'It's pleasant,' said Sir Thomas, 'to feel that everyone is concerned with the exact timetable of our day.'

Mrs Hoyland Leach laughed, ' "Three or four families in a country village is the very thing to work on," ' she quoted, twinkling, sure, as she could not always be locally, of her audience's literacy.

'Yes, yes,' said Sir Thomas impatiently, 'and a little bit of ivory and all the rest of it. But it's by no means certain that Jane Austen wouldn't have done a great deal better to extend her range. That's what they're saying now anyway. No, for novel reading in retirement, I recommend Trollope's horizons. But you didn't come here to talk about novels.'

'We don't know that yet,' Lady Needham observed; she added, 'My great-granddaughter is taking English Literature at her University.'

'Was,' interjected Sir Thomas, to Alexandra's fury lest he should say more of this silly idea they were trying to force upon her to keep her from everything that mattered. She closed her ears to protect herself from this ludicrous nonsense that was squeezing her life – her life that, since *it* had happened, had been shot out into space to travel in a time machine through one cruelly absurd irrelevancy after another in a cold outer-space wind of no love, or real human contact. But when she closed her eyes, she saw the row of paperbacks above her head in her second-year room at college, and smelt the faint pot smell that sleepy, loving Ned had left behind in that room, and the sharp, awakening smell of eau-de-Cologne with which thoughtful, protective Rodrigo had sprayed her room after Ned had gone. So astringent, so healthily awakening from the faint of Ned's dream stories that she opened her eyes even now as though Rodrigo had just sprayed her. How dare they try to separate her from all that, from all she loved? She was going to say to this silly woman, 'he's got it wrong, he's senile, he's in the plot,' but Mrs Hoyland Leach had taken the monosyllable simply for an old man's noise.

She said, 'You're not so cold after all.' At which Lady Needham drew her fur stole more tightly to her shoulders in protest. 'It *is* about a novelist. What we're worried about – the few of us that is who care and who have lived here all our lives – is that Mardwick town council or borough council – it seems to change every year now – are actually preparing to pull down Rhoda Broughton's old house. I know she isn't read much now, and of course she never directly wrote about this part of England ...'

'Why?' asked Lady Needham. Sir Thomas appeared to have dozed off.

'Oh, I don't really know,' Mrs Hoyland Leach had not the facts at her fingertips. 'She had such a wonderful knowledge of the London scene of those days, the smart set as they called it, the Season and so on, I suppose.'

'Oh dear me. Of *course* she wrote what she liked. And we don't read her because we don't want to. No, I mean why do the council want to pull it down?'

'Oh, you know what they are. No feeling for the past or the place. It's some sort of housing estate. You can be sure they've got a direct financial interest somewhere. Near the Hospital. What a place for a housing estate!'

'I sometimes wish that Tom and I lived nearer to a hospital, but ...'

'What we hoped was that we could have *your* names in a letter of protest to the *Advertiser*. Otherwise it's the same old list of names, just those of us who were born and bred here and think it's all far more important than it probably is. The Council will never take any notice of us, and as for the Ministry of Thing, I mean, of course, they've never heard of us.'

She would go to Rodrigo's week-end home. It was not far. Somewhere in this Wiltshire place, in fact. They'd be setting out with the pony club, his small sisters; and his mother to lie down upstairs with trendy women's magazines and a bottle. If darling, so beautiful Rodrigo was to be believed about it all, which he wasn't. Oh, the enchanting smile, when he agreed. 'Well, I made you laugh, Ally darling. And the reality's too plain boring, I promise. Not funny-boring like I've made it.' ... 'Oh, excuse me, I've come because I'm having a baby by your son.' That would make a funny-boring scene for him. No, no, she didn't want to hurt him, she wanted his eyes tender and loving-mocking, not frightened and hating. I'll go there and do it, I'll go there and do it. I'll make him cry in front of them. 'Roddy, who is this terrible girl? What a thing for your sisters to hear!' ... 'Mummy, I'm your new daughter. Yes, and I've got another man. And he's got a beard and sometimes, too, Rodrigo strokes it.' She must do it now before the hate went from her. Was she mad to think of doing such a cruel, senseless thing? And this idiot comedy went on, the absurdity of this woman's chatter and the old man asleep. At least there was not hate here, only death and absurdity. And then the woman said: 'But a distinguished name like Sir Thomas's, and, of course, yours.'

And the hate of *her* voice as she said 'distinguished'. Alexandra looked to see if her great-grandmother flinched before it, but the old dying forget-me-nots set in the withered parrot's skin showed no sign of recognition. Thay had all – the older ones – that thing about not flinching and courage; how could she get any tenderness for her own cowardice from these sort of hard-shelled stoics, from people like them?

'And then if you felt like being pioneer contributors to a fund to save the house, for we feel sure we'll have to offer to purchase, it would give the whole thing a more serious appearance. To outsiders, I mean. At the moment it's just us – Freddie Silchester, and Mary Wemyss-White, and Dolly Danby, and the old Marchioness and the usual local names. With your names we might even venture to get Sir James Langmuir, though the old boy is not always easy to get on with. Tycoons, I suppose,' she said vaguely and looked for Lady Needham's worldly support.

The old lady said, 'Do you mean rich people? Naturally they

make their own ways more than others. And the others must bend to them.'

Mrs Hoyland Leach was driven back on the generalized appealing voice she might have used for anyone. '*Do* help us, won't you, Lady Needham?'

'Well, Tom, as you see, is snoozing. And I never do anything that involves money without sleeping on it for three nights. I made that rule years ago when I had to entertain Commonwealth Prime Ministers and I've kept to it ever since.'

There was nothing for Mrs Hoyland Leach to do but to go, which she did with such a pantomime of tiptoeing as implied respect not only for the old gentleman's sleep, but for the old lady's senility.

Lady Needham said, 'We'll go and talk your little problem over in the garden while Tom sleeps.'

Alexandra had supposed that her great-grandfather's snoozing was a pretence, but, no, he was fast asleep and snoring. The behaviour of them both confused her so that she thought, now if *he* wakes up like the Red King, it may well be that I really am merely some part of his dream. She had to force herself consciously not to imitate Mrs Hoyland Leach's tiptoe. Lady Needham, putting on felt hat and woollen jacket and arming herself with an ashplant in the lobby, did the opposite. She clumped her feet on the floor.

'That's to make sure the old hag knows I've gone out. Then if we catch sight of her in the garden we shall know it isn't chance.'

She didn't explain this.

Alexandra said, 'Why did Mama have no more babies after me?'

The old lady cried, 'Labels! Now really, Alexandra, you should have reminded me. I'm afraid you've got into a lot of this mess through absent-mindedness. It's the case with most troubles of that sort. Ugh! this beastly garden! Tom never goes out in it and all I can think of is what a prison we've landed ourselves in, cut off from our friends in London. Those that are left. But labels! Your mother says you want to have your baby. She seemed most upset at the thought of it, if I understood her properly; but the line crackles so – living in the country! We had a clearer line when Tom was doing the economic survey up-country in Borneo. I can't think why she doesn't want to be a grandmother. She wouldn't have liked it, if I had objected to her birth. I think you're right. But are you *quite* sure?'

The old lady stopped suddenly on the lawn and, standing squarely before Alexandra, she took both her hands in her own and pressed them.

'You *really* want to have the baby?'

Her faded blue eyes stared vaguely out of the puckered parchment of her face; her stance suggested a direct, searching approach to her great-granddaughter, but her eyes, as Alexandra realized, were gazing furtively into the shrubbery.

'Quite, quite sure, darling.'

'Good. Now you don't want to marry the young man. He's not your type. Or you're not his or something. Lots of people would disapprove of that. But as Tom says we're too old to bother with what the world thinks. We gave our lives to it and we've a right to ignore it now. Of course, Tom only thinks he does. Those old memoirs! But *I* don't care a hang. No, if you don't want marriage, I'd be the last to tell you it was unalloyed bliss. The very last. But I *am* worried about the label you're giving yourself. It's difficult enough to be a real person anyway. Look at that woman just now and all the so-called "people" round here. Noises, not human beings, and irritating noises at that. If you fix yourself with a label, it makes it even harder to be yourself. And that's what it'll be – "unmarried mother"! To say nothing of the baby's ugly label. I don't want you to do it. Never be a pioneer of *anything* – first woman this and first woman that. Be yourself. And you can't be that, if every time you come into the room people are thinking to themselves a whole lot of silly opinions about "unmarried mothers". There's no end, my dear, to the stupid clichés people get into their heads unless they're artists or people of affairs. So what I suggest is that you marry this man, if he's decent. And if he's not, marry him just the same and then divorce. Then there'll be none of this stupid "unmarried mother" business. If the man's treated you badly, he'll agree to marry as long as he's paid. And heaven knows your mother's got enough money. That was the one good result of our son marrying a rich ninny. When they died, they left your mother very comfortable. Not that Tom and I are poor. We can contribute if your mother wants us to. Far better than for some unread novelist's house. Tom will give the bigger contribution. But I don't mind giving the young man a cheque for a hundred if that will help. Of course, if he's the thing, and if you want to marry him, we shall always welcome him here. And, if not, much better buy his name until you meet the man you want.'

Alexandra found the advice, in the abstract, rather touching, but she wished that it did not also, of course only by the wildest exaggeration, touch Rodrigo or Ned.

She said, 'Thank you, darling. But what I want to talk about is Mama and my grandparents. You see . . .'

But Lady Needham stopped her. 'Just go and look behind those lilac bushes, and see if anyone's hiding there.'

Bewildered, Alexandra returned to say that there was not.

'Hm! I probably did the trick stamping my feet in the hall. But look behind the escallonia, too, dear, over there. No, that's a potentilla – even a dwarf couldn't hide behind that. And they haven't started to use dwarfs yet. They probably haven't thought of it. Over there!'

When her fears had proved groundless again, she said, 'Now, Alexandra, I've helped you. I want you to help me. Not now. But I may need your help later, so you must keep in touch with me, dear, whatever you decide to do. You see, I may need somewhere to hide away for a week or two. I don't want to be down in the country here as I was telling you, but I think if I said I was leaving, they'd keep me here against my will. Or try to bring me back if I went away. Of course, I don't suppose they could do it because we're not living in the days of Rhoda Broughton and all those Victorian melodramas. I don't want you to think I'm fancying things. I can't prove it because I've never tried. But I am definitely being watched. There's always someone – it's either Harriet or the gardener or the woman who comes for the rough work, but always someone.'

'But, darling . . .'

'Now I know what you're going to say. You mustn't be shocked. And you mustn't let it put you against your great-grandfather. Men are very vain. Even the best of them. Not that Tom hasn't done useful things, putting colonies on an economic footing, drafting all sorts of important bills for ministers who were ninnies. But he's not been one of the *really* important people, so what's he want to add to the flood of books for? Sheer vanity! But it means that he'll sacrifice anything for those old memoirs of his. Even his wife's happiness. Of course, I don't think of him as the real Tom, now. This is just what happens to the old.'

'But, darling . . .'

'When did I notice it first? Well, there you are, dear, you see. I've had one or two horrid spells of dizziness and so on. And so I called in the doctor here. Not a very clever man, I'm afraid. But when I bullied him and insisted that I should see a heart specialist in London, he agreed that I was probably right. But somehow, I don't know why it is, I've never got there. Tom was determined I shouldn't.'

'Oh, darling, are you sure? It sounds so silly . . .'

'Not silly, dear. He realized at once that he hadn't got more than a year or two at the most to use me as secretary to get those old memoirs finished, and he wasn't going to have that year wasted with me resting under doctor's orders or anything like that. I don't mind. At present I've decided to make the sacrifice. But as I said to you we mustn't let ourselves become labels. So if I decide to run away, you shall hide me until they're tired of looking. You will, won't you?'

'Of course, darling,' Alexandra was about to add more, but she decided against it. 'Don't you think we ought to go back to Great-grandfather?'

'Indeed, yes. We don't want to make them suspicious or they'll put a double guard over me.' Lady Needham laughed bitterly. As they walked back to the house, she said, 'Do *you* ever read Rhoda Broughton?'

'I've never heard of her before, I'm afraid.'

'I thought as much. How lucky you were here.'

And so she said to Sir Thomas. 'You went to sleep, Tom. That silly woman wanted us to buy a house that belonged to Rhoda Broughton. But luckily Alexandra was here and she said at once that no one read her now. And when I said that Alexandra knew because she was a University student of English Literature, you should have seen the silly woman's face.'

'Rhoda Broughton?'

'Oh, really, Tom. The famous novelist: *Red as a Rose is She* and all that sort of book. You'll forget your name next. Anyway we mustn't have that Mrs Hoyland Leach here again. She tried to make mischief. Hinting that old people can't accommodate themselves to the young. It wasn't very pleasant in front of Alexandra. Do you like anchovy toast, Alexandra? I'll go and talk to Harriet and see what she can do for us. She's probably made some of her delicious little rice cakes. She's always so pleased to have someone to make them for. She can't do enough for any member of the family, you know, after all these years.'

She made a face over her husband's head as she left the room. But Alexandra couldn't tell whether it was a wink, or frown, or what.

However, there was clearly no time to lose, so she said abruptly, 'Is there any madness in the family, Great-grandfather? I mean is that why my mother never had another baby?'

Sir Thomas looked at her for a moment or two, solemnly, then he said very deliberately, 'I've always understood that she didn't *want* another child. It was in the air then, you know. Had been since the Great War unsettled people. And your father's a good enough chap, but he hardly rises above the *idées reçues* of the moment. Angry young man, as I remember.'

'You're not answering my question.'

'There are rather a lot of questions there, you know. Now to take one. Did your mother suppose that there might be hereditary insanity in the family? And then again, did this weigh with her in her decision not to have a second child? Now, those are two questions. If you were preparing a minute for a minister, you'd set them out separately. I can't answer either of them definitely. I've the greatest respect and affection for Zoe, but that doesn't mean that she doesn't get bees in her bonnet.'

'Well could there be any *reason* for such bees? Don't you see this is important to me. I've been so near breakdown and sometimes it seemed to me that it's more than breakdown. You see surely that, however much I want to, I can't have the baby if that's at risk.'

She spoke as a child to a child.

'I see that you've worked yourself up in a way that does no

credit to your education, my dear. The purpose of a University education, or one of them, is to teach people how to formulate questions. Get your questions straight and you may get the right answers to your problems.'

She tried to dismiss the look of patronage which he gave her as absurd; but then it suddenly appeared to her as a sneering emphasis of all the unfairness that life suddenly brings to the innocence and good intentions of youth. He was Sauron or perhaps the guileful Gollum, playing on her pity for the confusions of old age. If she refused all such pity and attacked him directly, perhaps all the forces of cruelty and hatred and unconcern which had brought blackness to the clear skies of a year ago – of the first happy love times of the three Hobbits last year – would burst down upon her in a storm that would end in the return of sunshine, of goodness and of love and innocence and the hope of a new world.

'And Great-grandmother? Is *she* normal?'

She had so expected him to blast her with lightning or to shrivel away to nothing before her eyes, that she was disconcerted when he sighed, as it seemed with relief, wearily it is true, but nevertheless with relief.

'Ah! So that's it. My dear girl, there are many good aspects about being very old. One doesn't compete, one doesn't act regardlessly, one doesn't expect. Very useful negatives. But it brings, of course, attendant miseries. Of body and of mind. Lucy's told you a lot of stuff, I expect, about her heart being bad, hasn't she? And probably a lot of other troubles too. All pure fancy! And you mustn't encourage them. She could become a miserable hypochondriac. But we won't let her. I shall need your help in that, Alexandra. No, it's typical of one of Hardy's life's little ironies. She'll live to be over a hundred, probably. The more the nervous imagination plays up like that, the longer the person lives. Just see if she's coming back, will you? No? Well, then I can tell you this: and I can do so with a clear mind, and, anyway, it won't harm you to have somebody else's woes to take your mind off your own problems. *I* shan't live long. It doesn't matter. I've had a good life. It's comedy not tragedy. Bowel trouble. I can tell the doctor knows it. Cancer. He doesn't say anything. No point in it at my age. Nor do I. But he's a humane man. He won't let me suffer more than is necessary. Meanwhile I must press on with the memoirs. If they do nothing else, they keep Lucy's mind off her imaginary ills. Ah! There you are, Harriet! And a smell of delicious newly baked cake. The fatted calf, in fact. Well, Lucy, I think I've been able to help this prodigal.'

'Alexandra's not a prodigal, dear. She's just been unlucky.'

'Ah, yes. "One more unfortunate, weary of breath." But we won't go on with *that* quotation. Trouble is she's got her questions all wrong, you see. Fatal when you have a problem. Now I've sorted them out. What you need, my dear, is intellectual discipline. You know what I think, Lucy? She shall stay down here with us and help with the memoirs. She can have her baby here. Harriet'll feed her up, won't you, Harriet?'

'Harriet – do you remember those meringues you used to make for Miss Alexandra when she was quite tiny? Coffee, weren't they?'

'That's right, my lady.'

'Could you make them again, do you think?'

'I think so, my lady. I'd be glad to for Miss Alexandra.'

'There you are, Alexandra. Harriet's not forgotten any of us.'

Their voices sounded so sweet and menacing, so tender and silken and cooing and cruel. How can you know what is siren song? How can you tell the purring of the great cats? How can you pierce the fair elfin mist, or penetrate the great Boig, when you're only beginning life?

'It's not fair. It's not fair,' Alexandra cried, and she began to scream as the faces closed in on her.

They sat at this chromium fitted table in the chromium fitted room that couldn't have altered for twenty or so years, for it had a kind of pink plastic sugar thing on the table that you pushed for the sugar, which the Little Mam said had been part of the war austerity. And there were those big coffee machines you still see sometimes that make a lot of hissing. The coffee was that kind too, all froth. And the Little Mam said He and Uncle Leslie had lived off it when they were students. It was all Italy then, apparently, like movies now, but shirts and suits as well then.

All this the Little Mam told her, as she could guess, to take her mind off things. And what with the shush, shushing of these chromium monsters and those awful clattering staccato voices Italians use to talk to each other, and sudden violent swooshes of traffic every few minutes, as though they were sitting under a fly-over, instead of in a dirty-book kind of little street quite a long walk off the Tottenham Court Road, she found it very hard to listen to her grandmother who spoke, as always but a bit more so in public, in a soft chuckling voice that she must have learned from exchanging intimate chaff with the customers at the bar.

As a result, Alexandra found herself brooding over this awful extra week away from the University, as always when her mind wasn't artificially filled. It made her feel ashamed because it was at her request, whenever she felt imprisoned, that the poor Little Mam heaved herself (well hardly, because she was so tiny, petite they probably said then) out of the comfort of Number 8 and went with her to cinemas, cafés, parks, even amusement arcades. As if she hadn't done enough, handing over the restaurant to an untrustworthy manageress and coming to London just to live with her granddaughter!

And Alexandra really did want to respond to this kindness, for the Little Mam had been so truly good – not the 'brick' that He had tried to make her out – but really aiding; not Gran and Granddaughter playing at being pals which His awful picture of the plucky Little Mam had made her fear; nor 'darling, there isn't really any difference between the generations, not when it comes to fundamentals, there isn't, I promise' that poor Mama sometimes tried out; but really concerned and loving. To begin with she asked all about Rodrigo and Ned often and about the way they moved and about the hair on their chests, though she pretended resolutely to think that only one of the two could be 'serious' and clearly hoped it was Rodrigo. She had seen at once why Alexandra loved the little line of blond hairs that ran all the way down Rodrigo's backbone. She agreed that being kissed by beards (although apparently for some reason she knew much more about moustaches) could, if you gave yourself up to it, be a good sensation in itself, quite apart that is from the delights of the lips and the tongue and the kiss itself. And then, except when

158

she was worried by one's being in a state, as now – and even that was probably because They'd got at her, or Mama and her doctors had, and exaggerated it all – the Little Mam just listened and sat and asked sensible questions and (getting on terribly well with Concepcion) saw to it that one had nourishing but also delicious meals with lots of kinds of ice-creams, and put one's swollen feet and ankles up.

But now, as she strained to catch the Little Mam's words and could not, Alexandra's straying attention began to wonder whether, this week late for term on the doctor's orders, and Them moving out, and the Little Mam coming up, was not a pacifying sequence too good to be true. If, here and now, the Little Mam proved to be *too* good and *too* patient, it would perhaps reveal that they were keeping her in London to prevent her from being with Rodrigo and Ned (although she had spoken often to them on the telephone), or that the mental illness had really begun, or that They were driving her into it so that They could have an excuse to abort, however late, and break her will with Theirs.

To test the sincerity of her grandmother she began, against the slow stream of the Little Mam's reminiscence, another stream, siphoning the sugar out of the horrible pink plastic penis-shaped device upon the table until it made the beginning 'Gand' in sugar writing, for she needed magic protection.

She did not, however, prove her grandmother false, for the Little Mam ceased her talk and said sharply, 'Stop it, Al. If you're not careful you'll turn into a slut. And if you're going to be a girl on your own, that way lies the gin bottle. I've seen it too often and too much not to warn you, duck.'

So Alexandra thought of another way of testing the Little Mam. She began herself to talk very fast.

'And you see, although apparently the kidney tests were all perfectly clear, as soon as she saw this swelling thing of my ankles, Doctor Dunkerley got into this state. And then Mama, of course, became quite hysterical. And She got Concepcion worked up. You know how superstitious peasants are about childbirth. I'm sure she didn't understand a thing about what Mama said to her about the Dreaded Toxaemia, although of course that was nonsense too, as Doctor Dunkerley said, I mean I'm only four and a half months. But anyhow, she, I mean Concepcion, had seen a mouse in my room, or said she had, but I don't believe it for a moment, for though Number 8's an old house, sort of not quite Regency, there aren't any mice, or if there are it's her fault. Anyway apparently mice are terribly unlucky for pregnant women in Spain and the baby's born dead or mad. And Mama was terrified I should hear all that, although why she should think my very real fears would be affected by Concepcion's superstitions, I don't know. So they all began screaming. Poor Pa! I mean, all those women, including me, of course. So there had to be this absolute promise not to go back until the end of the first week of term. And I agreed but not if *They* were to be there. It would have been awful having Them about, but mainly I think I just wanted to impose my will. It's part of an hysteric state, you know. And making Them go to an hotel from Their own home was quite a triumph, you see. I mean you could call it a sick thing, but still it's a victory. And for the person to be with me I chose poor you ...'

To Alexandra's real fright, the Little Mam brought her gloved hands flat down upon the table – bangers in Up Jenkins that she'd played with the Little Mam as a child – and a terrific bang it was with her many rings. And clouds of sugar Gandalf filled the air like Christmas Tree frost. You could sense the people behind looking round. Scenes are so awful. But the Little Mam was unperturbed, for she shrilled, 'Shut up! Shut up!' Not the intimate chaffing widow behind the bar ('Two bouncing boys? I don't believe it.' 'Sorry, duck, it's true.'); but another Little Mam, buried now in the past, putting those two out who had taken liberties. 'Shut up, Al. I don't want to hear any more.'

Then more quietly she took her hands up; and you could see people going back to their coffees and their pizzas and their bologneses.

'You said all that four or five times to me the first two days when I came to Number 8. You said it again only this morning. Why are you repeating it all now? No, don't say because you're worked up. We know all that. But you're an artful little thing. It's part of your charm *and* your trouble. Even this mistake of yours. You use it. And I don't say you shouldn't, love. Any girl on her own has to use anything to hand. But all that stuff. You were watching me, Al, when you said it. Why? I mean I expect I bore the tits off you, dear, as my friend Edna Ashe used to say. But I'm doing my real best, dear. I can't talk books. You knew that anyway. But all that stuff. Twice in a day. I'm not Lady Needham – a bit missing in the upper storey. Give us a chance. How old do you think I am, Al? I suppose a hundred and two to you. But I'm not senile, my memory's not quite gone.'

The Little Mam's Slav wooden doll face, with its funny all-over pancake sort of make-up, set, as she said this, in such sad, lost lines that Alexandra felt desperately ashamed. It was this stinky illness, making her suspicious of everyone. Soon she would have no friends left. Big tears formed in her eyes and began to roll slowly down her cheeks. But there was no hysteria, none of the usual shaking or sobbing; she was too tired for that.

The Little Mam left her seat, came round the table and sat next to her granddaughter, put her arm round her, pressed her tightly.

'Oh, Ally Pally! for crying out loud! You do make a fuss of it all, don't you, lovey?'

'I thought you were just being nice. I thought They'd got you here to stop me going back. And I do want to go back, Gran. I want so much to go back to life as it was. I don't want to be like this. I want to be like I used to be.'

'Yes, dear. I know. And up to a point . . .'

'Oh, I know I'm an escapist. Or I seem so. But truly I do realize that it can't be the same. Not with the baby. But I started it and I must give it all I can.' She sat up straight in her chair. 'That's why I must go back, Gran. I shall need a good degree if I'm to do all I want for that child. I should think another coffee, wouldn't you?'

'No, I shouldn't, Al.' The Little Mam burst out laughing. 'How you do act it all. It's like a play. But you're right about the baby. I know that winter I had the bad influenza, they couldn't stop me going back to work. At the Bag of Nails, it was. And a girl there. Ida. She always seemed a real bitch. But she stood in for me two or three times marvellously. You know, when I felt I couldn't stand on my feet. But I'd got three mouths to feed. So you see, Al, people aren't all that bad. There are swine, of course, everywhere. But people don't have the time for all this pretending and taking you in and making you do what you don't want to. Like you seem to think. Or so it seems to me.' She took her gloves out of her bag. 'I've had enough of this fug. Are you coming or not? Or do you still think that I'm pulling a fast one?'

'No, no. I want to come with you.'

'All right then. Just to show. I'm going to phone that Doctor Whatsit. She doesn't seem a bad female. And I'll tell her I'm sending you back to the University tomorrow. On my own authority. Get back with your boys, that's what you need. And your work. You'll take it easy when you ought to. Nature has its way. Zoe fusses too much. She was brought up differently. And Perry's an old sentimentalist. All this about my hard life bringing two boys up. 'Course it was hard, but there's more to it than that. Leslie knows. I suppose it's the compensation Nature gives them. Understanding a bit what we women feel. And now I'll pay and we'll get out of this fuggy dump. *That* doesn't do you any good. A bit of a walk would do no harm. London's changed and not for the better, but I may as well see what they've done to it while I'm up here. And as soon as you say, "Gran, I'm tired" – taxi.'

It was at the top of Gower Street in that new world of underpass and flyover that Alexandra felt, not tired, but as so often now, the need to pee.

'All right, you go to the ladies, love. And not to waste time, I'll phone the doctor. And we'll meet back here.'

When Alexandra emerged four minutes later she could not see the Little Mam anywhere. She gave her five minutes but then she became alarmed. Perhaps, after all, this had only been a ruse to try out whether she could manage on her own. To force her to admit dependence. All right, she would show them. She had come up from the underground by the Euston Road exit. She stood for a moment at the entrance in a world of thunderous emptiness. High above towered the great glass and concrete monsters, swaying down upon her as the clouds scudded by them; and she poor feeble insect on the pavement below. Not to look up then. But ahead. And there, whoosh, whoosh, cars, taxis, lorries, buses by some secret timing, by an indicator hidden from the pedestrians, known only to the cold metal brontosauruses that were hunting her down in the concrete wastes.

And ahead was waste land, half destroyed houses, hoardings with torn bills that flapped in the great sunlit dusty gale that was sweeping through this world and clearing it of all the human rubbish that was blown before it.

And she was following others, for that was how it worked – never get out of step – she saw where to go and when the lull was and why the crossing exactly there.

It was only when she arrived at the other side of Euston Road that, looking back to that alien land from which she had escaped, she noticed a little figure, legs shapely enough for its scarlet mini-skirt, but body too fat and heavy, and then above that, a face of a terrified pet animal. There she was – the Little Mam, at the wrong tapered end of the long central island that divided the throughway, standing on a narrow concrete edge, behind her a forest of landscaped shrubs, before her, within inches, a Birnam Wood of speeding traffic. A brave little vanishing species of chirpy robin in the concrete jungle. Alexandra watched with agony to see in her some stranger, all sturdy good sense, all sexy ease, all good fellowship, fun and irrepressible cheek gone, a little, oldish, frightened made-up woman lost. It was unbearable to see her so, to sense a panic imminent, more genuine than any she herself had probably ever known. To enable her to reach her grandmother, there came, piercing through the clouds of anxiety that swam through her brain, a quick, accurate intelligence she had forgotten that she possessed. With it her eye made out in a second the way to join this little shipwrecked sailing boat – arrangements are not made for those who lose their moorings – and in seconds her more youthful legs brought her to her grand-mother's side.

The Little Mam said nothing, but she was trembling. It took, in the centre of those rushing unending streams of traffic – people want to get there, get home, get away, get stoned, get stuffed – what Alexandra felt to be for ever to find a taxi, to attract the driver's attention, to secure his acknowledgement, to find a stopping place, to be on their way home. And by then the Little Mam's trembling had given way to tears (the age of stiff upper lips has given place once more to the age of sentiment, men are wearing their hair long again, an Empire has been lost).

In the taxi, with all the weapons of her time, compact and

mirror and powder puff and lipstick, the Little Mam set to to repair the ravages of her fright, the vestiges of shame.

'It was the telephoning that did it, duck. I just can't cope with the new public boxes and that's honest. As soon as I got on to the receptionist at the doctor's, I lost her over and over again, then those pips and I dropped all the money on the floor. But it's all right – I did what I said I'd do for you. And then, coming out, I got lost.'

Alexandra had taken her grandmother's hand, nor did the Little Mam remove it. After a long silence – indeed as Camden Town came into sight – she said: 'There was three men altogether that saw me standing there. I mean, you know, real men. Smart and all. And they looked away. Babies, bringing up children, money worries, hard labour, don't let them worry you with that stuff, Ally Pally. It's all in a day's work. Any woman can do that so long as there's men around to show interest. And I always had that. Plenty of men to pass the time of day with. Good lookers, too. Fun to be with, some of them. Now in the restaurant it's all women and women's talk. Or foreigners and the waiters – Arabs, Portuguese and such. It makes it hard to find a reason for going on.'

She took her hand out of her granddaughter's. They were home, though, so it was the natural thing to do. Nevertheless, it was done, not as an automatic movement, but as a deliberate gesture.

> *Ah! the rorty little things! ... how they*
> *tousled them, and mousled them!* – Beardsley

The great pink and white iced cake with its intricate tiers and columns was an edifice equally fit for a curious pantheon or for the Shrine of Kali – although to the uncles, especially the Northern uncles, it spoke also of half-forgotten nursery tales, of Grimm and of Perrault, of the Christmas Carol and of Andersen. Its fourteen candles of pink and white wax flamed and smoked, filling the room with a mysterious haze. The long chain of rose and white frangipani flowers running across the centre of the table could have been a scented molten stream of deliquescing candle wax. Even to Hamo's rational sensibility, the whole perfumed, steamy, murky atmosphere brought overtones of exotic and arcane mystery, initiation and rite.

Jonkheer Kerkelyk van Enkhuijsen rose to his full six foot height at the head of the table, turned his back upon the assembled company, let down his trousers and underpants: and from his enormous hairy arse emitted in rapid cannonade fourteen farts that resounded across the delicious cake, putting out the candles, giving an acrid turn to the cloying flower scent. A rouroulade of fourteen farts so consistently sustained in both force and note was an achievement that roused excited clapping from the boys and a warm shower of compliments even from the sophisticated grown-ups. Little Ian Wong, in whose honour the feat had been performed, buried his smooth saffron face in his white shirt to hide his delighted blushes and giggles at so signal a tribute to a mere boy from the greatest of all the uncles, the Dutch uncle himself.

The French uncle, Armand Leroux, apprehensive no doubt of English concern for the social aspect of events, said to Hamo: 'No. But really. This is quite extraordinary. One so easily forgets the deeply traditional quality of the Dutch noblesse. The cheap *Paris-Match* image of the house of Orange has obscured it. Something of this kind must have been the customary honouring of a favourite page by the Jonkheer's ancestors of the fifteenth or even, one may venture, the fourteenth century. We have nothing here to do with the vulgarities of Frans Hals' burghers of the dyke lands. No, this is the *petite noblesse* of Louvain and Brabant at its best – what in France we call the *hobereaux*. An aristocratic *franchise* that found an easy response in the *moeurs* of its own peasantry, in those broad-cheeked arses of the merry-eyed skaters and drinkers of Breughel or Jan Steen. No! No, really – such a lack of bourgeois *pudeur* is completely delightful.'

But the Jonkheer, his clothing and posture as host both resumed, gazed out of his great grey-skinned, sensual, flabby face with his usual empty, yet unyielding stare.

'Well, boys, cut away,' he cried, 'but don't forget, any chap who stuffs himself sick earns a stuffing of another kind.' He purred at his English punning, for all the uncles prided themselves on their wide linguistic powers. Then he added, titillating himself and others by a little self-conscious brutality, 'As if they won't all be stuffed before the party finishes.' And he roared in gargantuan ancestral laughter. But perhaps its very robustness put him into an *eheu fugaces* mood, for he said sombrely, 'Yes, yes, cut away. Is that a possible play on words, Mr Langmuir? But there should be no need for knives. My grandfather would have blasted that cake into pieces.'

The Dutch uncle was a great man – doyen, leader and organizer of this international club, and the elder English uncle, Commander Ensworthy, hastened obliquely to reassure him.

'I think, Langmuir, you know,' he said, 'that we've been privileged to hear the authentic thunderous note that put the wind up Charles the Second and his roistering pals at Whitehall when the Dutch came up the Medway.'

He frowned and coughed in tactful remonstrance when Hamo refused his large 'dollop' of birthday cake. He was frankly a good deal worried by Hamo's presence at this great triennial rendezvous of the uncles (made each three years in a different Asian land to coincide with a favoured boy's birthday). Not only because he felt responsible for Hamo's behaviour as a visiting Englishman, but because the younger English uncle (by a long way the youngest of the uncles, not yet forty years of age) had introduced this travelling scientist on a very inadequate knowledge of his tastes, finding indeed (so he had anxiously informed the Commander), only unfortunately too late, during the car journey up to the rendezvous, that the man's tastes were schismatic, if not indeed heretical. 'I say, I'm rather worried. He seemed to be one of the holy brethren when we got talking at the club. But now it appears that he's looking for milk that's gone off the boil. Coming up, we stopped at the resthouse and he started showing an interest in the houseboy, a great hairy chap of twenty. I didn't know where to look.' 'Well, for God's sake, keep him away from von Langenbeck and Poulsen,' was all that the Commander could advise on the spur of the moment, for the German and Danish uncles were notoriously strict in their practice. Hamo, however, showed no response to decent hinting.

'I'm afraid you *must* excuse me. My days of cake-eating are over,' he said primly. To mitigate any apparent standoffishness, particularly to the junior part of the company, with whom he felt particularly ill at ease, he addressed himself to the huddle of boyish faces of varying shades of yellow and brown, from very light ivory to rich dark chocolate, which looked eagerly, with a suitable mixture of respect and impudence, towards the uncles' end of the table. 'There'll be all the more for you boys,' he said, hoping that his voice did not suggest the embarrassment he felt at the words he had chosen. Not to appear wholly unsusceptible to these disgustingly immature charms, he searched among them, and, finding a taller heavier boy, who might have been an under-sized seventeen, he spoke to him particularly. '*You* have my slice.' Then he dreaded what might be the outcome of such par-ticularity.

He need not have feared. The uncles exacted a pre-1914 good manners from their various protégés, who, in any case, as the French uncle explained to him, came from 'the old Asian European-trained clerisy, brought up in the traditions of the grammar school and the lycée, very conscious of the advantages to their sons of association with European gentlemen'. As indeed were the boys themselves, each of whom now vied with the other in welcoming this new, elegant and probably rich English uncle. What greeted him from this display of shorts and open white shirts and crest-pocketed blazers was a barrage of boyish welcome that came from the pages of some shabby volumes lying half-forgotten on the shelves of his prep-school library.

'Please, Sir, have my piece.'

'Have my piece, Sir, have mine.'

'Don't bother with his rotten old bit, Sir.'

'Oh, don't encourage *him*, Sir. He's a frightful pig already.' This last from Master Singapore 1968.

And another, blowing out his cheeks in imitation of the rather fat-faced boy to whom Hamo had spoken, cried, '*Voyez vous, monsieur, comme il est déjà joufflu.*' This from Master Cam-bodia 1967.

Quick interchange from English to French and back again among the boys. But it was clear from the victim's blushes and his uncomprehending eyes that he had no lingua franca at *his* command.

The German uncle, in fluent Burmese, came to his protégé's rescue. It was a feat in these days to be the lover of Master Burma at all, as the Commander explained to Hamo. To have brought him out of that self-quarantined country solely for the birthday celebrations of Master Hong Kong was something worthy of Richard Hannay, Percy Blakeney, Bulldog Drummond or James Bond. Did Langmuir like good yarns as much as he, the Commander, did? Strange that the perfect playing of such a role should fall to a Hun; but strange really only if you forgot the knight errantry of Rudolf Rassendyll, in that finest of all yarns, *Rupert of Hentzau*. Langenbeck's bringing of his Burmese boy to this great occasion was the exploit which all there would have admiringly discussed, had there not lingered in the topic some flavour of criticism of the great Dutch uncle himself. As the Commander whispered, it was in some ways a prickly subject. After all, the Jonkheer, in providing Master Hong Kong as the hero of the day, was in that very offering, despite all his perfect Mandarin, Cantonese and a dozen North Chinese dialects, underlining the absence of Master Peking for whose Final Coming all the Uncles (as indeed all good South-East Asian Europeans) ever looked. But short of such a return to civilization, Herr von Langenbeck's Burmese exploit had something in it of the chivalry of the good old days.

The sense of a lost age first adumbrated in the Jonkheer's nostalgic reference to his grandfather's farting prowess, and unspokenly present in the thought of the imaginary Master Peking, lovely peony imprisoned in the Eternal City of Pax Sinica and civilization, year by year appearing more lost to them for ever, was reinforced by Master Burma's total lack of European tongues in which he was almost equalled by the Danish uncle's Master Ceylon – could it be some horrible portent of an alien iron-curtained Asia of the future? It was the American uncle, as much spokesman for modern political matters among the uncles as Armand Leroux was for social matters, who explained this to Hamo.

'Jesus! Do you hear that? Can you believe that a nation can be so dumb? The boy's going to be an engineer and this goddamned Burmese government doesn't teach him English. What can you do for these people?'

And the Danish uncle added that since Mrs Bandaranaike, his own lovely Laksman had to pick up most of his English from himself.

'I am afraid he will be practising Viking medicine.' His jokes were very simple. 'My English is not so perfect, you know. Also in the wholesale marketing of plastic buckets to improve the domestic conditions of Asian villagers, I don't think I employ so many medical terms.' As his lilting Welsh English ran on it was hard not to believe that he had taught English to all the youth of Ceylon and India.

'Oh, I shouldn't worry, Poulsen, if Mrs B. gets back a second time, it won't just be this "neglect of English" nonsense. The boy'll be learning ayurvedic medicine – eye of newt and toe of frog.' Commander Ensworthy, however, seemed more friendly to the reaction than the American uncle, for, fixing Hamo with a far-away occult look in his frank British blue eye, he added, 'I don't suppose that Langmuir here will agree but it may not be half a bad thing. Eye of newt and toe of frog it *is* in their minds and the mind creates the body's expectancies. I doubt if any Asian body expects or can be satisfied with the latest Western antibiotic.' He added something further, unintelligible to Hamo, which he addressed to his pouting-mouthed, drowsy-eyed Indian boy. The boy instantly replied very solemnly in equally unintelligible words. 'There you are, you see, the lad knows all right. I started the tantric spell against the piles he gets in his dear little passage to heaven and he completed it at once. *Their* language, *their* beautiful little bodies and, I'm inclined to believe, *their* medicine to go along with them – that's how it should be.' Looking infinitely melancholy, the Commander stared across the room, and said in a sort of chant, 'The boy across the river has a bottom like a peach, but, alas, I cannot swim. Ah, well !'

This was not the way to bring Asia, however screaming (and a few screams were surely a reasonable gratification), by its heels into the twentieth century. On the faces of the others – all agro-business salesmen, advertisers, development men, technological advisers, import-export experts – there could be seen that combination of irritation and impatience with which the rest of the world so often nowadays hears the voice of Britain. The Jonkheer spoke for them all when, with his usual courtesy, he addressed the senior English uncle.

'My dear Commander, let me congratulate you on your Gujarati and,' bowing to Master India, Banadakrishna Ghosha, upon the delicious partner whom you have chosen in which to exchange its poetry, but if this foolish nationalism really succeeds in reducing our singing birds to nothing but their native song, I must remind you that much of the fellowship, and most of the verbal delights, of our meetings would be lost to us. No, what pleasure will there be if we have to propose our traditional jolly British toast "Bottoms Up!" in ten or so different tongues before our charming guests realize what is expected of them?'

The laughter against the Commander was immediate, and he took it in good part, but unfortunately the second English uncle, Mr Derek Lacey, perhaps in defence of his countryman, but with real wistfulness said: 'I suppose it might mean that we could open our membership to some of the meaner beauties of the bazaars and the estates and the paddy fields.'

Even Hamo (bored, when not perspiringly embarrassed, and always with a distaste for conscious social snobbery) could sense that this was a gaffe more serious than appeared on the surface of the words. The French uncle clearly found it a socially unpleasant suggestion, but it was towards the great Dutch uncle that everyone looked in anxiety; and indeed his heavy brow was thunderous, but no storm broke. Ostensibly to change the conversation, but perhaps with malicious desire to push home this rout of the English, perhaps from some jealousy at Hamo's particularization of his Burmese boy, the German uncle said: 'Mr Chairman, I really think I must protest that our distinguished British visitor does not forgo his puritan refusal of the sweets of life, at least in honour of the delicious Chinese sweetmeat you have so generously brought to our tea-table. Mr Langmuir, you must have some of the torte or you will hurt the feelings of our beautiful Ian Wong.'

But the Jonkheer was too big a man to be influenced by such flattery from mischief-makers.

'No, no, von Langenbeck. We are proud to have with us a man whose rice hybrid has made so many Asian landlords and farmers wealthy enough to profit from all the many services we have to offer them whether in the sale of consumer goods or of technical advice. Where you have walked, Mr Langmuir, sowing your seeds of prosperity, we have, I assure you, not been slow to reap with our commerce. You will, I hope, eat exactly what you like.'

He summoned one of the servants with a clap of the hands and gave an order for special food to be brought to Hamo.

'And I am sure that any member of the club will be glad to offer you some more of the tender national specialities if you will choose.' He waved his hand towards the other end of the table.

'I'm afraid they are all a bit too tender for me.' Hamo feared that if icy courtesy could not carry him through this uninviting occasion, the unfortunate adventure might end in distasteful incivilities, even physical dangers in this hidden, high retreat.

'Oh, now we can see,' said von Langenbeck, 'why you do not eat the torte. You wish to keep a boy's figure for your *tough* friends.'

Looking about him, Hamo was conscious of real dislike, almost hostility in the eyes of his hosts; and, indeed, they practised their own precepts, for in their worship of the *truly* boyish they had rid themselves of every conceivable trace of vestigal youth – skins were leathery, necks bulging, stomachs vast, everything aimed towards a geriatric magnificence; even Mr Derek Lacey's thirty-five-year-old face and body were disguised under layers and layers of carefully acquired corpulence. In this company, Hamo was aware that his disciplined, lean figure was an ephebic insult.

'I have no taste for the tough. *That* I can promise you.'

'Oh, come, Langmuir, that was a pretty hoary, not to say hairy specimen you had your eyes on at the resthouse,' the second English uncle told him.

It looked to Hamo as though the birthday cake was acting like alcohol in releasing an ever-increasing coarseness among his hosts. He shuddered at the adjectives.

'A smooth nineteen,' he said sharply.

There were sneers at these incompatible words, as a company of sceptics might greet the paradoxes by which religious devotees seek to express their mysteries.

But the Jonkheer, grim though he looked, persisted in his courtesies. 'Perhaps somewhere in the compound something can be found to accommodate your tastes, Mr Langmuir,' he said loftily, 'I will make enquiries.'

At such graciousness, the French uncle was driven to cry aloud, '*Mais c'est tout ce qu'il y a de plus chic.*'

And the Commander said, 'I hope you realize, Langmuir, that the Jonkheer's being more than decent about all this.'

But once again the Jonkheer's essential breeding sought to lead them away from the impropriety of Hamo's presence. 'Before we give ourselves up wholly to fundamental joys, I must intrude upon your gaiety with a small matter of club business. Our good friend Iito Hashawabi, or more exactly, no doubt, I should say, Hashawabi Iito san, has asked to be allowed to attend our next dinner. As an observer, or a participating observer, rather than a member. I must add that Hashawabi has said – and it is an amusing conjecture, but perhaps not wholly jest – that in three years' time he is hopeful, or should I say hopefully in three years' time?' he bowed to the American uncle, 'he may bring with him our first guest of a paler colour – Master Australia.'

The two British uncles looked unashamedly aghast. Even the American uncle said sadly, 'I don't know. It seems just yesterday that one bar of candy from the P.X. could buy you a whole Japanese high school.'

But the French uncle quickly intervened : 'How depressing to find this Anglo-Saxon obsession with the past standing in the way of an increased pleasure.'

The Jonkheer said decisively, 'I must confess, gentlemen, that to invite a Japanese uncle to this sort of probationary membership seems to me exactly to fit what we all know in our hearts may be so necessary in the years to come.'

And his words, however chilly the future they implied, swayed the majority opinion.

'So I am enpowered to invite Hashawabi Iito san in – shall we say? – a proto-avuncular role. And if he tames us a little Koala bear, so much the better for the widening of the fundamental Asia of tomorrow.'

And now Hamo's special food made its appearance : a hundred dishes – a curry to which every nation of South-East Asia and the Peninsula had contributed – burning white curries, sweeter brown, bamboos and mangoes, brinjals and poppadums, chappatis, chilies, string hoppers, egg hoppers, and all the many rices that made so appropriate a tribute. For the next half hour, Hamo's palate was so scorched and tortured and his nostrils so assailed by acrid and forceful scents that he was in a semi-trance. Through it he could hear alternate snatches of grown-up conversation about currency deals and customs evasions, and excited boyish exchanges over the relative merits of the cricket and football teams of the Queen's College, the Lycée Pascal, St Wilfrid's, St Aloysius' and the Mandela High.

At last the first and divided step of the celebratory dance came to a close, and the two ends of the table began to mix. The Jonkheer, noting, with his usual sensibility, the eagerness of his members to follow a more abandoned measure, gave the call to engage with a double-entendre so drolly pronounced that no one felt any further difficulty in releasing all his avuncular feelings.

'Our aims are simple. We offer Asia expansion and, more gentle than our ancestors, peaceful penetration.'

At once there began an excited and noisy pulling of crackers, and generally a pulling. Here the Danish uncle, the most light-hearted and childish of the elders, was in his element. Above his heavy body, his head, alone of all the uncles, had kept a certain youthful spareness; his green eyes slanted below his white-blond hair and above his pouting goat lip. He gave the proceedings a satyr note, a note of monkey mischief. He was lucky enough to secure from his cracker a whistle which, when blown, sounded piercingly, and shot forth a long scarlet tongue tipped with a purple feather. With this, setting off squeals with as high a note as the whistle, he tickled nostrils and any other openings he could find. The party might have turned permanently into a riot had not the Jonkheer, always conscious of the educative role that the uncles offered in exchange for their nephews' favours, insisted upon the whole company sitting down to a game of Monopoly. If there was one thing he believed that the uncles should hand on, it was skill in the money market. Nor were his efforts wasted : many of the boys showed a remarkable talent in all matters concerning profit. Not surprisingly the victor was Master Hong Kong, and most appropriately for it was his birthday.

But now the same lessons of commercial skill were turned a little more to adult advantage in an increasingly riotous game of strip poker.

Through it all Hamo was in too much of a curry stupor to be aware of how much his failure to participate was a cause of offence. Straight-backed, he dozed and snoozed, so that the colonial cane-woven rocking-chair moved him backwards into sleep and forwards into wakefulness. He was woken by a nudge from the Commander.

'Wakey, wakey,' he said in a tone made more vulgar by the delights of an hour's strip poker. 'We're going to play forfeits. And here's A Ma Rang. The Jonkheer says you can go as far as you like with him.'

The older youth stood grinning beside the Commander; he indeed resembled a meringue in that he was of an extreme pasty off-whiteness, that he had a very hard-surfaced skin, and that, wherever possible, at the chin, the neck, the stomach, the hips, the buttocks and the thighs, he bulged with fat like a meringue over-filled with cream. The Jonkheer had tried to use imagination as well as tolerance in pandering to his distinguished guest's indelicate tastes.

The game began. Some protégés were called out, not always by their official uncles, to perform forfeits which did not allow of their return. At last, since Hamo showed no disposition to move, the usual role was reversed and A Ma Rang was sent out of the room. He speedily entered again and, wobbling with excitement, chose 'new English uncle to pay the penalties'. Outside on the veranda, Hamo did not wait for the youth's giggles to subside and his own forfeit to be announced. On the contrary, taking advantage of the Jonkheer's suggestion, he went as far as he liked. He gave A Ma Rang a friendly pinch on his vast bum, and fled under the blazing sun into the shade of the garden trees, almost falling over a cable-thick banyan root in his hurry to get away.

The bungalow's shrubbery, so long neglected, soon gave way to scrub and then to jungle: the glowing colours of hibiscus, the clinging scent of frangipani straggled into a shapeless, dusty, undergrowth in which the dull green was relieved only here and there by the white bracts and golden flowers of *mussaendi* – tiny by the sides of the huge cultivated trumpets, as the wild is always stunted by the nurtured. Beyond the low scrub soared the great trees – *canaria, grevillea, pittospora* – which shut out the sky in the near distance. But Hamo knew that not far behind *them* again was a sheer rockside drop of several hundred feet to the flat, flooded marsh land below where a few peasants still waded for a living in land too hopeless to enjoy the prosperity of a Magic crop.

Knew, because, as in Lacey's station wagon they had zig-zagged up to the then horn-giving prospect of the feast, the second English uncle had mused in his best house-colours sort of way about their rendezvous. 'Trust the Jonkheer to find it. Can't be seen. Can hardly be got at. The natives won't come near it because they believe some devil or other lives here. Shaped like a lion, you see. Or so they say, I can't see it myself. But I don't fancy things easily. Unless it's male, in shorts and just reached puberty, that is. But there may be something in it. Most chaps who've been out here for long believe these things. I'd look into it a bit myself, if I wasn't so bloody busy. And if it wasn't such a bore!' He had peered at Hamo, hoping that this second line, with its weary worldly overtones, might draw a friendly response from him. It was clear that Hamo heard all that he was saying, but he had only replied, 'If this was Africa, I should say that was *oryza glaberrima* that we passed a moment ago. These grasses really are very confusing.' 'Ah? Well, I'm a rubber chap as you know. But anyhow the place is like a bloody fortress. And it gets cut off by floods from time to time. Not regular monsoon time either, some tidal freak of the river. One hundred and twenty days of it last time, I believe. But not to worry. The Jonkheer's got it all fixed. Provisions of every kind for as long as you want. And delicacies too! I don't know how much your mouth's watered at the little hamper I've brought on the back seat, and remember that like all nice little parcels, you'll get some surprises when we cut the string and see inside. But alas, whatever you think of my little contribu-tion, I'm afraid it'll be the poor man's end of the banquet. The Jonkheer will produce the dish to end all dishes. He's a sort of genius in his own way. What he's done for the club! When I first came out here the whole thing was run by a Portuguese chap from Goa. I doubt if he was wholly Portuguese myself – Fernando. Anyway it was a pretty shocking show. More like a dockside brothel. But of course the Jonkheer's terrifically cultivated. Superb collection of Chinese bronzes ...' The head-boy praises of the housemaster had gushed on in genuine, stuttering hero-worship, but Hamo had been too conscious of the hamper be-hind, who, awakened from a healthy boyish, if faintly dribbling slumber, was now tickling the back of his driver-uncle's neck with a peacock feather. To a historian of English culture this combination of footer shorts and peacocks – emblems of the two rival factions of the Edwardian puerile muse – might have given erudite delight. It had passed Hamo by. He had become increas-ingly alarmed, as the English uncle became more and more ex-cited, at the serpentine ascent before them, and the infernal depths beneath. Only by concentrating on the instructive spec-tacle of nature's near recapture of a marginal paddy field had he been able to control rising fright, or to avoid giving a sharp nur-sery word to Master Java that might spoil the fun.

Seeking now for a pathway out of the ruined estate garden, he thought of those perilous heights, of cobras, of Russell's vipers, of whip snakes and tarantulas, of Lacey's 'I believe a leopard made a nasty mess of a lad round here recently,' perhaps most of all of floods and the sinister possibilities of the Jonkheer's fertile ferocity at the end of another one hundred and twenty days. The stillness, above all, made him remember, with a desperation that shocked him, how much work he still had to do, how much of that work needed now rethinking, and surely, too, there must be some hope of pleasures undiscovered before death closed in. He broke a stout branch from a bush and began with an officerly gesture to beat out a path of escape from the high tanglewood. Immediately the silence was broken. A chattering stream of jade flowed fast and sheer from the highest treetops hundreds of feet down into the valley below. Scurryings, gruntings, cracklings of branches spread out from his feet in waves into the undergrowth. The grinding and clacking crake of a great billed bird (some hornbill?) came now from this depth, now from that. But drown-ing all other noises, a hollow boom echoed continuously above his head. Looking up, he saw for a moment four or five large im-passive black faces wreathed with magisterial grey dundrearies gazing judicially down upon him, and then at once the whole society of langur monkeys were bounding off away through the treetops, putting a decent distance between themselves and him. The message of all alike, large and small – parakeets, hornbills, mongooses, wild pigs, monkeys – told him to go back to his own kind. Somewhere behind him, however, he could hear whoops of joy, and boyish giggles; his fear was greater to evade *them*. Rigidly controlling panic, so that his limbs seemed hung weights from their tautened muscles, swinging his stick from side to side, sword-sharp grass and cleaving thorn thigh-high to his tall body, he made his stately, independent, civilized and rational way from confusion towards some hoped-for clearing, some surely inevitable decently roomy viewpoint where he might consider so much afresh.

Such an open prospect came before he had even time clearly to be sure that it was fresh air, wide horizons, broad vistas that he was seeking. Striking with his branch at the brutal spiked arm of a huge thorn bush that barred his way, he broke both the monster and his weapon. The two parts of his stick flew one away from him and one towards him, and, avoiding a blow across his eyes, he stumbled on a half buried rock and fell, arse over tip, deep into a stone hollow. Then, with his breath for a moment beaten from him, he rolled over painfully two or three times, suddenly, strangely to feel the firmness, the smoothness of another human body beside him. He opened his eyes to see two wide frightened dark eyes turned towards him with jungle alertness. There beside him on the sun-baked rock lay what seemed to him the most perfect, the most desirable youth he had ever encountered. Chest 30, hips 35. The measurements and lineaments of Hamo's ideal are sufficiently well known. But what crowned this extraordinary encounter was that when the large black eyes had looked out for a moment above the smooth creamy skin tight drawn across the bones of the cheeks, they closed again behind their long eyelashed grille, and the youth returned to a gently breathing, kitten-purring sleep. Only two or three large tears rolled down his face to form little dew ponds in the declivities at each end of his small, cunningly curved mouth. He sighed as he nuzzled back into sleep, and his firm but slender arms met round Hamo's long rigid neck in a loose but determined embrace.

What Hamo might have been in the boy's dream, he did not

speculate. He was too overwhelmed with amazement that a dream which he had so frequently created to warm himself during the last weeks in the polar air-conditioned solitude of modern Asian hotel bedrooms, should now draw him in, to cherish him and his sore limbs after their heavy and painful fall. Looking at his surroundings, he realized that they lay – he and his amber wonder – in a crumbling limestone pool, three feet in depth perhaps, but six or seven wide, its sides indented to make the petals of a lotus flower – relic of what forgotten age: an Edwardian planter's suburban exoticism? Recent Buddhist piety? An ancient civilization inbuilt with the Master's teaching? – whatever it was, now dead, devoid of content, empty of water, empty of flora, empty of fauna save two basking lizards, a six-foot English plant breeder in a ruined tropical linen suit, and a perfect native youth with a bare glistening chest and shabby, faded, torn, pale blue sarong. A blood-stained sarong.

His first feeling was of aesthetic self-disgust that in his clownish clumsiness he had spoiled a perfect object. And then admiration for the wounded youth's stoicism – his own most esteemed virtue – came to muddy the clear water of his sensual pleasure with a sudden weakening sensation of tenderness. He raised himself gently, took off his coat, carefully with his nail scissors cut off the left sleeve of his cream silk shirt, and, lifting the youth's sarong, instead of a wound, saw two perfect thighs. It was then that he realized, with the disgust of fastidiousness, that it was himself who was bleeding. The raising of the sarong had brought the boy to inquisitive, giggling life, but Hamo, rolling up his trouser leg, was now seeking fruitlessly to pull the many small black leeches from his hairy calves down which blood was pouring profusely. The youth, unrolling what appeared to be his sole possession, a fresh sarong, took with grave pride a small cake of soap and, sharply rubbing Hamo's flesh, watched with delight this giant stranger's pleasure as, one by one, the withered leeches fell from the leg.

Now the youth stood up and the slender dignity of his spare figure in his rags again threatened Hamo's lust, but this time with an injection of splendid pathos. The youth unbound his sarong, knelt beside Hamo and wiped away the blood from his leg. He then stood and bound the other garment, green, but even more faded, tightly round his figure. He turned away, as though, having done all he could in service, he must now efface himself; tears were again trickling down his cheeks. Hamo sat, crouched on his haunches for a few minutes, too excited to extend a hand, then gently he stroked the back of the boy's leg up to his firm buttocks. Instantly with a strange grunt of content, the boy turned, unbound his cloth, lay on his face, and, handing Hamo the precious soap, looked over his shoulder in a smile of gleaming white invitation. Hamo's sole fear was of being too ready for the feast, when suddenly, in the trees above, the boom of the great monkeys sounded again, and a second later a ripe mango followed by a shower of squashy fruits exploded disgustingly over the youth's glorious nakedness, and over Hamo's clothed neatness. Looking up in anger, his rage was redoubled when he saw, not the Wilberforcean Victorian features of a wanderoo, but the malicious ape-cat face of the Danish uncle, who, leader in a follow-my-leader, was now calling up reinforcements of the boys to hurl their disgust at the prevented coupling below. Who so casts the first *stone*? But at the dictation of the scandalized German uncle, it *was* cast and, with it, great coconuts, one of which half stunned Hamo's companion as he sought to drag his new lover up the slippery slopes of the holy flower. To the squealing, delighted lads above they must have seemed – this giant uncle who had proved no uncle and this low-born, over-grown passé servant boy – like two absurd insects struggling to get out of a saucer. Nor was the pack's treble howling lessened as, continually pelted, Hamo forced his furious way back through the thorny scrub to the hibiscus-edged lawn.

There the elder English uncle, very red in the face and naval in language, met him.

'What the hell do you think you're doing, Langmuir, messing about with the bloody servants, and the outside servants at that? The Jonkheer doesn't make many rules, but eating yesterday's dinner out of the kitchen cookpot goes too far. I think the best thing we can do is to get young Lacey to drive you straight back to the Club. There's clearly been a grave mistake, not only about your tastes but also about your manners.'

But Hamo was too angry to take heed of the quarter-deck. He marched towards the bungalow, his arm around the youth, who struggled, from fear of the Jonkheer no doubt, to leave his grasp. Even the disgusted and haughty uncles, let alone the pranksome boys, parted their ranks before Hamo's determined steps. But not the proud Jonkheer. He stood on the back veranda ready to meet the erring guest. Framed in cascades of black-centred yellow thunbergia, he looked, in his formidable size, like an early photograph of a returned colonial hunter. He wanted only a rifle and Hamo's dead body on which to plant his triumphant foot.

Some such thought may have been in his mind, for when Hamo, reduced to a stuttering incoherence by his anger, got out at last, 'Can you explain to me what your friends . . . ?' he looked down with vast grey-faced contempt and his voice came through the creeper as thunder from the mountain.

'I want no conversation with you, Mr Langmuir. I had no special regard for Nikita Khrushchev and his Russian friends, their business methods are not mine, but he had a remarkable power of illustrating his point of view with stories of the animal kingdom. May I explain to you in the same terms? The tiger, no doubt, is aware of the skulking presence of the jackal and the vulture waiting to feed from the offal that he leaves; but I do not suppose that he holds conversation with them. I suggest that instead of insulting your host by buggering his servants, you look for your leavings in the slums of the cities of Asia. Luckily your very valuable scientific rationalization of our local agriculture has made sure that the bazaars and public places are filled with the scum overflowing from the waters of hopeless paddy fields. If anyone has such low tastes, they are always ready to oblige for the price of a bowl of rice. And now, if Lacey wishes to atone for his mistake in bringing you here, he will gratify us all by taking you away again.'

He turned his back and went into the house. Perhaps this time his fart was unintentional, for he was an ageing man who had just eaten, drunk and fornicated heavily in the midday heat. Indeed it was this sapping humidity that decomposed, which made Hamo decide that he would not pursue his host. In any case, at that moment, he was almost thrown off balance as the lovely youth with a violent jerk pulled out of his grasp and ran off into the scrub, pursued by stones and fruit from the boys. When some of those high up in the trees showed inclination to pursue the fugitive, however, the elder English uncle, representative in the gathering of his nation's common sense, genius for order and moderation, called out to them, 'No, no, stop that, you fellows, we don't want any more of a shambles than we've got. Now, Poulsen, what about you and I picking sides for a game of tip and run?'

The Danish uncle, in whom there was clearly far more mischief than malice, readily agreed. And as Hamo, seated beside a sullen and silent Lacey, was driven away down the hairpin bends, he could hear the clack of bat on ball, the innocent laughter and the excited cries behind him. His was clearly the exit of a defeated spoilsport.

For many miles of their return journey, Lacey's swollen, purplish face wore a more than usually Neronic scowl beneath its Roman crewcut, and Hamo was too possessed of a superstitious fear that the Jonkheer's sinister rule might still not be ended, that they had not gone far enough from the fearful bungalow, that they were being pursued and would be taken back, to feel collected enough to broach the silence.

At last it was Lacey who spoke.

'My God! That was a balls-up,' he said, then he added, laughing though harshly, 'Do you always have a genius for picking them like that?' And to Hamo perplexed, he explained, 'Didn't you realize that you'd picked up the old boy's leavings? Hence all that jackal stuff. Look, three years ago, when we celebrated in Laos, there was one hell of a row, because the Jonkheer brought that very boy along. Of course, he was a peach then, not the scrawny half-starved scarecrow you seemed to delight in. But still he broke the old boy's own first rule – "Nothing low." Quite honestly, I confess,' and the Englishman turned with a near complicit grin to Hamo, 'I have certain vulgar tastes myself. I suppose,' and he seemed to be watching for some spark of interest in Hamo's set face, 'you see, at school at Radley, it was so dinned into us that we mustn't talk to the Teds, that that sort of thing was bound to happen. At least that's the kind of thing they say,' he added rather sadly as Homo's interest failed to come alive at this social analysis. 'Anyway, the Jonkheer picked him up at that very estate bungalow. His family is one of the few left scratching a living down in the valley. With the new sort of bumper crops your Magic has brought, that irregularly flooded land isn't worth the irrigation and there's only a pocket of half starvers like him left there. Well, you know all that better than I do. The boy was a smasher three years ago. Quite good enough to make the Jonkheer ready to face the music when Leroux and the others got on their hind legs about the club rules. He'd have been wiser to have his piece of cake at home, but he couldn't help randying the others up. *And* they knew it. Anyway he paid for it, as his own teaching should have told him all along. You see, with the right sort of boy, this uncle lark really works. They're going to be engineers, doctors, ad men, even parsons, some of them. But you can't do anything for these illiterate types. To the strong and the brainy everything, to the weak the wall. Well, you know that, as a scientist. Anyway another trouble is you're left with them on your hands. Mind you, the Jonkheer was very good to him. He went on until he'd almost got indigestion from tough meat. He must have been sixteen before he told him to get to the kitchen and stay there. Then there have been tears ever since. Crying for his lost looks I suppose. Anyway this weekend it all blew up. Weeping and hysteria because Master Hong Kong – God! he's a dish – arrived on the scene. So the Jonkheer had to kick him out. Silly little tyke! There aren't too many warm corners for the starving in this country. Trust you to find him though,' Lacey by this time seemed to have acquired an affection for Hamo. He took one hand from the wheel and smacked him on the shoulder. 'Feet first every time, is it? God, your lab must be a shambles.' He gave a look of mock disapproval, that would have suggested to one more attentive than Hamo some real softening of feeling, even of admiration in a man clearly given to hero-worship – perhaps the Jonkheer as Commanding Officer or Housemaster was to be replaced by Hamo as the Chap who's Always on a Charge, the Clumsy Idiot of the Remove.

But Hamo was hypnotized by the heat, by the car's motion, and by the somnambulistic rhythm of the gaily coloured women and children as they waded backwards in the mud passing their shining yellow-green bundles of seedlings from left to right hand, jibbing them in endless lines into the richly fed and well tended black soil of the vast estate of paddy fields on either side of the road. For they were passing through land where Magic had clearly found a home. Through his ever more shadowy thoughts ran professional unease that made his body twitch, and a lustful regret that made it twitch again; a longing for sleep, in which he would know no more of such twitches than a cat or a dog before the fire, dominated all his thoughts and feelings. But alas for Hamo, the dream of his driver was for mutual aid, not for oblivion.

'You seen any of the temples yet?' he said, stopping before a white, gold and vermilion dagoba of more than usually rich confection. Hamo, coming to from his daydream, thought for a moment that he was being offered again a slice of birthday cake. Then, fully awake, was about to say, yes, that he had visited one or two such temples, and also, that having no understanding either of their religious purpose or their architectural form, he had not found his visits particularly rewarding. But Lacey cried, 'We can't have you go away without seeing the Temple of the Tigers. That would never do.' As it turned out, they went away seeing only the tigers, who, three in number, were as morosely, stingily and mangily engaged with a few bloodstained bones in their sunk pit in the temple forecourt as any old Western circus tigers in their cages on wheels.

'Of course, it's strictly very un-Buddhist all this,' Lacey commented, 'probably some local superstition, that goes back to the Ark, that's got attached to the place. You ought to have come with an old Asia hand like the Commander if you wanted to know the religious ins and outs of the thing.'

He seemed annoyed at Hamo's supposed expectations. But his attention was immediately drawn to the young meat vendor who stood beside the enclosure selling, to the pious, bones to give to the tigers as well as frangipani and lotus to offer to the Buddha.

'I say. What have we got here? He seems a likely sort of lad.'

What they had got there Hamo found embarrassingly young (? thirteen years old) and embarrassingly naked for approach to any kind of worship, so he looked instead studiously down into the tiger pit.

He could hear from behind him Lacey addressing the boy but without response; and then suddenly there was a jabber of both voices. He turned to see Lacey standing with his arm encircling the boy's naked waist, his fingers tickling his smooth, flat little belly. He put on his black glasses; the sight was no less unpleasing but his disgust would be less apparent.

'Just choose a couple of these juicy chops and throw them to the wretched beasts, will you? I think it'll please our friend here if we buy his wares.'

Lacey winked at Hamo, who, feeling that, whatever his own uninterest, he could not be responsible for a sabotage of his host's amatory plans twice in a day, rummaged with head averted from the fly-covered mass in the meat basket, and dropped in turn two high-smelling, blood-slimy bones to the ambiguously sacred animals. He then occupied himself rather longer than was required in wiping his hands in order to leave Lacey time to make his assignation or whatever. He supposed the tedious, distasteful business done, for a minute later Lacey was at his side taking his arm and moving him towards the car again, apparently forgetful, in his fulfilled excitement, of the proposed visit to the temple.

'Well,' he said, 'I shall have something to talk of at the club. Do you know what that chap was? I had my suspicions from the first that he wasn't a local Indonesian lad, though I tried him in each of the five local dialects. So I took a very long shot. My Batak's pretty rusty, but it acted like magic. He started jabbering away. God knows how he got here. One of our peasant lads looking for gold bricks again, I expect. They walk bloody hundreds of miles. Looks as if he could do with one of those chops, doesn't he? But then they're probably sacred. Anyhow, I told him he was as beautiful as the teat ends of a full ewe. That's the way they pitch the story in his lot.' He stopped. It became clear that Hamo was intended to comment. He spoke as interestedly as he could sound, but he was most unwilling to be cognisant of any details of the encounter or party to any future meeting.

'And what was his reply?' In nervousness, his voice took on a treble note that sounded in his own ears unbearably arch, but Lacey appeared not to notice it.

'Well, it's difficult to give an exact translation for *imaguta-si*. But I suppose "barmy" would be the right word. Yes. He said, "You must be barmy."'

Hamo could not stop himself laughing out loud.

Lacey frowned, and for the rest of the journey remained silent. The familiar lagoon, with its doleful mangroves, brought additional depression to Hamo, underlining the watery world, but at least announcing the coming of the city and a release from this disastrous expedition. Lacey, looking more firmly to the road than his usual standard of driving demanded, spoke again.

'We're not trendy here, you know, if that's the word we're supposed to use. But we're not fools either. You thought it very funny that I said "barmy". I'm quite aware that it's out-of-date slang. I use it because my father was very fond of it and that happens to be enough to make it a special pleasure to me.' As he stopped the car at the Club door, still looking ahead, he added, 'Of course, you can tell everyone that Lacey's very soppy about his father. But it wouldn't be true. I've never mentioned my feelings to anyone before. I wouldn't now, only thanks to you, today's been such an appalling washout. It seemed to me only fair to give you some idea of the way you balls things up.'

Hamo reflected, as he took a shower, that he had already been given some idea of this earlier that day. Nevertheless the man's piety towards his father touched him very nearly. He felt weighed down by a sense of being a double murderer. It took indeed a lot of soap and hot water and splashings and blowings to make him feel himself once again: Hamo Langmuir, plant geneticist and gentleman eccentric, and not just a too long body exposed to the disgust of those upon whose privacy he had obtruded his repulsive tastes. The boys' mocking, sportive laughter, the uncles' malevolent distaste still rang in his ears.

The Erroll he met on the hotel's dining terrace was in high spirits. He had had success with the secretary of the Commercial Counsellor at the Embassy, a girl named Jane Dare, who had prepared for him, in addition, a first-rate curry lunch; not the sort of thing the bazaars ponged of, but tasty and authentic.

For the first six weeks after she left the Tangier hospital, where she had been so devotedly fêted and blessed by the loving, disapproving nuns, Alexandra sat or lay hour after hour every day and for many of the still warm nights on exactly the same stretch of sand, her right arm either holding Oliver to her as he sucked her breast, or holding on to the rim of his carrycot as he slept.

Only some ten kilometres to the north-west stood the Msûra circle of cromlechs around an eight-foot high menhir – great limestone monuments brought somehow, somewhen to a sandstone region. Señor Ramón Lopez y Garcia gives them a 2000 BC date and refuses to conjecture about their neolithic purpose further than to agree that it must have been 'religious'. Brigadier Foxways-White, however, considers that only prejudice can refuse to recognize in them the sole-surviving, millennia-ancient, Atlantean *mainland* scientific achievements, infinitely skilful, religious only in the sense that Atlantean science was, of course, occult, and still extraordinarily powerful in their cosmic vibrations.

This view has called forth a vexed rebuttal from Doctor Stéphanie Gautier who considers that such excessive claims do immense harm to the study of Atlantean science. It is evident, she points out, that the Msûra columns are very inferior in execution, in sacred measurement, and, indeed, in cosmic force, to even such outlying, provincial Atlantean engineering projects as Stonehenge (itself the work, no doubt, of members of the inferior trading caste of Atlantis absent on some barter mission among the outer savages when diluvian disaster overtook the great civilized continent and all its highest caste of initiates). Msûra, she thinks, could possibly be the work of some similar but less instructed trading group, or more likely a very much later and inferior imitation of Stonehenge made by descendants of the Atlantean traders isolated in those northern parts who had come south over the ice in an instinctual search for more powerful solar cosmic rays. That this view is correct, she, in fact, *knows* from direct psychic communication with the Atlantean initiates, but such information being arcane she can only hint at it (a hint, however, that with its undertones of power greatly excited Sir James Langmuir when he read her book).

Berber and Arab peasants alike, despite all Allah's disapproval, worship or propitiate spirits there. La ilaha il Allah, Muhammad il Rasul Allah, they cry illogically, but find no blasphemy, because the propitiation of spirits strengthens the Oneness of God and the single voice of his Prophet.

Elinor has felt the force of its vibration and has persuaded Ned, on occasion, to take his troupe (an entity this, like the Community, changing from day to day) to perform their mimetic movements within its rhythm-enhancing circle. She regularly performs her own spiritual breathing and postures (pranayanas and asanas to her, for she is ready poised for flight to India) within the shadow of these mysterious limestone columns. Rodrigo, immaculate in clothing, if in nothing else, walks there (in the absence of Elinor or members of the mime) for its regularity and symmetry soothe the outrage that the flux and muddle of the Community daily inflict upon his nerves.

Alexandra glimpsed the cromlechs as she was jolted down from hospital to the communal beach in a car hired and paid for by Elinor's mum, old Thelma. She registered it, in that glimpse, as a sort of Stonehengey thing, but her intense bliss both in herself, and, if she could ever separate them, more still in herself and Oliver together, did not allow any external objects to impinge on her for more than a second or two.

A few more kilometres, but to the south-east of the sand space she now occupied (with the fiercest pecking if her rights had ever been threatened, but given the flux and muddle of the Community as well as its deeply self-centred peace, they never were), lay the Garden of the Hesperides, orchard of the Golden Apples, according to that source of all ancient knowledge, Hesiod. Of this, Alexandra was more aware, for she passed it within view on her frequent, stifling, crowded, roller-coaster bus journeys to spend the night in Elinor's unoccupied room in Thelma's hotel at Larache. And these bus trips became increasingly frequent as the ever-colder nights threatened her and more still Oliver with the stenches and noise of the half-ruined ex-Spanish colonial shore fort and barracks where the Community sought refuge from the cold and wind and rain. She saw the Garden of the Hesperides and registered it as a kind of dreary marshland sort of place. If it remained with her at all it was as one of the few distresses of her wonderful existence, for she had seen there a tall chocolate-coloured camel seeking, with hobbled front legs, clumsily to reach her delicate cream-coloured calf that had stumbled and fallen. She certainly had no thought of its being the Garden of the Golden Age – all the golden ages were inside herself or in the movements and cries of little Oliver as she watched him sleep and yawn, feed and sleep, cry and play. Surrounded by those still seeking for nirvana and Utopia, ecstasy and bliss, she alone seemed to have arrived.

187

In fact, there was something else that possessed her, day and night, as she lay on her own special private piece of the beach that the Community had succeeded over the years against sporadic police raids in making its own. It followed her even to the various public beaches where, clothing her body, she (often with Rodrigo) sought refuge from Communal peace. It stayed with her in the assiduously scoured and swept, bare stone rooms of the barracks refuge which nonetheless stank, in their draught-ridden fug of pot and steaming clothes and orange peel and sweat. It echoed above the sound of guitars and of mantras. It was there on the rickety brass-knobbed bed in the little Larache hotel room which still wore its 'style jazz' wallpaper and fabrics of its nineteen-twenties beginnings. That other thing was the sea.

For hours – often as she later realized, when she had believed that she was intently feasting on the kicking, naked Oliver – she had gazed at the ocean. Its glossy swell was directly in her eyeline, a mirror flecked and stained with floating seaweed masses. Its smooth surface would swell at last to burst into white spume over the shingly ridge of shells that rimmed the edge of the sand. And, as it burst, it would fling the tangled slimy seaweed masses upon the dark wet sand; and, as often, gather them again to float and bob away out to sea. Hours of gazing at the ocean, hours more of hearing its perpetual slop, slop, slop and sudden surge, its slop, slop and sudden surge, its slop, slop ... until the whole of her gentle, sweet daily round of life with her baby was taken up with the rhythm of the sea.

With Oliver well within range, safely sleeping or lying soothed or happily kicking in his carrycot, she joined each day in Ned's mime sessions on the sands. The steps and rhythms were for ever changing as he heroically sought to improvise new mimes to instil his shaped visions into the fluctuating, coupling, fusing muddle of carefully cultivated individual innernesses that called itself the Community. But, for Alexandra, Ned's steps and rhythms, like everything else, became part of the rhythm of the sea. She knew that though she danced a giraffe, or a swinging girder, or a river, at Ned's bidding, she did it deep down, no longer as a Trilby in search of an heroic Svengali, but merely as part of mothercraft; not as the act of human community that Ned sought to instil, but as an exercise demanded by sensible voices from outside the Community's limits – Zoe's, the Clinic's, even Thelma's whisky-sour rasp. The more that she saw Elinor seeking to turn Ned's mimes into yoga and incidentally to dissolve Ned's heroic ego, the more she herself participated in the rituals with a determined sense that she was any welfare mother doing the proper thing. And yet, in some part of her still, she could feel herself a spectator of the tournament she had long ago devised – the proving of her hero. In this remote emotional region, she still hoped that Ned's strength of will, sense of form, sweet determinedness would rout both her and Elinor and mould them to the shape he wanted, so that in him she could recognize and crown her knight. But even the touch of self-mockery with which she voiced such thoughts evaporated in the general joy of her daily life. The hero-search was so far away that it needed no laughing self-correction. The mime was no more than one of the happy daily chores in her idyllic life, as they rocked back and forth (she and Oliver), for she was, they were the sea, and her life was its smooth unceasing rhythm.

A rhythm broken but never shattered by the heavy seaweeds that, clotted and tangled, were thrown out and sucked back. As, to begin with : 3ς3 – the secret name they had always given to their Birkin-Ursula-Gerald tripling.

The 3ς3 trouble with Elinor had always loomed in the distance, but then finally broke one evening soon after she had returned from hospital in Tangier. She had fed Oliver. He was sleeping. The sand was still hot, almost too hot for her naked body in the evenings. She lay murmuring happily to Ned and Rodrigo about the hospital, what she could remember of it, that was, for just like people always said it was fading very quickly.

Ned said, 'I believe you had an ecstasy !'

But Rodrigo told him 'not to be obscene'. 'You know perfectly well something nearly got torn. Don't let him make you sing a hymn to disgusting Nature, Ally.'

But she told him, 'Yes, it was very wonderful.'

'Christ !' from Rodrigo.

'Well, I mean I don't know what word to use. And anyhow, how can you remember what "wonderful" means? But I think that's what it was. And horrible and painful too. Only I never felt *miserable*, I mean, angry. Except when I told the nuns my thighs were hurting and they said they couldn't be, that wasn't where the pains came from.'

'How could you know what they said? You don't know any Spanish.'

'Thelma told me.'

'How does she know?'

'Lots of Americans learn Spanish, it seems. Especially in California where she comes from. And then she was in Mexico. To take evidence about Trotsky.'

'That can't have pleased the nuns.'

'I don't think they really understood. And then you see she was at a convent as a girl. Apparently no matter how much they lapse, Roman Catholics keep a thing about the sacraments. And so *she* agreed with the nuns about Oliver's being baptized. And *they* forgave her about Trotsky. Anyway, she'd only let it out to them in one of her whisky bouts.'

Rodrigo said, 'I can't think it was good for you to have a Mrs Gamp for your lying-in. Even a wealthy American Trotskyite one. What would your mother say?'

'It was Thelma who wrote to Mama to tell her about Oliver. I *was* pleased though I had forbidden it. And anyway even when she was a bit maundering, all that about Trotsky and Charlie Chaplin and McCarthy the devil incarnate made a sort of humming distraction when the pain was bad. Like when he nearly tore something because his head was so big. It is, isn't it? And she held my hand. *All* the time. No one else did.'

'No one else was allowed.'

'No, Roddy. I couldn't choose between you two, could I. And then to have *both* of you! After all my *body* was being torn in two as it was ...'

'Elinor, like, would have been there, but she has this thing about blood. She knows it's shameful. It's the worst for her. I mean to achieve this peace she's after and then to find shit and piss and blood and that won't leave her mind.'

When Alexandra saw that there was no trace of smile as Ned said such things, she had to tense her muscles not to shout at him.

She said, 'Elinor said "The pain rhythms work along with the fruition and in a proper birth they cancel each other out into non-being." That's what *she* said. It was sent as a message of comfort for me. Thelma told me. And we both laughed so much the nuns stopped us as it might have split something.'

Rodrigo began kissing her hair, her eyes, the tip of her nose, all little brushes of his lips that changed to a delicious biting.

'Darling Ally, I do love you when you still hate people.'

She put out her hand and stroked Ned's belly.

'Does it hurt being so red?'

'I like it,' he mumbled and ran his hand down her thighs. But when Rodrigo tried to move her head down towards his prick, 'No, no. I'm sorry. Only just tenderness. I can't think my way into anything completely. I'm sorry, Birkin and Gerald! I can see how shameful it is for you both. But you must accept it for now.'

And tenderness it remained. So much so that for the first time for months, since that happiness had first swept over her when she knew, for sure, that she would have the baby, Alexandra felt as though she could make some contact outside the swelling sea, with the seaweed ... when she thought what *that* made Ned and Rodrigo, she began to laugh.

'Flotsam,' she said. And they began to tickle her to make her tell.

But a lengthy shadow had fallen upon them and as suddenly fell away again. There was Elinor, reclining on the sand in front of them, her elbow resting on the sand. She fell into such postures very quickly because of all the spiritual exercises she did. And she fell into them often. So often that, though there was so much of her, one usually did not notice her sudden crouches, her wild leaps, by now. Even when, as now, she was dressed in some diaphanous tulle kind of a long garment somewhere between something Arab and something Eastern and something in those Art Nouveau posters and postcards that had got so boring. Usually when she reclined like that, as though an odalisque or a caryatid were lying sideways, she quizzed you with deep gentleness in her large grey eyes. And, thought Alexandra, you knew that what she was aiming at was to look lovely, and intolerably she usually did look so. But this time she stared at their three naked bodies as though she were looking at a Cubist picture and trying to make out which were legs and which were arms and which were heads in the formal shape. Clearly the picture disappointed her. Stretching out her long plump arm, she traced with one long slender finger '3 ⊆ 3' in the smooth sand. Alexandra was filled with anger at Ned's betrayal of their secret sign, such anger that she could not speak.

'So this is the famous tripling,' Elinor said, and leaning back her lovely head so that they could see the lines of her long lovely throat, she let out a coloratura of stage mocking laughter. 'No, thank you, Ned. No thank you, so *very* much. We won't make it a quartet. Birkin can have his Ursula *and* her Gerald; but not Gudrun. She doesn't play. I just don't reckon to being a babe in the wood. Not even to play such an innocent Wordsworthian game on Mr Lawrence's grave and have the pleasure of feeling him turn over under me. Poor boob! It was fine, fine of you to ask me,' as she could always do to order, she exaggerated mockingly her own usual earnest tone, 'but I guess I'm too tall a girl.'

Alexandra determinedly continued to stroke Ned's reddish matted belly, and buried her face for sheer misery in Rodrigo's armpit.

It must have been some look of Elinor's that whipped him, for the next that Alexandra knew was that his smooth, elegant body had slipped from under her. At Elinor's cry, she looked up and there, as he crouched over the long body showing white beneath the transparent grey blue tulle (Elinor never lay in the sun), all the little notches of his backbone, that Alexandra had so often counted, showed in bumps through the smooth golden brown pastry skin of his tautened back. He had plunged his long powerful fingers into that Raphael Madonna's calm softness and, with the long black strands of her hair as levers, he was beating that great gentle head backwards and forwards against the hard-baked sand, so that tears were flowing from those great grey eyes, wetting those long black lashes, falling down those beautifully structured high cheek bones to moisten those firm full lips that were opened unusually wide to let out such screams. Alexandra knew that she did not care twopence for Elinor's pain. Madonna turned to 'cow in pain', for that's what those great Zen eyes spoke of – a cow's vacuity. She knew that she was indifferent. She was not ashamed that she might even be glad. She only feared that the noise might awaken Oliver.

Sensing the anger that was filling Ned by the tautening of his stomach muscles, she tried to restrain him, saying, 'No, Ned, no.

Of course, Roddy hates her. He must do. We don't blame *you*. She *got* you to tell. She's indecent.'

But he pushed her arm away, and leaping on Rodrigo, he caught his throat in the crook of his arm and pulled him back from Elinor so abruptly that a bone snapped somewhere. Rodrigo screamed with the pain. At once they were rolling and struggling together in one of the worst of their fights.

Elinor rose to her feet. She was Hecuba by the waves, a Beardsley Cassandra, her hair streaming down her shoulders, her tulle torn, one smooth white breast caught in the golden sunset. Alexandra fed her disgust by thinking, she's a vulgar tele-ad. But now this tall girl was kneeling down before her and crying to her.

'Stop them! Stop them! Oh, Ned, please, please, leave me alone. You're making all my life ridiculous.' She turned on Alexandra. 'You think I'm just some common fraud, don't you? I'm not. It's his weakness making me. He's so vulnerable. He makes me will things. And I've worked so hard to be rid of all this will. Oh, let me be, all of you. You've made me act jealously, like a sour old maid. Don't you understand how difficult it is for someone like me not to be absurd.'

That Elinor had such insight and such honesty about herself was unbearable to Alexandra. And to stoke her anger, Oliver had been woken by the noise and was crying that desperate cry that she had always feared from the memory of other babies. A cry of fright that he had never uttered before.

She pushed Elinor away from her so that the great graceful figure rolled clumsily across the sand.

'Get out, you silly cunt. And you two, go to hell. I won't have my baby mixed up with all this stupid emotional rubbish.'

Rodrigo and Elinor stood side by side on the sand, shamefaced, their arms dangling, like two mental patients on a seaside outing, waiting to be snapped. But Ned had gone over to the carrycot and within seconds, as always with Ned, the tiny fingers were playing among the hairs of his beard and Oliver was chuckling.

Elinor started to sob and then to hiccough, and then, in shame, ran off across the sands.

Rodrigo said bitterly, '*I'd* better not go near him or he'll start to scream again.'

But Alexandra was determined that, with her baby's fear gone, it should all come to an end, so she turned her face away from Rodrigo's misery.

That 3¢3 incident was only the first smack, smack of the seaweed, which broke the gentle rhythm of her life, but most of the time this rhythm itself was punctuated by another less violent yet teasing sound, just as the sea met regularly not only the sudden full stops of the seaweed, but also the commas of the shingle.

For many hours of the day, voices from the Community talked at Alexandra, though only from time to time did they break through the sea spell that lay upon her, cradled with her baby in a soothing world of chorus. When they did, they meant little to her – hardly more, she supposed, than the rustling of the shingle meant to the sea. The voices were always young, mostly male; but the accents changed and changed again, so many American, and European in all Western varieties to season, but even then the phrases seemed to Alexandra a kind of American. The bodies that lay naked beside her were scorched all shades from pink to near black, mostly male, mostly bearded or whiskered, always skeleton thin.

Most of the sound was reminiscent and content – 'I need not have bothered, within a month everything was happening everywhere' ... 'That was the good time. We were just making love – making love with God, making love with ourselves, making love with women. Yeah, 1964 through 1966 was the good time, look at it anyways!' ... 'Quite a lot of us about had got fed up with plastic. So we started to play it differently' ... 'We were kids. We dropped some L.S.D., sat around, giggled and watched the wallpaper do funny things' ... 'Y'know, like it wasn't happening any other place the same' ... 'Often here I'm so full with something that's happened between them and me that it's like I'm on a trip, had a mind click that's all good' ... 'So we lit up and watched the scenery go by through the elevated clarity of a good high' ...

But sometimes the reminiscence moaned sadly – 'He was the first guy I ever balled with. In a back seat. The whole bit. Stoned and drunk. Do you think it ought to start that way?' ... 'She knew just where I was, but I couldn't tune her in at all' ... 'I was sixteen years old, right? A knight in shining armour, huh?' ... 'So what did they have to offer me but words. Words is the biggest hang-up of them all' ... 'So they told me, man, it's in your head and it's two billion years old and it's got every control switch that I.B.M. ever thought of and a million more. But every time I tried to get my fingers on that switch, I just crashed.'

Once, Louise, a white-faced, ill-looking girl (who wasn't a girl any more, but twenty-seven) with a sad, yellow, creased little body and shrivelled paps that her swollen-stomached baby turned away from, screaming, voiced a general lament. 'Why can't they love us? We aren't up to putting anyone down about anything.' She was probably speaking of the Moroccan fishermen who the day before, as Alexandra, through her swell of bliss, vaguely learned, had thrown stones at four members of the Community straying inadvertently and naked outside their conquered stretch of sand. But it sounded like a general lament about humanity.

All that Alexandra could offer was some share of the humanized milk food mixed with hemolac and lucidac which a guzzling Oliver was now taking as his first variation from her breast. But the swollen baby was more difficult and spat out the spoonfuls of macrobiotic infant health all over its mother's sad little pallid naked body. Alexandra at least was able to wipe it up. But the mother was cheered at the sight of the food. 'Just because we've substituted a vegetable culture for *their* mineral culture of technology.' It hardly seemed to apply, Alexandra thought, to the fishermen she had seen.

Wiping up was one of her principal services to this endless chorus. She could offer them no words – men or girls. She held their hands as they talked, or stroked their hair, or when, as occasionally, their eyes or their noses or their mouths exuded excessively from some ecstatic habituation that she could not identify, she would wipe them up. Occasionally she would embrace or kiss, but few were lusty enough to be importunate, and none succeeded in turning such eroticism as her involvement with Oliver had left in her away from Ned's now delicately bisque clean flesh and rought red bristles or from Rodrigo's now golden silk hair and smooth cinnamon flesh; nor, for all she could tell, did many of them seek to have her.

Some liked to quote to her – 'Like Mailer says, we must set out on that uncharted journey into the rebellious imperatives of the self'; or more often, 'Like Leary says, if we could once again dance around the phallus and grow golden corn from our dung'; or, 'Like Laing says, the Dreadful has already happened.' Alexandra, in part, did not fully listen because she could seldom contribute to what she heard. Once when a man, returning to Sweden to a peasant life in television, excused himself by explaining that 'media people enjoy their work, media is substitute play', she tried to refute him by explaining how little Perry enjoyed his work with the B.B.C. But when she was forced to explain that her father worked in administration, her illustration seemed without conviction. Another time a young German told her that L.S.D. was the electron microscope of psychology; and this led her on to speak of her godfather's work on rice hybridization. For a while the German appeared to fear that Hamo had performed some vile technological rape on the sacred food, on brown rice (*zezania senolica*), but when she said that no, it was the sort of rice that Indian people ate and Japanese and that, he calmed down.

There was a time, too, when she had thought for half an hour that she was making something constructive. A young man came daily to read to her from his meta-novel; try as hard as she might she could not fix her attention to this narrative of events on the inner cosmic plane. Then, as her attention wandered, she found herself making a montage of words and phrases that she happened to catch when his voice came through to her. His delight at this adventitious art proliferating from his own was gratifying; but then Alexandra found that the very few phrases or sequences that offered any satisfaction to her ear, her reason or her sense of the absurd were, without faking, so very small. Gradually she allowed chance events and chores – a small crab surfacing from a hole in the sand, the smoke hieroglyphs of a high-up jet, the sandflea settling on Oliver's leg – to create an adventitious visual pattern that drowned the meta-novel's words and her own derived montage.

But if Alexandra had nothing to say to her fellow Communards, Rodrigo made up for it whenever he found one of them engaging her company. He would appear, late in the morning, like a Wodehouse drone, having spent many hours of swimming, sunbathing, exercise in seclusion, and lengthy because inept care for his clothes and his small tent, before he felt prepared to astonish the Community and, with luck, detach Alexandra to a public beach. Every encounter with Rodrigo or Ned seemed to Alexandra a threat to her gently rocking, swelling happy life, a call to decision, to an unnecessary future time. Much though she loved their physical presence, indeed was habituated to it (why else should she be there?), she was glad now when Rodrigo's impact was broken by the presence of a Communard in full spate. And not for herself alone, because to see Roddy loose himself upon these intruders into the privacy that he wanted, was to see for a moment a break in that glacial, dandiacal misery which had now frozen tight upon him in these uncongenial surroundings, a frozen misery that made Alexandra feel herself to be the Ice Maiden, for she could not bring herself to end (or even to seek to end) the hang-up which kept him by her side.

He found a special fierce delight in quoting at the Communards from their own sacred books in inapposite contexts. When a billowy, naked American girl with a childlike, owlish, spectacled face began suddenly to vomit on the sand at her side, he stood, superciliously looking down, asking with one superb golden eyebrow faintly raised, 'The sickness attendant on living with the Bomb?' And when a long thin Vercingetorix-whiskered English wandering bird squatted to crap within Alexandra's range as he continued the saga of his migrations, Rodrigo explained with mock admiration, 'How splendidly you nail the old Pauline lie that people neither shit nor piss nor fuck.' The Communards were unaffected by his sarcasms. They thought him an up-tight misfit; and so, of course, he was. But, for Alexandra, his evident delight in these ironic releases gave her some feeling that her elegant, relaxed, fun-sharing lover was still alive to escape out of the Englishman Abroad frozen in starch, if and when they should all three escape from the dilemma into which their frivolous, happy, ironic adventure into half-magic had led them.

Delighted at such times at the almost dancing movements of Rodrigo's figure as he celebrated victory (however unnoticed by the defeated), she would reward herself and him by an afternoon's escape to the public beach. Delving into her many carefully packed bundles, she would put on her white bikini and long gold and white silk robe she had bought in a phoney tat shop in Tangier, and he would get out his white shark-skin trousers, kept so immaculately pressed and cleaned at the cost of so many hours' inexpert, incompetent attention, and don them over his gold strap.

They would swim and lie in the sun for an hour or two, among the autumn's surviving tourists, and the Moroccan emancipated bourgeoisie, and, if they were lucky, perhaps a splendid group of Moroccan grandes dames hidden in black djallabahs pacing the sea's edge like so many chess castles as their children paddled. Local youths who would pester her if she were alone, now circled around to decide whether Rodrigo offered profit enough to allow them to purchase elsewhere.

Small Moroccan children, drawn by the sight of the spoon-fed Oliver, would accept in turn helpings of macrobiotic health with giggles that vied with physical nausea, until Rodrigo began to urge caution when she resumed Oliver's feeding with the same spoon.

'But, Roddy, you don't object to that pinchy faced Louise's baby or those Swiss children with the scabby legs.'

'The Community has rightly been cordoned off by all decent Moroccans, Ally. But that *does* have the advantage of cordoning off Moroccan bacteria.'

'"The Natives"! You go on like one of those stories that are always on tele – Somerset Maugham or Noël Coward or something.'

'It's just true. That's all. Of course, these people are much nicer. Those elderly black ladies are enchanting. So discreet! Covering their faces! If only all old women did. My mother and aunts! But there just *are* diseases and dirt here. And Europeans even when they've dropped out just wash much more and have better health. Especially with Elinor's Community discipline. *Though* I'm always cheering wildly when somebody defeats her vigilance and shits in the Council Room.'

Rumours of Elinor's battle to control the Community physically as well as spiritually were always leaking through into Alexandra's sealed happiness chamber, but she determinedly refused to give them attention, lest they should increase Elinor's power to erode her contentment. Suppressing her interest in this, however, only made Rodrigo's natural colonialism more annoying to her.

'All Moroccan people I've seen wash and wash and wash,' she

cried. 'I see it's not good, Roddy. At least not until I marry a
suburban business man. Then you can call again. You're *made* for
all that adultery and stuffy, weepy meetings in railway stations.'

'That's not fair. It's just that this awful place makes me atavistic. My adulterous aunt weeps buckets just by thinking of Noël
Coward's *Brief Encounter*. You've no right to put me in a leper
colony and then jeer when my nose falls off. Yes, you have the
right, because you're so lovely.'

And then and there, despite the enchanting black djallabahed
ladies, he embraced her with flailing excitement. And then they
trid to reach each other again through solicitude for Ned.

'Why does he stutter so much when he talks, Roddy, *and* talk
so much for that matter? Is it acid or Elinor?'

'Not acid. No, I think he's always high on pot. And then
Elinor's taking all her hang-ups out on *him*. But he *enjoys* it all,
Ally. We've got to face that.'

'What? Changing the mime four times a week? And having a
fresh troupe every other day? He *can't*. He was such a perfectionist with "Batteries".'

'Well, so he is with "Territoriality" and "Megalopolis" and
"The Lost Eden" and "High but Cool". The truth is that he did
drop out because he'd have got a very bad degree.'

'No, I *won't* believe that. He's much more brilliant than us.'

'Yes, much more *brilliant*. But not *half* as clever. Certainly as
you. And anyway his brain's working now at about three times
the speed it should, what with finding that the Community was a
kind of non-thing with no hope of a proper troupe, and rolling
joints all the time, and fighting his thing about Elinor who's half-
crazy anyway trying to crack her own hard-boiled ego. He's like
the Red Queen, you know, running twice as hard to stay where
he is. Mentally, I mean.'

'Yes, I *did* understand that. Anyway he's not any sort of a
queen whatever you may have wished.'

'I just liked to stroke him, that's all. If you don't know the
limits of my bisex yet, I really don't see why we're talking.'

'*I* don't either really. Let's go.'

Holding each one a handle of Oliver's carrycot, they set off
from the public beach back to the Community beach just like any
mum and dad driven off the Costa Brava by rain.

Ned's irruptions into the almost ceaseless sound of the Community voices were less violent, but infinitely more voluble. Whatever his motive, he always ostensibly came to Alexandra on mime business. And since this allowed him to evade open distress at their trilemma, Alexandra welcomed it for him and for herself. What he said, then, simply cut off the wash, wash of the Communards' confessions on the instant. 'Look,' he would say. It was always 'look', though he meant 'listen'. During the Territoriality mime, 'Look, you're one of the hartebeestes!' to the Communard, 'don't, like, look towards her while you're talking. She's an eland. She has her territory, you've got yours. That's how you feel. Let your body show it. No bloody charm, like, no communication. Just talk to yourself like you were browsing and chewing the cud. It's what you're doing anyway. Only time you notice is hartebeestes' rutting season and that's not in the mime. Or if a leopard comes or a lion. Then its scent. Head turning so. Body quivering. And sway. Not all this human needs and stuff.'

Alexandra said, 'When the chocolate-coloured camel whose front legs were hobbled couldn't get at her cream-coloured calf, *she* noticed all right, Ned.'

'Motherhood,' Ned dismissed. 'Anyway,' he took a pink oleander flower from the Communard's shoulder-length silky fair hair, and stuck it in his pubic hair where it nodded absurdly at the youth's prick, 'he's got *that*. He can't be a mother hartebeeste. Go and, y'know, get the movements from Elinor,' he told the young man. 'She's got a breathing exercise to make the body relax in indifference. Spiritual unconcern, she calls it.'

'That Elinor's got hang-ups you can see a mile away. Why do you let her do her thing here. You're just gonna bum each other out, man.'

'Go and see her like I say.'

'What you say. You're the director. It's your hassle. It's no skin off mine.'

When he had gone, Ned sat with his back against Alexandra's knees. His arms came above his head. His hands stroked the inside of her thighs.

'All this mother stuff,' he said, 'you and him. That little twerp.' He made sucking noises at Oliver who immediately began to chuckle and kick with pleasure. 'And Elinor being spirit mother to the lot. Or trying to be. Only they won't do her thing.'

'Don't let's talk about her.'

'All right. But it's harder for her than you. Trying to lose her will by imposing it, y'know, and not being able to anyway. It's all stupid. Women and wills! When there's a man to fuck them! All the same it's better than imposing your will on a poor little bastard baby who can't even stick his prick up at you. Isn't it, Olly?' He cooed this time at Oliver, who in turn burst into ever more delighted giggles. Then, sitting relaxed, Alexandra and Ned sang in a low voice together their half-mock version of 'We shall Overcome'. They were quite like any mum or dad on the Costa Brava when the sun was shining, until Ned was on his feet again, stuttering about 'The Lost Eden'.

'It's like, y'know, the yokels have got to use their limbs in double joint so that they give the kind of Wordsworth sort of natural joy, but what Marx said is all there too – rural idiocy. Kind of happy slobbering. Like him.' He pushed his finger into Oliver's plump knee. The baby chuckled, then Ned was gone.

Otherwise the Communard talk had just gone on as a regular background like the tidewash upon the shingle. Or as she had come in the end to think, like the bleating, the urgent bleating of sheep. For they were asking all the time for something she could not give. 'The hungry sheep look up and are not fed, But swoln', except that only Louise's baby was swollen and most of the rest were skeletons.

Nor had it been much different in the increasing hours, increasing as the days grew rainier and the nights colder, that she spent with Thelma in her hotel – Thelma, rake-thin, legs matchstick and knotted with blue lumpy veins for all the world to see below her stained, pleated skirt, skeleton-white face out of which looked two incredibly beautiful eyes; Thelma shivering and twitching, wrapped in her food-clotted mink coat.

'I was there at a good time, hon,' she would say, and the ice cubes would clack against her glass as she shakily refilled it with Scotch, 'but I had a lousy time while I was there. Why? Because I was a louse. And loused it all up like lice do.'

Later when they had been downstairs to the dining-room and

Thelma had piled all her share of the special couscous made for her at double rates on to Alexandra's plate and drunk two more Scotches instead, she would come back to one of the highlights of her own lousiness.

'Yes, hon,' she would say, pulling the mink tightly around the tweed trousers she had donned against the long, flyblown mirrored dining-room's draughts, 'I was one of the brave ones. I *didn't* testify. I told McCarthy go chase himself. How come I didn't go for a stretch? Because I was in hospital, hon, having surgery. Excused from testifying on account of having surgery. Women's surgery! Can you sink lower? To be exact, having my Fallopian tubes blown. Oh, yes, they excused me. While men like Chaplin and Brecht and Hammett either gave as good as they got or went inside. Women's surgery! You can hear the old buzzards on that bastard's committee laughing over that bit of filth. Their chuckles must have reached the ears of my dear Senator husband. He was in the House of Representatives then. And if he heard of a piece of filth he had to get his hands on it. He heard of me. So a year later he married me.'

And afterwards, upstairs in Alexandra's room, bending over Oliver in his cot who, as usual, chuckled and reached out his little hands as soon as he saw her beringed, rheumatism-swollen, whisky-trembling fingers making pokey-pokey at him – she laughed her rasping, cough-spluttering laugh and said: 'He's gonna be quite a man. Quite a beautiful man. Aren't you, lover?' And then as she tottered her way to nembutal and bed, she finished her usual saga, 'And I know. For I had three lovely men for husbands, hon. Before I married the jerk I've got now. And I threw them all in the trash can along with the rest of my life some place, somewhere, some street, but I don't remember the name or number. Did you ever hear Beatrice Lillie sing, "You're rotten to the core, Maud?' No, of course, you didn't. It's way back. But in the cool currency of our time we thought it witty. Well, let me tell you, Maud, *you* were lucky. I never had a core at all.'

Jesus said, 'Feed my sheep.' But Alexandra saw no way of doing it. She only hoped, perhaps, that by letting their bleating break into her sweet content, she could atone a little for her happiness. Oh sweet content, oh punishment. Oh damn Eng.

Lit., that brought to one's mind always metaphors, symbols, quotations, and characters from books. The truth was, she thought, as she swung a little yellow-feathered bird on a string in front of Oliver's spellbound eyes, she didn't, looking back from Goa's beaches to Morocco's, really care. She had been there with her baby, and now with a new ocean swinging to and fro, they were here. That was all that mattered. And the Indian ocean slapped a great mass of seaweed, brighter red, brighter emerald than the Atlantic offered, upon the seashell line in front of her and she was forced to remember two special heaps of seaweed that had swept into her Moroccan bliss, and being swept out again, had left her life different.

First, there had been the business of the comforter. She had seen these rubber objects in a shop in the left-over colonial main street of Larache when walking with tottery Thelma. Suspended from a hook by loops of blue or pink ribbon they were. She hadn't any idea what they were for.

'No, you wouldn't, hon. They went out around when I was weaned. Rubber tits and babies' bottles. Why even in the thirties they were a crime in any decent modern mother's home. And by the time I had Elinor, it was breastfeeding or count yourself poor white trash. But my mother saw to it that we all had them in turn as babies. It was that or suck the thumb, she used to say in her homey way. Maybe she was right too. Look at the way that Elinor of mine bites that thumbnail of hers. Comforters they called them. But it was a pretty unhygienic sort of comfort, and psychologically – well, Anna Freud took one look and placed them on the banned list. Trust the Arabs to still live that way. Probably the latest fashion in Larache.'

Something in her tone made Alexandra go defiantly into the shop and buy two of them immediately, one pink bowed, the other blue.

Oliver rejected the pink, but refused from then on to be without the blue. And Alexandra, watching his delight, blessed the comforter.

'It's the Holy Ghost, that's what it is,' Rodrigo said, when he came upon the beatified mother and child. 'I don't know what that makes *you*, Ally. But if it's a Virgin, then I'm absolved from all guilt at last.' And in this unusually friendly mood, he even saluted Elinor with the whimsy, 'Do look, Elinor,' he cried, 'Do look. The Holy Ghost or Comforter. I bet you always thought it was a dove. But it isn't. It's a piece of rubber with a blue bow.'

Elinor smiled at him or rather at his direction as though he were not there. She knelt down by the carrycot and put her face close to Oliver's. 'That's not a nipple, Oliver. Don't you be fooled. That's just a rubber placebo.' She said it all in a special soft and gentle version of her deep voice which, she had once told Alexandra, allowed one gradually to condition babies to adult language, since in any case it was the tone not the words to which they responded. 'You don't need that to sleep. Not that to sleep. Sleep. Sleep, Sleep.'

Her voice grew softer and softer. Oliver was fascinated, for he lay quiet and his eyes never left her lips. But if she had hoped that she had willed him into sleep, she was wrong. When she put out a hand to take the rubber dummy from his mouth, he let out a terrified yell, and then began such crying of mixed fear and anger that he became redder and redder in the face with convulsion. Elinor drew back.

'It should never have been given to him,' she said sharply, then, softening her tone, 'Alexandra, what *was* in your mind? You've lived so wonderfully with him in natural rhythms. It could not have been that terrible mother of mine. No, even she, with all her plastic culture for the masses, doesn't live in the pre-breastfeeding age. Oh Lord ! *Why* has there got to be this pain? Look, I know we can't speak. And where I'm at it takes all and more to endure the sensitisation. All the noises of the world seem to crowd in. As if all the stupid parties and foolish clever talk of all my wasted years was deafening my ears, and all the tastes and smells I'd let take hold of me over the years were ... well, let's say it's bad. But it'll be done as long as I don't fight it.'

Looking at her, Alexandra saw that she indeed looked old, her beautiful modelled face was pinched, the skin wrinkled and scaly, the nostrils red and translucent like someone with catarrh, the lower eyelids pouched and khaki-coloured. She looked away; it was no affair of hers.

As though to echo this, Elinor said, 'We're not working on the same planes. But I know living to the full with the body, as you were, is hard too. All the same, if I couldn't help you, surely you could have spoken to Ned. Or – because I know you respect his life style – to Rodrigo here.' She made a suppliant gesture, but Alexandra was busy now trying to soothe Oliver with the soft tapping on the forehead and chest she had learned from the Arab mothers.

Elinor tried another tack, 'To have spoiled such beauty. For you *were* beautiful, Alexandra, feeding him, and he was beautiful sucking.'

Alexandra had taken Oliver in her arms and was walking away from them along the sands. Elinor suddenly shouted.

'It's no good talking to you except in the old dead language. Very well, rubber teats! Dummy teats!'

Alexandra forced herself to make no reply, but Rodrigo answered for her.

'Christ! You are a snob, Elinor.' And assuming Cockney, 'Orl right then. Wot's the matter wiv rubber tits? The kid likes them, don't 'e? Orl right, it give 'im wind, so what? We all 'ave wind, don't we? Or don't you fart up on Nob 'ill. No, I suppose you wouldn't. It's all piss up there. Piss elegant.'

'My God! The British! Wherever you start from it ends up with class! You live all the time with triviality, immediacy. Dandy! You're just a sub-person, sinking into a dreary, ageing round of malice and gossip and posturing to escape from the boredom and fear that comes from being a robot nothing.'

Later, Ned came to Alexandra. 'Look, it's been brought up at the Council. I know, like, it isn't important but there's lots think it is, y'know, against the natural living of the Community. *I* don't care. Rubber, flesh, I mean it doesn't seem important. But it's plastic to them. I think you ought to know it was Elinor stopped them expelling you, she explained about the pain of living in the body intensely as you had and that. But, y'know, it's just impossible to get coordination with all this tension. I mean Territoriality's indifference or it's nothing. And they must live it in their movements. And now all their muscles are knotted up.'

Alexandra said, 'I'm sorry, Ned.'

But he scowled and sat throwing stones into the sea. Then he burst out.

'All this mothers! It's got to stop, Ally. What we want is not you with your rubber teats or Elinor's deep breathing, spiritual mother. We want the Great Mother here. The White Goddess. Yes, I mean it. We've got tangled up in conventional Reason. We've got to go back behind that. We need older cults, Binah or Devi. P'raps even Durga or Kali. We could satisfy *her* with the sacrifice of this little bastard.' He hardly seemed to be mocking, but Oliver, hearing his voice, put out an arm and delightedly touched his beard.

Rodrigo came back the next evening from a trip to Larache Post Office. 'Ally, I've got this letter from my awful mother. Can I read it to you? It's rather important to me.' And he read. ' "Daddy heard the other day that your hero Sir James Langmuir talks of wanting a third private secretary" – she's put two exclamation marks after the third. Moderately rich people are always fiendishly envious of the very rich – "someone quite young. Apparently he has all sorts of financial interests in these trendy firms for clothes and records and restaurants that the young go to and spend all that money they have, and he wants a young man who'll keep him in touch. Knowing how much you admired him, I couldn't help feeling a tiny bit sad that you were so determined on this year of travelling before you look around. Of course seeing all those places is a wonderful opportunity though the Community sounds as frightful as its name, but you *would* do the job so beautifully and Sir James seemed to like you that time we met at the Ashtons which considering his usual behaviour was quite something. And then again you do have the most expensive tastes, darling, so that it isn't going to be easy for you in the sort of job most young men have to take today. And your degree wasn't exactly brilliant. Mary Bond's eldest boy, the one you've never met, is getting £12 a week! I can't see *you* managing very far on that. And then to work with Sir James would be such *a wonderful entrée* which is the most important thing of all. Of course, Daddy, as always, poor darling! isn't able to say the right thing to the right person. And given "the right person" here I can't altogether blame him. But then as you know Sir James is not my favourite person . . .'

Alexandra said, 'I thought an entrée was what people like Mama call what people call starters.' Then looking at Rodrigo,

'You wouldn't really want a job with that man surely. He's a sort of terrible tycoon.'

'I think I would. Oh, it's all very well for you, Ally – you went and got a two one. And Ned dropped out. But I got a two two. I can't even hope for anything but the dreariest jobs. I shouldn't complain, of course, if I had to teach in some dispiriting place. I'd even try to do it well and so on. But I don't really want to be a stoic. It isn't at all the same as being a dandy. It's only that both can be austere. Whereas with this thing of Sir James's, I do really believe there could be what she calls entrée. Not, of course, into the silly social world *she* means, but into cultivating my own way of life, being elegant and separate, and a bit austere and arrogant in the right way.'

'It sounds awful.'

'No, you know it isn't. It's one of the only personal protests left. It doesn't mean at all being arrogant to the *weak*. Only to the awful and to the petty bosses. And living with some style. I *think* Sir James does it that way. Only his being rich makes it difficult to tell whether he's a dandy or just a shitty bully. At least, working for him, I shall find out. What my father calls "the hard way". All that occult isn't very promising, I admit. We've seen enough of that guff here. But there must be an explanation. I just don't believe that people who run large enterprises are stupid. That's a University sort of illusion. They're much less stupid and boring than academics. Anyway, I can't stay here much longer.'

'No, I don't think you should.'

'Well, then. What I really want to ask is could you write to Hamo Langmuir and ask him to write to Sir James to say I'm the person he must give the job to. He said Sir James would do anything for him and I know *he* would do anything for you. He had worship in his eyes if ever a man did. I mean I have it, of course, but not in that way.'

'If you really want it, I must. But, Roddy, a tycoon person! What *will* you turn into? It'll be awful if you start wearing bowler hats and umbrellas, and flowered shirts and frills for dinner, and giant roses in your buttonhole.'

'I'm not going to be that Sir Gerald Thing, M.P. He's not a dandy. He's what's called a British "act". Being a dandy in the real sense isn't like that. And you know it. And if you think I'm too corruptible then you should marry me. If you believe that Elinor bitch when she says I could become a flamboyant robot, it's your duty to save me from it. Just as it's my duty to rescue you and my son from this squalor – spiritual, physical, aesthetic squalor, every sort of it. For all we love Ned, it has to be said. And it's not just priggish to say it either. I know Oliver loathes my very touch, and I'm not going to pretend I love babies smelling of salt and covered in sand. But it would all be different. We'd be reasonably rich, especially when you earned as well, which you'd want to. And I'd want that too. Being a dandy doesn't mean being a Victorian husband, you know. Just having everything appropriate and elegent, which we could do. And we'd look elegant. And he'll be handsome, with my looks and yours. All that *does* matter. It's a taking-off ground for protest against second-rateness. Whereas this sloppy place is just a dive into a treacle well or a treacle midden. Just because my ghastly parents and yours live in middle-class taste and awfulness doesn't mean we can go on all our lives reacting. Anyhow, you and Oliver mustn't stay here any longer. It's getting far too cold. I don't mean just now, although this wind is freezing.'

'Yes. I know what you mean. I can understand general statements if I try. Even though I'm a female.'

Alexandra was immensely relieved that they could end on a joke, because she could not bear at that moment to be driven from her routine. But she promised to think over going back to London if she could resolve the intolerable problem of being in the same city at Zoe and Him. And also if Ned was all right.

Meanwhile they agreed to put on lovely clothes and go into Tangier and a day's luxury which Oliver should share. They could visit the British Library and find the address of Hamo's Institute to which to send the letter for forwarding that Alexandra would immediately write. She would urge Hamo also immediately to write to this Sir James person saying that Rodrigo Knight, who would already have written to him, was the only young man who could possibly do what he wanted as his secretary.

The next morning when they left for Tangier the south-west wind blew behind them from the sea carrying squally rain so that their delight in for once appearing elegant was spoilt by all the leather they had to cover themselves and Oliver with for protection. Nor was he any happier than usual with Rodrigo for his cot bearer though he stopped short of crying, making only a face that would have brought in large funds to an N.S.P.C.C. appeal. But if Oliver's suppressed misery caused Alexandra disquiet, it was almost forgotten as they came upon the three small children under the trees. The two Swiss children – the four-year-old boy in torn, thin pyjamas trousers and the three-year-old girl in an oversize pair of dirty linen slacks – were apparently burying Louise's baby under a mound of pine needles and leaf mould.

'She's cold,' they said in explanation to Rodrigo's anxious questioning, 'she's cold.'

And it seemed very likely, for the wizened little creature had on only a pair of cotton drawers. Rodrigo clothed it in the embroidered military tunic he was wearing under his long leather coat; the tunic went round the little thing three times, the roughness of the frogging against its skin made it cry. Alexandra took the large Turkish shawl she had draped over her head and wrapped the Swiss girl in it; it trailed on the ground like an Edwardian illustration of a small girl dressed in her mother's ball gown. There was nothing left for the boy except one of the many covers on Oliver's cot, it cost Alexandra much irritation to part with this and Oliver began to cry.

They waited for the bus in a light drizzle. Some village children, pinched in the face, thin and lightly clad, came and stared at them. To keep themselves warm they drank hot milky coffee and, in pouring it out, spilt some on the ground. A cat, so thin that its ribs made stripes on its black furry side giving it a false tabby look, crept out in an attempt to lap up the spillings; but it was first stoned by the children and then chased away by a large half-starved mongrel pointer who barked so loudly that Oliver's crying increased. But then, they weren't, after all, called upon to 'do anything' about the village children, the dog or the cat.

On the bus, they stood with Oliver in his cot suspended between them, just as on each side of them stood sesame-smelling peasants with live fowls suspended upside down between them.

Alexandra said, 'I believe I'm having a presentiment. I mean a bad one. Something's going to happen to the Community. Something bad.'

'It's happened,' Rodrigo said, 'oh dear, I do hope you haven't caught psychic gifts from Elinor. Do you think you've got those faces coming on again?' This made them laugh a little.

In Tangier the sun shone.

They could get out of the wind. They ate a delicious potage and a daube of kid at a small French restaurant. They had sherbet. They drank a bottle of red wine. They bought Oliver a vulgar comic rubber camel intended for tourists which they swung on a stick above his carrycot. He was delighted. They found the address of the Institute and posted Alexandra's letter to Hamo. By now the sun was shining warmly. The stormy time was done. Alexandra decided to sleep at the Community instead of going into Larache. She fed Oliver from her breast on the bus and he sucked so contentedly that Rodrigo was able to stroke his arm gingerly without his objecting. They both felt rather happy.

It was the more disconcerting, then, that when they reached the village in fast fading light, they were met by a little crowd of people who stood at the entrance to the path that led through the wood to the Community beach. It was not a crowd that made way for them, and when they decided to go round it, stumbling among the trees through increasingly sinking sand dunes, they were followed by the noise of shouting that sounded angry and some stones that were not aimed at a cat.

However, the weather turned really hot during the next week or two and Alexandra, lying sea-rocked, forgot the whole bad presentiment. Her happiness was ambiguously reinforced at the end of that time when Rodrigo, concealing childish excitement under extra urbanity, produced a summons to an interview, all expenses paid, with the great Sir James. She felt happy for him, she was almost sure; and worried for herself without him, she almost knew. He was to leave by air from Tangier in five days' time.

But before that time, many more of the Community began to leave as the stormy cold rains returned in full force. Going to the bus for Larache and Thelma, Alexandra fell in with the Swiss couple and their children and Louise with her baby, all seeking to hitch their way south to Marrakesh. She noted with amused annoyance that all three of their children wore thick bristly little fur coats and fur hoods that stank in the rains. There were no signs of the clothes that she and Roddy had given to them.

The shouting children of the village were reinforced this time by some youths, who really frightened Alexandra by walking round the little group of Communards in closing circles and laughing jeeringly. The Swiss youth was so thin and his ginger beard and whiskers so straggly that his evident weakness made the situation more frightening than if there were no man with them.

Louise said again, 'Why can't they love us? We aren't up to putting anyone down about anything. I want to build a House of Love.'

The comment seemed more apposite now, but hardly more effective. It was some time before any vehicle came along the road. A group of unveiled women, presumably Berbers, with red and yellow plastic buckets, gathered round the communal tap. They looked angrily at the little white group and chattered volubly. Then they began to shout directions to the youths. Alexandra felt so frightened for Oliver that she always remembered with pride afterwards that she hadn't been frightened for herself. But at last a large lorry appeared from the north, raising clouds of dust behind it. She wondered if the others felt as relieved as she did, but she did not ask them, for she felt safer not to be associated with them. The lorry stopped and the Swiss couple began to hoist their children into the back. When Louise sought to follow them, one of the Berber women, accompanied by laughter and shouting, rushed forward and tried to pull the little fur coat off the baby but succeeded only in tearing its ill-sewn seam. For a moment Louise seemed about to hit her, then she burst into tears.

The driver's mate shouted, 'Antrez-y. Nous pattim.'

The Swiss youth took the child from Louise, then pulled her in after it. The lorry drove off, trailed not only by dust but by shouts and jeers and a flurry of stones from the villagers. Her fellow Communards had said nothing to Alexandra – shown no more interest in her than a herd of hartebeestes next to a herd of elands. But the villagers she now feared, as a single doe might be afraid when left to the mercies of a jackal pack. She need not have worried. Once the lorry was a distant vanishing point, the villagers resumed their lives, except for one small child who stood and stared at her until the bus arrived. Nevertheless Alexandra stayed at Larache until the day before Roddy's departure.

When she returned to the Community she was stopped in the holm oak wood not by the villagers, but by the police. And she and Oliver were put into a lorry and taken to Azilah police station. There she found the few remaining Communards – most of whom, since they had been too disembodied to follow the general trek to warmer climates, were too disembodied to be feeling the despair or desolation which clearly showed itself on the faces of Ned and Rodrigo. As for Elinor, she sat, not, Alexandra noticed through her own alarms, with the dull vacancy of the others but in a calm passivity that was a triumph of all the disciplines she had endured in the previous months. She wore an expression, not of the zany beatification which showed on the face of the stoned Danish boy at her side, but of a peaceful, happy absentness. Yet she also looked ill, old, tired, shivered continuously, and ran at the eyes and nose with a hideous cold.

Their stay at the police station was so frightening to Alexandra in its suddenness, its uncertainty, and its menace that she scarcely felt the indifference, the contempt, and the roughness of the policemen. She fed Oliver at the breast and as far as she could tried to go with the sea into a deep trough of oblivion: but the sea swell brought her not rocking contentment, but lurching sickness in the stomach.

She was not questioned for long, for she had no hesitation, once she knew what had happened, in telling how Louise and the Swiss had gone south. And the fact that she did not know the registration number of the lorry caused no surprise, for neither did the village family who had stood by and seen their goat livelihood disappear into the south on the backs of three white children.

She had very often to interpret for others, since, except for Elinor, she alone knew French at all fluently: and Elinor would only reiterate, smiling vaguely, 'Rien à dire.' And in fact Elinor was right, Alexandra reflected. There *was* nothing to say. The goats had gone. The peasants to whom they represented their sole livelihood might with satisfactory assistance from the police of

Marrakesh regain three badly sewn goatskins. Three white children would then be without warm covering, and, as they were likely to be compulsorily repatriated with their parents to England and Switzerland, where the climate was inclement, they would be the worse for the loss. As to the Robin Hoods, who had supplied the needs of the children of the new Kingdom of Love at the expense of the children of the old Kingdom of Greed, they had disappeared into the etheric void from which they claimed that their life energies, on which presumably they had depended in the very exhausting task of transporting, killing, and skinning goats, derived. So a bewhiskered German youth, the only one of the dozen who had ever talked with them, informed the police.

Alexandra, remembering the clients waiting in the Larache police station where she had gone to register, thought there is nothing really for us twelve people to do but sit on the stone benches or the floor until we are released. A Moroccan brought into a police station, with nothing to say, would no doubt wait patiently until the righteous anger of the police gave way to their normal indifference and this in turn to a strong desire to relieve their cramped quarters of the presence of an intruder. But then a Moroccan, no doubt, would know how long all these psychological influences would take to have effect. But not so the Europeans. Like those Wilcoxes, it would be telegrams and anger, or rather, telephones and consuls.

Herself, after the first half hour, she was no longer frightened. Her sole thought was for Oliver. But even into this capsule of maternal concern, there was from time to time injected a shame for what had happened, a disgust for being associated with it which was in no way lessened by the theatrical anger with flashing teeth and glinting eyes of the dispossessed peasant nor by the theatrical grief with hair tearing and wailing of his wife. Indeed this pantomimic display seemed to make the Community Robin Hood heroics even more shabby, as being committed against people too simple, too suppressed, to command any personal emotions, only these formal, traditional expressions of their desperate loss. She wanted only to make one gesture – to produce the cash to recompense the losses of the poor. But she had only just enough money to ensure independence for herself and Oliver for a month to come. There was no room for the luxury of buying decency.

Rodrigo's disgust was as great, but his anger was greater, for the whole of his future life seemed to hang on his early release. And Alexandra understood. For some people, at some times, telegrams and anger were necessities. For Rodrigo it was the telephone and the British Consul at Tangier. This official, enormously impressed by Sir James's summons, took little time, especially with the aid of cash, in securing Rodrigo's release. Other consuls were to act as effectively, but much more slowly. Meanwhile there was one snag in Rodrigo's course of action: Alexandra refused to go with him while Ned's position was in question; indeed she could not go with him for the police insisted on her remaining as a witness to the departure of the children in their ill-gotten goatskins. She might stay where she liked, but not on the beach, for the rule of love was now officially forbidden. So Thelma was summoned and arrived in a hired luxury car, dressed in all her diamonds and a clean mink coat, her skeleton body almost plump with dollars and travellers' cheques. Such ostentatious wealth and the flourish of her husband's name – an American Senator! – threw some of the police into a frenzy of hostility that Alexandra feared for a moment might be counterproductive, but luckily it threw a lesser number of them but these the senior into a salaam of sycophancy. And it was not many minutes before Alexandra and Elinor were free to leave.

Then came Alexandra's hardest fight to persuade the generous Thelma to recompense the peasants for the loss of their goats.

'But it's charity, Alexandra. You can't give charity. Just think now, hon, what a chance this is to expose to these kulaks – for that's what they are – the realities of the system they live under.' It was hard to say whether her American ethic of self-help or her Marxism was more outraged.

And, for once, mother and daughter were united, since Elinor declared that any such acceptance of surrogate guilt would chain them once more to this area – an area which events so apparently casual, yet, because so casual in their appearance, undoubtedly cosmic, showed to have become emptied of vital fluid.

'I just can't breathe here any more,' she said. And instantly, to the alarm of the officials and of Thelma, showed real signs of convulsive asthma.

But Elinor's dismissal of the goat-owner's right to recompense had in turn a violent effect upon Ned.

'Look,' he said, 'someone's got to pay for this. I mean like we shall leave a whole community up-tight with injustice.'

'But, Ned, it's all so banal.'

Elinor's lofty manner plunged him straight into action. With the translating aid of the unwilling British Consul (for neither Elinor nor Alexandra would act), Ned made a Dostoevskyan confession of guilt on behalf of all the Community. The confession puzzled the police, but offered them a scapegoat, and Ned was immediately hustled off to a cell, where it was evident – or so the Consul told them – he would have to remain at least until the goatskins were recovered, probably until the thieves were caught.

It was only then that Thelma agreed to pay the peasants, but she gave double the sum asked for through the police.

'If I know these goddamned cops, that'll shorten the guy's time in this stinking place.'

With Ned in prison, there was reinforced reason for Alexandra to obey the police order. She could promise Rodrigo no more than that she would seriously consider returning to England as soon as Ned was released.

And so she did, for the situation at the hotel became intolerable: Oliver cried so much when Ned never appeared; Elinor, refusing to eat more than a cupful of brown rice and to drink more than a cupful of water, was judged by the doctor, whom Thelma insisted on bringing in, to be in a dangerously weakened condition – the postures and breathings to which she gave large parts of the day he declared to have produced a state of physical hyperaesthesia, in which the mucous membranes were sensitized to a dangerous degree.

To this Elinor replied, 'I should hope so. That's got to be the preliminary to any transcendence.'

Thelma shouted at her, and, when the doctor cautioned that any such state of tension could be highly dangerous, she shouted at him. Paying him three times his fee, she told him to take his incompetence out of her daughter's room. Then in her remorse, she went on a heavy bout of Bourbon (the local Scotch supply having run out), repetitive self-recrimination, swearing at Elinor, cursing of the absent Senator, and tears. Through it all, Elinor just sat or lay, apparently quite remote from all that was happening. The spectacle of Elinor's distaste for her mother, the mother's bewildered, fuddled concern for the daughter, and the hatred and contempt of both of them for the apparently corrupt and double-dealing Senator Tarbett was like a terrible parody of her own family situation to which she now seemed committed to return. Alexandra could only keep her sanity, she thought, by locking herself day after day through three weeks of almost continuous rain into the sad little cheaper bedroom in which she and Oliver were now installed. Living in and for him minute by minute she shut out all but the immediate feeding and potting and nappy-changing and rocking, to a background, an insane surrealist background, of the complicated plots, the highflown sentiments and overcharged French of seven George Sand novels that she found in the hotel lounge and which she read at every moment when thought could possibly invade.

Thelma she had to listen to, Elinor she tried not to see. She tried also to keep Thelma's desperate loneliness from invading, in the self-deceptive guise of parental duty, her daughter's search for nothingness. After all Elinor was someone of her own age; and, however she disliked her, she must help her in her right to do her own thing. And, it seemed, she really was doing it. Until one evening she burst into Alexandra's room and hysterically attacked her for preventing Ned from expressing himself; and then equally hysterically begged her to take Ned away when he came out of prison.

'Help me, Alexandra! It's not a small thing I'm trying to do. I don't aim to some cranky life living in an ashram, or hanging round a guru. I'm almost through it. I'm almost free. And when that's done I can go back into the world. Oh, say in a year's time. Why I could even teach literature in college and do it well without it meaning a thing. I'd be so secure on the plane I'd reached. What have I done this Ph.D. for if it's not to work in the world?' And she laughed in a natural way that Alexandra had never heard before. 'But I've got to free myself of him, of all thought of those muscles working in that strong white neck, of the crazy way he talks when his ideas come too fast, of the way all his clumsiness turns into grace when he starts showing us the movements of the mime. Help me to run away from him!'

So Alexandra did just that. She closed her mind to the bitterness Ned would feel when he came out and found Elinor gone. She never ceased to back Elinor in her resolution. One part of her felt a terrible treachery to Ned, another part felt that she was doing him a great service. It appeared that in Goa in India there was a certain Swami Sant Sarada Maharysh, usually called the Austrian Swami because he came originally from Salzburg, who was the master of pranayana.

'He's a genuine magister of the occult, an adept too,' Elinor said, 'but that doesn't interest me. Oh! and I guess he's quite a charlatan too, which is how it should be.'

So it was arranged that Elinor should fly to Bombay and then join the Swami's classes in Goa. So she would escape both Thelma and Ned.

Two days before she went, Ned came out of prison, miserably thin, muted, diarrhoeic, and a bit the worse for blows and kicks. Alexandra had hardly begun to organize ministration for him, Oliver had only just greeted him twice with delighted cries, when suddenly he was gone, at Elinor's expense, with her to Goa. For there he would be close to the real Community, the one that had begged to perform "Batteries", which was assembled or would soon be assembled farther down the Indian West Coast in Malabar, probably at Cochin. And the group led by the girl from Warwick was rumoured to be in that area, at Trivandrum.

Alexandra was so angry that she nearly left at once for England. But then Thelma got gastroenteritis, verging on dysentery, and, with it, a morbid misery that frightened Alexandra when she was near her. Yet near her she had to be, for there was no one else to care for the old tramp. Near, and, at the same time, constantly vigilant to see that no infection of Thelma's, physical or emotional, should reach the baby. And anyway, baby cried because Ned had been taken away from him.

Rodrigo – darling Roddy – sent her a first-class fare to England, and announced with triumph that Sir James had engaged him. But a few days later when Thelma was enough recovered, *she* announced that *she* was travelling to Goa.

'Hon, I conceived Elinor without any love. I just was the lowest crawling creature on God's earth after I'd sold the piss on the McCarthy thing. And being that low what could I do but marry the lowest bum I could find, Congressman Tarbett. God rot his two-timing soul! But that didn't say I had to get a child by him. But I did. I gave poor Elinor that rotten, stinking father. So I've got to stand by her, hon. She's all out on a limb, walking to the end of the jetty. And the drop at the end could be pretty big.'

Somehow, at last, Alexandra decided that, given Ned and given Thelma, she too must go to Goa. And so here she was lying on the sands, feeling the baby and herself to be the swell and roll of the warmer ocean, where the dugong replaced the manatee, where the seaweed was more vermilion and more emerald, where sometimes, they said, great shoals of red and blue Portuguese men-of-war, with deadly stings, were washed ashore instead of seaweed. The sea they were, she and Oliver, and it was warmer here, hot so that all the Community lay naked day after day, and the trees had scarlet blossoms, and flashing blue-green birds flew zig-zag before one's eyes, and it had been Portuguese, and a Saint was buried there, an abbé to do with Dumas had hypnotized there – his statue was in the town – and once it had been the sea-god's but he had given it to Vishnu, and Ned had begun 'Batteries' again, and Elinor her breathing exercises, and Thelma's room had a little wrought-iron balcony, and Oliver made noises that must surely be early speech, and it was warm, and she and baby were the ocean, slop, slop, slop, slop ... and suddenly she was entangled in the seaweed, Oliver's little head struggled to break through its brilliant, transparent coils, and they were sinking, down into warm sucking water, the swallowing ocean. Then she woke and Oliver was crying. The sun beat too strongly on him in his cot on this new beach.

The fear that Hamo had experienced as he clattered through the scrubwood in escape from the uncles' dreamfeast, the sense of their malevolence bombarding him from the trees, of their pursuit through the labyrinthine descent from the fortress bungalow, did not entirely leave him when his aeroplane took off for Kuala Lumpur. Erroll talked of Janey Dare's curry and afters, and compared them with Gillian Fail's version of sukiyaki ceremony and even with May Latimer's T-bone and starters. He then sketched a comedy short based on the bazaars. In which two drolls (likely English lads) fell tip over arse again and again.

Then, seeking to dispel Hamo's continuing dark brooding, he went on to speak of 'Magic' so praised everywhere, jealously a little in Japan perhaps, grudgingly a little in the great Los Baños, but with awe and gratitude in Hong Kong and Taiwan and Thailand and Indonesia. Then he ventured to criticize the workings of the labs even in the mighty U.S.A., in giant Japan or the great Philippines. 'Oh yes, the gear's all right but let them come back when they've learned how to us it as the tart said to the well-hung apprentices.' Finally, he chose another muse. Well, he said, with some effort in breaking through the Great Barrier Reef, and what were they like, the lads of Indonesia, different he supposed from the Bangkok lot, the sister-boys on bikes in mini-skirts and frilly blouses! Oh yes, he'd heard about *them* from a G.I. in a bar – bastards those G.I.s too, shouting their big mouths off – telling how, when he felt her up and found it was a boy, he'd beaten him up, and he, Erroll, had told him he was a dirty fucker and, if he'd seen him at it himself, he, Erroll would have bashed him so much he'd have wished his old mother had died a Virgin in old Virginney. The Filipino boys looked a hot lot, he thought, though you heard ugly stories of night life in Manila. But not, he supposed, for those like the Chief who knew how to look after themselves. And treat others right.

At first Hamo felt every heat flush from anger to embarrassment, from shame to affection, at this first open speech on the tacitly understood, unmentioned subject from his faithful follower. He ached to respond as it had clearly cost Erroll much to bring it out. But he simply could not open his mouth to speak. But, at last, Erroll's shock-tactic words blew him out of his depressed inertia. He knew what he had to do. He took out his silver pen and his leather writing-case and very neatly penned a letter:

Dear Lacey,

I have continued to feel most distressed by the unfortunate interpretation you put upon my laughter when we stopped at the temple on our return journey last week. The laughter was aroused by a very misplaced sense of absurdity which visited me at that moment. I had thought that I had left such sudden visitations behind me with other irrational, emotional spontaneities of youth. I can only plead the heat and fatigues of the day. Had you been saying 'barmy' under the misapprehension that it was on the lips of every frequenter of Carnaby Street or of the King's Road, Chelsea, it would have suggested to me an ignorance of fashion-dominated England which I entirely share. That, as you tell me, you like to use the word because it was a favourite of your father's altogether delights me, if that does not sound patronizing. I assure you that it is not intended to be so. Since we are not likely to meet again, I feel emboldened to confide in you what I should hardly tell an habitual acquaintance or a business colleague. My own father's memory is very precious to me. I honour it in many ways that the modern world might find comic. For example I continue to use his hair brushes and clothes brushes and I postpone arranging for their re-bristling, though the need for it has long been apparent to my housekeeper. Such a thing could easily, and would, no doubt, be mocked by most people today. I should not care. So you may see how far I was from laughing out of the frivolous motive you supposed.

My sympathy for your attitude to your father leads me further to encroach upon your kindness – despite the unfortunate misunderstanding which led to my presence at the Jonkheer's tea-party. I cannot forget how, by my clumsiness, I may have further harmed the fortunes of the extraordinary youth, who, you tell me, was already in disfavour with his employer (now, I very much fear, ex-employer). I realize that, living out here, and accepting the desperate quality of much human life, as you are bound to do if you are to manage your estate efficiently, you will find my request sentimental. However, I can assure you that it is heart-felt. I cannot believe that some provision of work, shelter, clothing, perhaps even further education could not be of service to the youth. I venture to trespass upon your sense of justice, so close to the sense of respect you show for your father, by asking you to dispose of the enclosed cash on the youth's behalf as with your knowledge of these parts you think best.

Yours sincerely,
Hamo Langmuir.

P.S. There can be no need of telling him the source of the help, for I have been the cause of enough distress for him not to wish to be reminded of me.

He wrote out a cheque for £100 to Lacey's credit and addressed the whole to the Club where he had met him.

But although his heart was lighter, the threatening sense of the avenging uncles and the mocking boys remained with him. Each time as his eye caught sight, through the thick safety of the window of the plane, of the vast rush of steam and air that hissed and shrieked through space away behind him, he felt as though the Jonkheer with his crown and sceptre, as in the German song they had learned at school, was threatening him with an intruder's punishment. Their plane, hurtling indeed through night and wind, came, unwontedly in that perfect sky, into the edge of a typhoon's cloudy turbulence. Strapped, but jolted and bumped, he felt himself riding desperately away from anger to which as it grew more violent he was less and less able to give a specific, even an avuncular name. But it must be the uncles. After all, he had insulted them (those trolls) beyond anything, for he had declared their dream to be his nightmare. As most men would think his dream. So now, as when we try to leave a nightmare, its phantasms hold us to them, the uncles' hot breath was fast upon him. So hot, that, however he assured himself that the pursuing figures were but figments built of cloud and vapour, he felt himself fighting for breath and had to ask Erroll to ask the Stewardess to adjust the air control, but he felt sick to death of it all. A nice thing it would have been for Erroll to arrive with the Chief dead in his arms! But 'Ladies and Gentlemen, we are about to make our descent to Kuala Lumpur airport. Will you ...' And he stepped out on to the tarmac alive, temporarily purged of irrational fears, glad to help Erroll count their many suitcases against the baggage receipts.

After Indonesia, Malaysia brought the now rather mechanical round: The Institute for Tropical Crops, the University Department of Agriculture, the Ministry, the British Council, the Commercial Counsellor of the Embassy, some field work among native grasses allied to *oryza indica*, visits to the paddy fields. It was pleasant, but now a little mechanically tedious, to hear again the miracles that Magic had performed (after all, why else call it Magic?). It was less surprising now, but increasingly disturbing, to learn by chance how two years before, when Magic gave an especially miraculous surfeit, it had all been eaten by rats and weevils. However, storage difficulties are an endemic teething trouble of developing countries ...

But all this was familiar enough now to Hamo. Each day and week he heard more purely tourist talk with its varying yet inescapable flavour of the advertising people, and more purely business talk with its varying yet inescapable flavour of the entertainment world. As he did so, he became aware that he belonged to a third group, an inter-group, growing indeed every day in numbers, as people a decade or two ago used to warn that intersex was growing. This hybrid army, neither tourist nor business, but a bit of both, whose service being intended as perfect freedom, somehow, he felt, failed to be either quite free or very useful, had, he began to suspect, just enough engagement disguised as leisure or leisure disguised as concern, to hear, because they moved camouflaged, what tourist, business men, and officials all missed – a high, distant overtone of perpetual, desperate woe. Could it be the natural noise of the world, as he began to fancy? More likely, with insufficient occupation, unsatedly randy, the noise was simply present in his own too little disciplined head. Certainly he *heard* it; and with increasing frequency, as soon as he was alone, he ran gushing taps and cascading showers to cleanse his sweat and drown the sound, but to no avail.

The monstrous joviality of the uncles, echoing across the flooded valley, came back to Hamo even in the civilized and controlledly picturesque tropical landscape of Penang's huge-treed Victorian botanical gardens, or among the absurd Moorish domes and minarets that English Edwardian taste thought appropriate for the railway station of Malaysia's capital, or in Singapore harbour, when watching the great steamships basking like friendly docile sea cows, as though George V, our second, better sailor king, were still with us and the Nips had never come. Yet in the end such constantly fresh scenes – some natural, some colonial – proved too strong for the nightmare's mood. The grey thunderclouds of the Jonkheer's implacable anger rolled away from the brilliant blue sky. Nevertheless there remained, as with nightmares, visual fragments, aural fancies that came back, even on beyond Malaysia into Ceylon, to catch Hamo unawares.

Such, encouraged perhaps by Erroll's continued entertainment of him with the saga of the exploits of his two likely lads, were his sudden apprehensions of the Danish uncle and another – was it the German uncle or the American uncle who had been led by the jokey Dane into such partnership? – but certainly two of the uncles appearing in unlikely guise wherever schoolboys, grubby or clean, mealy or chubby, made their, by now to Hamo, nauseating appearance in groups of three or four.

At first, these apprehensions turned apparitions so disconcerted Hamo as to bring him near to deserting his habitual dignity in company. But in the end these very vestiges, these last uncertain shadows of his Adventure with the uncles, led him on by means of the Fairest Youth he had Ever Seen into his next Adventure, that of Cinnamon 7, where the lovely suburban homes and gracious gardens of Colombo's élite bid fair to outvile man.

No apparitions, of course, perform their seductive task at our conjuring summons quite directly – that would be too crude for our credulity, or for theirs. The Danish uncle's and his companion's visitations, on the edge of Hamo's vision, were no contradiction to this. At first, indeed, instead of barking him Cerberus-like towards a new circle of adventure, they seemed to be regular dogs in a manger. As witness their appearance on the evening of Hamo's fourth full day in Colombo.

'Phew!' said Erroll in relief as they watched Mr Watteratne's hysterically rattling, ten-year-old Peugeot disappear out of the hotel forecourt into the quickly darkening streets of the capital city; and then, 'Oomph! Aah!' as, turning towards the surf-thrumming ocean, he breathed in the first cooling breeze that they had known in four days. The car's retreating clatter sounded the end of a day of sweaty frustration, of indignation pent up in apoplectic heat, of the endless irritation of Mr Watteratne's soothingly intended stream of aimless flattery and promise, and, in climax, of a dismal dinner that had undone all the refreshment of the evening's three lengths of the hotel swimming pool. Hamo's sense of relaxation at its close was doubled by Erroll's noises. He alone of all people that Hamo had ever known used such sounds, 'Phew!' 'Oomph!' 'Aah!' 'Ugh!' 'Wheee!' – so much for those who saw his assistant only as a Cockney character, he was much more than that – a real original, basic, knowing yet unspoiled, as solid as these ridiculous yet absolutely apposite monosyllables that he and no one else emitted.

'Well, no complaints about this. The Isle of Spice at last.

Spicey! My old dad would have been looking for a bit of fun on the promenade as soon as he heard *that* word. Shocking what repression did to all that lot, wasn't it?' He waited for Hamo's reply which didn't come. 'All the same, I can never quite relax on tropical evenings until that bloody great sun's made its sudden bump into the sea. Doesn't seem right, does it? I mean the sun ... Well, you know, it ought to go down stately, like one of those old dowagers taking the waters, not like fat Phyllis falling off the deep end. "And so we say farewell." Funny to believe they could ever have said that without taking the mickey. I can remember it as a kid though. Travelogues! The breeze and the surf and the ... no, not a bloody coconut palm in sight,' he surveyed with exaggerated disappointment the flat distance of the Galle Face Green that flanked the promenade, 'Wimbledon Common on a windy evening, Southend without the pong.'

'I've never been to Southend, I'm afraid.'

'Well, that's two of us.' He chuckled, teasing himself, a habitual, pleasing Erroll sound. 'Shockin' admission for a Cockney. After that dinner, old Water Rat'll have some stories to tell to make the baby rats' mouths water when he gets back to his homely hole. Mulligatawny soup! I ask you. When we've had bloody great rivers of soupy sweat running down our backs all day. Peculiar odour the sweat has here, hasn't it? I thought Janey's parting present of perfume had got rid of it. But back it came with that soup. Hot ham. Hot hams is about it. Cumberland sauce. Well, they can put *that* back in the lakes they drained it out of. And Queen's pudding! No wonder the place is a Republic, if that's the little leavings from the Royal Table.' As so often, Erroll's cheerful Cockney send-up of the scene, his total extroversion, gradually relaxed Hamo. This time to the extent that he could give his attention to the groups of strollers who made up the evening promenade.

For the most part, respectable middle-class family parties, their children, especially the little girls, all fluffs and frills and ribbons so revoltingly feminine that it made him, with a start, think for the first time that he would *not* perhaps have been happier living in the more ordered early years of this century. In the centre of the vast Green, stolid, blazered little boys flew hired kites, strange black dragons and bats with scarlet figurings, that seemed ab-

surdly to be threatening to darken the turquoise sky before night-
fall. But little boys, too, now, however neat ...

There were lovers, also, almost all in Western dress – indeed,
as Erroll said, it could have been Southend, or to choose what he
knew better, Eastbourne – the middle-class promenade that must
have been Leslie's social apogee as a boy; but, thank Heaven,
lovers here were more modest, more circumspect than the unpleasing permissiveness of England now decreed. And, yes,
knots of young men ... somewhat drearily trousered, or seduc-
tively saronged; seldom a sartorially mixed group. But there was
one, as it passed him, which contained in the centre, flanked by
shapeless trousers, a smooth white sarong that suggested, in its
darkening creases shaped to the gracefully moving limbs, all
manner of thoughts of sheets and of bed. Surely the perfect
length of thigh, tightly swathed waist and hips; and the whole,
though short, barely 5'8", certainly quite twenty years of age,
certainly no horrid schoolboy.

' "So Monday, Dr Longmoor" – poor old Water Rat! "Your
car will be at your hotel at 8.30 a.m. on Monday. A very early
hour for a V.I.P., but then you are also a working bee. Hee, hee,
hee." Honest, that's the noise he made. I thought it only came in
comics : like "Ugh !' and "Wham ! !", you know. But that's the
genuine water-rat squeak all right. Then old Watton has to
correct the obvious, "Look, you said Thursday, Mr Watteratne." '

Erroll, as so often in re-telling, presented himself in a highly
authoritative light, not at all the breezy Cockney, but the ser-
geant taking charge. And so of course he did; or he would not
have been in Ceylon at his side. Yet the tropical air had brought
out some old-fashioned, almost atavistic streak – could his grandfather have been an N.C.O. in the army in India? It threatened
at times to embarrass – he surely would drop a little insularity,
a little prejudice, as their voyage continued. Up to now it had
seemed to grow. And yet, when he was on his own, he appeared
to fraternize with the local people as happily as ...

For example, Hamo remembered this very afternoon, coming
out of the University talking to that bright young postgraduate
about his work on the hormone stimulation caused by the decom-
posing of *crotolaria juneca* and wild indigo, he had seen Erroll

225

with a whole group of Singhalese, chatting away happily. He would like to look into the question of green manuring: it was clear that the sunflower *tithonia diversifolia*, for example, while plentiful of leaf, was unhappy in many soils ... But this was sheer agronomy. Nothing to do with him. All the same there had been something quite beautiful about the young man's workings; graphs that delighted the eye in their symmetry. A year ago he would have come away from such work unable to think of anything else. But now there appeared to be no power to concentrate, to escape every manner of nightmare, of ludicrous irrelevancy. At least he must go back and talk to the young man, see more of his workings, encourage, criticize, give his mind ...

The groups had turned round and were moving towards him, giggling surely intentionally loudly, and, as they came nearer, large dark eyes, shy but inviting, fluttered across his own intent gaze. And then – he was younger, slimmer, smaller than his companions – they passed, chattering in staccato, preening awareness, through Erroll's imitative flow, like a flock of lorikeets flitting above a miming mynah bird. Yes, there had been Erroll deep in matey laughter with two Singhalese business men, or so they seemed ...

'"No, no, Mr Wootton, I assure you there can be no question of Thursday. Thursday is Poya. Do you know what is Poya? Ah, Mr da Souza, *you* must tell them what is Poya. Mr da Souza does not believe in Poya. He is a Roman Catholic. He follows the Western Sunday. But now we are a Buddhist country. So all holidays follow the moon. Many from the U.K. find the computation hard. But you are no doubt a mathematician, Mr Wootton, for you it will be easy. Poya is the holiday for all in Ceylon – Buddhist, Hindu, Muslim, Christian. So Thursday I am afraid is not possible. But I will send you on Monday with a very good driver. A Mr da Silva, Anthony da Silva. He has been with many important people from the U.K. And given them great pleasure. You will tell me, please, what pleasure he gives you. So Monday ..." And then of course the interfering bastard Wootton has to wave his little diary. Sorry I just couldn't help it. "You're wrong, mate. I've got this Singhalese diary here. And your next Poya's on Monday."'

The note jarred. There were moods of confusion, hesitation,

expectancy in this tropical world ... Erroll's inflexibility, of course, was one of his great virtues. But ...

The red ball had all but tumbled into the sea. The braziers of the roasted nut vendors with their no, not nauseous, rather their bizarre scent, were the brightest points of glowing red light beside the now black, still mysteriously surf-booming ocean. High above a few kites showed only their sinister outlines of black bats' or dragons' wings – but only a few, for the children, the families, surely all the respectable, had moved away at the approach of night. The hideous government offices, hotels and business houses – with which the British had shamefully made uglier this ugly crowded corner of a miraculously beautiful island – were fading in the dimming light to ruinous indefinite shapes. They would not now have seemed too disgraceful beside the fine ruins with which earlier conquerors – Dutch, Tamil, above all the Singhalese in their ancient cities – had, as he had seen in their preliminary weeks of tourist discovery of Ceylon, fittingly decorated the magnificent natural scene. Everything was mysterious. Not the least, the chatter and laughter, the glances in the dying light from the beautiful youth and his group once more coming by.

' "So then, Thursday. Please make a note of that, Mr da Souza. Do not forget your photographic equipment, Mr Wootton – you will pass a bird sanctuary ..." '

'I suppose you've got a date tonight.'

Erroll stopped in his tracks.

'Well ... Yes, as a matter of fact, I have. Room 49. Sharon Gray. Nice little blonde. Bourbon she's got and a chicken sandwich. I'll see to the rest, I told her. But it's not till ten o'clock. She's gone on a conducted moonlight coach tour to Mount Lavinia. "No bathing lark, mind," I said. "I don't want any shark's leavings." '

But the youth had separated now and surely his head was nodding slightly towards the far end of the Green where some conduit or waterway ran out towards the sea.

'Look,' Hamo said, 'I think I'm going to leave you now.' And he tried to cover his answering nod to the youth in a gesticulatory accompaniment to what he said that he feared must seem very uncharacteristic to his assistant.

'Oh! Well, don't let me keep you.' Erroll sounded offended at being cut off in his skilled recital.

Remembering the many weeks ahead, if not the many years behind, Hamo sought to appease him.

'It's all this intolerable shillyshallying and hanging about in this frightful town when we could be finding out what Magic hasn't done. All these generalities and mutual self-congratulations! These ghastly speeches from officials in country after country. One expected it, of course ... but I couldn't gauge how it would affect me. It makes me antipathetic to the human voice. I disgracefully failed in my attention today to a really excellent piece of work at the University here. You must come with me tomorrow and meet this young chap. He's working on hormone stimulation of some of the green manures. My suspicion is he's held up by lack of equipment. His structural analysis rate is horribly slow. In terms of weeks. And he's go so much material to hand.'

'Analyser?' Erroll asked.

'Archaic really, though he's made ingenious improvements. But enough of that now. I just feel like walking it all off. And I've no intention of taking account of your assignation in the length of my peregrination.'

He sought for a less pompous word, but his attention was confused, because the youth, misunderstanding his gesturing perhaps, appeared to be returning towards them, towards the lamplight and the braziers. Ludicrously, as he knew, he sought to motion him away into the mysterious darkness with a flapping of his hands that he hoped might seem justified by a few flying ants feebly circling one of the sparse street lamps some hundred yards ahead. The gesture's success was partial; Beauty halted, and began deliciously to dawdle; Erroll seemed to take the gesture for a general hysteria brought about by the events of the day.

'Oh, Christ! Trust me to cut capers at the wrong moment. Watton, you've ballsed it all up. I hesitated whether to tell you earlier, Chief. But I felt a bit jokey, so I didn't say anything to-night. I was playing Water Rat along. Not to worry. It's all in the bag. You saw those two saloon-bar type blokes I was chatting up in the University courtyard. Executive types in the Ceylon

Tourist Service. I've fixed it all up. A Chevrolet and *I*'ll do the driving. No need for official cars and Mr da Silva can go and pleasure someone else. And as to Water Rat, we can tell *him* tomorrow just where he can put his long, bare tail. Now don't say ...'

But Hamo could say nothing. His wild gesture had drawn towards him two of the kite hirers surrounded by a small mob of older blazered schoolboys anxious to see what this eccentric, middle-aged tourist giant would do with the black bat Night on the end of his string. Distracted by listening to the comforting words of his loyal, efficient assistant, by keeping in view the uncertainly hovering idyllic swathed-bummed figure, and dismissing the absurd, mistaken offer of a kite, he turned sharply to recognize, as for a moment it seemed, in the two vendors' mock-obsequious smiling, the Danish uncle and another *en travestie* surrounded by a knot of grinning nephews. He reeled back from the malice, caught his foot on a kite string, felt another wind round his ankle, then another round his waist, and more and more, until he realized that he was properly parcelled. A sudden heave brought him to the ground, to lie at last a Gulliver, bound and helpless. Pinched and pummelled by boyish fingers pretending aid, mocked by dark eyes that, lit in the brazier light, were no longer liquid and caressing but snakelike and cunning, confused by alien chatter, Hamo would have felt no surprise, though much dread, if he had been brought (intrusive stranger in this Lilliputian island) before a diminutive yet terrible Jonkheer with crown and sceptre. But he had (and he remembered it with shame as he ached in bed that night in the air-conditioned chill) reckoned without his faithful Erroll who with a ready shove and a well-placed kick and 'Come on there. Out of it!' soon had his employer on his feet again, and had dragooned a couple or so of motley bystanders to support the tall figure, bruised and cut, back to the safe unmocking caverns of the spacious prosaic hotel.

Hamo's body did indeed feel to him a Man Mountain's when he woke the next morning; acres of bruised flesh and jarred bones floated into his consciousness like an endless flat landscape. He exerted every strained muscle, every strained nerve to put behind him present pains with last night's lusts. Two vigorous if painful lengths of the swimming pool did much to help. If they were to stay here many days more, he must make enquiries about squash.

Erroll was already seated in the stately dining-room, relaxed and sated in a cloud of delicious tea scent, when Hamo, painfully refusing himself an easing limp, came to their table.

'What, no pawpaw? You're making a mistake. That's one thing about all this East of Suez – funny how you can't help thinking of it that way even though we've come to it through the Rising Sun – everything not only looks bloody marvellous but tastes it. Everything not human, that is. How are you this morning, Chief? Sure you oughtn't to see someone? Could be there's a British doctor if we rattled our bones at the Embassy.'

Hamo waved aside the solicitude and countered with enquiry about the delights of Room 49. Erroll, with tact and compassion, played it down.

'Oh, fair to middling. Not bad at all.' Then bursting into a grin of sated contentment, 'In fact, bloody good.'

'By the way,' he went on, 'I got talking to a bloke last night in the bar. While I was waiting, you know. Some sort of Scandinavian in the agricultural machinery racket. Seems one has to keep away from the front at night. They're a shocking lot of bastards apparently. Some old boy from Germany, professor or something, was trying to cut a caper with something that had taken his fancy. They lured the poor old thing down to some cave in the rocks. Knocked him about badly. Took all his lolly *and* his clothes. There he was stark naked knocking on the hotel door at two in the morning. Better in this climate than at Southend, but still it took some explaining, I dare say.'

So the uncles, perhaps, *were* fairy godmothers, protective guardians – if it *had* been the uncles, for by the time Hamo had been able to distinguish the real stars of that magnificent sky from the fictive stars of concussion, Erroll's righteous wrath had driven the kite vendors from Galle Face Green. Good uncles, then, or so it might have seemed but for the events of a few evenings later.

Hamo hardly remembered his bruised thigh and compressed ankle, hardly thought to limp, so delicious was the cooling evening, so happily did the Flame of the Forests above them supply all those hot colours which tropical lands need in order to replace the burning sun when it is going down, so cool was the contentment he could gauge in Erroll, so burning the excitement that he knew in his other companion, Mohan Wickramanayake, so pleased was he in his sense of something useful promised. It was hard to believe that the sheer inchoate ugliness of Colombo lay beyond this delightful park through which they were strolling after seeing in detail the young man's lab work – they to their hotel, he to – where did these innumerable professors and students and government officials in all Asian countries go when at last they left their ill-paid labours to return home? What might be disagreeable in the conjecture was happily on this occasion banished by the automatic amino-acid analyser which he had promised to raise heaven and earth (Sir Alec and the Rapson) to get for this clever post-graduate, a promise so splendidly suggested by Erroll, so happily made by himself, so delightedly (no, overwhelmingly) accepted by the young man. Happiness, indeed, had loosened his tongue and he had chattered with captivating coyness far beyond the bounds of his immediate research, so that Hamo found himself listening intently to an account of the contrasting nutritional needs of the highland soils and the lowland soils of the island.

'Of course, Mr Langmuir, Magic has transformed much of this. Nevertheless education is slow and it is wiser to make issues of phosphate to the wet zone farmers, and of nitrogen and potash to the dry, highland farmers only in conjunction with the traditional green manures. And, you know, these old chaps are not always wrong. For example those wild varieties of grass allied to the oryzas which the new young farmers, who are reared on the transformation created by your Magic – *ischaemnon ragosum*, for example, or *fimbristylis milacea* – see as pernicious weeds, the village doctors use them for medicine, and remember we have two universities teaching that very same ayurvedic medicine.' The young man giggled, then changed, as so often, to an earnest tone, 'And again, they are very valuable in fish rearing. And perhaps in the flooded paddy fields the protein of fish … But these things only apply to the *hopeless* cases – lands too minutely divided by some old legal customs or farmed by remote temple

landlords. Much of our land *is*, of course, of this kind. It is difficult to educate where the peasant has no concern. And again
some hopeless *areas* ...'

'*Hopeless* areas?' Hamo questioned so sharply that Erroll
thought, hullo, the maniac's got on his wick. By their names
you can tell them. And truth to tell, though the bloke had constructed some beautiful instruments for himself, this history of
bloody farming was a bit too much for a quiet stroll home. He
must come to the old boy's rescue. But he couldn't break into the
flow.

'I speak of the exceptions, of course. But now that our population is rising – unwisely in my opinion – Magic produces its own
problems of prosperity ... You will excuse my ironies ... the
contrasts are very great between bad lands and good for those
who work them. Some of the wet lands really are not capable of
adequate irrigation. Flooding is too frequent, salinity is too
great, the monsoons too uncertain. And many of the highlands, I
must say, for I come from these parts, are ill-adapted for rice,
too little soil, too close to the rock. You must persuade your
people to be more British, Dr Langmuir, please. America,
Europe – these orientations make for too much coffee drinking.
And *we* have too much tea. "What about a cuppa?" I have
read.' Giggling again for some reason, as they all did.

'You mean then that you're trying to farm lands where Magic
can't be cultivated?'

'Bad lands. Marsh or desert. Hopeless lands. Hopeless people,
I'm afraid. But these are *social* questions ...'

His words were drowned in a sudden high shrieking and a
violent clattering in the air as fifty or more bunches of fruit
came alive on the trees of the little island in the park lake's
centre. Above them, and in all directions, the great bunches
turned to be flapping black leathery wings, red furry bodies,
beady eyes, greedy mouths – hanging grapes had turned to flying
foxes. No one in the park looked up. Mohan Wickramanayake
merely raised his voice.

'There are too many pressure groups ...'

Hamo and Erroll both followed the last black shadow into the
far distance over the town. Hamo muttered and looked down at
the ground, as though he had been personally responsible for the

shame of this hideous flight. Erroll determined to throw off his discomfiture.

'Oh Christ! and I haven't got my bloody Zoom with me. What a perfect kick in the pants for Bela Lugosi. Just look at it. Off they go, thirsty for the slender necks of a hundred blonde virgins. And then look at that old lady over there, or those kids playing football, no bloody notice at all. Virgins come cheap in these spicy isles. Hammer Productions (Inc.) Ceylon must have come under the hammer years ago.'

'They go for the evening's feast upon the fruit and vegetable crops. I am afraid that these are more important to us than virgins.'

'Jesus! Why don't you poison the brutes? Or there's the old remedy of a silver sword through the heart at the crossroads. Complicated and messy but guaranteed effective.'

'We are Buddhist people, Mr Watton.'

The Chief tried to paper over the crack with some question about some weed or other; or was it tact? or was it madness? Because for the next five minutes of so, he seemed to go crackers, with his questions about green manuring. It seems there was a pith plant, *eesti* something *aspera* that would grow in standing water – well, that *was* the news they'd all been waiting for. And now it was weed control; and harrowing which 'Dr Langmuir, you know, is very beneficial for it strengthens the tillering'; a whole fucking Farmers' Hour, as if they hadn't seen enough of paddy fields in the last months to choke your guts up. At last it appeared to be getting on the little maniac's wick, too, for his words came more hesitantly, his giggling ever more irrelevant.

'I am afraid all this bores Mr Watton and I owe him so much.'

'Oh, don't worry about Erroll. It's just his evening thirst coming on.'

They turned into a main road. The sight of the usual bundles of rags preparing for sleep in the doorways of the closing shops came to Erroll as a heaven-sent opportunity to relieve his feelings, on his behalf, on behalf of these poor bloody down and outs, probably untouchables or some such crap.

'Funny country this,' he said, 'the bloody bats take off for a feed just as these poor bastards settle for empty bellies and a night's kip on the sidewalk. Always seem to choose the corners by the main road, too. Must make for a noisy night with all that traffic. You'd think they'd go for those leafy quiet streets among the desirable residences of the Cinnamon what's it Quarter. But there you are – these are social questions.'

He had truly not intended it, but the last sentence came out as an exact imitation of the voice of the Maniac Wick. Oh, well, if he got a two-column Piez and Morris out of them, he hadn't much bellyache coming. And because, after all, in for a penny, in for a pound, he went across to where an old woman and two small kids were settling down in their rags and handed out a chunk of lolly all round.

His only worry was that the Chief would blow his top. 'Manners makyth man' – that it seems was the old school motto. And he never forgot what they'd taught him at school, didn't the Chief. But hearing the well-known voice, all officer, 'I don't think that's necessary, you know, Watton,' he suddenly thought bugger that for a lark. Walking farther up the street to where an old man was spreading a threadbare blanket on a step, he handed out more money. Even remembering things that brought tears to the eyes, he added, 'How's it going, Dad?' Turning back for his expected rocket, he saw at once that he'd properly got on the maniac's wick, for the dark, calf's eyes blazed at him for a moment – maniacally, as you might say. But no Chief!

'Where's Mr Langmuir?'

'He also has the tourists' preoccupation with the beggars of Asia, I think.'

And sure enough there across the road was the Chief's tall figure bent over a youth who stood at the door of an ancient Humber parked outside a grocer's store. Christ! he'd have to watch their steps or Maniac Wick would put too many twos together.

'Unfortunately the boy is a servant and not a beggar. But all alike will seem very poor to a Great English scientist. So, Mr Watton,' and Mr Wickramanayake bowed, 'unfortunately, I have to go to my home. Postgraduate students do not live in the rich Cinnamon Quarter. You will say goodbye to Dr Langmiur for me, please.'

Erroll felt repentant. 'Look,' he said, 'the Chief doesn't praise work easily but what you're doing's really excited him. I'm only a technician so don't bother with me. But I can promise you this

234

that if he says you'll get a new analyser, you'll ... well, he'll bloody well see that you get one with three analysis panels running at once. That's Rothschild stuff.'

Why was he wooing the young bugger?

The young man bowed.

'I wish it were as easy for us to accept gifts as for you to present them. Luckily our bureaucracy protects our pride. It will be a decision of the interdepartmental scientific committee of the Universities. Whether we can accept, I intend to say. The Chairman is Professor Samarasinghe. A very fine scientist and a proud patriot. So we must hope for the best. He will no doubt make the decision known to Dr Langmuir.'

Behind the young Singhalese graduate's retreating back, Erroll could find no more to make than the two-finger sign. 'Up you, mate,' he said.

'Look, Mr Wickramanayake, please don't take any notice of Watton's failure of taste,' Hamo had said earlier when Erroll had so embarrassingly departed on his tour of largesse.

'Mr Watton is generous. He is moved by the poverty of our country.'

'Look here, you know you don't really feel that. The management of your society is your affair. All we can do is to put such skills and resources as we have at your service. But this sort of tourist vulgar gesture ...'

'Charity is a well-established function of Buddhist life ...'

'Yes, no doubt your own. But not this sort of thing. I can only say that Erroll's intention is good. Or at least I think so.'

'Most people from the U.K. think this.'

'Yes, it's exactly that that I want ...'

But Hamo could not really tell what he wanted, except that he knew that what he had just said had been welling up in him during these last weeks. That and lust. Yet really to burden this unfortunate, able young man with the explosion of his emotional tensions was hardly ...

He said, 'You must excuse me ...' Then, on the other side of the road, an old Humber had drawn up. A noise, an event, something that allowed him to look the other way while he recovered his thoughts and found some way of soothing the young man's hurt pride without any further embarrassing intimacy. And He got out ... there had been so many perfect visions in the last months, visions that once seen, had vanished. It seemed strange, then, to encounter a true repeat, a verification. Here was the Fairest Youth he had Ever Seen: 5′ 9″ in height, waist 24, hips 35, chest 30, all that went without saying; but then too, long shapely but strong legs boldly outlined, as he stepped down to the pavement, through the close shape of the sarong, so white, so clean, it was an advertisement for the tight firm buttocks it enclosed, but no flaunting poster, no tasteless television cliché, nor again anything furtive, no 'well-built lad seeks fatherly guidance', rather (this damnable itching lust knew no limits of absurd juxtaposition) a *Times* column insertion, modest, direct – 'well-shaped buttocks with every accompanying elegance, including exceptionally finely moulded, unusual and intriguing face. View any time after six in the evening.'

If only such were true; but the wonderful, half-smiling, near black little marmoset's face, after a moment's provocative return of his stare, was bent in humble passivity to assist a tall, handsome middle-aged lady in the most splendid of blue and silver saris to sail from the car into the hugger-mugger, semi-bazaar, little general stores like an ex-queen or an ageing film star going to her apartment at the Crillon or at Claridges. The wonderful features then set in diminutive footman dignity as he stood to attention by the car door until his mistress returned.

Hamo thought, it was now or never; that in such beauty alone lay escape out of all his problems. Without turning back towards Mr Wickramanayake, he crossed the street.

'Hullo,' he said.

He *knew* himself to be a ludicrous, if not frighteningly grotesque, moustached stork peering down at a gulping little frog (yet there was no gulping, only a dignified somewhat worried frown); but he *felt* it to be a meeting, casual, hands-in-pockets, class-and-creed-forgotten, between two youths, such as long ago somewhere he had somehow missed. He knew with despair; he felt with desperation. But, however class and creed might melt, language divided. There was no answer. With delicious panic he scribbled his name, his hotel, on a page out of his pocket diary and, wrapping it in a fifty-rupee note, folded it into the smooth

skinned, sinewy blue-veined small black fist. There was no delight, no alarm, no anger in the black eyes behind the lowered
sweeping black lashes – only the forehead's frown grew deeper.
And then, at the sound of the shopkeeper calling, the money and
the note were rapidly returned. Hamo could hear Erroll's voice
and the postgraduate's, could sense the bewilderment, feel hovering in the air that word of such horror to all Asian people –
scandal. Now was his chance to withdraw, now especially, as the
lady once again sailed forth with the youth in tow, his arms filled
with piled-high packages hiding the delicious little snub nose,
obscuring the resolute steady eyes, revealing only a worried
forehead and the neat short black hair above. Shopkeepers were
there to open doors and to bow. Incongruous as a decade ago some
Mother Superior (before 'modern nuns'), the stately lady took
the wheel, pressed the starter, the Fairest Youth Ever to be Seen
sat sedate in the back surrounded by the parcels. As the gears of
the (so beautifully polished, so wonderfully washed, no doubt by
those beautiful, wonderful hands) car ground with age, there
sounded another noise, tinkling, loud and ludicrous. With the
cutest of Disney-wisney bell chimes there came round the corner
a two-man pedal-cycled, ice-cream vendor's sales box. For a
second, as the car set off with a bump that shook the stately lady
up in her seat but not out of her stateliness, and set the youth to
holding a dozen or so parcels from sliding to the floor, the frown
disappeared, the eyes lit up with laughter at the ice-cream musical
chime, the bowed lips parted to reveal tiny perfectly white regular
teeth – a miracle happened, in fact, for Hamo, and something
happened in turn to *his* face that he could not remember feeling
before – he supposed it must be a 'broad smile'. He pointed to
the ice-cream cart, and, through the car's back window, he could
see the marmoset's head shake from shoulder to shoulder in a very
deliberate Asian affirmative – but, of course, as usual, all too late.

At least he was determined not to act sourly because fate was so
sour. The two ice-cream sellers, their little tune arrested, were
surrounded by a group of boys of all ages – the blazered and
pocket-moneyed as usual, busy fulfilling their needs, the
saronged, or even the ragged, seeming to get as much pleasure
from the satisfaction of their betters' appetites as if they had in-
dulged their own. Disregarding Erroll's call to him, trusting to

237

some obscure sense of luck, making, indeed, as he was embarrassedly conscious, his first social challenge and experiment, he went over and bought ices and snofrute and lollipops for all the poor and forgotten. There was, no doubt, he must conclude, of the result of the experiment: the lowly found more pleasure in self-indulgence than in the satisfactions of their betters. But none were more satisfied than the vendors, their skinny arms and greedy looks poured blessings on Hamo. It was only when, setting off once again with their maddening little tinkabell tune, they turned to bow their gratitude, that Hamo saw at once how in all probability, perhaps, and given the nature of random action, these grinning (mocking? encouraging?) dispensers of joys to boys were that mischievous Danish uncle and the up-to-any-old-trick other uncle at their little games again. It surely must be so, for their nods and becks, if not their smiles, were so triumphantly European despite all their dhoti drag.

He did not even consider telling Erroll Watton of his decision. He set off at once to follow the gay little tune to whatever gay little end it might lead him.

In fact he had not walked more than a leafy scented street or two of this once ancient spice-merchant's nabob quarter, had passed only one embassy and not more than two consulates, when he turned a corner to see the Ice-cone Wops doing a lively ding-dong trade with a mixed-gendered crowd from the two junior schools of the élite of the district. Mopping his sweating brow with a large silk handkerchief, seizing with relief the opportunity to relax, if only for a moment, his exhausted body, he stood back and watched the scene.

But only for a moment, because the uncles, with awful glee, hailed his appearance by a particularly loud playing of the little tune and an excited address to the school children which led, not to the whole crowd, but to the schoolgirls alone, all knickers and niceness, descending upon him with teasing cries of 'Please treat! Please treat!' To be pinned to the ground by the ladies of Lilliput was a nightmare from which he *must* wake up. He turned to run, then the nightmare turned to My Happiest Dream, for there standing at the open doors of a double garage, standing at the end of a passage beside a carved stone screen of a no doubt sumptuous patio, indeed at the rear of the ancient Humber, was the Fairest Youth, who bowed low, head to the ground, and then, coming to attention, very lightly winked.

Hamo needed no second call. Leaping like a giraffe in slow-motion safari sequence, he was with him in a second; the garage door slid to, and girlish giggles, feminine fingers and avuncular vengeance were alike shut out. Hamo put up his sweating hand to stroke the bristly black hair at the nape of the neck, but the hand was as firmly removed and as firmly held in another, firm, cool, and smooth; by it he was led out through the back of the garage into a narrow, whitewashed, walled-in yard in which stood a pump and bucket. And on into what from outside looked like a lean-to privy or wood shed, but from within, by its mattresses, its small tin trunks, its drawing-pinned portraits of Indian movie stars, its crêpe-paper-edged shelf of articles wrapped in towels, showed clearly as the servants' bedroom. Hamo bent down and kissed the Fairest Youth. His delicious lips tasted unaccountably salty and Hamo was instantly seized with an intolerable thirst. Not even the tense excitement of the emerging naked limbs as the sarong was unwound could fix his attention. He asked for a glass of water; pointed towards the pump, but to no avail. He simply was not understood. To avoid any further delays of bliss, he sought to allay his thirst by the skilful management of swallowing his own spittle.

The coughing fit which ensued brought on such convulsions that the youth, no doubt in alarm, left smiles and frowns alike for an expression of total blank. Then, on a sudden decision, he took the sweat-pouring, scarlet-faced Hamo once more by the hand and led him by a short passage, out of which in an open recess stood the servants' privy, into a large, and even to Hamo's high demands, excellently equipped, spotless kitchen. His choking and the apoplectic heat it generated were soothed and cooled by the mere sight here of the ice-white cookers, the large refrigerator, the washing machine, those very aspects of a modern techno-logical civilization, otherwise vulgar and trivial, which he liked for their hygiene, for their efficiency in a tediously necessary sphere, those which he allowed in his own otherwise quietly machineless home, those which he expected to find in the houses of his friends, those which alone reminded him of laboratories that were far more 'home' than any home to him. But somehow after the yard, the shed and the passage – he had not expected such things here.

Especially not as the setting for a tiny young girl, demure with a neat bun and starched apron, who, like something he had seen once, before he could read, in some picture in his maternal grandfather's set of Dickens (the sole relief on Sunday childhood visits), now bowed before him. Beauty filled a glass at the tap and was about to hand it to him, when the little old-looking girl took it from his hand, got ice from the refrigerator, and, with a look of rebuke to the youth, placed it on a small lacquer tray and handed it to Hamo. Solemn, she bowed again.

'Leela,' she said, and pointing to the Fairest Youth, 'Muthu.'

'Hamo,' he said, and 'Thank you.' Then he added, 'Is it all right for me to be here?' But it was clear that no one spoke English. Indeed this was made plain by Leela, who, evidently in charge, gave some reply in Singhalese and then went from the room. Muthu put his face into his hands and simpered bashfully. In a moment Leela had returned with a glass decanter of whisky from which she liberally spliced Hamo's glass of water. Hamo realized that the odd pair were watching him with hushed expectancy. Looking at them in turn, he knew at once what he must do. He took a great gulp of the whisky and water, then exhaled an exaggerated breath of delight, banged himself on the chest, and said loudly,

'Ah!' and then, 'Ha!'

The response he had intuitively expected came at once. Both solemn onlookers burst into fits of laughter, clapping their hands and rolling from side to side in their glee. It was impossible not to follow their delight, yet, even as tears of laughter and relief ran down his cheeks on to his moustache, even as he mopped them away with his large silk handkerchief, he made overt glances at his audience. No, they were *not* children! not even immature! Hamo Langmuir does *not* like chicken. Beauty, it is true, was the younger, but he must, seen now in full light, have left twenty behind him; and as for little Old-Fashioned Miss, she could have been a stunted twenty-four. His, then, was no wicked unclery. But there was of course childishness of mind as well as childishness of body. He took a considered sip of his whisky, while the shadow of a fresh moral Angst loomed in the distance.

But its threat was instantly banished by alarm, as the sound of a motor-car grinding into the garageway stopped every vestige of fairground glee with which the Man Mountain's antics had been greeted.

Solemnity hurried with the decanter from the room. But Beauty stood tensely at attention by the splendid sink fixture. Hamo made signs that they should take refuge in the bedroom, but the youth might have been Sebastian pinned to the sink by arrows. In any case it was too late. From the yard came a man's voice shouting orders in Singhalese. On the other side, from the patio, a woman called 'Boy! Boy!' in impatient staccato command.

To Hamo's horror he saw that every inch of the Fairest Youth's body was shuddering. His eyes were round, set, expressionless.

Clearly they must not be found together. He made through the kitchen door into the house. He could announce himself as a strayed English tourist, a rare European salesman of encyclopaedias, an admiring if over-impetuous domestic architect, a nostalgic colonial, an astronaut, an immanence – yet none seemed likely. His imagination, as seldom before, leapt into the absurd and the fantastic. He could risk hue and cry by simply rushing past the owners without explanations. He could say that he had mistaken the house for the Ministry of Agriculture or for the Residence of the Professor of Biochemistry, though neither, he knew, was remotely in this area. He could pretend to have been taken with a vomiting attack and to have sought to avail himself of their lavatory, but this, as well as being generally impolite, might involve certain religious taboos that could cause an 'incident'. 'Scandal' – that dread word – seemed inevitable, as he found himself in the vast lavish salon decorated in the most contemporary of styles. There seemed no way out from it save down a seemingly endless covered-way glowing with brightest bignonia creeper. From there came the woman's voice. He saw that if he ran, he would be caught there like some intruder in a harem; if he announced his presence at all, indeed, he must implicate the servants, for either he had come in through their quarters, or they had let him in by the front entrance of the house. Something in the whole situation demanded an operatic aria in explanation, but for this the bathroomly resonant tenor with which on most mornings he performed his repertoire of hymns, songs learned at his prep school relating to England's mariners and the vagabond life of the English highways, or even parts of the Hallelujah Chorus, was surely insufficient. The only operatic piece he could in part at least attempt was Leporello's 'Ma in Spagna' and that would only give the game away. In any case it was for the absent Erroll to sing not he.

Seeing the whole incident as the culmination of a life, now for the first time clearly marked as ludicrous, he felt lightheaded, even lighthearted, but dedicated at all cost to protect Beauty. Yet thumping heart, pulsing temples, stifled breathing were surprising companions to this new exhilaration.

He stifled an incongruous giggle and stood at the back of the deep room in the shadow of an elaborate arrangement of tropical plants in a white painted wrought-iron 'indoor garden'. Let surprise at least remain on his side.

The great glass door from the covered way was slid open impatiently, and a young Singhalese housewife flew into the room, corncraking loud cries of anger at Leela invisible behind her. Her thick black hair was piled high and ornamented with frangipanis and one glowing ruby, her ears and throat glittered with jewellery. Her sari was of a glorious emerald silk touched with gold leaf. There was no puff of air, yet the fringed ends of the long gold-threaded scarf draped over her inviting sweetmeat shoulders rippled slightly as she came in. Everything was light and trembling and airy; but everything was also greedy, cross and pecking. He had seen her, he thought, already as some tropical bird – a roller, a bee-eater, a hoopoe, an oriole – grubbing up, with toss of beak and head, insects from the great lawns that lay between the ancient ruined temples of Anuradhapura or Polonnaruwa, as she now plucked crossly at a cushion here, a curtain fold there, snapped on an electric fan, kicked with her brilliant studded slipper a wastepaper basket that got in her way, never ceasing her craking at the little brown bird that followed her. If women must obtrude these bird images then let them at least keep to demure dunnocks or linnets like Leela; of all detestable things an exotic woman stood highest with Hamo for the attention she drew to woman's form. And above all now, for, looking at this extravagant creature, he was forced to admit, with almost as much a gasp of surprise as of annoyance, that he had seldom seen such a delicate, beautifully modelled face, so delicate a pale skin – a beauty neither wholly denied by the ample feminine rounding of her small breasts and hips, nor wholly spoiled by the petulant, pouting mouth, the flattery-fed nagging voice. Her naked belly was flat, firm and smooth as a youth's, as the Fairest Youth's. Hamo turned his eyes away from it.

'Boy,' she called, 'Boy,' on a cracked contralto note that bid fair to dispel for ever the enchantment, always diminishing in Asia, that once hung around that magic word for him. Her eyes, like most birds', flaunting or faded, were hard round buttons. Even when suddenly she saw the tall unexpected foreigner in the shadow of her salon, she showed no alarm, not even embarrassment, only an annoyance that she might have felt at a film of dust, a light that did not work, or a miscarried telephone call – any failure in the service she expected but clearly did not always receive.

'Yes?' she asked sharply. I'm glad I'm *not* selling encyclopaedias, Hamo thought.

Before he could answer, Leela, a demure apple dumpling to her mistress's triumph of the confectioner's art, stepped forwards and made her little bow.

'This Mrs Jayasekere,' she announced, as though Hamo had been inquiring for the mistress of the house with ruthless importunity. He could have kissed the dumpling on its suety lips, for it must have the most ready address and cunning – but the face was all solemn dutifulness as she turned to the mistress. 'This English gentleman you tell.' She stumbled over the foreign words. 'Dotty Man come.'

'Oh! Dr *Mal*colm! I am *so* surprised. We did not at *all* expect you until next month. How is it that the Ministry has made such a mistake? Where are you staying? Do you wish to stay *here*? Kirsti! Kirsti! Dr *Mal*colm has come. Please sit down. What can it mean? We are going to a party. But our car has broken down. Even a new car. You will come. All will be happy to see you.'

All her self-possession seemed to desert her. Her voice now ran up and down on a wild scale of henlike, housewifely concern that ill accorded with the magnificence of her tropical plumage and her petulant, blasé air. Her smile was so desperate, so near to panic that Hamo began to seek only a way of extricating *her* from his predicament; but then she addressed Leela in Singhalese and her voice lost its anxious crescendos and took on again the short driving note that, even through the unintelligible words, sounded to Hamo like a blunted cudgel.

'And, Dr Malcolm, you have come on an evening when our old servant is out. Only these *young* servants are here. And she gives you no drink, no seat, no fans. Please sit down. Do you like the leather sofa? When Kirsti was in England, he bought it. It was very smart. That was five years ago. But nothing can be imported. So we don't know. Our country people are so ignorant. It is impossible to train them, Dr Malcolm. Kirsti was so surprised at Professor Lamplugh's. There were *no* servants. On Sundays even the Professor took part, washing the plates. It was in Macclesfield. Number 47 Harbour Street. But there is no harbour. Kirsti will tell you. I am not very fond of jokes. Do you know Macclesfield?'

'No. I live in London.'

The metropolitan sound did something to assuage her anxiety, for she spoke in lower tones nearer to her Singhalese speech, and through the sing-song of her English accent there was perceptible the sort of charm once fashionable with his smart great-aunt, Dorothy, Sir James's long-since-dead psychic wife.

'Of course. And *I* live in Colombo. Really, Dr Malcolm, it is too amusing. People from the U.K. ask me, do you know the game reserves – Wilpattu, Yala – elephants, wild pigs, crocodiles, I don't know what else, or the ruined cities? But why should I go to such places to see such things! Of course, I have been to Kandy. And when we were young our parents always took us to the hills, to Nuwara Eliya. It was still the old British season, you know, and a dressmaker to make new frocks for the parades. I was so excited as a little girl. But now we younger people prefer to go water-skiing. Everything is water-skiing now, isn't it?'

'I am a very keen swimmer, but I know nothing of water-skiing.'

'So you like the *old* ways. The old British season. I am afraid only very rich people ride horses here now. All the race courses are closed. Can you imagine anything so absurd? But before we had a mad Government and now this Government is afraid to go back on it. As if our losing money on a horse makes things worse for the peasants. The old people like my parents simply don't understand it. And they're right. Where is my mother? She will talk to you about the old British days.' But now she called, 'Kirsti! Kirsti!' again and, getting no reply, seemed once more to lose her poise. 'The party is at Maisie Goonasekere's. Why didn't the girl give you a drink? What is she doing in here? She should be in the kitchen. They are peasants, you see. They can't learn. Do you believe in women having a hobby, Dr Malcolm? Maisie Goonasekere is starting classes in bonzai. Bonzai is the Japanese flower decoration. Everything is bonzai with her. You will like her. What will you have? Where is the boy – to serve the drinks? This girl should be in the kitchen.' She spoke fiercely to Leela, who retired.

'No really, she was *most* helpful. I've only been here a few moments. The servants looked after me splendidly. I wish mine were as good.'

These words produced yet a fourth mood in his hostess. Indeed Hamo felt astonished not only at her changes of manner but at his own concern to register them. Such must be the painful and continual alertness forced upon any impostor, not the more generalized habit of wary concealment that his private life had bred in him.

She spoke still in her blasé contralto but with some excess of assured ease that made her once again seem at his mercy. He winced as the emotive thought-word pulled him up short – 'mercy', with a stranger and a woman, how much command of himself was he losing?

'So you have servants, Dr Malcolm, like us. That's not the usual old U.K. at all. When Kirsti went to visit Lady Arcott – my father was a barrister when Sir John was Governor here, you know – no servants, poor woman.'

Hamo's dislike for pretension inclined him to deny himself the plural – it felt disloyal to loyal Mrs E. But then one couldn't tell how essential social grandeur was to the imposture, so, throwing in Erroll's faithfulness and the ever-changing daily woman, he acquiesced in the tacit lie.

'But then, of course, you are a great V.I.P.' She looked at him with a teasing look that she clearly hoped would please. 'Everyone speaks of your visit. Even the Minister is afraid. And the students! Will the great man give permission? For them you are the great Inspector, the Inspector General, the Head Man from London. But I am telling stories away from school. You will have seen all this for yourself. But here with us you will have no panics. Only straight business talking. Kirsti! Kirsti! Ah, here is the boy. I shall tell him to fetch my husband.'

Hamo was about to urge her not to disturb Mr Jayasekere, to say that he would return the next day, and so to make his getaway from the ludicrous and potentially harmful embarrassment for good. She was, however, so intent on scolding the impassive Muthu, that his good-byes could get no hearing. So violent was her fury with the servants that some of the frangipani flowers were shaken loose from her hair and her corsage. With a strange mixture of annoyance at Hamo being present at such a predicament and a genuine girlish modesty, she moved into a corner of the room to make all right again. In that instant, Muthu's stern obedience changed to a smile, at once so impudent, so shy and so flirtatious that Hamo knew he could not leave. He must establish himself, even in his fictitious role, so that he could visit the house, make assignations, rescue the Fairest Youth from his bondage. To smack Mrs Jayasekere's face for her disgraceful treatment of such beauty would not, he knew, be helpful in achieving these ends. Yet somehow and immediately aloud he must express his feelings for the boy. Keeping Muthu lustfully though gently in image, he searched among all the horrid contemporary furniture for something he could praise, then he saw suddenly an antique colonial chaise longue of some local wood and canework.

'*That's* a very attractive piece indeed,' he said, and felt relieved of his anger.

'You like the old Burgher furniture? My mother will be so surprised to hear you say that. She wanted to throw it out as rubbish. But I told her, "All that's coming back, Mother." Maisie Goonasekere has started a small factory to make some imitations. The same but more comfortable. And now the great Doctor Malcolm likes Burgher. Do you hear, Kirsti? We must buy some of Maisie's Burgher pieces. Dr Malcolm tells us this.'

But the short, stocky young man in the tight dark suit and the striped club tie appeared to hear nothing. He went straight to the telephone and engaged in a voluble and angry conversation that moved from Singhalese to English and back again. It appeared to relate to the back axle of his car. He spoke so loudly that he could not hear his wife's protestations, although, every now and again, he directed a fierce 'shush' at her. At last he put down the receiver and turned towards them, mopping his forehead in recovery from his exertions.

'Kirsti, why do you not listen? This is Dr *Mal*colm!'

It seemed to Hamo that Mr Jayasekere had indeed been aware of his presence, probably even of his supposed name, but that he had no intention, perhaps insufficient control of his anger, to change his original priorities. Certainly there was a perceptible moment before he registered his amazement, horror and delight at this doctor's presence (was the title medical or academic?).

'Doctor Malcolm! My God! And here was I giving those chaps at the garage a rocket, with a V.I.P. sitting in my rooms listening to all that slanging match. So who will get the rocket now? I think it may be me. And from very high places. But what are you doing here, Sir, after we've said we're honoured to see you and so on and all that?'

'Doctor Malcolm is admiring the old Burgher sofa. It is made of jacaranda. It is a pity that you will not see the jacarandas in flower, Doctor Malcolm. This is not the time of the year.'

'Oh, bother the jacaranda, Jayantha, the question is why has this chap not got a drink? Boy! Boy! So what has the great man decided? No, I know. Ask no questions, hear no lies. What poison do you take?'

Before Hamo could choose this ever-deferred drink, voices sounded from outside the room.

'Why are you back again, Jayantha, what does this mean?' a man's voice, solemn and fussy.

'Is there an accident? I was always afraid of this automatic motor-car,' a woman's voice, shrill and querulous like Mrs Jayasekere's in her panic, but older, and higher in pitch.

The door at the side was opened for a minute or so, and Hamo saw a gentle, elderly, spectacled man in a sarong and what appeared to be his pyjama top; and, more indistinctly behind him, coming from some floor-sweeping lacey garment, the head, yes surely, the splendid Roman matron's head of the lady who had driven Beauty in the old Humber, her black hair now let down and cascading around her noble countenance. Disorder, he felt, must be infectious here to affect *that* stately head. At once the door was shut again, but the effect of this interruption on the younger couple was immediate.

Mr Jayasekere yelled out, 'It is only an adjustment required for the Renault. But I have no time now for adjustments. So we shall take your Humber. At the moment we have business.'

His wife shouted scoldingly, 'Dr *Mal*colm is here. Don't you see, Father? Dr *Mal*colm is here.'

The importance of Dr Malcolm alarmed Hamo; but he was exhilarated. It had never happened to him before to be anyone else; he had never contemplated it. But he had never entered a drawing-room before through the servants' entrance. Leslie's voice came to him, commenting – 'Well, if you *will* make use of the back door . . .' Mr Jayasekere was deep in apology.

'I am so sorry about these interruptions. We wanted an architect-built house. But that is expensive. And so we must adapt this old house with parents-in-law on the top floor. But the old people are often very useful. I am afraid this time you've caught them on the hop. Now, what are you going to have? Whatever's in the house is yours.'

Hamo said, 'I should like the boy,' he paused self-indulgently, 'to get me a whisky.'

'Why did we not receive an announcement of your arrival from the Ministry? Oh, my God! That's this damned business of the servants going away. "Days off" they call it. These young ones don't know how to answer the telephone. I know what it is. That's so like you chaps from the U.K. You have to come to talk over the publication arrangements in a fireside chat. We are not used to that, you know. We have no firesides.' He chuckled nervously, spilling his whisky on his shirt. 'But I like informality. I wish our chaps would use it. No, it's always "The Minister requests your attendance." Stuffed shirt and damned silly. So you'll have a bite with us while we talk things over. That's the informal U.K. way, isn't it?'

'But Dr Malcolm is coming with us to Maisie Goonasekere's. Everyone is there.'

'Everyone! Do you think Dr Malcolm wants to talk business

with Everyone about. Do you want to meet Everyone, Dr Malcolm? No, of course not. You telephone to Maisie, Jayantha, and make the usual apologies and so forth and all that women's rot. The social soft soap, eh, Dr Malcolm? No. Better still, you arrange some food for us, and then shoot off to Maisie's. And take the old folks with you. What do they want resting for now? You're only as old as you feel. Isn't that so, Dr Malcolm? But fix a bite for us first. What do you like? The boy can serve us. Do you feel hungry?'

At the sound of such service, Hamo did feel peckish.

He said, 'No. Really. Well, if you insist. Something rather light.'

Mrs Jayasekere shimmered before him like a humming-bird in search of nectar. 'I'm so sorry that we do not have any pineapple chunks, Dr Malcolm. When Kirsti went to the U.K., my mother thought it would be all cabinet pudding, but at Professor Lamplugh's everything was pineapple chunks. I have no pineapple chunks. Sometimes people from the U.K. like to try Singhalese dishes. Would you like to try a Singhalese dish?'

Looking at the demurely waiting Muthu, who even in servitude was excitingly like a small trapped wild animal, Hamo said, 'That would be delicious.'

'Then I know what we shall do. We shall give you egg hoppers, not rice hoppers, but egg hoppers. And brinjal. Do you like brinjal? Not too hot, of course, the curry. Not a white curry. And then for dessert, what about some buffalo curd with djagaree? Do you know what is djagaree?'

'Oh, my God! Don't worry the poor chap's stomach with all that stuff. Besides the cook is out. Now you see what happens by listening to your Maisie – "Everyone is giving the servants a day off."'

Mr Jayasekere's imitation took him from his throaty Welsh rumbling to a note higher than his wife had struck in her worst confusion. But she was clearly not to be put down where etiquette and hospitality were in question.

'Leela can cook it.'

'Oh, no, no, no.' Her husband groaned facetiously, he reminded Hamo of a long-forgotten ragging of a weak form-master at his prep school.

'I know,' his wife clapped her hands. '*Mother* will cook it for him. Mother! Mother!'

Into the room came the stately matron, dressed now in the most significant crimson sari, her shining ebony hair piled higher even than her daughter's beneath drapes of black tulle spotted with gold leaf. Her voice when she spoke was light as a young girl's, but her words demanded full attention, for they enlarged his pretended self in a peculiarly unexpected religious direction.

'If we had been Roman Catholics, you know, Doctor Malcolm, my son-in-law would not have needed to ask you such favours. But we are not. We are Buddhists. So we can go only to Bihar. But why should we go to Bihar? We are not Indians. All there is Hindu. At Kandy we have the Sacred Tooth. Have you been to Kandy? It is very much liked. And Kataragama, too, we have. A very holy place. But there you must take sleeping bags.'

'Oh, never mind all that, Mother.' Mrs Jayasekere forestalled what was obviously going to be an angry reaction from her husband. Her own irritation with her mother flowed over into Singhalese that had a note, to Hamo, much the same as that she had used in addressing Muthu and Leela. However, it worked.

'Mother will make you a fine egg hopper. That is settled.'

'Please, really, something quite light.'

'I don't know what is light,' the older lady was definite. 'Is a hopper light? Perhaps then only the sweet for Dr Malcolm.'

'Mother, sweet is a bad word,' her son-in-law corrected her, 'I remember in Lyons tea rooms, the waitresses are always saying "Two sweets coming up."' Once more his voice rose to awful heights. 'But Lyons is for clerks and typists and accountancy students. Dessert is now what they say, isn't it, Dr Malcolm?'

Before Hamo could answer, the plump elderly father, dressed now in dark trousers and an olive-green buttoned cardigan, and also, wearing a club tie, but differently striped from his son-in-law's, ambled towards him.

'Allow me, Sir. Mr Dissawardene. The young lady's father. I believe, Sir, that I have read that dessert is an Americanism. But I cannot find whether Americanism is the common speech of the U.S.A. or implies only the words borrowed from the American speech by the British. What do *you* say, Sir?'

'Well,' said Hamo, 'actually I say "pudding".'

Remembering suddenly the laughter that had greeted his 'gun room' on that last evening at Zoe's, he looked around in vain for a smile. Everything was, as Mrs Jayasekere might say, blank consternation. But he reckoned without the matron's girlish toughness. With infinite shyness and downcasting of eyes, she said firmly: 'Buffalo's curd is *not* pudding, Dr Malcolm.'

'Well, whatever it is, get us a bowl, Mother. We'll keep the Great Man company. And plenty of djagaree on your famous sweet.' He mimicked her voice on this last contemptible word.

'That sounds delightful.'

'Quite marvellous, doesn't it?' His hostess was back in her most social role. 'Imagine! An impromptu supper with Dr Malcolm! Maisie Goonasekere likes everything impromptu. But she is on the telephone for days beforehand telling us all about it.'

Hamo found himself smiling across to her in complicit fun about this ubiquitous Mrs Goonasekere's hypocrisies – she might have been Zoe in less serious mood.

The splendid matron's words were downright.

'Maisie Goonasekere has a very disagreeable voice. I do not understand why she uses the telephone so often.' Then turning to Hamo, she said gnomically, 'You have broken the joke then, Doctor Malcolm. Jayantha will be able to get to Harrods without visiting Lourdes. We always make a joke, you know, "the Roman Catholics must go to Lourdes before they can go to Harrods". But now we shall not need that joke.'

She offered him her laughter as an unintelligible tribute, as she hustled Muthu ahead of her into the kitchen.

There was such an embarrassed silence that Hamo felt he would be driven by the sheer tension of it into saying at last, 'I'm afraid I don't quite understand.' And who knew to what unmasking of imposture even so negative an assertion of his state of mind might lead?

He was saved by the old gentleman's long years of legal tact. Indeed it was clear that both his daughter and his son-in-law were looking to Mr Dissawardene to release them from whatever net they felt had been thrown over them by the matron's inexplicable words.

'Doctor Malcolm.' The retired barrister stood before Hamo in suppliance, nevertheless he did not speak until he had taken out a piece of chamois from his spectacle case and had slowly cleaned each lens of his tortoise-shell rimmed glasses – Hamo supposed it was a vestigial gesture from his legal days, a means no doubt of unsettling an important, recalcitrant witness by delay.

'Doctor Malcolm, how is it possible for a Roman Catholic to be a Freemason? In my encyclopaedia I find that the Freemasons accept only the Great Architect. What, in your opinion, is the Great Architect, please?'

'I have no religious convictions, I'm afraid, and I know nothing about Freemasonry, though I don't think Roman Catholics *are* allowed to be Freemasons.'

'Arthur da Souza *is* a Roman Catholic, *and* a Freemason.'

Hamo bowed to fact. The silence took over again. Then bravely and doggedly Mr Dissawardene resumed the hearing – this time he coughed and fully cleared his throat before speaking. Hamo still had the impression that these gestures were as much aggressive as defensive. An impostor's role is not a happy one.

'In my encyclopaedia there is a cross-reference from Freemasonry to Rosicrucianism. In the old British days here, there were many important people in Ceylon from the U.K. who were Freemasons – Sir John Arcott, Mr Avery, Major Reith, Mr Justice Carpenter. But I never heard that these gentlemen were Rosicrucians. Why is there this cross-reference?'

'I really don't know. I expect because they're both secret societies.'

'These noble old chaps were very open-hearted, sincere men, not at all secretive.'

Hamo felt rebuked. He must also have looked it, for Mr Dissawardene said, 'I think, Doctor Malcolm, you are saying to yourself, what is the old fellow driving at?'

He murmured, 'No, no.'

'Father, Doctor Malcolm's finding all this listening thirsty work, poor chap.'

'Kirsti, I am talking seriously with this gentleman on things that trouble me. Not money and government licences. Let Jayantha give him another whisky and don't disturb us.'

Silently Jayantha did as she was bid; and Kirsti made no more protest than to squirt the soda loudly into his own whisky.

'I am a Buddhist, Doctor Malcolm. We have our Way. But now here in Ceylon there are confusions. I don't speak of all the mad chaps with their strikes and violence. But even amongst the bikkhu, saying foolish things to the village people. And then I look back and regret the wicked British. I was proud to serve under Sir John and to plead before Mr Justice Carpenter. A white face like a mask. Seeming asleep. People laughed. A judge for *Punch*. But I remember him. He was very quick. His tongue like a chameleon's. But then what can we learn from you now? Everything seems confusion in the U.K. also. And then I remember Sir John and Mr Justice Carpenter were Christians and also Freemasons. It was C. of E., not Roman Catholicism. But even so it is difficult to understand. So I must ask – was it *always* confusion? Perhaps I remember only rosy pictures because I am old. So I consult the encyclopaedia. And the encyclopaedia is confused.' He looked sadly at Hamo, and then, as though apprehensive of his reaction, or, perhaps, of the impatient movements of his daughter and son-in-law, he spoke suddenly in a jaunty tone. 'Anyway, keep in touch, ask questions. Read books. That's the recipe against old age. That's what the new chaps tell us. The geriatric science. Are you familiar with the geriatric bigwigs, Sir?'

To forestall any harsh words from the young couple to this old man who stood before him, confused and pathetic like some old Chelsea pensioner in mufti, he said, 'I think perhaps a general encyclopaedia is insufficient for your needs. An encyclopaedia of religion, for example, might give you more detail. The *Britannica* is excellent, of course, but . . .'

'Oh, I do not use the *Britannica*.' Mr Dissawardene looked guiltily towards his son-in-law and said a little wistfully, 'Though I have an old set from my student days upstairs in my apartment. No, of course, I use the Dugong Encyclopaedia.'

Mr Jayasekere said with hearty unease, 'Good Heavens, Father, Doctor Malcolm doesn't know the Dugong.'

But some counterfeiter's sense of guilt warned Hamo that here was hot money.

'I know *of* it very well.'

Mr Jayasekere jumped up from his chair, hurried into another room, and, returning, dropped a heavy book on to Hamo's lap.

'There you are, Doctor. See for yourself. A volume chosen at random. So I think you can say, "no faking", eh? Did I ever tell you, Jayantha, of the conjurer I saw at Macclesfield? Lamplugh engaged him for a children's party. The tricks were very poor. We should be ashamed of them here. But the man's talk was brilliant. They call it patter. "No faking" they say.'

Hamo said, 'I haven't seen a conjurer since . . .'

'Oh, no, no, please, Doctor Malcolm. Read the book. I am talking so that I don't distract, so that I don't seem to be breathing down your neck. Otherwise I should seem to be a salesman. Also I am nervous. "Here it is at last. What will he think?" '

'But Doctor Malcolm *must know* the Dugong work or he will not be here.'

'Ssh! Ssh! Let the chap browse, Jayantha. Now, Father, I wish you had heard this *patter* as they call it . . .'

Hamo opened the book at random. He forced himself to read the blurred print: 'CAMEL: We are not surprised when this ungainly beast claims the title of Ship of the Desert, for the camel may make another boast . . .' But the boast he never understood, for Mrs Dissawardene appeared at the kitchen door, behind her the shadowy shapes of attendant servants and the clatter of trays.

'Doctor Malcolm. I have brought *bees*' honey as well as djagaree. Perhaps Doctor Malcolm likes *bees*' honey I thought . . .'

'Violet, Doctor Malcolm is reading the encyclopaedia.' The old man's husbandly rebuke was firm, kind and effective. It brought the stately matron to so sudden a halt that those behind had no time to halt with her. She must indeed have received so sharp a dig in her well-corseted waist that she was thrust forwards absurdly. She was aware of the loss of dignity for she turned in anger upon the servants behind her.

'This boy is very bad,' she began, then she recovered her sense of the high occasion, 'Albert,' she asked her husband in a penetratingly considerate whisper for the benefit of Hamo, 'what does Doctor Malcolm think of the illustrations? Everybody is praising the illustrations.'

Hamo, turning over to the shiny thick-papered photography a few pages forwards, saw a misty over-exposure, a blur out of which two crescent-shaped objects vaguely loomed. Imagining

Erroll's scorn, he decided at once that he could answer no more questions, solve no more problems, encourage no more promises, chide no more incompetence, unravel no more knots, waste no more anger or compassion, indulge no more lusts. He would get up and leave this house at once, with honourable discharge; calling for a napkin and bowl at the hotel, he would wash his hands of it all – Ceylon, South-East Asia, the developing countries, the Third World – all the things without which his father had been perfectly able to live an upright life in Perthshire and die an upright death at Arnhem. He would return to England tomorrow.

He looked up from the blurred pale hemispheres of the photograph to the view of two deliciously firm buttocks bent beneath their white sarong over the dining table, as Muthu arranged the bowls of buffalo curd for their delight. Looking again to the photograph the blurred shapes took on another meaning too delicious to accept the caption: 'Camel's humps: On a long journey some Arab nomads allow themselves the luxury (!) of a pitcher of camel's milk (!!).' Ah well, the encyclopaedist was not alone in finding foreign customs strange. He allowed himself the pleasant prurience once more of sweeping his eyes from Beauty's clothed buttocks to their imagined nakedness in the blurred camel's humps.

'This photograph of a camel is quite delightful!'

Something in the warmth of his tone released all the pent-up hopes and conjectures of the family he had invaded.

'Photolithotype on a rich, thick cartridge paper,' said Mr Jayasekere, attempting an easy professional insouciance, but he collapsed into a schoolboy's delighted smile. 'So you've got some good marks for the Dugong Press! Your visit is one of friendship then. I bet the Minister didn't want you to come. And the Permanent Secretary chap – "Mr Jayasekere, I must inform you that the Government does not favour the granting of exclusive licences to private enterprises." "What the hell did we get rid of the socialists and Mrs B. and that lot for, then?" I asked him. "Mr Jayasekere, the new Ceylon will not be built upon cynicism but upon co-operation." It will be built upon hard work and profit making, I told him. Did you meet the chap?'

'No. I have met none of the officials nor the Minister.'

'You came here without seeing the Minister! Kirsti, do you hear? Doctor Malcolm has snubbed the Minister! You are my idea of a hero, Doctor Malcolm.'

Looking at the light of admiration in Mrs Jayasekere's now suddenly wildly lively eyes, Hamo feared that her excitement might prove orgasmic and that her orgasm would be in honour of himself. He was relieved when her father rebuked her.

'The ministers in our government are sometimes foolish, Jayantha, but they are good men. They are steering our country through stormy waters. Steer the ship through stormy waters – is that a good phrase, Doctor Malcolm? I think it was used by Sir John in his parting address, but I don't remember such things exactly now.'

Mrs Dissawardene came to support her husband's authority. 'The Minister's wife is Winnie Wijelawala. She was at school with me. A fat girl but a *good* girl. The Wijelawalas are a *very* good family.'

Mrs Jayasekere looked for support from her husband, but he had gone from the room. She contented herself by saying, 'Doctor Malcolm, I take you for my champion.' And she repeated her fiery, hero-worshipping look.

Hamo's embarrassment was moderated by the return of her husband who handed him another heavy volume of the encyclopaedia. With a well-manicured finger he indicated a passage for Hamo to read. It was headed DEGREES, University – subheading, Ceylon, and read, 'At present the University of London has unfortunately withdrawn the granting of external degrees to students in the Universities of Ceylon. Their decision, however, is under reconsideration. Enlightened opinion in Singhalese educational circles is pressing for the restoration of the external degrees both in the sciences and in the sister arts so that the island may take her place beside other lands in the rapidly growing technocratic world of today. Parties of the Left, however, playing upon the nationalist sentiments of their countrymen and seeking to confine the outward-gazing students to the narrow confines of a so-called "Asian" culture, are opposed to the said restoration. One specious argument – that of the supposed high cost to the island's hard-pressed economy of foreign text-books – may easily be met by the almost limitless expanding potentiality of Ceylon's indigenous publishing industry (see PRINTING, Asia – Ceylon)'.

'So, Doctor Malcolm, there is our back line volley. Now the ball is in your court, please.'

'The buffalo curds are served. Hurry up to table.' Mrs Dissawardene gave this order with mock severity that involved much coy laughter; but also with an air of routine which suggested that she supposed it a facetious remark inseparable from the etiquette of all dining. She added, 'Nowadays men are always eating when they are doing business. Do you have the Chamber of Commerce and the Round Table in the U.K., Doctor Malcolm? When Albert was at the courts, the Chamber of Commerce dinners were often so very late.'

Her husband looked at her sternly, affectionately, over his glasses. 'Such things started in the U.K., Violet. The men know how to make their escape there.' Then more lightly he added, 'They also have the Buffaloes, but I don't think they enjoy your excellent buffalo curd.' He turned to Hamo to motion him to the table. 'But perhaps you call this now a working luncheon. Can you have a working luncheon in the evening, Doctor Malcolm?' He looked at the table. 'There are three places, Kirsti. I shall not eat however.'

'The third place is for Jayantha, Father. After all, if Doctor Malcolm is happy with the proposals, she will be our partner.'

'Yes, Albert, Jayantha will not need to go to Lourdes to buy at Harrods. Or at Jaegers. If Doctor Malcolm agrees with Kirsti.' Mrs Dissawardene paused in her scolding preparation of Muthu's setting down of the innumerable small bowls that were accessory to the curd. She bowed her noble head at Hamo with a modest but friendly smile.

Mrs Jayasekere almost bellydanced as she preceded Hamo to the table.

'I do not know what Maisie Goonasekere will say when she knows that I also am to be a business woman.'

'The first rule of business, Jayantha, is to be silent and discreet. Even for a woman.'

'Kirsti is angry with me, Doctor Malcolm. Are you also angry? You will not want me for a partner now.'

'Doctor Malcolm is not to be a *partner*, Jayantha. He is to be a patron.'

'Aren't you going to eat all these delicious things with us?'
Hamo, seeking to distract, asked first of Mr Dissawardene who
stood by the door like a *maître d'hôtel*, and then of Mrs Dissawardene, who stood beside his chair like a formidable waiter.

'No, Sir. My wife and I do not eat in the evenings. But we
wish you every success in your generous espousal of my son-in-
law's cause. May I say "espousal"? Or is there perhaps some
offence in the term?'

Hamo did not answer. He did not feel at that moment anything either of quaintness or pathos in the old man's question;
nor indeed in any of the family. On the contrary their remarks as
they jostled him gently to the table appeared each in turn to shut
a gate to his evasion of the fraudulent scene – gates which he had
sought by his silence to keep half-opened. Only Muthu's presence,
stiffly standing to attention by the kitchen door, kept him in his
seat; and even that might have been insufficient had not the boy
sought unnoticed to scratch the back of his right calf with his left
foot. The small manoeuvre so whetted Hamo's lustful appetite
that he surrendered himself for the moment to whatever Dr
Malcolm's apparently undercover activities entailed; but he re-
tained enough of his senses unheightened to seek to make sure
that whatever he was letting himself in for gave him some promise of return.

'Now, Mrs Dissawardene,' he said, 'I'm not going to have
you waiting upon me. It isn't our way in England and I shan't
enjoy your delicious dishes if I know I'm being watched.' Pressure, he could see, was teaching him a whole new manner of
talking to women.

'But you *must* be *waited* upon.'

'If you insist, let the boy wait on me. It'll remind me of my
childhood days when we still employed a page.' He gave a small
laugh he had never heard himself use before – the apologetic
laugh of those who have seen better days. His hosts, knowing
none of his days good or bad, made no comment. His imagination, too, was stimulated by adventure. 'It's pleasant to meet the
old ways again.' As he said it, he thought that there *had* been
somewhere, even if only in dreams, some such happiness in his
childhood – 'Master Hamo' at the table, but 'Race you up the

bank, Hamie,' as they ran, two naked lads, from forbidden bathing in Farmer McGregor's stream.

Mr Dissawardene looked quizzically over his spectacles. 'I think that with your liking of the old-fashioned ways you must have some troubles with these radical rascals in the U.K. nowadays, Doctor Malcolm.' But he gave orders in his soft but definite Singhalese and soon Muthu's beauty had replaced the Matron's stateliness behind Hamo's chair.

It's amazing what you can get away with if you try. Hamo got away with a good deal of covert stroking of the most beautiful thighs in the world and even a pinch or two of the most beautiful buttocks; the most beautiful knees, in their turn, caressed on occasion the small of his back, the most beautiful hand gently once or twice flickered across the nape of his neck. All this he got away with, perhaps because he so astonished his hosts by the amount of food he consumed.

'Bee's honey *and* djagaree! Doctor Malcolm is eating the candied guava! Do you like the plantains? They are very big. We usually eat them as vegetables. No, please help yourself to more of the shredded coconut. I am so pleased that you like it. Doctor Malcolm likes the shredded coconut. He has had *three* helpings.'

But, in for a loquat, in for a bread fruit. The excitement of the unknown increased as much Hamo's appetite as his lust; indeed he hardly felt the two as separate when opening his seventh mangosteen he sucked the delicious sticky white coating from the pulpy seeds. And he learned, indeed helped to outline, the shape of the role he had taken on.

As Doctor Malcolm, Secretary and Representative of the London University Examination Board, he could and did safely say that the Board's inclination, no, let it be put more strongly, its earnest wish was for the restoration of external degrees of the University to candidates from the Universities of Ceylon in the nearest possible foreseeable future. Candidates, let it be understood, who satisfied the examiners. That went without saying. A certain sternness, a certain reserve, a certain insistence on academic standards seemed to him his best bargaining counter; and then again it appeared impossible to move completely from one personality to another without carrying some of one's personal luggage – intellectual rectitude, at least, and a concern for the good name of British Institutions, these were as indispensable to him as his dressing-case and his hair brushes. Whatever the other Doctor Malcolm might dispense with in professional decorum (and the whole affair appeared to be in some degree shady), Langmuir-Malcolm was to be a stickler for correct form. The man was, after all, a representative of English learning, even science, after his fashion (although the administrative fashion was hardly of the most elegant). Nevertheless he found himself, when Mr Jayasekere told of the Minister's concern, in the event of a resumption of London degree-giving, that text-book supply should be left open to the bids of British educational publishers, despite all the claims to efficiency, local knowledge, and, above all, saving of foreign currency that the selection of a prominent native publisher would entail, astonished, even a little (though as a foreign visitor, cautiously) shocked at such an – unpatriotic was hardly for him to say – but certainly unnecessary, and he must say, yes, frankly misguided attitude. If as was being said (by Mr Jayasekere, in fact) the Minister feared that, without commerce with the English publishers, the University would not be interested in the deal, he could say at once and with a good deal of hauteur (and he did so) that the Minister sadly misunderstood the independent standing of the English Universities. Indeed he must altogether deprecate the use of the word 'deal' which, unknown in academic vocabulary, totally failed to describe the independent decision of the University which would be made solely in the interests of Singhalese education, or, he would go further and say, global education.

As soon as he had said it, he wanted to recede; to find himself using Sir Alec's vocabulary threatened some dreadful take-over by his new and administrative personality. But he concentrated on the positive side of things: it was evident that a Singhalese publisher, provided that one could be found that could undertake so considerable an enterprise (and it looked as though one could) was the obvious solution to what was probably the one single most important factor in a complex decision. That, indeed, had been the thinking behind his surprise visit.

If he had not been excitedly resisting an absurd giggle as Muthu, for a daring second, tickled his armpit, he would have got up and fled before Sir Alec entirely took him over. He could not, of course, commit himself immediately, but he would venture to say that he was deeply impressed by what he *had* seen of the – he must look to see how it was spelt – work of the Dugong Press, such a good and easily memorable name. He had not as yet had an opportunity of visiting the other presses. ('Oh, you are going to the *other* publishers, Doctor Malcolm. Who will you go to? You will not *like* them. There is Aloysius da Souza. Not at all a smart man. Their house is very vulgar. They live in Dambulla. That is not a smart ...' 'Oh, my God, Jayantha, don't rock the boat. Of course he must see the other chaps' work. That's only trade etiquette. Justice must be *seen* to be done and so forth and so on.')

Exactly, and Langmuir-Malcolm's main idea, it seemed, was to be around a good deal, have a look at what people were doing, particularly, if they could bear it, drop in on the Jayasekeres themselves for a run-over of various blueprints, 'talking the thing through' would perhaps be the way one could put it (it was certainly the way Sir Alec would have put it). If he could browse about a bit among the Dugong publications, familiarize himself with them, so that he could put the best possible case to the University and to the Minister when he did eventually make his arrival public – but browse *here* in their lovely home, not at the publishing house if Mr Jayasekere would not mind leaving a representative selection of publications here at his house. He feared he was sounding sybaritic but this *was* a working *holiday*, if that expression could be used, and just to relax, say in this attractive lounge or under this beautiful creeper, to come and go without fuss, was that taking a terrible liberty? (Mr Dissawardene spoke from his attentive *maître d'hôtel* position by the patio door – 'So you are going to snoop, Doctor Malcolm.' 'For heaven's sake, Father, this is a business talk.' Sadly the old man went upstairs as though to convey a complaint to the chef.) Mrs Jayasekere really mustn't give a thought to his being there, to seek to entertain him or anything of that kind or he wouldn't consent to come; the boy could see to his wants, which were simply told. In any case the last thing his beautiful hostess would wish was to bother her head with all this business.

As soon as he had said it he realized that his role-playing had run away with him ... Sure enough the shapely mouth that had followed his every word with open delight now closed in tight chagrin, the wide sparkling dark eyes went small, and tears trembled on the long eyelashes. And out at last it came – from a sob-trembling Mrs Jayasekere, and from her worried but now defiant husband, with occasional excited glosses from her Matron Mother.

At first he was doubtful, definitely doubtful, so deeply had he sunk into his other self. After all, if Mrs Jayasekere were to be visiting England, how could he be making sudden descents upon this island where only Muthu was beautiful? But then the reality of the situation came to him. And really it did seem an impossible situation for a young and elegant woman – no possibility of leaving the country except on business or pilgrimage, and the Buddha's birthplace so far from Harrods. Indeed particularly unfair that her Roman Catholic friends should window-shop the whole length of the Brompton Road simply because some cretinous peasant girl had suffered from religious delusion at Lourdes. Of course, such a deprivation was not comparable with the hopeless cases, the hopeless lands, the dispossessed, and they were no doubt, as all told him, a mere handful beside the teeming urban derelicts that he would see if he visited Calcutta or Bombay. Probably some economic purist would show a justifying connection, some point about scarcity of foreign exchange, but he distrusted such bureaucratic red tape, he had never permitted the Sir Alecs of England to disrupt his work, why should a Singhalese Sir Alec impose his priggish nonsense upon this harmless, elegant woman?

'Imagine, Doctor Malcolm! What can it do harm for Ceylon if my daughter visits Harrods? Harrods is such a beautiful place. I was there in 1937.'

And really it seemed a sound point – his own mother, he remembered, had laid great store by her Harrods account, and, although that was hardly a recommendation, his father had started the account for her so that it must be the thing to do.

'Perhaps, Doctor Malcolm, eh, you think that the publishing

chaps in the U.K. won't like to deal with a pretty woman? That won't be the British way. But I can promise you that Jayantha has a very good head for business.'

And here Langmuir-Malcolm surprised himself with his sociological knowledge, for he told them that, on the contrary, the greater part of publisher's representatives, at any rate the leading executives in the major firms, were indeed young women. As he said it, the claim seemed not improbable, for certainly he found no wish to associate what must be so very dreary an activity with the magic words 'young men'. Finally, then, all was concluded, or rather left pending, on the happiest of notes.

And now Muthu's touch as he covertly stroked Hamo's arm felt listless, suggested boredom. Hamo himself was aware of rumblings in his stomach and of extreme heat after all that food and the anxiety of all this role-playing. A tightness of his abdomen that told him he should defer more feasting to another day. He could leave now with the prospect of days of exciting and probing experiment – a week at least, he hoped, until the inevitable (but really rather irrelevant) intrusion of this no doubt upright (he would judge no one unheard) but surely bumbling administrator. ('Once aboard the lugger and the girl is mine,' he remembered his father to have sung in the bath – a singing he had inherited.) Himself he need never, thank heaven, shake hands with his double or put to the test how bumbling his conduct of this tedious affair might eventually be, for he was due to leave Ceylon, to see the effects of Magic in the paddy fields of India, in ten days' time. If, as now seemed likely, his inspection of the working of his Magic in this island's fields might well have to be curtailed by the demands of this new chivalric errand – for he fully determined that the Fairest Youth should not be left in such unseemly servitude when he departed – he knew that he was secretly relieved at a respite from any further discovery of how often the great white intentions of his Magic seemed to have worked the blackest of spells upon so many beneficiaries. He said good evening to them all, with a smile of courteous thanks to the boy for his service, and particularly enjoined upon them to keep the news of his arrival a close secret for the next few days.

The goodbyes among the white datura trumpets opened to the clearest moonlight by the garden gate were as warm as the hot night air. Mrs Jayasekere in her delight found a touching, un-affected directness that was winningly incongruous with her glamour.

'Kirsti, I do not think I have ever been so happy. I shall go to Maisie's now and I shall be nice to *every*one because I am so happy. And I shall not make you come there, Doctor Malcolm, because I think you are a shy man. Imagine, Mother, the great Doctor Malcolm is shy. And I think you are shy of women, too. But do not worry when you come to the house, you will never see us. It will be like in the houses of the Muslims,' and she laughed at the absurdity, 'we shall be there to look after you, either Mother or I, but you will never *see* us.'

And Mrs Dissawardene, giggling now with real girlish happi-ness for her daughter, said, 'I shall be no more than a lizard on the wall. A very big lizard you are thinking. But I can be very quiet, Doctor Malcolm, even more quiet than a lizard. And like a lizard I shall see everything. Is the boy giving Doctor Malcolm what he wants? *I* shall see.'

Here, indeed, as his delights and hopes crumbled before him, was a facer! Yet, driven on by the tantalizing near-farness of the taste of perfection, Hamo's brain worked with a rapidity that he had not known since the last stages of Magic in what now seemed years ago. What were the essentials that would bring the experi-ment at last to consummation? Propinquity, distraction, darkness, absorption. He would rely on Muthu for the ravishing rest. In that momentary intuitive flash, which is so often the culmination of a hidden but no doubt severe series of logical deductions, he saw that, with a little judicious preparation, he could still enjoy if not the week's leisurely browsing he had hoped for, then at least an hour's greedy gobble that, he hoped, would slake his lustful thirst for ever. The new scheme, too, as it formed in his mind, had the additional advantage of giving satisfaction to the faithful and shamefully neglected Erroll Watton.

He turned to the Jayasekeres.

'You know,' he said, 'I am a little concerned that I shall have so little opportunity of knowing the arguments that will be used *against* the re-introduction of our London degrees . . .'

Roger Sudbury stood in the corner of this elegantly furnished salon (a little too 'smart' for his old-fashioned bachelor taste) and made himself as unobtrusive as his exceptional height allowed him. He felt most beholden to his chance travelling companion, Charlie Keaton (the name worried him a little), for securing an invitation for him, a simple tourist, to this charming Singhalese home – hardly typical of Ceylon as a whole, of course; but, no doubt, representative of the lives of a privileged few. He could not say that the prospect of Keaton's cinematic showing appealed to him, although in all politeness he *had* said otherwise. He was not a great cinemagoer, not indeed a cinemagoer at all. But still the chap was clearly master of his art and the subject, being world travel, especially Ceylon, would help to round off, possibly to sharpen his own impressions of the island during his all too short a stay.

Frankly, however, the gathering itself was of more interest to him. It appeared from what this chap Jayasekere had said of himself – extraordinarily kind of him to allow an unimportant passing tourist like himself to tag along with the evening's notability ! – that he was rather a distinguished fellow in both the business and the cultural worlds of Colombo. The guests were an interesting crowd: made up it appeared of all sorts of people who were by no means friendly to British, indeed to European influence. Buddhists, gentle fanatics so one was told, with a sincere belief that they had a way of life to offer to the world far more harmonious than the restless technologies of the West; some poets, dramatists, and chaps of that sort, who wanted to go back to their own deep roots, their own fascinating legends, to free their thoughts and sensibilities from what they saw as the distorting medium of the English language that colonialism had imposed on them; some who were not so hostile to Western thought of *another* kind – chaps who looked to Moscow – but perhaps only as a means of cutting their Western cables, of rendering Asian what the Kremlin crowd had to teach them, as Peking perhaps had done, indeed Jayasekere had hinted that there were not a few who had visited the Celestial City at Mao's invitation (for foreign travel for the Singhalese was difficult in the ordinary way); and then, predominantly, no doubt, chaps like the smoothfaced stout man dressed in some sort of national dress, though not the Buddhist monk's saffron, softly but firmly making his points to a respectful little group by sweeping gesticulations of his glass of orange juice – nationalists, for whom – and however little we had succeeded in leaving behind that impression, this was surely what the best of our colonial men had intended – things Singhalese were as vital and revered as the English way of life still was to a dwindling crowd of fogies like himself at home. (Sudbury was becoming much easier to find than Malcolm had been.) Not probably the easiest crowd for a shy Englishman to meet. He envied his travelling companion, Keaton, whose cheery Cockney voice he could already hear across the room, ribbing the men a little and giving the ladies a little heart's flutter.

'No, no, ta all the same, but I use handshots a lot, you know, so I have to keep off the booze, can't afford to have the shakes.'

Surely he was growing more traditionally Cockney as the days went by. To their hostess it was clearly all unintelligible, but something in her distinguished guest's look clearly appealed to her – or was it the way he had said 'handshots' – it was to be hoped not.

'I'm afraid I have no beautiful movie stars for you, Mr Keaton,' she said.

'That's all right, darling. I'm not choosey.'

Which wasn't even true – ah well! He could not suppress satisfaction that his voluble Cockney companion should be playing his part with such total and pleased self-absorption when all the while he, the author, was not only acting – better perhaps because less accustomedly – but directing as well. Surely it would have delighted Perry and Zoe, such unguessed-at powers; Perry certainly, Zoe perhaps not with her puritan conscience. There were no scientists present, he understood from Jayasekere, unless it were one of these doctors who practised native medicines which had found its way now even into the University curriculum. Frankly, it had surprised him that so Western a chap as Jayasekere should have known so many people eminent in the anti-Western camp; but his host had explained that, politics being so unstable in the island, it was necessary to maintain a foot in all camps. Business, he said, was business. Nor, it seemed, were many of these apparently most vociferous opponents of the West entirely closed to similar considerations.

The tall tourist felt his mouth grimace in dislike. He smoothed his small moustache to hide his expression, for his host's mother-in-law, a handsome, still youngish lady dressed to kill, was bearing down upon him.

'Why have you not got some buffalo curd? I said to Jayantha I will take him some buffalo curd. I know we are not to take great notice of him. That is *quite* forbidden. But some buffalo curd cannot hurt. And with lots of djagaree, isn't it? We remember how he was eating the other night . . . Oh my goodness!'

The lady's olive neck was suffused with pink embarrassment. She looked in alarm to see if her daughter or son-in-law were near enough to have heard her gaffe. She felt her mistake too greatly even to make good her offer of food to her visitor, apart from spilling a little of the golden brown djagaree at his feet.

He knew a moment's vexation, for, to tell the truth, his hosts were observing the imposed neglect of him so rigidly as to make him very ready for the offer of some food and another whisky. He pushed his annoyance aside in a determined effort to master this new personality, for he must soon, however much a second fiddle to his cinematic fellow traveller, come in for some introductions to these improbable people, else the Jayasekeres would think it odd. He must be ready to meet all as the undistinguished tourist they expected to be bored with. He felt a certain affection for this new personation, increasingly proud of a creation so near to his heart and yet so touched with decent comedy (he could not help thinking how Leslie would have applauded him, or would he? 'Kid's games, love, and at *your* age.') He felt warm towards himself as he had not for a long time. So untouched by Dr Malcolm's unattractive leaven of Sir Alec's large talk, Sudbury, he felt, was a cleansing wind to blow away many layers of dirt that had accumulated in the last months.

He was not very happy, then, when Mr Jayasekere advanced upon him winking broadly.

'All on your own, Mr Sudbury? That will never do. You must see a bit of Colombo society while you are here. Well,' he went on, in low, conspiratorial tones, as he jovially splashed whisky into his guest's glass, 'how have I done, eh? It was pretty short notice, you know. I said to my wife, this chap Malcolm is mustard, he expects his people to work magic. But that's good for us. It keeps us on our toes. It's what we need in Ceylon. I was straight on the blower, I can tell you. You can imagine their surprise. "Jayasekere! Good Lord! That materialist, that capitalist lackey, that westernized bastard! What does he want me at his house for?" But they've all come. "What is there in it for me?" Isn't it? That's the way of the world. Anyhow all we chaps at the top in Ceylon, left and right, we were at school together, you know. Besides, most of them are damned glad to be published by the wicked Dugong. Remember that, when you sound them out. By the way that chap Keaton's quite a genius with the camera. What a scoop for Dugong if we could get him to illustrate some of our textbooks. I told Jayantha, "That's what the big man has in mind." Was I right?'

Delighted though Hamo was by this part of his scheme (where would it end?) Sudbury-Malcolm had only time for the quickest smile of approval, which he turned to a silencing frown, as the gentleman in the maize-coloured robe bore down upon them. Though he wore no monkish saffron, his manner, Hamo thought, was indefinably clerical – soft, humbly self-pleased, rosy-viewed, yet not hearty. All these people! The necessity of observing them! However, these purgations must be borne, these dragons fought, these monsters met – but, oh, beautiful youth, little do you know the trials, the perils! And just for a moment, rather sharply, Hamo thought, 'Beautiful youth, you'd better be good after all this.'

'Has this gentleman also come to bring us the latest culture of the West?'

Suppressing without too much regret two of his identities, Sudbury said, 'A mere tourist, I'm afraid. Enjoying the beauties of your lovely country.'

'Mr Sudbury. Chandraranthera Thera. Or do I say Dr Chandraranthera? At any rate he's the chap who keeps our culture pure. Superintendent of Monuments. Superintendent of Religious Education. Representative for us all at the world's great cultural congresses.'

Dr Chandraranthera stood back to let a few of these credits flash on to the screen, then he waved them to one side.

'Oh, Jayasekere, stop all this nonsense. Don't worry the poor man. W. R. Chandraranthera. That's enough. Now may I ask you again, Sir, why you say "mere" tourist? You see, for me a tourist is a very fine person, a very special person. Understand, of course, that I didn't always think so. Oh no, when I was young, I was still susceptible to the British teaching. I made a trip to Europe – St Peter's, Westminster Abbey, Michelangelo, the Eiffel Tower – all marvels! The highest expressions of man's achievement. It was the phrase of one of our Professors here – Professor Martindale – a very fine British gentleman. Then I changed. I was travelling in Europe on my country's business. I saw again these buildings. Monuments of man's folly I found them. A hardness of will, an expression of egoism that produced only vain beauty. I was then still young, arrogant. Now I think differently. All have something to say, if we listen and if we hear the voices as part of a great symphony – yes, even the voices of cut stones. That is why I tell you don't be ashamed to be a tourist. A humble tourist who truly seeks something beyond himself in all the great monuments is a fine man. Poor Mr Tourist. Let him hold up his head. Are you afraid of rats, Sir?'

At the far end of the room a young man was intent in conversation with a student-like girl – the ugly, earnest face struck a note of sympathetic memory in Hamo. And then as he saw it more clearly, he knew that there were things he feared more than rats – young plant physiologists in search of laser beam equipment, for example, Wickramanayakes. Trying to make his cursed height small behind the bulk of W. R. Chandraranthera, he answered crouchingly.

'No, I think I can safely say that rats don't worry me.'

First things first for the Thera. 'May I suggest, Sir, that you correct your posture. Posture and breathing are the first steps, you know. So, you are not frightened by rats.' He seemed cross. 'Many Europeans are. I can tell you a story of it. There was a lady. One of your compatriots. An actress but a very fine person. She was seeking. Rather like a child I am afraid. I want to learn the True Path, Pandit, she asked me. She confused Ceylon and India, you know. So I answered as to a child. "Madam, you tell me you are afraid of rats." For she had told me that, you see. "But you have many pet cats." I knew this because she had spoken of them. "I advise you to procure also some pet rats. And all can live in harmony." She screamed. Then when I told her, "Rats too are living creatures," she cried, "But the cats will eat the rats." We shall see, I told her.' He paused to allow a thin, pale but very elegantly dressed elderly man who had joined the group to say, 'May I?', and then dramatically announced, 'A letter came two years later. From Dawlish. Dawlish in Devonshire where this lady lived. "I write," he said, "on a beautiful spring day in my garden where with my darling marmalade cat and Bianco my white rat I am sharing a bowl of milk." By the way, I was glad that she too was drinking the milk. There had been some problem of alcohol for the poor lady.'

Hamo saw with relief that Mrs Jayasekere was making her rounds, urging people to take their seats for the film show; but Mr Wickramanayake, too, was moving nearer. It would be a neck to neck. He felt quite angry with his host; he had specifically said 'no scientists'.

'Oh yes, I know the old story. Here we are all together – you, the spiritual saviour of our country, and I the dangerous revolutionary, and Kirsti Jayasekere, the wicked capitalist. And we are all drinking together with an Englishman. The reign of love has broken out. The sun shines on Sri Lanka to please even the late Bishop Heber.'

To Hamo the drawling voice of this elegant self-announced revolutionary gentleman reminded him vaguely of visits to the theatre, a performance of some comedy of Wilde's that was done at his house at Winchester – for a moment he remembered a boy, dressed in a blue satin gown with a train, on whom he had had a crush. It seemed a curious association for revolution but he was too concerned with watching Wickramanayake to give the ambiguity much attention.

'Or shall we prefer to say that the dialectic moves in a mysterious way its wonders to perform? In the struggle against neo-colonialism, there are many apparently strange alliances. Even with travelling English gentlemen with consciences about Imperial history. They can be most useful, such consciences.'

The Marxist dandy slightly inclined his slim-waisted figure and grey coiffure towards Sudbury, the nobody from the U.K.

Even through his alarmed distraction, the heavy ironic politeness, the undertone of sheer hostility that now marked the artificial drawl, suggested to Hamo something more appropriate to revolutionaries. All the same, *stage* revolutionaries, he thought;

but then he had hardly known revolutionaries at all, except from the occasional cinema or theatre performance. In any case all these plays within plays were only further complications by which *his* play, the play he had put on here this evening, was getting out of his directional hands. He must treat the whole thing as a controlled experiment, allow no extraneous irrelevancies. He did not answer.

'Perhaps you have *no* conscience about the late British rule, Mr Sudbury. My congratulations. I can assure you it is most refreshing for us not to be asked to excuse or forgive the process of history. We find it hard sometimes to view the long exploitation of Sri Lanka as an aberration in the consciences of our liberal British visitors. The absolution so many nice gentlemen and ladies from England ask for it is not in our power to give.' He laughed softly and pressed Mr Sudbury to accept a nut.

Even W. R. Chandraranthera's fatty chuckle of benevolence had an edge to it now.

'Oh dear! Conscience! How the poor British tried so hard to teach us this conscience. There was a nice chap, the Anglican minister at Kandy – "search your conscience," he said to his servant one day. That fellow was looking for many hours, but he didn't know where to search. Was it under the master's bed? Oh, yes, for nearly two hundred years we were learning about conscience from the British. And what a mess we made of it! The Singhalese conscience was always a most distressing hybrid. And now Professor Pereira wants us to learn about dialectical materialism. I am afraid we shall be at the bottom of the class again. But what is your impression of our country, Sir? May I say, "poor tourist that you are"?'

The Professor, too, seemed ready now to be less acid. 'I hope you haven't been left to the tender mercies of our tourist industry, Mr Sudbury. We made some beginnings during the last Government. Some experts came from Intourist. But now with free enterprise back again we can offer you only Jayasekere's Dugong Guide. Most of it advertisement. Well, that's all right, milk the rich Americans, why not? They expect it from those goddamned gooks. Trouble is the pictures are so poor. They don't know, these poor Daughters of the Revolution, which I believe those blue-haired, thin-legged ladies are called, whether they've ordered rubies from Ratnapura or bought the Buddha's tooth.'

W. R. Chandraranthera's smile was against rather than for this joke.

Kirsti Jayasekere said at once, and rather haughtily, 'That's all being looked after now. Mr Keaton, the celebrated photographer, whose movie, Pereira, you will see tonight, will be undertaking the supervision of all the art work for the Press.'

Hearing his own pronouncement, he was clearly disturbed by its audacity. He stopped short and glowered at his father-in-law who was approaching the group, beaming with benevolence.

'Here I am snooping,' he said. 'By the way, I looked up that word in the dictionary. I am afraid that it has rather an unfriendly meaning. I was most distressed that I should have used it to so distinguished a gentleman the other evening. May I say,' and he made a little old-fashioned bow in part whimsical, in part deferential, 'that our house is open to your snoopings at every hour.'

His son-in-law turned his irritation on the silent visitor, 'Well, Mr Sudbury, we are waiting for your answer. What is it that interests you in Ceylon? Education, isn't it?'

But Sudbury was deaf to Malcolm overtures, for Hamo, in following Wickramanayake's approach, had caught a sudden sight of Muthu's slim figure slipping nimbly into the kitchen.

'The vanishing wild life, really,' he said.

W. R. Chandraranthera's sweet smile of universal acceptance of life was swallowed up in Professor Pereira's angry sarcasm.

'The contradictions within capitalism, I have no doubt, will in the end bring that historical phase to a close; but long before that I am afraid they will have destroyed the Third World. At this moment, although I have not met the gentleman, I understand that the distinguished British scientist who has enriched our economy with the hybrid rice Magic is visiting us to see the results of his work in our plentiful rice harvest. I hope that he will see how his benevolent discovery has been exploited to the detriment of the poor peasants under a government which is so sensitive to the demands of Western investment. But no doubt, poor chap, he has to play the double role of the scientific white wizard and the needy rentier. Oh dear, his poor conscience! And then to make matters worse along come you, Mr Sudbury, and other gentlemen from England who are asking us to preserve most carefully the elephant and the buffalo who will trample down that same harvest.'

W. R. Chandraranthera giggled like a schoolgirl. 'Your examples are not well chosen to touch the Western conscience, Pereira. Remember that in Western countries all is forgiven if it is useful. I recall when I was in my primary school, the teacher told us "the horse is a useful animal". I only knew horses from passing the racecourse, so I told him, "Excuse me, Sir, the buffalo and the elephants are the useful animals." '

But Mr Jayasekere had seen his chance to bring Doctor Malcolm to his senses.

'Mr Sudbury wishes to save the rare species, I think, for example the dugong.' He smiled with self-teasing charm.

At that moment, Wickramanayake, talking earnestly with an elderly man, registered Hamo's presence with surprise and a formal bow – but, thank heaven for his earnestness, continued his conversation. And now Charlie Keaton's voice came to them.

'Right you are then, boys and girls. Take your seats in the shillings. Old-age pensioners first. What the butler saw through the aeroplane window.'

Mrs Jayasekere, trying to follow so cheery a lead, clapped her hands and cried, 'Everybody to their seats, please.'

'I don't know anything about dugongs,' Hamo said, for he felt at last free to shed all personation, 'We must take our seats.'

But he spoke too soon, for Leela announced loudly, 'Mrs Goonasekere,' and immediately, in the lightest of jade green silks and the most glittering of emeralds, shrieking like a jay, a tiny little woman flew down upon her frightened hostess.

'Oh, Jayantha! I am so late. But those who are not invited often come late, isn't it? Somebody told me Jayantha Jayasekere is giving an impromptu. Only last-minute telephone invitations. And I have been out so much this week that I knew I had missed your call. But here I am come impromptu. So many people I have not seen for years. So many people we do not *usually* see. Professor Pereira, Dr Chandraranthera, Mr Premaratne,' her bright little eyes took in each and every guest. 'Edith Dhammaratna will be so interested for her column. She has gone to the first night of *Paddy the Next Best Thing*. These old plays the British left us from our grandmothers' time! But I told her, who wants to see those old Players, when we have Mr Premaratne's Singhalese ballet, isn't it? Now I must see the famous photographer. Where is he, Jayantha? Introduce me, please. Oh, I shall report *all* to Edith.'

The whole room, including Hamo, was riveted to her announcement.

'Oh, my God!' cried Mr Jayasekere, 'the chattering mynah!'

But once again Mr Dissawardene came, however unwittingly, to save Hamo's embarrassment. He brought a Dugong Encyclopaedia volume.

'The entry for dugong is *here*. "A curious creature of the order *sirenae*. Often called the sea cow. It inhabits the Red Sea and the Indian Ocean. It is found in diminishing numbers off our own island coast near Mannar. This aquatic animal is vegetarian. The animals are said to be the origin of the legend of mermaids." '

Professor da Silva laughed. 'Mermaids or not, I am afraid there will be few left for Mr Sudbury's liberal conscience to preserve. The Puttalam Muslim fishermen, you know, kill them. Oh yes. The flesh is like pork. No doubt the Wheel of Being included such creatures to provide Muslims with a seemly means of eluding the Prophet's commands.' He smiled pointedly at Chandraranthera. 'And like all vegetarians, they are easy to knock on the head. But why do you want to preserve such creatures, Mr Sudbury? I see you are not a liberal at all but a lover of lost causes. An *Oxford* man of the dreaming spires. Oh dear! You should talk to Premaratne over there. He is performing the magic drama and folk mime in all our villages. But my word! he'd better watch out when the Indian movies arrive to those places. There's a piece of private enterprise you haven't considered, Jayasekere. How about Dugong Movies Ltd? *The Mermaids of Mannar*. But all very tame I am afraid, Mr Sudbury. Modesty is still a virtue with us. That's why I feel more at home in Moscow than in swinging London. But magic drama and dugongs! Oh my God! All this putting the clock back, when it doesn't even tell the time properly. Why you might as well try to encourage the peasants to grow their rice on the Mihintale rocks or in the flood waters by Kataragama. It's all very charming if you're a Count Tolstoy, but we have no room for Counts in Sri Lanka. By the way,' his voice took on a new drawl, 'did you ever stay at Yasnaya Polyana? No? Well, I suppose they don't accommodate tourists. I was guest of honour in Moscow for a big conference and they put me up there at the week-end.'

No one had much to remark to this, so Mr Dissawardene continued his reading: ' "The dugongs are allied to the manatees of the Gulf of Mexico and the lagoons of Florida." What does that tell us, I wonder?', he asked.

The pretty, plump, spiteful old face and blond coiffure of Lorelei of Little Rock came back to Hamo; he saw that skinny, spiteful hand tightening on the full flesh of a smooth amber buttock.

He said, 'It tells us that Professor Pereira is wrong. The dugong like the manatee could do much to clear exactly those swampy areas he referred to of choking weeds like the water hyacinth, and so make possible rice growing in places where it has up to now seemed hopeless.'

'Oh good heavens!' Professor Pereira cried, 'don't voice such views here. Do you see that gentleman with the spectacles there? He is Professor of Ayurvedic Medicine. He is teaching us all how to combat the cancer virus by eating iguana fat. Surely that's enough of such stuff for one little island.' And he laughed in a reversion to his most silky rudeness.

But a more direct anger now met him. From behind Hamo a familiar, earnest voice spoke.

'I think, Professor Pereira, that you are stepping dangerously. When one of the most distinguished authorities on rice in the world proposes a suggestion ...'

But once again Mr Dissawardene's simplicity came protectively, angelically to hide Hamo in its wings. Before his elderly authority, young Mr Wickramanayake, even in earnest professional anger, gave way. The old man raised his puzzled face from the encyclopaedic volume.

'Ah, I understand it now. These creatures were mistaken for mermaids because, to speak frankly, and without the presence of ladies, the sailors of the old days saw them giving suck to their young. So they are called *sirenae*. Because of the siren song of the mermaids. What sort of song was that, do you think, Sir?'

Hamo, in despair, had fixed his eyes upon the Most Beautiful Youth – in what was probably to be a Famous Last Glance. The boy was chattering volubly in reply to some order of Mrs Dissawardene.

'It was like the chattering of a little monkey. And infinitely seductive,' he said.

'Oh ho! So the mermaid was a monkey. That is very dry.' The old man in his delight forgot all caution. 'I think Kirsti that we must ask Doctor Malcolm to revise the encyclopaedia.'

The whole theatre was falling about his ears. The play trap he had devised threatened now to spring its teeth upon no one but himself. In his panic, he forsook alike Sudbury's nullity, Malcolm's self-importance, even Langmuir's wary reserve.

'Put out the lights!' he shouted. 'Put out the lights! It's time to start the show.'

In comfortable crepuscular disguise, in a specially selected seat at the end of the back row and nearest to the kitchen door, Hamo reflected with shocked surprise that panic (so forbidden to him by his father, his housemaster, his most admired professors, and Leslie) appeared to have its proper time and place, so docilely had the company followed his lead into the darkness – a lead which Erroll, aching to woo an audience for the first time by art rather than charm, had been quick to support; a darkness which the Jayasekeres, beset by Maisies and Wickramanayakes, were eager to embrace. So attentive and silent was the audience that the faintest giggling from far down the servants' quarters seemed an explosion. Mrs Jayasekere sharply ordered the elderly servant, absent on Hamo's first visit and now in attendance on this company, to convey her anger to the banished juveniles. The scolding that followed produced even more noise, but it gave Charlie Keaton his impromptu clue – as important to a likely lad's soft-sell as to Maisie Goonasekere's fashion-setting.

'There you are, boys and girls. The laughs have started already. Now all we want are a few tears. And by the sound of things they shouldn't be long in coming. It's all my own work, Ladies and Gentlemen. Done with my very own B. & H. All I aim to do is to make them laugh and cry. And if I can't do both at the same time, I'll return my medals to the President, as the

Yankee General said when he launched the first napalm attack on a Vietnam village.'

Led by Professor Pereira there were a few isolated bursts of clapping at this sally.

'Thank you all very much. Thank you very much. And we're all ready. The first sequences by the way, Ladies and Gentlemen, are of your own island paradise. After all, Charity begins at home. And if anyone knows the bloke at the head of the Tourist Department, I'm open to offers. But strictly for large lolly.'

Singhalese life flowed and raced and streamed and flashed before the bewildered company. For the most part they sat in dazed silence before it, although after ten minutes or so, coughing and a restrained, restless rustling provided subdued comment on the Life that they were being offered as one man's view of their own daily background.

Hamo, alert for noise under cover of which to make his getaway, without wishing Erroll failure, could have welcomed louder coughing. He saw, with impatience, sweating and dusty camera-packed tourists, passing with self-conscious disregard the wheedling-bullying whispers and nudges of the illegal money touts outside curio shops, change to a stout rich Singhalese gentleman with old-fashioned topee and umbrella allowing himself with grandeur to be conducted by bowing clerks up the splendid staircase that, beneath the vast cool, colonial magnificence of the Chartered Bank's roof, led to the holy sanctum of the manager's office. Why Erroll couldn't give them ... well ... something noisy, for tediously now the camera had fixed upon the carved detail of a post on the Bank's mahogany staircase rail; it circled again and again among the frets and over the smooth surface of the ballhead. Mr Dissawardene spoke to his wife in what no doubt deafness led him to think was a whisper.

'I remember those old ball posts. When I was a boy, my father used to take me to the Bank. Sometimes I would sit for an hour on the stairs while my father talked with the manager. There were big transactions in those days. I came to know those posts just as we are seeing them now. But I was always rewarded with ... Oh my!'

For the camera was now dwelling in detail upon the smooth

roundness of the ice-cream that crowned the cones seized eagerly by the hands of noisy children jostling one another at the corner ice-cream cart. But Charlie Keaton gave the old man a word of recognition.

'Aren't they wonderful old posts?'

The children's squealing delight changed to the honking of pelicans suddenly sailing out with greedy power from the banks of the great Topawera tank at Polonnaruwa towards the fish shoals. Hamo had just time to notice with satisfaction that the ice-cream vendors bore no likeness to uncles, before, under cover of the din of assembling waterbirds, he tiptoed out to the kitchen. But pictorial Life swept on regardless of his lust. For a moment, as a snakehead cormorant's sinewy neck slithered voraciously down into the fish-thick water, there was a glimpse of the lakeside resthouse veranda.

'That is where Queen Elizabeth stayed on her visit in 1954,' Maisie Goonasekere told everyone, but her information was brought to an abrupt 'Oh!' for the camera was now making another snake-ladder descent which proved to be down no bird's neck but through the S of Cargill's store sign as the scene moved from the feeding birds, via the outside of the famous emporium, to a stall where a number of elegantly clad Singhalese ladies were deftly picking over silken materials. Professor Pereira, anxious no doubt for any moral he could draw from this unenlightening show, said: 'Cormorants of another kind. The luxury goods that keep the wheels of capitalism oiled.'

But the evident sincerity of Jayantha Jayasekere's fashionable little cry, 'Oh, Professor Pereira, I don't think you can have been there for a long time. What can we buy, we poor ladies, when nothing is imported,' rather underlined the banality of the screen's social comment. It was Jayantha's mother who held to the sequence, when already it was replaced by the half-naked temple attendants at the Dalada Maligawa beating vigorously upon their drums.

'Oh, that is *so* interesting. When I was a little girl, I always said to my mother, "I am frightened of the big gold S on the Cargill shop. It is like a snake." My mother always laughed at me. And now I see that it is not a snake, it is a bird.'

'Well, it could be a snake,' Keaton told her, 'Beautiful bit of lettering anyway. Can't find that sort of thing in England any more.'

And now, as the sacred drumming changed to the concentrated industry of an old man in the Kandy market pounding his little heap of turmeric, there was a sudden whirl and the reel broke.

Maisie Goonasekere had years of practice in making celebrities feel that all was well with their fame.

'So that is our little Ceylon,' she said, going up to Mr Keaton, while the servant filled the impromptu interval by distributing coffee and candied guava under the supervision of the hostess and her mother.

'And how do you decide what pictures to take?' Maisie continued.

'Oh, well, you know, you've got an idea like before you start, haven't you? I mean even abroad you know what you want. And then you look for it. But you'd be surprised at the little details that come up.' Erroll was pensive and proud.

A little detail was worrying Mr Jayasekere. 'Where is that fellow Malcolm?' he whispered to his wife as she bent over the coffee cups.

'Oh, I don't know, Kirsti. I am angry with him. This movie is not so interesting for everyone, isn't it? Senator Peiris has been yawning.'

'What do I care for his yawns? What do you expect? Entertaining all these Reds. But that's what Malcolm said he wanted. To sound them out. But he has not said a word about the examinations. What does it mean?'

In answer came the lively lad's call. 'Back you come, Ladies and Gents, to another whiff of the isle of spice.'

Across their vision walked with deliberate long-legged gait the extraordinary figure of the painted stork, majestic above the common flocks of egrets and ibis and herons that thronged the shallow waters of the Yala lagoon. As a tufted duck dived beneath the water, the stork's stately leg was poised above in martial step; and then Muthu's delicate little body came into view bowing to receive parcels and behind him, in superb matronly regality, Mrs Dissawardene moved processionally towards the waiting car.

'Oh my!' the good lady reeled from this vision of herself.

'You look most elegant, Violet. I am pleased with your appearance on this screen.' Her husband's firm praise appeared to be addressed to the whole audience as much as to his wife.

'But the *boy* is on the screen. How funny that is! He will like to see himself. Go and fetch Muthu,' Jayantha told the old servant.

'Ah, Mr Sudbury, *you* are in the picture,' cried Mr Chandraranthera jovially to encourage that undistinguished, uncommunicative tourist.

'What is Doctor Malcolm doing there?' cried Mrs Dissawardene. 'I never saw him.'

'Oh my Gawd!' cried Erroll.

But Mr Wickramanayake could not allow all this to pass. 'It is Mr Langmuir,' he said. 'He wished to give money to the boy. And all the time you were photographing, Mr Watton. I never realized.'

'There we are. The Great Buddha himself,' Erroll cried desperately as the vast rock-cut Gal Vehera statue came into view.

'It is not the Buddha. It is Ananda. In any case no such photographs are allowed,' W. R. Chandraranthera announced.

'*If* you please, mate. I got the special permit. And a proper charlie I felt too with all the questions the bloke asked. Religion!'

Kirsti Jayasekere almost knocked Leela down, who, obeying her training, had moved fast to answer the loud telephone ring. He saw in the service a desperate means of escape for himself. Some minutes later, the older servant whispered in Jayantha's ear.

'Oh my Lord!' she cried, 'What fool has showed Doctor Malcolm to the servants' toilet?'

Her husband turned in rebuke of her indiscretion, perhaps of her impropriety, but also in rebuke of all the humiliation that life entails.

'Doctor Malcolm is not coming to Ceylon,' he told her; and in some reassertion of his status, he gave special announcement of the news to the whole company. 'The London examinations are not to be restored in Ceylon. The Minister has rung to inform me. He said that he did not wish my hopes to be disappointed,' he told his wife bitterly. And then, for he could not bring himself to make one of this audience of God knew what trick any longer, he left the room to seek, whatever the impoliteness of the place, some retributive explanation.

In the servants' bedroom, Hamo found himself greeted by such soft, pliant and yet teasing tenderness that he was quite disconcerted—though very pleasantly. Dalliance, as Leslie mockingly had called it, had never played a great part in his love-making; yet now, when the situation demanded an expeditious coupling, he found himself, with Muthu no more than half-undressed, giving way to all manner of lingering kisses and fondling. Gently he sucked the ear lobe, let the tip of his tongue slide round the hard shell outlines of cartilage, buried it deep into the heart of the ear. Then, taking the rough but soft palmed hand, he began to suck in turn each finger. He had just reached the thumb, when Mr Jayasekere flung open the door.

'You are not Malcolm,' he shouted, 'Why do you want to be called Sudbury? And who is Langmuir? The Minister says Malcolm refuses the examinations. Oh my God! What are you doing here?'

Muthu, in terror at the shouting he did not understand, sought to jerk free of Hamo's grasp. Hamo, in alarm and resistance, bit the thumb.

With a presence of mind that amazed himself, he spat on to the floor before he answered.

'I think this boy may well have poisoned his thumb,' and, despite Muthu's reluctance, he resumed his sucking. Before Mr Jayasekere had protested further, his wife's plaintive voice came from behind him.

'That young man from the University that Senator Peiris brought with him says Doctor Malcolm is a famous man.'

'This is not Doctor Malcolm. I told you he is an impostor.'

'No, Kirsti, no. It seems he is famous. It is to do with rice and magic. Oh! Why is he sucking the boy's thumb? And why is he in the servants' room? Muthu was going to bed, I think. He is undressing.'

'Mrs Jayasekere, this boy has been badly bitten.'

'Bitten! What has bitten him?'

'I wish I knew,' said Hamo solemnly. But then, more foolishly, he pointed to a lizard peeping out from behind the framed picture of a voluptuous highly coloured Indian lady film star.

Mrs Jayasekere's expression was contemptuous.

'Those are geckoes. They do not bite.' She spoke sharply to Muthu in Singhalese and he answered haltingly. 'The boy says he caught his thumb in the door. What does it all mean?'

Mr Jayasekere jerked back into authority.

'Thumbs! Boys! Shut up with all this nonsense, Jayantha. Don't you see that we have been fooled. I call this man an impostor.'

'But this is an *important* gentleman, Kirsti. The University young man says so. He is the big rice man. The Magic man.'

'Stuff and nonsense about magic. All these names and pretendings. What do you think our friends are saying? And they are not even our friends. Thanks to this chap, our home is full of Reds and anti-government people. What a scandal!'

The word electrified Mrs Jayasekere. She knelt before Hamo.

'Doctor Malcolm ... Mister ... I don't know the name ... Please do not bring *scandal* to our house. Doctor Malcolm, we here are a *small* community.'

'Now, now, now. What's all this about? God Almighty! What have you been up to with this lad?' Erroll's imitation of a police constable only feebly hid his real anxiety.

'Doctor Malcolm has been sucking the boy's thumb.'

'Oh! Is *that* all? Well, chacun a son goo. That's all right then. Now don't you worry about scandal, Mrs J. I've settled it all in there. All the boys and girls have gone home, and some very nice chicks among them. I told them my mate Sudbury here had had a coronary. Shocking thing! But we'd been expectin' it. I thought I'd have a bit of trouble with young Maniac Wick. He would keep telling them all how he knew the Chief. Boastful little bastard! But I pitched the tale. 'Fraid I put you in the shit, Mr J. But it was all in a good cause. I told him the Chief was worried that some monkeying was going on in Ceylon with the Abstracts of their work from the *Plant Genetical Journal*. Wanted to watch the publisher without being noticed. Bit of nonsense. But he wore it. Sorry, Mr J.'

Mr Jayasekere pushed the door into the passage wide open.

'Both you fellows will leave at once, please. I don't know what fellows you are, but you have come here to make us look stupid. I thought it was business, but I see it is some *bad* affair.'

'Look, you don't know what the Chief is . . .'

'I don't know anything. I am an ignorant fool. That is clear. But I know that you have insulted my wife and you must go.'

Mrs Jayasekere began to cry.

'Doctor . . . Mister, what is it? All my life I wanted to go to London. You tell me that you can arrange it. You lied. You have no feelings.'

'Oh, now, look here, if that's it. I can tell you the Chief never hurt a flea. I don't know what it's all about, but you don't have to worry, my darling. He's rolling in it. He'll fly you to London, put you up at the Ritz, pay for the lot. As to business, Mr J., this is Hamo Langmuir, the biggest plant geneticist in Europe. He'll get you scientific publishing on a scale . . .'

Before Hamo could dam the torrent, Mr Jayasekere interrupted. He appeared no longer angry. He was even faintly smiling. But he was firm.

'I think you are a good fellow. I don't know. But after what this chap has done, whether he's a big man or not, he must go. The scandal will blow out no doubt, but no thanks to him. The sooner he gets out I am better pleased.'

Hamo prevented Erroll from speaking further.

'Mr Jayasekere is perfectly right. There is no point even in apologizing. But I must ask you, Mr Jayasekere, please, please do not dismiss this wretched young man. He is in no way to blame.'

'Muthu? Why should I dismiss him? He is a very good servant. I don't know what you have said to him. Anyway he can't understand English. All the same I shall scold him about it all. But it is *you* who should not be here. This is a poor boy. He works hard. He comes from a poor village. All our servants come from that village. How could I send him away?' Mrs Jayasekere dried the last of her tears. She settled the folds of the delicate pink veiling on her head. 'I am the mistress of the house,' she said.

'Please go,' her husband insisted. But as Hamo and Erroll turned to walk to the back courtyard, he said in shock, 'No, no, through the front door, please. You are guests.'

They walked the bastinado of Mrs Dissawardene's puzzled aloofness and of Mr Dissawardene's reserved bow. Only when they reached the patio, did Mr Jayasekere come striding after them. He handed Erroll a visiting card.

'You – the other fellow! Your movies were damned boring, but a lot of your photographs are superb stuff. If you want publication with Dugong, you see this chap – Lionel Nicholas, the Art Editor. Tell him I told you to see him.'

It was this, perhaps, that made Erroll for once say, as they returned to their hotel, 'Look. I don't want to know any of the reasons for all that. You're the boss in this outfit. But another time, mate, give us a chance. And the sooner we get down to the business we came here for, the better.'

But meanwhile, Hamo, walking ahead into the leafy, flamboyant-flanked, opulent street, superstitiously dreading the mocking echo of the uncles' bell, even their laughter, found only Leela final witness to his expulsion from Eden. To her, he said, 'Please, if they treat Muthu badly, tell him to come to me. I'll look after him.' Towering above her, unaccustomedly waving his arms, he sought to pierce her solidity by astonishment. 'I'd take him back to England, you know, if need be.' She broke her dumpling surface but the giggling that poured out was not sweet. It seemed to Hamo more like jeering.

Paddy might be the next best thing in Colombo, but in the south-west wet lands of Ceylon it was, thanks to Langmuir's Magic, a triumphant success. Hamo returned from there with spirits revived, hopes refortified, mind cleared of large, irrelevant social doubts, ready for discussion with workers in his field at Peradeniya University of the small but relevant problems that were his true concern. Magic in those wet lands had worked. His years of labour had induced the mutation that exactly relieved all the deficiencies under which these heavily monsooned lands had for so many centuries suffered: three harvests where one alone had been reaped before, and this in country where no crop rotation could make up for a too-light yield; a quickly drying seed that allowed for early threshing; no matter that the deep waters inhibited tillering – so much the better, for Magic stood firm and strong but low without unwanted tillered progeny; with successive harvests, the ratoon will of stubble for survival had been killed and with it the great pest ecology that had grown up with it. Where H.4 had only partially succeeded, Langmuir's brainchild had conquered. The house that Hamo built stood firm. Everything, as Mrs Jayasekere would say, was Magic.

As Hamo watched the long rows of men, women, adolescents moving forward in the ballet dance of transplanting the two-week-old green shoots; as he looked at the neat groups of bissas, great jungle roots so neatly compacted with plastered clay and lime, and within them the hundreds of bushels of threshed harvest; as he saw those separate bushels of Red Magic, the rice so acceptable to sub-continental palates, previously so foolishly excluded by those with Japanese or Anglo-American circumscribed tastes, he felt that he had been right for so many years to leave the final fruition of his work as a hazy dream of pastoral Utopia, for so it seemed, or near enough, it was. He was conscious of a lordship, of his tall figure (the Lodger, let them call him) who had brought to these small people the sturdy dwarf rice that they needed. Spurred on by a sense of mastery, he broke through his usual despairing acceptance of Ministry intermediacy, helped by the faithful Erroll who held the voluble, self-important government guide in check by a double dose of his double talk. Thus released, Hamo found a charming (but not too charming) elegant (but not too elegant) young (but not too young) bilingual local farmer, and felt himself for the first time really touching the roots of his creation. So the smallholdings were only 25 per cent; but so the smallholders had reaped such crops that they had dropped suspicion enough to combine for storage and marketing; but so the shared smallholdings, long impoverished by rotating owner, gave forth goodness enough that all, even to the youngest, were satisfied thereby; but so even those great men – merchants in the cities, the big families of the island, yea, even the bikkhus in their monasteries and the great abbots, who absently owned three-quarters of that fair land – reaped such great crops and were so satisfied thereat that they rewarded their labourers justly and did not turn away such as were old or temporarily sick or slow, neither did they seek to remove the landmarks of the small peasant holdings, and for new seed and even for new animals (Magic required few machines) they gave of them gladly to their labourers. Hamo saw it all and it was very good.

So, then, how delightful to return at last to his proper sphere of concern in general exchange of ideas in Colombo with the chap come down from Peradeniya University, a man whose tendency to generalization Hamo felt he could overlook, even interestingly contest, in view of the very fine record he had shown in the laboratory. The high, dark but spacious sparsely furnished Colombo colonial hotel suite had, despite the periodic clatter of the antiquated air-conditioning machine, a sense of stoic yet patrician bachelor orderliness left over from the old British days to make Hamo feel as though he were at home in his flat. Hostlike, he urged more stale-edged chicken sandwiches and orange juice upon Professor Abbegurewadena and his shy young technical assistant, while replenishing his own glass and Erroll's with good Scotch whisky. The Professor crammed an enormous sandwich and, with the cress still poking out of the corners of his mouth, said ardently – with his protruding eyes and protruding vegetation more than ever like a delightful frog: 'No, no, forgive me please, Mr Langmuir. Such puritanism if I may call it that,' and he giggled, 'would make impossible a great deal of scientific advance. Now take totipotency. Supposing I had gone to a chap in 1945 and said to him, "Don't discard that dead datura plant. You will be able to breed from any single surviving cell." He will laugh in my face. Laboratory experiments showed it was impossible. Yet already forty years before in Germany Haberlandt had pointed the way. And now today ...'

'Yes, of course. But if you'll excuse me, Professor Abbegurewadena, for one such fruitful unestablished hypothesis, there are hundreds thrown out by egoists who have neither discipline nor patience enough ... And the waste of time involved is appalling. No, people speak of scientific philosophy, but they should more properly speak of scientific ethics or even, in my opinion, scientific etiquette ...'

'So you would find no place for the increasing concern with the history of science, the discovery of fruitful hypotheses that seemed ridiculous when the chaps put them forward.'

'The history of science is a very proper occupation for retired professors. And very elegant essays they may produce ...'

They were both at once vehement and yet laughing at the familiar patterns of their arguments. It was just such a *pas de deux* as he liked best, found it most fitting to dance with a colleague after some hours of fruitful detailed discussion and examination of work in progress. And Hamo's delight was complete, because his faithful Erroll was having an equally good time, for he and the professor's young technician had set to in a country dance of their own. That was how it should be: everything forgotten except their proper skills.

'Our trouble, you must understand, Mr Watton, lies with lack of money. We need an electron microscope. All right. The salesman comes to me. "Mr Fernando, I can promise you a high physical performance from this machine. And the price is not very high." But then I begin to ask, can we make use of the microscope for this and for that? Well, this chap tells me, for this perhaps, but not for that. We cannot afford such machines.'

'All right then. Let me do a little sales talk,' and Erroll assumed the manner of a cocky representative. 'Not to worry, Mr Fernando, we've got your answer. The Zeiss E.M.8 offers you not only high physical performance at a low price but also universal applicability.'

'Oh my goodness!' the Professor intervened, 'don't raise the poor chap's hopes. We have no money.'

'No, seriously,' Erroll carried it on, 'this is a real proposition. You see ...'

But Hamo had to exercise some authority, even at the cost of Erroll's exuberance. But that, too, was like old times. 'As to price,' he said, 'I feel quite sure that we ... but it is essential, Erroll, that the microscope should meet their particular problems. Too often, with such a small market, the stereotyping ...'

'Yes, and, you see,' Mr Fernando broke in excitedly, 'we have *many* specimens of a very thick circumference. Now ...'

'Ah! This is exactly where the E.M.8 provides the answer.' His audience, except for Hamo who was trying not to laugh at the perfect salesman voice, looked so grave that Erroll assumed an American accent in hope of the smiles that had not yet greeted his parody. 'You have problems, Mister. Our unique intermediate accelerator provides the answer. Thiswise . . .'

But how wise they were not to learn, for the telephone rang. Erroll, answering, said, 'No, I'm sorry he can see no one. He's busy.'

'Who is it?'

'Some name or other. Dissawardene.'

Hamo leapt from his chair at the immediate vision of Muthu; then he sat down again, signalling his agreement to the denial. He had done enough harm to the boy. But almost immediately the dignity, stateliness and simplicity of that old couple amid the confused inferno of international travel that usually marked the hotel lobby restored his sense of courtesy.

'No. There may be something I can do to make up for . . . Say I'll be down immediately.'

'Oh! for Christ's sake,' said Erroll, then, 'Well, it's your affair.'

But as Hamo left them, he heard Erroll say, 'What a bloke! There isn't a day he doesn't land his well-polished brogues in a cowpat. Then polishes them up again ready for the next. Even if he wasn't the world's best geneticist, how could you help loving such a natural for taking his punishment standing up?'

Hamo hoped that the words were unintelligible to their Asian guests; otherwise they would be embarrassingly personal. He was not even sure that he understood them himself, but he was glad that Erroll had said them.

It was, as Hamo emerged from the lift, worse than he had feared. The old couple's visit had coincided with the arrival of a winter package tour of French and Italian tourists. Latin *laissez-faire* volubility was meeting a match in its Asian equivalent of Singhalese happy inefficiency. Exhausted by their long journey, denied access to their bedrooms, the French and Italian bourgeois, dressed in a Gauguinesque mixture of coloured clothing for the tropics, milled about each other and the staff, falling back upon their last defences of high-pitched shouting and competitive pushing. Mr and Mrs Dissawardene, solemn in the darkest of clothing, were the principal victims.

Hamo said at once, 'Let us go and sit down,' and led them to seats. 'Well?' he said.

'It is not well at all, Mr Langham,' the matron rebuked. 'It is very bad. What can you do with the boy in England? He is a good boy. But he is ignorant. What will he do there? My daughter has forbidden us to see you. As to Muthu, good riddance to bad rubbish, she says. But I am not happy to say this. The boy is good.'

'Oh, God! What has happened to him?'

'If *you* don't know, nobody does. You said you would take him to England. Leela has told us it ...'

'I was upset. I didn't wish him to come to harm.'

'He *has* come to harm, if you don't know where he is.'

'It is what I said, Violet. The boy has run away.'

'Oh my God! You mean he hasn't gone to his home.'

'Mr Langham, the boy has no home. These people are very poor. Once they had a little, now they have nothing. They were going to sell the boy to the fishermen of Negombo. To Roman Catholics.'

'These are stories, Violet.'

'They are *true* stories, Albert. Then a Tamil man, a government servant, is travelling there. He took the boy for a servant to his family in Colombo. It is better than Roman Catholics, but, all the same, these Tamil people are Hindus.'

'There are many very fine judges and barristers who are Tamils, Violet.'

'We do not know Tamil people, Albert. Then these people are leaving Colombo, Mr Langham. What will happen to the boy? My daughter heard it. The other servants are from that village. So she accepts him to our house. She is angry *now*. But she is a kind mistress to her servants.'

'Yes, I'm sure she is. But where is the boy? Are you sure he's not gone to his home village?'

'Mr Langmuir, these people have many children. Formerly they could feed them and buy a little more by selling the rice they did not eat. But now, with the new agriculture, they can only feed the very young ones ...'

'But what about the government subsidies?'

'This land is bad. A little soil on rock. The government cannot subsidize such hopeless lands. I think you should know this, Mr Langmuir.'

'Mr Langham, is the boy *with* you?'

'No, Mrs Dissawardene, he is not. But I shall do all I can to help you to find him.'

'I do not know what you can do. Albert, this palm is very un-comfortable, always brushing upon my face. I think we shall go.'

'Mr and Mrs Dissawardene, you have every reason to be angry with me. But please, before you go, at least let me offer to help. For example, a reward. Suppose we offer a police reward of what? Two hundred pounds?'

'Police? The boy is not a criminal. Everyone will hide from us. No. We must make our own enquiries.'

'Well, then, don't punish me too much. Let me contribute to the expenses. I insist, Mr Dissawardene, as a matter of justice, let me make out a cheque for a hundred pounds. At least, if you find him, it could help to . . .'

'I do not know what is the use of this cheque, but if it is a matter of justice . . . Strict account shall be kept. Now, Violet, we must go.'

But before the couple had reached the still furiously milling crowd through which they must make their way, she so vulner-able and stately a ship, he so chunky and secure a vessel, the old man turned to Hamo.

'Mr Langmuir, I will tell you what Mr Justice Carpenter used to say sometimes in the club after a day's work in the Court. "Dissawardene," he would say, "you failed today in your duty to your client. You did not master your brief properly. A profes-sional man must always know the details of his job." '

With pride his wife filled out the rebuke. 'Mr Langford, we are here a *small* community. You have come among us without respect.'

They drove in an old open car. Mr Subramanian, that is, drove – well and cautiously, seldom turning his eyes from the road, so that Hamo in their conversation had to guess at the degree of courteous irony, of proud assurance from his profile – from the patterns of the little wrinkles at the side of his flashing eyes, and by the creasing of the high smooth dark-chocolate forehead beneath his elegant grey hair. It was all so different from the giggling, the laughter, the nervous appealing of eyes and body that he had come to expect from his Singhalese hosts. He liked it. It seemed more English. But he did not voice this; partly because this very Tamil reserve, thank heaven, checked the impulsive intimacy into which he had fallen lately and because to involve himself in the island's racial tensions was his very last wish.

Behind them rode only Erroll, for Mr Subramanian had quickly disposed of the Colombo official as soon as they had arrived at Jaffna and had suggested definitively that the smaller number of visitors who descended on the paddy fields the better. Now, as they returned from their day's inspection of the agriculture of the canal-crisscrossed flat peninsula along a causeway between two wind-ruffled lagoons, Erroll was happily engaged, leaning back across the lowered hood, in recording the jade and turquoise swoops and dives of the rollers who crossed and recrossed the dusty road behind them in intense pursuit of insects.

'So, you see, Mr Langmuir, your Magic has worked.'

Hamo gave no answer. He did not want fulsome praise to break the image he had formed of this civilized Tamil government official.

'Oh, yes it has, you know. A very considerable increase in yield, less tillering, therefore less pests, and so on. It wasn't the miracle here that I am sure it has been in so many parts of Asia. But then we didn't need miracles. We're very lucky with our soil. Mr Watton, I see a pied kingfisher ahead, on that flood-level post, if you are quick you will catch its dive as we pass.' He spoke without turning his head . . . And there a moment later a revelatory streak of shining black and white hit the water with a splashless thud.

'Did you get him? Isn't it superb? And then to have made your journey by car all the way up through that endless scrub jungle! I hope the green manuring we were making from the jungle saplings and liana growth today made you feel less haunted by those endless hours of dusty scrub. It does serve man a little. Not just the hornbill or our famous loris. I've never seen a loris, by the way, or met anyone who had.'

'Doesn't the jungle cut you off very seriously from the central Singhalese world though?'

'I hope so. No, no, don't mistake me. I am no lover of communal strife. But I had enough of Colombo in six years there.'

'I understand that. It's so beautiful here. And then, although as you say it's very Dutch, it seems to be somehow more English.'

'Ah! The British always loved us Tamils. Unfortunately that hasn't been of the greatest help now that we must live under Singhalese rule. But then look how private we are, how discreet.' And he indicated the high hedges of hibiscus and corrugated iron which marked the beginning of the properties of Jaffna. Over the top of the hedges broad leaves told of tobacco cultivation. 'Our homes are our castles! And gardens so well cultivated! Such pride in hard work! The British liked all that.'

Hamo could almost feel his limbs relax in the decent distancing that the man's civilized irony provided. He felt a familiar very faint smile, such as he had sadly missed almost since London Airport, twitching at his lips. Erroll, too, in his own way, clearly felt an equal relief.

'That's what I can't get over,' he had turned towards the front seat now as he changed reels, 'the way you speak English. I mean, you know, after Colombo, it's like having come away from a novel by that bloke Wodehouse.'

Hamo looked at the closely hidden farmsteads, gazed towards the distant, fortressed island of Kayts across the shimmering waters. He agreed, but the observation was one he would have left unspoken.

Mr Subramanian said, 'Ah! Jeeves!' Then he remained silent for a moment or two. 'You mean "the old chaps" and "the old fellows".'

'Yeh, ghastly, isn't it?' Erroll said.

'I never cared for it with the British, certainly. It seemed patronizing and yet insecure. But that was mostly the planters and engineers and so on. I was luckier in my associates. I mixed mainly with ...'

He broke off, as if embarrassed. Hamo, understanding this, said, looking towards the massive curtain wall, 'The Dutch castle alone, of course, gives a dignity that Colombo lacks.'

'Oh, the Singhalese had that symbol of conquest, too, you know, at Galle. Like the Welsh. But still, the Singhalese are making a profit out of it now, with the tourists. It's all a matter of time before injustice is righted.'

He began to hoot a little irritably as, from behind a line of nearly collapsed buses, juddering and spluttering as they halted like drunken derelicts dying of the shakes, there poured crowds of villagers come to market with squawking baskets of hens and beasts tied by their legs, a cacophony of bleating and squealing and shrieking. Straight-backed, silent, impassive, unheeding men and women, even children, moved randomly, uncaringly before the car's demands.

'In Colombo, Mr Subramanian said, 'they would be chattering and shouting, making a hell of a row. But *they would* scatter. Here they don't. The British liked the Tamil dignity. But it's inconvenient. I shall take you to my home now. The residence is like a charming English rectory in its own park. Not the local Palmyra palms, you know, but great trees like oaks. They aren't, of course, but it make us feel as though at home in England. And we're all supposed to want that. Even those of us who only stayed in South London digs. No, really,' he cried as two boys rolling ancient tyres passed within inches of the front wheels. 'I think we must go round by the esplanade. The roadway is part of the market and must be respected as such. The weak, you know. My wife will have a civilized meal ready for us. Or we like to think so. Out in the wilds here, you know. Not Colombo 7. We have very good lobster. Is that all right for you?'

Hamo now fully smiled his pleasure at the whole of the man's tone.

Erroll said, 'Do you dress for dinner?'

'Well, on this occasion, since you've come so far, we'll excuse you.'

Hamo felt a bit shut out by their laughter.

'Oh, God!' cried Mr Subramanian, 'What the hell's this?' For the broad esplanade was blocked by a huge crowd that spilled over from the water's edge. 'It must be a turtle catch ... Well, it might amuse you, Mr Watton, to photograph those melancholy creatures.'

When the crowd parted before Mr Subramanian's authority and they found themselves beside the deep tank, they looked down to see no lugubrious turtle beak or sadly waving flippers; instead there looked up at them two round surprised eyes coming from a brownish-grey furred body so flat that it seemed two-dimensional. Turtles, by their slow bewildered grief, command our tears, but this creature, by its human eyes in a body drawn by a child, wrings our hearts. And Hamo's more than most, for each side of its nostrils – holes in a cardboard model – above a blubbery upper lip, were suggested whiskers. A dugong is a dugong. But this to Hamo was Old Bill. Old Bill of the trenches, Bairnsfather's Old Bill – a sacred figure, for had not his father in distant childhood days when Hitler was only 'this German chap who's probably what they need there', when Arnhem was a name unknown, shown him, a small boy perched on a tweed-clad knee, the Old Bill drawings – 'If you knows a better 'ole, go to it' – and said with a special voice, 'We must hope this sort of laughter will never be needed again,' thinking, no doubt, of his own father, killed at Loos?

Mr Subramanian, shocked into Wodehouse by the unusual spectacle, said, 'By Jove! A dugong! That's a pretty rare chap in these parts I can tell you. He seldom comes north of Mannar.'

He peered down at the too-shallow water in the tank too narrow to allow the creature to move.

'It's not a he, it's a she.' He spoke to two proprietary men who stood by (but they were not, Hamo saw to his relief for his own sanity, uncles, skinny not fat, dead-eyed not grinning). 'Yes, it's as I thought. They're selling it to the Moslems here. They eat them. Their flesh is said to taste like pork. And again the blubber has properties. Magical, medical. I don't know. It's all the same. Of course, I ought to forbid it. If the wild-life people knew ... but these religious differences. The last thing one wants to do in a small community is to upset the minority groups.'

Erroll said, 'You're not going to let them kill that, are you?'

Hamo cried, 'But they're so rare. Look, let me buy it from them and ...'

Mr Subramanian's reactions were lost in a sudden pushing and shouting that nearly capsized Hamo's long legs, as a group of youths shoved their way through the crowd; in a moment they had climbed on to the slender rim of the tank – four youths swaying a little in their delicate but sure balance with a sweet-spiced, warm breeze playing around them – and had begun to throw small stones at the helpless dugong. Most fell into the water and were dulled, but one caught the puzzled head and cut the skin above a nostril hole. Strange and horrible to see blood ooze out from fur-covered cardboard. Mr Subramanian shouted louder than either Hamo or Erroll, perhaps to excuse his former handwashing. In a moment, men among the crowd had secured three of the four youths for authority's verdict, but the fourth, more slender, more agile, had swung himself from the parapet. Turning a moment his wonderful simian smile upon them, afraid yet mocking, he dived six feet into the water below.

Hamo shouted, 'Muthu Muthu!' But, by the time he had forced his way through the jabbering excited crowd, Muthu was making his strong overarm strokes almost as a distant object through the smooth green waters. 'We *must* get him back. Find out where the boy's living, please, Mr Subramanian. I must speak to him.'

'Oh, let him go. I don't intend to do more than reprimand these three others. They're bred in a hard school, Mr Langmuir. The R.S.P.C.A. means little in their lives. But I'll order these men to release this creature in one of the lagoons near here. Who knows, poor cow! she may find her way back to the herd. After all,' and he turned a shamed face into a laughing one, 'I committed myself to the defence of the weak.'

He turned to talk to the men, but Hamo with his huge strides was already running along the great causeway towards the disappearing figure. 'Muthu!' he shouted. 'Muthu!' Once it seemed to him that the youth hesitated for a moment and looked back, but surely the eyes showed only fear, for he immediately redoubled his strong swimming and was soon only a distant point in the far-stretching waters.

When Hamo returned, six men had lifted the great tank and were carrying it shoulder-high, but the puzzled look in the dugong's eyes was no different. We supply our own puzzles. This one at least would be registered for posterity on Erroll's film.

'It's hard to think that mermaids appeared like that,' Mr Subramanian said.

'Look, I must speak to you about the boy who swam off. I have reason to ...'

Erroll interrupted, 'Isn't there a Scotch phrase – something about the end of an old song? If there isn't, there should be.'

Mr Subramanian was puzzled, 'Oh, you mean the mermaid's song,' he said.

'The Chief knows what I mean.' Erroll spoke in tones so harsh and abrupt, even fierce, that Hamo believed he could actually *hear* the breaking of some link between them. But he couldn't afford to repair it now.

'I must explain to you, Mr Subramanian,' he said, turning his back on Erroll to exclude him from the confidential stance he took up with his Tamil host, 'that that boy who swam off is a boy from Colombo. He's called Muthu. He was in the service of some, well, acquaintances of mine. And he ran away. Largely through my fault. It is vital that someone should persuade him to return.'

'Oh,' said Mr Subramanian. '*You* are the Englishman. I know the boy. He was in our service in Colombo. A few days ago he turned up here asking my wife for work. But his manner was very strange. He talked of some British gentleman. In any case, we have servants here from our own people. And also my wife does not care to employ anyone who has been with a Singhalese family. They spoil their servants, you know.'

'I don't know anything about that. I only know that I feel very responsible for his running away and I believe that he has no family.'

Mr Subramanian seemed about to lead the way back to the car, but Hamo's agitation defied his reluctance to become involved.

'This is not the kind of thing I care to be mixed up with. But you are a V.I.P., as the official gentleman from Colombo so repeatedly reminded me. More importantly you doubled our rice harvest. I shall do what I can to trace the boy. But it will take many days, if it can be done at all.'

Hamo got out his cheque book and pen and he began to write. Mr Subramanian raised his eyebrows.

'Perhaps you will add a few pounds to recompense the men for the dugong.'

It was hard to know whether he was speaking ironically. 'By the way, will you be kind enough to say nothing of this to my wife? Our women are not broad-minded as they are in England, I am rather happy to say.'

As they sat in the car, Hamo ostentatiously took out Alexandra's letter from his wallet. Reading it, he composed a letter to his great-uncle: 'Dear Uncle James, I believe that you have received an application from a young man named Rodrigo Knight for the post of ... I cannot believe that you could do better than to give him a trial ...' If Alexandra wanted it done, he should do it. If the young man was a good thing then it would enable them to marry as they should; if he was a bad thing, Uncle James's testing authority would soon reveal his weaknesses to all, including Alexandra. It made him feel a bit better, in face of this Tamil chap's disapproval, to be remembering his authority with someone so weighty in the world of affairs as his great-uncle.

But then, sadness overwhelmed him. He knew why he was sad, even if he couldn't exactly say what that sadness meant – like the victims of the mermaids of the Rhine. The Commander's breezy shanty came back to him:

> The boy across the river has a bottom like a peach,
> But alas I cannot swim.

And something sadder from his schooldays:

> Children dear, was it yesterday, call once more,
> that he went away?

or something like that.

Ahead of him, directly in sight, as they bumped, interminably, and too fast he thought, along the dusty road, was always the chauffeur's thick, bristly neck. He had occupied many long stretches of time, when silence seemed the only dignified way of expressing his growing anger, by counting and recounting the little pits, some blackheaded, some not, in this neck – the counts never came to the same figure, but then he could never remember exactly what he had fixed as the qualification for a pit on previous rounds. The figure was about twenty-five. Sometimes, to break the charged silences, and sometimes, to stem the many and unaccommodating questions that poured out when Hamo's anger burst into flooding words, Mr Padmanabhan or some such name, anyway the annoying man who had taken charge of him at Tanjore, would indicate once again the great rock that always dominated the endless flat distance ahead of them.

'They say it is like a three-headed demon, Mr Langmuir. But I can't see it. I think you must be an artist or a magician to see such shapes.'

Occasionally, but decreasingly as Hamo made his loss of temper apparent, he added, hopefully, 'But of course, I forget, *you are* a magician.'

For a good two hours Hamo had kept his eyes steadfastly on this rock, for there, at Trichinopoly, he was to take plane and leave for what might (Good heavens! to be thinking in such terms) prove the better because more revolutionary state of Kerala. Right-wing Madras, go-ahead right-wing capitalist Madras, for there were areas so Right that they banished his Magic altogether from their conserved peasant economy. Anyway, Right, Left, for in some such ridiculous terms had he now been reduced by events to thinking – Left, Right; left, right. A refrain that was only not futile in an emergency, when a dark age threatened once more to engulf decency and knowledge, when men like his father had to put on uniform, drill and go to war. Left, right – silly enough terms when some lunatics to catch votes started to set up Ministries of Technology, to lay down interfering plans for national research, or with ignorant or, worse, half-ignorant committees, attempted to interfere with the Institute's budget; but in such a cliff-hanging world as India, where in a second the sea or the opening ground can swallow up all, to be confronted with such silly sheep-dip marks – red, put your mark here, and so on. It was an outrage! His own voting came back to him, for he had felt the ritual necessary since it was part of the English scheme of life – three times Conservative and once Labour; once, too, Liberal, but he regretted that gesture, it had had a senseless theatricality ... But now, once again, he recalled the little group of young men with their foolish banner, or only foolish really because it was ragged, but then they were all in rags in these parts, the foolish and the weak ... they had been hustled away when they wished to speak to him, and, for he could not get away from it, he had been, however politely, hustled away from them. Pulses he had not known to be in him – at the temples, beneath the ears – throbbed as his anger rose again. Whatever the rights or wrongs of it, it was clear that the Right was not all right here, had something to hide. He forced himself to speak very deliberately.

'Mr Padmanabhan, do I understand correctly that the owners of the large estates we saw today are absentee landlords?'

'Yes, Mr Langmuir. That is right.' The weariness of the reply grew each time, no doubt as a rebuke. 'As you had in Ireland, I think. Or today in the U.K. many businessmen are investing in farming.'

'Yes, yes, but that's to do with income tax and making a loss.'

'In India we have no money to lose.'

Hamo heard for the first time in many weeks laughter that had no shy giggling intermixed.

'No, Mr Langmuir, thanks to your Magic, rice growing is now very profitable. Many of our richest men, our most responsible citizens are interested in farming. And so we can feed our great city populations. This is our chief problem.'

'But these responsible citizens have taken away the small-holdings of all these people . . .'

'Taken away? Come, Mr Langmuir, I don't think sociology suits you, Sir. How can a scientist who has trebled our crop by his mutation wish to preserve this farming where mass selection, all varieties mixed together – the more kinds the prouder these peasants are – has led to decades of deterioration of grain. I don't understand how you favour such things.' He looked at once earnest and desperate. 'Mr Langmuir, nobody supposes that we are bringing the millennium – is that what you say? But we bring prosperity to some and, with prosperity, education and, with education, birth control. Then less people, less bad stock, less hopeless cases.'

'Ah,'' said Hamo. He felt ashamed of all his roles, as they had been and as they were. Mr Padmanabhan perhaps sensed this, for his hard-pressed courtesy took on a teasing note that was hardly disguised aggression.

'Now, I should like to ask *you* many questions in *your* field. Is the D.N.A. the same as the life force? for example. But I don't ask them, because I know that they will seem foolish to you. Isn't it?'

'Yes. I am afraid they would. But it's not the same thing. If I understood that little man aright, these people have just lost all they have, because a mutation in rice that I induced has produced a sort of farming from which they are excluded.'

'Not excluded, Mr Langmuir. But these peasants are often very foolish. They borrow money from the village money lenders, the *jotedars*. They get into debt. The crop is too small, the holdings are too small. This is hopeless cases. Now we have, for example, a system of traditional leasing by payment in kind, *batai*. If these men ...'

'Nevertheless, from what that little man said ...'

'Mr Gupta's English is very poor. I think you misunderstood him. In any case he is not of this country. He is from the North. He does not understand how hopeless many of our peasants here ... These people can all have employment on the big farms.'

'Yes, at such wages it seems that only those in rags will accept. And so when the less ragged ones tried to hold out for better pay, there was fighting. And people were killed. With mattocks. That's true, isn't it?'

Oh, if only Erroll's faithful Cockney tones could come to calm him, to prevent such an outburst. But Erroll was far away, had had enough for the time being; and then this man Coates ...

Mr Padmanabhan said, 'The story is very garbled. It was all some time ago. I shall get the Ministry to send you a full account of the affair since you wish it. Please say nothing until you have read the facts. By the way, you know, I suggest you do not speak of people in rags. These are their clothes. They are very poor.'

And, indeed, Hamo could not think why the word 'rags' was so tenacious. Something he had seen, something he was avoiding, somewhere in the swim of his vision ...

He turned his eyes firmly to the car side-window and confronted it. All along the roadside sat cross-legged, wrinkled, toothless old women, rows of their withered soles turned towards him like one of their temple friezes. The skimpy rags, yes rags ... of cotton that served to clothe them seemed often insufficient to hide their stringy paps; yet their skull-like grey heads were always decently veiled. Before them, in the dust and cow dung, were squares of rag, extensions of themselves, and on these arranged in lines, drying in the sun, rows of rice grains, some scarlet, most ivory white, all wretched and quite unMagical. Before he turned away in misery, he realized that the chauffeur, in avoidance of two great dewlapped cows lying in the road, had driven over two or three of these little rice hoards. He seized the man's shoulder.

'For God's sake! Watch what you're doing.'

The driver turned in alarm and in so doing swerved towards the second cow. Mr Padmanabhan cried out. Just in time, the car avoided the beast. But sacrilege had been close enough to rouse shouts from the crowds by the roadside. One of the old women shook her fist. Mr Padmanabhan said something in command to the chauffeur. They increased their speed and were away in clouds of dust. Mr Padmanabhan said nothing to Hamo.

'Look at them dipping. Like huge birds, cranes or something, feeding in the water. Beautiful. Clean lines too. Just like those Chinese drawings you see. And you won't believe it, they *are* Chinese. Seems the Chinese came here fishing centuries ago. And they've kept the design of the nets. Very old place this, you know.'

'Yes,' Hamo said, 'I did know. All the same, it's very peaceful.'

He leaned back in the cushions of the cane and mahogany chaise longue. He knew that what he had said must sound contradictory, but Erroll had startled him from a half-sleep, and he could not explain that in the peace of this tiny island, of this finely proportioned Dutch house, of this huge over-hanging bread-fruit tree with its great shiny fretted leaves, of the miles of blue water beneath the endless blue sky, he was minute by minute shedding the desperate sense of ageing that had weighed him down in the last months of disillusioned bustle. 'Did you say birds? What birds?'

'No, *no* birds. I was just saying how those Chinese nets *looked* like birds.'

'What Chinese nets?'

'Oh!' Erroll had clearly been brought to a surprised stop.

A moment later he asked, 'Haven't you really seen the nets going up and down out there from the shores of that cape towards the ocean?'

Hamo, once more dozing, forced himself to peer out across the vast bay towards the narrow neck of water that led to the sea.

'Yes. I do see them. Like huge shrimp nets. Though I shouldn't care to eat the fish brought up out of this bay, however colourful the water. A lazy life, too. Dipping and hauling in your livelihood. But that's Asia all over. Some people live a lotus existence, others starve their life out scratching a bit of rock to make seed grow.' Seeking to dismiss the whole subject in easy generality, he fidgeted with the cushions. 'Has Coates taken his film crew to Cochin? Why didn't *you* go? He asked *me*, but I really know nothing about these Jews.'

Erroll made no answer, but, after a silence, he said, 'Look. It's not for me to criticize and that. But I'm worried about you, Chief. Honestly I am. You've come all this way and all you can do is to bellyache about the social conditions. In this wonderful country! Not to say the Philippines, not to say Thailand, not to say Java, not to say Malaya, not to say Ceylon. Living conditions, starving poor, exploited masses. I don't know. It began all right in the States and in Japan. Or I think so. And in Darwin everything seemed fine. But now. After all, every day's a revelation in these places – something new to see, quite little things sometimes, even things that we've got at home but you wouldn't notice them there, and then great extraordinary things like those nets sticking out from the shore. And you don't even see them! I'm getting all the kicks and you're paying for it all. After all, we came here part to see the labs and part to enjoy ourselves. Or so you kindly said. Well, we've seen some labs and *I've* enjoyed myself. But what have you done? Walked around a lot of muddy paddy fields and got yourself a bloody conscience. At first I thought, why not? They make a fuss of him and he likes it. But you don't, do you? First it was agricultural conditions. Now, judging by these interviews you've given to the papers here, it's reached politics. It's not my affair. But I don't think you know what you're getting into.' He looked at Hamo in enquiry, only to find him nodding his head in agreement. Erroll shrugged his shoulders. 'Honestly, you're hopeless.'

'Yes,' said Hamo, 'I am among that sad class. And to answer your other observations: It isn't. And I don't.'

'Well, then, why don't you take a rest? There's nothing you can do to help the poor buggers. It's the same the whole world over – and you can't alter it. Stop here and rest for a few days.

No larks and no lamentations. Just sun and sleep. Doctor Watton's prescription.'

'That's just exactly what I am doing, Erroll.'

'Good. Well, you couldn't have chosen a better place.'

Hamo lay back among the cushions. He looked up for a time at the intricately shaped glossy dark green. On one of the leaves a mantis bright as grass in Technicolor was in prayer. He tried to give himself up to the shapes, to the contrasting colours. But they brought no thoughts, no satisfactions. He gazed across the smooth water to the line of the coast. A staring white splash must be one of these Roman Catholic churches. Baroque, perhaps, or modern. Roman Catholicism seemed as flourishing now as then, or, then as now. He tried to make another sort of connection – the mantis in attitude of prayer, the kneeling fishermen in the church. But there was no satisfaction. Anyway the Jews, here from very ancient times, it seemed, had almost all left. He closed his eyes and dozed.

Yet Erroll's restlessness prevented him from sleeping. First the man sat in a near-by deckchair. Then he picked up Hamo's empty glass, turned it upside down, and let the last few drops of fresh lime juice fall on to the coarse lawn. All this Hamo could sense, felt forced to verify by peering through half-closed lashes, but then he slept and was woken by Erroll's getting up and walking towards the water's edge. Hamo saw him craning his neck around the little island's clump of trees towards the mainland, saw him relax as the sound of a motor launch chugged towards them, saw him sag as it passed by, churning its frothy way in and out through the nearly motionless black dots of fishing boats. Erroll, then, began to whistle tunelessly.

Wearily Hamo forced himself to be there. 'Why didn't you go over with them? Coates wanted you. He said so.'

'I dunno. Well, yes, I do. Ever since we met him in Madras, I've been following along with the camera team. I didn't even go with you on that Tanjore lark that seems to have mucked things up so. I mean commercial photographics for mags and that on the side is one thing but . . .'

'You think he's a really good producer, do you?'

'Kit Coates! The only really imaginative bloke on the tele today. And from what he says he'll break into the movie world

303

any day now. The things you can pick up just from what he says in a casual way. Half that team, even old Phil, his top camera-man, don't appreciate what they're getting, working with him.'

Hamo patted his moustache, allowed himself a moment's squaring of his shoulders, a faint smile, as he said, but softly, 'I can't imagine any fate worse than spending more than a day in his company.' Then he said, as though giving the day's orders, 'He plans to go up to Goa and then fly from Bombay to Ceylon. He wants to photograph the whole agricultural scene there. "The working ecology of a naturally idle people" is how he described his approach. He was anxious that we should accompany him because of our official contacts. As we had just come away from there, I was a little surprised at his request, I admit. But he ex-plained that in his profession one must never lose anything from not asking. Of course, *I* couldn't consider going through all that again. Nor am I sure that the contacts I made would prove exactly amenable after ... But *you* left with good marks all round. I want you to go with Coates. You can help him. He can interest you. I'll pay all expenses. No, those are orders. I shall rest here and write up my reports.'

'I dunno. Well, if you're sure. And you're *really* going to rest. It *is* paradise, you know. You think Kit Coates wants me along?'

'I'm sure of it. And with no need to feel obliged on either side. Because I may be doing him a further service which will also serve me. I imagine that's the sort of language he'd use. Or if not language – I haven't your ear for all that – at any rate the sort of sentiments. But I can't tell you about that yet.'

'What you going to do then? What you got on your mind? Old Kit's a crafty customer, you know.' Erroll was a Northern likely lad again. But he was not to learn whether imitation had once more eased the tension enough to inspire confidence.

'Oh my Gawd!' he said softly. A motor launch had stopped at the residency jetty. From it came, not Kit Coates and his crew, but Mrs Kovalam, the liaison provided for them by the Government Information Office.

All yesterday, as they toured the rice communes, the Storage Cooperatives and the Government Mills, Hamo had lain back, as he now lay back on the chaise-longue cushions, cradled in the kind severity of Mrs Kovalam's management of an eminent visiting capitalist scientist. The severe fold of her unadorned sari, the homely plainness of her pince-nez, the maternal strictness of the tight bun into which her thinning grey hair had been wound, the stately homeliness of her tall, ample figure, the infelicity – political and aesthetic – of her gold teeth, her total lack of humour, and the official brightness with which she compensated for it – all these had left him hovering between childish alarm and childish laughter. He supposed, as he saw her advance towards him through the hibiscus-lined path, putting the scarlet and apricot flowers to shame for their parasitic luxuriance, that she was simply the Indian version of all the Left-wing political ladies in England whom, thank God, he had never met. So impressed, indeed, had he been by all he saw of what they had done with his Magic (so different from what private capital investment seemed to have made of it elsewhere), that he had let himself be taken charge of, had surrendered, as he had once before done to capable hands at the London Clinic when his appendix was removed. But now, as she approached, he feared for what his exhaustion might be accepting; he felt a sense of challenge; a premonition of a showdown. To prepare for it, he rose from his supine comfort, despite her deprecatory gesture, as he always had for women. Mixture of Nurse Cavell's statue and of Madame Curie she might be, but he would not take it lying down, although neither would he use unfair weapons by dwelling inwardly on her gold teeth. He stood until she was seated.

'No, don't be worried, Mr Langmuir. I have not come to disturb your well-deserved convalescence from the shocks of Asia. I promised you some days of rest, and I keep my promises. I thought you would just like to know,' and she waved some newspapers at him, 'that you have put it among the pigeons.'

When Hamo closed his eyes at the weary remembrance of the interview, she added, 'You must not allow that overestimated English modesty to underestimate the importance of what you have said here to the reporters in India.'

But, if Erroll was soon to relinquish his watch-dog post, he was clearly the more determined to bark now.

'Look, Mrs Kovalam, what Mr Langmuir said was just an off-the-cuff statement for the local chaps. It wasn't for the world at large.'

'Mr Watton, I am afraid you do not understand the social pressures at present working in India. Mr Langmuir, one of the greatest architects of the famous Green Revolution, comes to India and makes criticism of the effects of landlordism, and even of the great god of capital investment programmes, and the use made of Western aid. This is not the so-called disinterested role that the capitalist world expects of its scientists. They are not to question the exploitation of their discoveries, that is not one of the freedoms permitted in the so-called free economies. Do you suppose this will not be attacked and vilified? Today it is reported, in garbled fashion of course, in Madras. Tomorrow it will be in the *Bombay Times*, and in the *Times of India*, in the Hindi press, and, more important, in the vernacular newspapers.'

'Well, I can tell you this, Mrs Kovalam, the Chief's very over-tired and if any bloody nosey parker reporters start fussing him here, they'll get such a bash on the nose that they'll never come to the surface of that beautiful blue water again.'

Mrs Kovalam smiled soothingly. 'Do not worry, Mr Watton, such schoolboy fisticuffs will not be necessary. Mr Langmuir is the distinguished visitor of the State of Kerala. His peace and quiet will be respected. Indeed we can hope that he will feel relaxed enough to see more of the cooperative systems and the communal agriculture that we are working here. His favourable opinions, expressed to me yesterday, could have great weight in the Third World, where naïve conceptions of the value of scientific objectivity inculcated in the education of imperialist days still have great weight.'

'Oh Gawd! This is going to be a ... Look, Mr Langmuir's resting ...'

'It's true, Mrs Kovalam, I cannot be drawn into any local controversies. I need some rest and then I should like to avail myself of your hospitality here to write my reports to the Institute. There are many technical recommendations that I have in mind which are far more relevant than the rather random social observations ...'

'Our scientists are waiting for them eagerly, Mr Langmuir. They will receive full publicity in our technical journals. But I think meanwhile,' and she twinkled as never before, severely and kindly behind her pince-nez, 'the dialectic has caught up with you. These attacks which you have called forth will, I am sure, force you to synthesize your subjective feelings of compassion and pity with your objective technical findings. If they give you time, these angry capitalist gentlemen. In their fury, by the way, their typography has deteriorated below even its usual poor level – "Go home, Homo, we don't need your homilies or your home-spun theories." Well, how do you answer that. You see I appeal to the sense of humour with which so many British protect themselves.'

Erroll's cheeks turned red even through his acquired suntan. Hamo looked to see if the lady intended any insult. But it was clear that she had read what was printed; and, no doubt, she was right in supposing that the distortion of his name was due only to typographical ineptitude.

With gymnastic clumsiness, he raised his long body from recline and stood looking out to sea. 'I propose to answer it by having a refreshing swim.'

His decision was answered by shouting, even screams, from the motor launch which awaited Mrs Kovalam's return. From under the central awning on to the open deck appeared a short but muscular man of thirty-five or so in a singlet and canvas trousers, his teeth below his feebly sprouting moustache flashed in doglike rage. He pushed backwards before him a youth whom he held by the neck. The boy's near-nakedness, veiled only by a pair of ancient bathing trunks holed and bleached of all colour, seemed to make the assault more brutal. As he shoved the boy towards the deck edge, with his free hand he smacked him hard from side to side across the face.

'What the hell are you doing?' Hamo shouted and Erroll moved to intervene. But Mrs Kovalam was stern.

'This is no affair for visitors, please.'

'Then will you stop that man at once,' for the youth, dark brown, almost black, waist 24, hips 35, long-legged, was nearly the Fairest Youth who had Ever Been Seen. And he was a youth in distress.

Mrs Kovalam got up gymnastically from her chair. 'Oh, my goodness,' she said, 'Don't worry, Mr Langmuir. There are always some fights in these boats.'

'But he'll kill that boy.'

'I don't think so,' she laughed, a dry, calming laugh. 'But if it's upsetting your nervous system, I shall order him to stop.'

She called out sharply, and the man stood holding the youth as he would a chicken whose neck he had been absurdly ordered not to wring. The youth was crying.

'Why has he attacked him?'

'Oh, he was probably stealing, or something. These casual labourers on the boats are often very anti-social elements.'

'Tell him to take on someone of his own size,' Erroll said, hoping so to dismiss the incident.

But it was Hamo now who was severe and kind.

'Mrs Kovalam, I insist on knowing what this is all about.'

She looked, for a moment, annoyed, then, seeing Hamo's earnest expression, she decided to accommodate his whim. She spoke to the man for a few moments, sharply, dismissively, and once she elicited a long, rapid flow from the youth which she cut short.

'Yes, it's what I thought,' she said, 'this boy is lazy. He comes from up-country. Some family of peasants who failed for one reason or another to cooperate satisfactorily in the new agricultural programme. Inefficiency, stupidity, backward-looking notions, all these present great problems. The achievements you saw yesterday, Mr Langmuir, in the paddy fields for example, were not brought about without much patient teaching by the central authorities, and, of course, there are incorrigible elements who inevitably drift into a kind of parasitism. It is one of the problems in all our cities. Rehabilitation is not an easy thing. In my opinion the pill will do much to root out these weak strains, as you have done with our grains of rice. Education for the pill is more acceptable to our male tradition than the older methods.' Again she laughed. 'Meanwhile the inevitable result is some violence. I am sorry you should have seen it.'

Hamo's answer was to walk over to the boy and give him a wad of notes from his pocket book. He dared not look towards Erroll, for he remembered the beggars in Colombo. The boy broke into a happy white-toothed smile. For a moment the magic was so powerful that Hamo had to control his tired muscles in order not to throw his arms around that half-naked body. At least he could relax his mouth muscles in an answering smile. But then the cruel effects of his own Magic upon the boy's life came back to him, and he resolutely responded with a frown and moved away. He went up to Mrs Kovalam and shook her hand.

'Well, goodbye for the moment,' he said, 'I'm going to have a rest and then a swim.'

He walked away from her towards the Residence. She saw nothing for it but to board the launch. As the mooring ropes were hauled in and the engine sounded, Hamo turned to see the youth spring from the deck into the garden and run off into the flamboyant and mango trees that masked the kitchen quarters of the perfect eighteenth-century house.

The water's warmth was, all the same, cooling beside the intense heat of the sun which blazed down upon his head. He willed himself to think only of the calming contact of the little ripples that splashed against his nose and arms and thighs, ripples that reached him as the last outer circles of the great swells thrown up by the chugging motor boats. Yet he could not wholly banish his anxieties, his cares. They formed themselves now into the fussing thought that he should have worn some sort of cap to protect the nape of his neck from the intense burning of the sun's rays. The very immensity of the water stretching away from him, for, at his breast-stroke level, he could see nothing of any of the coasts before him, might have been the mid-ocean, and he the flotsam cast out from a wreck. The aloneness threatened to bring him not composure but panic, not to banish the decision before him but to double the force of its absurd isolated necessity. He turned to look back, and, in the crook of the vast trunk of a flamboyant tree, set off by soft green leaf plumage and vivid scarlet flowers, crouched the Very Fair Youth, a delicious black cat purring to be fondled. He changed to a vigorous crawl, resolutely setting outwards into the bay. He sought some object in all the vast space before him, just some objective, however idly floating, that would give some definition to his healing swim. Some way over to his left he thought he glimpsed in the gentle swell's rise and fall a small floating mass, green, brown – a seaweed? He had noticed none before in these waters. He would have an aim. He would investigate. Now the warmth of the water played caressingly, easingly against his skin, the heat of the sun was delicious only and his fears seemed absurd. Taking his time, he moved towards his goal, which yet appeared to move away from him.

He heard a shout but he refused to look back; the shouting continued, and, turning his head, he saw the youth's face contorted – could it be in righteous anger on behalf of all youths, all the hopeless? The very sentimentality, the weakness of his thought made him aware of how tired his body was, how unwilling his muscles. But he must drive on. An agonizing pain shot through his right leg muscle, so that for a while he could do no more than tread water; but he was nearing his object. Then suddenly he felt his legs entangled and pulled down by some slippery creature, some entwining slimy ribbons, and his leg was rock-hard with cramp. He was under the heavy pulverizing water, but he fought up to the air again. Behind him from the bank came the clamour of voices and a loud crash of the water. He turned himself with a desperate effort, but he sensed that it had taken all his strength. He sank and rose again to see a dark face, all the muscles distorted with effort, the eyes staring, the mouth set in some laughterless grin. Arms encircled him, hands sought to hold him up, but he knew the gesture for the deception it was. He had to free himself, he had to have freedom, freedom from youth, freedom to live again. He kneed hard against the taut body pressed against his own. Sensing by the softness that he had found the testicles, he sought to wrench the snakelike arms from him, he forced the small head down below the water. He was terrified, terrified of all help.

He recalled later only a forced, breathless hiccoughing and vomiting.

When he woke in the great four-poster bed in the air-conditioned panelled room, he sensed Erroll's presence, but he turned over on his pillow and slept again.

The next morning he was intolerably weak but recovered. Erroll then told him.

'For God's sake,' he said, 'everyone feels for you. Drowning men are bound to panic. The poor little bugger didn't understand life-saving anyway. I've made that starchy bitch stir her stumps to inquire about the family. If we can help the poor bastards, I knew you'd want me to.'

And then as if by pre-arrangement to distract him, to prevent his despair, Kit Coates, in immaculate high-lapelled cream linen suit and scarlet silk cravat, was at his bedside and chatted generally.

'I wish you'd seen the synagogue,' he said. 'Only two hundred of the White Jews are left and very few of them are under forty. It's the sort of thing that appeals now. Not that there's any chance of conservation there. They're bound to die out in the next few years. They accept the fact. But still the tele audiences lap up doomed groups. Their morbidity's insatiable. I won't tire you any further,' Coates said, as Hamo closed his eyes. 'The doctors think you'll be able to leave here in a day or two. So we're postponing our departure for Goa. Watton and I have put our heads together and you're to come with us. Nothing comes of unnecessary suffering, you know.' Then he added, 'Drowning, not waving.' He said it as a quotation.

'I flung me round him. I drew him under. I clung, I drown'd him, my own white wonder. Father and Mother, weeping and wild ... calling the child (Roden Berkeley Wriothesley Noel [1834–1894]).'

Only, of course, the wonder wasn't white; on the contrary, almost black. And there was no calling, no Father and Mother could be traced. The boatman asked for recompense for the boy's lost services, but Hamo refused it. However he left one hundred pounds with a reluctant Mrs Kovalam – for the parents, if they could be found.

Alexandra couldn't pay much attention to what Elinor was saying as they clambered up the slippery sandbank away from the beach in quest of audience of the Swami. Her mind was with Oliver in the small hotel bedroom in Panaji – without herself, without his totem Ned. As Thelma said, 'He just loves peeking through these balcony curlicues. And they *are* kind of nice and ornamental too. It's a rococo generation, hon, right upon your heels.'

But if he fell, or if Thelma's grasp, shaky despite her fortnight-long Goan bout of sobriety, proved too feeble, he would at best grow up with rococo legs that would make people shudder. Shudder as she found herself shuddering again and again here in

India – at limbless trunks that propelled themselves about the streets on wheeled boards, at a man with a vast pendulous lip like an orang-outang, at a woman with empty eye-sockets burning red like Hallowe'en pumpkin eyes, and at a giant, nearly black, naked man daubed with ashes, with ash-filled hair, and eyes all too much there, violent bloodshot eyes seeming to spark with a strange demon flame as he rushed from a temple, shouting, howling and flailing his arms.

She saw the Divine Idiot as clumsy, yes; but neatly made, well-fashioned. I suppose, she thought, I want my Gothic tamed. And truth to tell, although she believed more and more that to solve all the complex horrors and the desperate boredoms of the world, only a simplicity near to absurdity would suffice – not Roddy's dandy elegance, nor even Ned's intuitive mind-body synchronization; she did not want Oliver to be the one to save the world by his idiocy. Dear Thelma, don't let him come to harm, dear God, because I'm not sure of you and Thelma doesn't believe in you, don't let that stop you keeping an eye on Thelma (for you must be everywhere or nowhere) so that she keeps an eye on my baby.

Elinor said a little more loudly than the deep but nowadays subdued tones of her normal voice, 'Don't fret about the child, Alexandra. Can't you let all this gentleness, this selflessness, yes, wait for it, this *love* that you've shown in coming with us today be complete? Just let it grow and breathe in you until there's no place left for the deadening, cramping maternal fears.'

She talked like that now, and did it so naturally that it was hard to laugh, especially since she seemed more often than not to know in advance what one was thinking. How laugh at a vatic manner if a real seer speaks the words? And she had ceased to bitch; for most of the time she had even ceased to rage after Ned.

He called it Death, a hateful sort of false spiritualized death, like a Victorian marble tombstone. But it was hard to say whether this wasn't simply because he was angry that she no longer raged for him and also because for a second time she had misled him about the Community, for the Malabar people had dispersed, and the people on the famous Goan Colva Beach were such a motley collection of self-conscious, worn-out, stoned-out, guru-seeking, old-fashioned hippies that there was no getting even a semblance of mimetic coordination out of them.

But it wasn't only Oliver that filled Alexandra's mind. More immediately there was the toe she had stubbed on a rock last night when putting up the tent, here at the Dona Paula Beach, among palms and cashew nut trees and the massive roots of banyans, which, sacred or not, proved death-traps for those who had no Hindu faith. It was her left big toe and the nail was half torn away so that the flesh bled and a nerve kept throbbing.

Once again Elinor had made it hard to complain, for with her new-found inner grace or whatever, she no longer sailed about like a stately schooner or a lovely swan, but was always tripping and falling over, so that, under her long skirt, her calves and knees were a mass of bandages, yet she never complained or even bothered about replacing the hastily knotted, swathed handker-chiefs when they slipped down and hung around her ankles. She had bruised her face, too, her now so thin, so translucent face. And the more she breathed and postured and fasted, the heavier, because the more shapeless, her long body seemed to look. Yet with all that, and with all the silly spiritual-sounding words she used, she looked more beautiful every day, more complete, more detached. And not beautiful idiocy, for, though living this life of positions and breathings that appeared to deny any mind, she could still be, whenever she wished, as practical in an academic-ally exact sort of way, as highly intelligent as she had always been – but she didn't want any of these things, she said, unless what she called 'the outer world of seeming' demanded them.

As now, when she said, 'Mother will be sober, Alexandra. No problems there. I just know that. She senses that I am near the end of my disciplines. She is beginning to understand that when I say I'll go back and teach college – the Metaphysical Milton, even Emblem Books if that's their thing – I'll do just *that*. *Only* let me do two months of this man's exercises and I'll be free to live on my own plane wherever I am. Why! the way I'll be then, I could teach high school in Dayton, Ohio or Mobile, Alabama or even in lovely California where Mother's got some atavistic urge to return, and no one will guess that I'm floating way out on my own etheric wave. So if you can't flood your body with more gentleness and love, please let the so-called facts of the situation stay your fears.'

Alexandra, as far as she was able to communicate, when seeking not to slide downhill on a mixed surface of sun-glazed sand and time-polished banyan root, and this in the long skirt said to be decreed by the Swami, sought to convey her acceptance of this reassurance of Thelma's new contented mind. Yet it hardly convinced her, for only yesterday that pathetic old voice had croaked at her, as that trembling old hand crashed down on the dressing table a glass full of ginger ale, 'God blast this lousy liquor! It tastes like sacred cow's piss! Come to think of it, it probably is. But I've got to stay sober, hon, until we're quit of this goddamned guru. One of these days when these phonies have put Elinor way up into the etheric, she's gonna get raped in her beautiful trance. I don't know the law in these parts about rape in the ether, but I know that if it happens, I'm gonna get that guru's guts. And Elinor's gonna need me around then too.' It hadn't sounded like a trusting and contented mind; but, by now, Alexandra had learned that all too often when Elinor said she 'just knew', it was true, she did just know.

In any case, even if, at this very minute, Oliver was cooing away happily as Thelma, no doubt, fed him on Turkish Delight and Chocolate Corn Flakes and other outrageous foods, that couldn't really banish all her fears. She couldn't speak of them, but quite simply she was in dread of what might come by seeing this famous Swami, feared even what he might look like, that he might prove to be one of the 'faces' come true. She had felt this absurd fear of him from the first moment that she heard of all these fantastic occult powers that he was said to possess. She had vigorously refused to be drawn into it all. When she accompanied Elinor on the long bus and ferry treks up from Colva Beach to Panaji to stay, in respite from the sand and the ocean, in Thelma's Portuguese little hotel, she would never go near the Swami's shrine or hermitage or cell or wherever he hid himself, though Elinor lined up there every day, desperately begging to be admitted to the classes. And now had come this mysterious summons. This Swami, this man with creepy powers, wanted to see *her*, or so Elinor and Ned insisted; and weakly, to help Elinor, to please Ned, she had agreed.

314

Once again, as they at last reached the top of the steep sandy bank and took in the jungle village, or really the sort of suburb among the palms that confronted them, Elinor went straight into her thoughts.

'I think he only asked to see you to impose another obstacle on *me*. In part he's quite right. If his *prayanas* have half the efficacy, the innerness that I'm sure they do have, he must do all he can to deter idly curious or sloppy-minded people from diluting the classes with their spiritual weakness. In part it's a bit of his publicity stuff. Making himself scarce, playing hard to get. But I *must go* to those classes. He knows the techniques; or rather, by now, it's this Subrindath Rao or one of the other Sadhakas who can do the tricks, not the Austrian Swami himself at all. That's what makes it such a drag. The disciples won't allow anyone that hasn't been accepted by the old man in *satsang*. But then again that may be just another trial, a *sadhana*. So one must fulfil what he asks. And thank you for coming.'

'But how could he possibly know about *my* existence?'

'Oh,' Ned, who had joined them, said, 'the way he lives and that, he could have knowledge we don't know of. Like his E.S.P.'s only got to extend into his courtyard to sense *my* thoughts. And, of course, you'd be in them.'

He took Alexandra's hand as rarely these days – and they went, swinging hand in hand, as in the past.

'Of course he does,' Elinor said, 'but that's not important. It's the *being* that matters, not what you do with it. If you're a Mutra you're free to be in any place, in any mind and all minds. As I shall be. Then I can teach college or high school or dance striptease but that won't affect my being. Just the same way with him. He may be the avatar of Vishnu or Francis Xavier or who you like, as some say he claims. He may speak telepathically with Atlantean initiates in Tibet or possess all this rumoured Lemurian wisdom older than Atlantis. It's probably all charlatan rubbish. Or it may not be. It doesn't *matter*. That's all *meaning*. Meaning doesn't matter. Only *being*. That's the trouble with your mimes, Ned. You want to make meanings.'

'I don't agree. In this uncoordinated, flabby state we're in now everywhere, any chance, y'know, of sort of superconsciousness's important. If he's not a fake, then what he's done with these disciples, I mean Atlantis and so on, could be just a symbol for some higher knowledge he's tapped. And we oughtn't to turn away from it. I shan't anyway, if he says anything that seems to mean more than all the usual stuff.'

'But the being *is* the knowledge, Ned. The other may be true. It probably is. But it doesn't *matter*. If you let it matter, it could just get in the way as much as all this.' Elinor waved her hand towards the world of natural objects before them.

And certainly, Alexandra thought, the real world before them *did* appear both very impeding and very improbable. So improbable that it prevented her from questioning either Ned or Elinor, for though it was likely that what each had said was nonsense, or at least so it seemed to her, yet Elinor's fasting and breathing and postures had changed her soul or whatever, even if they looked like killing her body; and if *that* could happen, a lot more could, things like these stories about this Austrian Swami's occult powers of healing and so on; and if that, then the faces and all their horrors might be true. She would rather not know, she would not ask.

And as a matter of fact she could not, for the natural world, whether real or not, in the shape of a heaving, pushing, swaying crowd of people hoping to have audience of the Swami made keeping her arm linked to Ned's which in turn was linked to Elinor's, an overriding, all-absorbing concern. She was frightened. All this mass of flesh and clothing and rags and sweat would smother her. All these feet and knees and thighs, elbows and buttocks that kept pushing against her would keel her over, trample her down, pulp her. It had happened so suddenly – first they were in a queue like at a supermarket exit, and now, from pressure behind and blockage ahead, they were in a tumult. She dug her fingers into Ned's muscley arm, she bit into her own underlip to stop herself from crying like a frightened child. How could Elinor (however tall) have made those daily importuning visits to this heaving mass, how could Ned (however sinewy) have so often escorted her? Her face was buried in the blinding magenta silk of some plump Indian lady's back, she was stifled with its patchouli scent. Her free arm kept brushing against some sweaty nakedness that, at last, freeing one eye from the billowy magenta-clad rolls of flesh, she could, squinting for a moment, see in close-up as a yellowy, smooth flesh marked with white patches and a horrible puckered scar. Her buttocks were alternately kneed and then rubbed by what she felt to be a vast tautened distended belly. Someone spat red betel like blood on to her grey linen sleeve. She was not now, as for so many past months, a current, a swell in the calming monotony of the ocean's rocking, but a trough that might at any moment go down, down into the profoundest horror or that might be thrown high into the air, to dissolve in spume. And that wasn't figurative, she told herself, fearing that this vague symbolic shaping of her thought might be the result of some awakening mass hypnosis; the trough is my body to be pulped into the dusty ground or thrown high and spun apart bleeding in the air by some uncontrollable movement of this human mass. These are bodies, smelly bodies most of them, including mine, there's nothing of symbol or spirit here.

But then, as the swaying crowd came to some halt that held it rocking to and fro on the same spot for what seemed minutes, her absolute fright began to lessen – she could feel once again her throbbing toe, fear for its safety, become aware of the dust that filled the air, filled her ears, her nose, her throat, making her splutter and cough, become aware, at last, with a new fear that this turbulent human ocean was not alone flesh but resounding with strange noises that went up and down and deafened and faded like the pounding roar and soft hissing retreat of the ocean. The crowd was never quite silent. Always a murmur.

Then, from a distance, a sound would pierce the low hum – some howling, of a single madman surely, or of an agonized ecstatic. Now far away on the other side, a high voice was raised in eunuch note, then joined by others in an eerie singing of a Vedic hymn. Now they were chanting the Swami's name. And now a hundred voices chattered and lilted in what could have been as many tongues – Conakry, Hindi, perhaps Sanskrit, how should she know? – but all, like birds or monkeys, were another race, unconcerned with her, yet infinitely menacing. Starlings in Trafalgar Square at dusk ready to take over the city like in that nasty Hitchcock thing.

Here and there in all this alien tossing, storming sea came European voices, ridiculous in their familiarity, and in the total powerlessness of their words to protect her against the darkening hostile mass. English, grand and female: 'I suppose it's the extraordinary inversion of the dead-weight of Western logic that refreshes,' and in answer, male, soldierly, yet giving thought and consideration: 'I don't know so much about that. I suspect the real truth is that it has its *own* strange logic.' German, earnest, female: 'But no, Ursula. You are quite mistaken. It is the *chatras below* the navel with which these *asanas* are concerned.' American, mid-West, formidably defiant and female: 'He *says* he sees us as so many fountains in a lake. Now where does the petty self lie in that, huh? It's neat.' And, at last, absurdly, French, and feminine: 'Mais non, il m'a demandé dix millions. C'est ridicule. Non, non, Ernestine. Écoute. Je ne m'y mêlerai plus. Entendu?' Alexandra thought of a phrase she had read somewhere which it seemed people had used a lot at some time. 'Same here,' she said aloud. And blushed as though she had been detected in folly by the whole vast gathering.

But embroiled she must be, for suddenly the swaying sea before her began to part. She wondered if, as with the Red Sea, the magenta lady would be cleft in two, but her fatty mass lurched to one side, wobbling. A cream-skinned, handsome, black-moustached, pale young man, in long loose grey linen tunic buttoned from neck to shoe and a black fur-trimmed cap, was bowing before her. They – she and Ned and Elinor – were the Children of Israel and all this neat, miraculous parting of the waters was to make a passage for their entry into the Swami's presence. 'How had this man known where to find them in this dense crowd? His eyes were soft, large and romantically dewy, but his thin pencil-line moustache above his pale thin lips was cruel. What was the special power of knowing that the Swami possessed, and did his handsome disciple share that strange knowledge, since he had been able to find them so exactly?' Well, Alexandra thought, trying to cool it by mockery as much as she could, there's nothing for it but to 'read on' – next episode: 'Inside the Sinister Swami's Cave'. But she couldn't stop her fast heart-beats and the disturbance in her stomach.

Her fears were not lessened as they all three passed through the crowd to the low-walled edge of the Swami's compound. It was magical to her that a great raging sea of people should stop short, as this one, in an orderly line before a mud brick barrier that came no higher than knee-level, if to that. Yet so it was. Not one wave, not one spray had spilled over into holy ground. 'Invisible fuzz,' she whispered. And to her comfort, Ned joined in, 'If this gets to Scotland Yard, it's the end of sit-ins.'

Their guide voiced that kind of intuitive, tangential answer that so scared her. 'The welcome *only* approach. The unwelcome are as a still ocean. Their stillness also pleases the Swami.' Yet, as he added, 'You are welcome,' he did not look as though he had heard, let alone understood, their facetious whispers.

It was all absurd. Here they were in a suburban garden of the most hideous kind – the cushiony coarse sort of lawn they seemed to have in these hot places a vivid green under the sprinkler's spray, bright orange marigolds, some other flowers, with cactusy sort of leaves, every rotten colour, but mostly magenta like the fat lady's dress, and bushes of those bright scarlet and pink and apricot flowers with the long spikes coming so rudely out of the trumpets – all this garish mass against the most awful suburban villa – red brick, set with diamond shapes and things in a kind of bruised purple. She ought surely to feel reassured, particularly when the handsome guide in a voice no longer gnomic but like any casual host said, pointing at the magenta flowers: 'The Swami loves all flowers, but especially the portulaca.'

She ventured to stimulate her emerging ease by whispering again to Ned, 'There ought to be those stone mushrooms that you hear about but never see.'

And he answered aloud, 'He's certainly achieved a powerful state of unbeauty.'

Elinor turned on him. 'Oh! for God's sake! Who knows what positive etheric waves you're neutralizing with all that infantile defensive humour?'

Immediately Alexandra's spark of reassurance was extinguished. It was exactly in just such hideous suburban bungalows with just such hideous front gardens that lived all the most sinister destroyers of reason – half-charlatans, half-magi – in London suburban terraces and in South-coast seaside villas, in undistinguished apartment blocks in outlying Paris arrondissements and probably in dreary decayed Spanish-style residences with empty pools in Hollywood. There they sat, the fat ear-ringed medium women, the pale thin clairvoyant men with suave white hair and burning eyes, waiting like half-gorged spiders for specially thinned-up flies like Elinor to walk into the loss of their fortunes (or Thelma's, or the Senator's), to the loss of their virginity, of their reason, of their lives. It was all in the horror comics. They had been warned from childhood. And now, to keep Elinor doom company, marched Alexandra Grant straight into the trap.

How would the cruel silken web appear? Bead curtains, dimmed lamps and burning incense? Or Hindu drums and fearsome masks and mantra scrolls? Or emptiness, a bare cell room to isolate and startle the victim, a sting to paralyze the nerve centres?

When they came up the steps of the villa and in through the half-open yellow pitch-pine door with ornamental ironwork facings painted in silver, they found themselves on a cheaply tiled floor of the diminuitive hall of a diminuitive bungalow. Led by their guide, they walked in ungreeted.

No more than three or four rooms, all little more than large cupboard size, all with doors half-open. That pervasive nose-prickling scent of curry came surely from the kitchen; there was a foot-rest Asian privy where a youth squatted, his dhoti half unwound; in a larger room were six bunks made up for sleeping, and on the floor a plate of orange segments and some liquefying white cheese; in the largest room, another bunk, and, beside it, some chewed-over paperbacks stacked in a pile.

'That is the room of Sant Sarada Maharysh. When cold winds blow from the Ocean he receives all here.'

But in the present sweltering heat, it appeared, he received upon the back porch; and, from it, Alexandra could hear a din like a cow bellowing from the pains of over-swollen udders, and against that, some high crowing noise, perhaps a cock's, and then peals and peals of giggling laughter as from a busload of schoolgirls. Wild though the sounds were, they calmed her down, although as a rule she thought uncontrolled laughter rather scary.

'A holy woman and her daughter are with the Swami,' they were told. 'They are the cause of the cosmic laughter.'

And, sure enough, as they came out into the sunlight, that dazzled them the more for winking and glittering at them through the thick meat-safe mesh of the old-fashioned mosquito wiring, Alexandra found herself peering straight down the pink slobbery almost toothless open mouth of the holy man himself, as his huge body rolled back and forth on the old motor-car seat on which he was perched cross-legged and helpless with laughter. To her relief he appeared not to notice their arrival and they were led by the guide to a far corner of the large and various circle of people who were seated on the ground a little below the Master's level. All of him worried her – the huge fiery multi-folded face into the creases of which his little eyes seemed to have disappeared entirely, his bristly pendant jowl, his large bald ostrich-egg head on which some mysterious lost continents had been sketched in patches of scurfy copper-coloured skin, his great, heaving, smooth shoulder, protruding from his shapeless white gown draped like a robe – a monstrous great dowager, or a sergeant-major in drag, and, dangling over the edge of the dark red imitation leather seat, beyond the hem of the white cotton gown, two scrawny hairless legs, two feet as neat and small and shapely as the Little Mam's.

In the centre of the circle was a dark-skinned Indian girl with long black matted hair, dressed in some greenish filthy rags that appeared to Alexandra most like a washing-up cloth long due for replacement. She was crowing loudly and scratching the dusty concrete of the veranda floor with her left foot, striking backwards like a hen, so that clouds of minute reddish particles had filled the air. Coughing and suppression of coughing came from all parts of the audience. The Swami, however, was untouched by the dust's contagion as his mouth opened wider and wider with convulsions of hysteric mirth. Looking at the girl's sad vacant eyes and her idiotic-looking loosely hanging jaw, Alexandra felt a revulsion from the Swami that was more than the physical disgust with which he had immediately inspired her.

But even more titillating to the Swami's glee was an old stout woman, also raggedly dressed, who stood beside the crowing girl. This shapeless creature, all rolls of fat around her vast waist and buttocks, but exposing a pair of the skinniest dugs, had raised her voluminous skirts high up to her huge loins and, squatting, was pissing energetically in turn into the pink and black of a row of half water-melons which, at the Swami's orders, one of his austere young grey-robed attendants had placed before her.

Suddenly, in the midst of a bouncing fit of apparently helpless laughter, the old man sat bolt upright and pointed at a thin, white-faced, red-haired European woman in a lemon-coloured sari who sat with an array of expensive groceries before her – her offering to the Master. One of the attendants came forwards and, removing the packets of Ceylon tea, Kenya coffee, marmalade, jam, biscuits, rusks, candied fruits, and pickles, placed them between the crowing girl and the pissing woman. Instantly the two creatures set upon them like hungry beasts, as no doubt they were, but for the half of what they swallowed of coffee beans and tea leaves compounded with wrapping paper and jam, another half they threw wildly into the air or spread upon their faces and bodies. For a while the Swami seemed intent upon the spectacle, but then he grew bored and ordered the removal of the two women who were led out, crowing and moaning.

The Swami turned to the red-haired woman and gave her what, to Alexandra's astonishment, truly appeared to be, despite his monstrous face and figure, a gracious smile and a gracious bow. He spoke in English with a very guttural German accent. But his tone and the words he used, she thought, were more like a conventional English vicar.

'We are very blessed, you and I,' he said, 'to give to the simple is to receive the divine scattering of their wits.'

The words, Alexandra noticed, served, like those of some artful stage manager, to distract attention from the less edifying spectacle of the attendants sweeping up the remains of glass, torn packets, and mess of marmalade stuck with coffee beans, all that was left of the lady's offering.

She seemed delighted, however, and was about to answer equally graciously, when a loud squawking rose from the far side of the circle and a boy of twelve or so, with pale greenish-coloured skin and a half-open mouth, suddenly stood above the seated people. Tearing at his tunic collar, he let out a series of shrieks that were choked in his throat before they reached their full note. The Swami listened to them gravely, 'as though,' Ned whispered, 'he's trying to measure the inaudible scale of bats.' But when Alexandra, cheered by the joking tone, turned to look at Ned, she saw that he was following the Swami's looks and movements with intense concentration. Elinor wore an expression of highborn disdain. The boy's choked crowing stopped as suddenly, and he fell rigid to the ground. The Swami signalled for the body to be brought to his side. Almost as soon as it was laid there, the fit or whatever it was came to an end. With a convulsive heaving of the limbs, an awful high scream came from the boy's grey open lips, through which his teeth glistened white as pearls set in grisaille. The Swami stretched his arm down and touched the boy's forehead. Immediately his own fat body began to shiver and his apoplectic face broke out in sweat. The boy's cries ceased abruptly. He sat up. The Swami smiled and stroked his hand. Then he began to fill the sloppily open mouth with toffees which he unwrapped one by one. And he continued so to feed the boy during the rest of the audience. A murmur of astonished awe ran through the assembly. A Japanese young man in horn-rimmed spectacles crouched over Alexandra's head and took photographs in rapid succession. A group of Indian pilgrims began chanting.

The Swami stopped all this with a gesture. Pointing at one among a number of pretty, choir-like American youths and girls dressed in cream linen gowns like surplices who were ranged in a row beneath a banner which read 'San Francisco Chapparti', he asked : 'What is actionless action?'

The youth, blushing beneath his crewcut, said, 'I guess it's sleepless sleep.'

'You guess. What do you mean you guess? No. Good boy. You are right. And what is thoughtless thought?'

'Sightless seeing?'

'Sightless sight,' amended the Swami. 'Very good, my dear boy. Now you ask your Swami a question.'

The youth looked at a loss when confronted by so positive a command, but the girl next to him asked, 'Swami, can we young ones also learn the initiate wisdom?'

The Swami smiled with infinitely tender pity.

'You will not learn it from the Brahmins,' he said. And suddenly shouting wildly, he pointed now at one Indian and then at another. 'No, not from you, who give service to the merry Lord Krishna and yet never laugh. Nor from you who are baptized into the Church of the travelling Lord Francis Xavier and sit like a filthy toad at your fireside.'

This second, stout, European-dressed Indian gentleman protested, 'But Swami! True, I am a Christian Brahmin. But I am

323

not from Goa. I have travelled from Malabar. From the country of Saint Thomas.'

'More fool you to come away. We want no doubters here.' He turned with elaborate courtesy to the American girl. 'Please forgive our Brahmins their manners. Now, I will tell you a thing. There is a God for you also. Ten miles from here is a stream. The name is Pahadavi. The God of that stream is called Cabolim. Give him offering. The people's gods, not the gods of the Brahmins, these will lead you to the True Wisdom. Among the simple, the divine fools, like those whose blessed presence you have seen here today.'

'Can't we learn it from you?'

'I? I am only a seeker, my poor dear young lady.' He tucked his huge head down as well as he was able into his armpit and simpered. 'You are from San Francisco? You are welcome to stay. Welcome in the name of Chapparti, spouse of that merry fellow Vishnu. Please see my secretary.'

He turned to a group of hippies, some of whom Alexandra recognized from the Colva Beach community. 'And you too. But remember – no careless collective living. We are in the age of Smritis now. We have our code of behaviour as well as our Veda.' And he laughed sympathetically. As both groups were filing out, he called after them, 'And no Esalen please. No touching, you from California. Do you think you can reach the true *cakras* by such childish means? My dear, what an absurdity.'

He shrugged his shoulders with a high giggle. A little appreciative laugh ran through the audience. One of the youths among the Bay area worshippers of Chapparti commented: 'That's the Swami's famous high camp.'

Elinor, from the heights of Nob Hill, looked away with contempt.

With the hippies and the San Francisco devotees gone, the audience was greatly thinned out. Alexandra felt at once more exposed and yet more at home. She shook herself. Whatever happened she must not allow herself to be drawn into this nonsense, perhaps shameful and pernicious nonsense.

An elderly pale-faced Indian gentleman, exquisitely dressed, with a fur hat and pince-nez – like someone out of Chekhov, Alexandra thought – stood up.

324

'Swami, is it true that you predict that with the end of Ramadan there will be some divine sign?'

The Swami looked intently at the questioner. Smiling to himself, he turned and whispered to one of his attendants. Then, addressing the well-dressed man with great severity, he said: 'I think you know very well that God has given his sign once for all in his holy law of the Koran.'

'I am of Islam. Yes. But I ask what *you* think, Swami. They say that because Ramadan this year begins on Divali and ends on the day of the procession of Saint Francis Xavier that you draw strange auguries from these conjunctions?'

'They say. Who say? Look at your diary. The dates are there. I am sure that an important man of affairs like yourself will not be without a diary for his grand arrangements. For centuries your Indian brothers in Islam have set forth for Mecca in all devout simplicity from this very port of Goa and you come here with guileful questions.'

The Swami's voice had turned to an angry shout. The man began to protest in his turn, but the Swami would not listen.

'What of your beautiful mosque that adorns these very shores at Namazyah. Wasn't that built by your Akbar on his visit here? Akbar, that merry fellow, who loved to give pleasure and smile, and *you* bring here nothing but anger and suspicion. Go away.'

There were murmurs from all over the gathering against the Moslem gentleman and he was jostled by his immediate neighbours. Wisely, as Alexandra thought, he withdrew. But as he went the Swami called after him.

'Come back again tomorrow. But let your heart speak, not your nerves. I like you. They'll tell you it's for your money bags, but it isn't. I like your face.'

Then he leaned back relaxedly and began to skin and eat a large plantain.

'Give fruit all round,' he ordered, belching. As the attendants went round with baskets of oranges and bananas, he said, giggling slyly, 'Any more trap questions for the poor silly old Swami? No?' A plump, spectacled elderly European held up his hand. 'Well?'

'Was können wir hoffen, von dem weisen Hermes Trismesgistus zu lernen?'

325

The Swami burst into delighted laughter and clapped his hands. He answered in German in a mocking childish falsetto. Then he translated, 'This gentleman asks what we can hope to learn from that great learned man Hermes Trismegistus. I tell him *I* hope to learn nothing, for Hermes Trismegistus never existed. Er hat nie existiert, wissen sie das nicht?' he shouted. 'My friend, I will tell you a thing. No, better, I will show a thing.' He gave some orders to an attendant who returned with a long loaf of bread and a paperback book from the house. The Swami broke open the loaf, smelt it, felt it. 'Stale, dry,' he said. Then he showed the cover of the paperback to the semicircle before him. It read *The Mysteries of Paris. By Eugène Sue*. The Swami irritably tore out a leaf from the book and, putting it between the two halves of the opened loaf, made a sandwich. 'There is your Hermes Trismegistus, my friend. A bit of fake mystery to sweeten the dry doctrines of Christianity.'

Ned said, 'Oh, Lor' !', and Elinor, 'My God !'

Alexandra felt the elaboration was embarrassingly feeble. The audience was clearly unimpressed, for only one pretty young Indian girl in a silver-starred pink sari and silver shoes gave a trilling laugh. Perhaps she hadn't understood. But the Swami understood failure at once.

He called out, 'Where are these dancers? Let them dance.'

Alexandra sat back, thinking, well at least that would be a change from all this super-quiz stuff, when to her horror, she realized from their handsome guide's demands that *they* were the dancers. Ned had only time to say, 'Not "Batteries". That batty girl's stolen our thunder. Let's try "Territoriality".'

As soon as they had started a few steps, Alexandra felt, well, really, yes, they were rather good. The audience was held, too. But not the Swami. He was hoisted up by two attendants and led to a small altar at the end of the porch where he set about prostrating himself before some figure, placing a bowl of rice or something before it; then he looked as though he was smearing it with some kind of butter and a bright scarlet powder, then at last, taking a garland of frangipani from one of his acolytes, he decked the god with it. Once more he prostrated himself, and, rising with great difficulty, smeared his head and cheeks with ashes. All this, as Alexandra could see by squinting, he did very perfunctorily. The attention of the audience was drawn away from their dance to this ceremony, but their trio kept dancing, and she could tell from Ned's expression that he was proud of their performance.

The Swami now gave it his notice. He returned and stood watching them, arms akimbo, like some washerwoman giving a moment's attention to her children's hopscotch. Then he shouted: 'Rubbish! Rubbish! You can't dance at all! This is terrible. Stop it at once. Go back to your places. Never mind. You are good souls I can see that. But the English are not for dancing. Who ever heard of the English dancing? No, no. The English are in this world to give orders and to look dignified.'

Ned said, loudly for him, 'She's, like, American,' and he pointed at Elinor.

'Don't be angry, little redbeard. I like you. I think you will find what you are seeking. Come here often. And the American African giraffe, she has achieved some posture. Is it she who wishes to attend the classes in *prayana*? Permission is granted. Sit down. Sit down. Even the great ones of England are now showing some spiritual concern. I have letters from Sir James Langmuir. Wise letters. The little girl is related to him, nicht wahr?'

Alexandra longed to run away in fear at his knowing even so much. I must stop him knowing about me. She concentrated very hard.

'No,' she said.

It was true, too, she wasn't *related*. Perhaps the truth would stop his power of getting at her.

Ned said, 'Our best friend's his secretary.'

Elinor said, 'It's happened quite recently, Swami,' as though he would be pleased to have such up-to-date news.

'Ach, so,' said the Swami. He gave no indication of how interested he was in this information, for he returned to Alexandra. 'I think you *are* related to Sir James.'

'She is,' Ned said, 'it's through her uncle or something who's a plant geneticist.'

'I'm *not*.' Alexandra was near to tears. 'Hamo's only my *god*-father. That isn't a relation. And anyway this Sir James is only some sort of distant relation to *him*.'

'Ah! Langmuir, the discoverer of Magic,' the Swami laughed. 'The Magician of Rice, the symbol of fertility. Is this rice magician as fertile as his magic?'

Alexandra did not answer. She thought the Swami's remark impertinent as well as unfortunate.

'He is now in India, I think, this great rice magician, nicht wahr?'

She was annoyed not to know this before the Swami, so she kept silent; anyway she had no right to involve poor Hamo with this charlatan.

'You make no answer,' the Swami said. 'Do you fear *his* magic also as you fear mine? Never mind that I know your secret. You must learn that all ways of knowing are good. And now,' he said, addressing them all, 'we have made our morning *puja* to Vishnu. Let us go our ways.'

But a young, ardent-eyed Indian youth in Western dress called out a question.

'Don't speak Conakry,' the Swami shouted. 'It's rude to this young lady who's related to such important gentlemen. Ask your question in English.'

'Sir, do you believe that the body of Saint Francis Xavier, for so long miraculously preserved, has now decayed to dust? Is that your opinion, Sir?'

The Swami produced what Alexandra recognized as a real mocking laugh from somewhere deep down in his belly.

'Oho! Another spy! Go and ask your Jesuit fathers. Ask the Father Provincial. They are custodians of that holy body. And don't look angry at me. Remember how it is said that when Saint Francis Xavier came to Goa the people were given up to excesses. He saved them, but not by angry looks. No, he dined daily at their tables and laughed at the absurdities of their sexual indulgences. Francis Xavier was, like Vishnu, a merry fellow. All divine science contains laughter. The ancient Lemurians had many jokes in their mathematical system – jokes that they could not convey to their more austere, wooden-headed Atlantean disciples. And I don't mean the obscene jokes of Russellian mathematical logic. Now go.'

Before they could break up, the anaemic red-haired lady in the lemon sari said timidly in a faint Cockney voice: 'How can I free my mind, Swami, from the enslavement of the body's shame of Hellenic reason-worship?'

The swami rolled over and took her hand. 'Little one, I am afraid you are not far enough advanced for me to help you. Go and see the Greco–Buddhist sculptures of the Gandhara School. Stand naked before them, glorying in your body, in all those cavities by which the magnetic fluids enter and leave your psychic centre. This may help you as a first step of unfreezing from the Valhallan northern ice of rational logic. Buddhism may be your way. Perhaps for a first step. Go to the bikkhus. But follow Mahayana not Hinayana, even a neophyte may allow herself such a step in the renunciation of the egocentricity of monism. Go first to the Buddha images here in India. Then go to Japan. Go at once.' He patted her hand and then turned to the departing audience, 'You see. To the simple and spiritually advanced I may speak directly. But to those still imprisoned in the absurd chains of reason, like our sister here, I must talk this spurious intellectual language. And now, you and you and you and you, and, yes, you my little girl, stay. I have more to say to you. You may keep the bearded fellow with you to protect you from my magic spells.' He laughed.

Alexandra was horrified. 'I have a baby ...'

'Your baby is feeding happily. Sit down.'

They were not more than twenty in all, but still a mixed bag; and while they drank tea and ate chappatis, the Swami gave them his discourse.

'Now, we are near to the moment of crisis. In one week, the procession of Saint Francis Xavier will go once more from the Bom Jesus to the Cathedral. Many hundred pilgrims will be present. The concourse of bishops and priests, of monks and nuns and friars will be large. But I tell you a thing – there will be hundreds but not thousands, the numbers will be large but not great. Why is this? Because at the fourth centenary in 1952 of the Christian calendar those worthy gentlemen the Jesuits, having gained control, decreed that the great magus's coffin should not be carried again, his body not exposed. Until the Day of Judgement, they said, it shall not be shown to the simple. Perhaps the Day of Judgement is nearer for these worthy gentlemen than they think.

'By the way, my dear young lady, you will not repeat these matters elsewhere, for you will not understand them. And even if you are so foolish as to repeat what you hear, you or the good redbeard fellow, it will not matter, for my words have secret meaning, known only to these ladies and gentlemen here – adepts. And not to *all* of them. Indeed the words I speak have many meanings that I cannot know myself and must not ask. But I wish you to hear them so that you may tell Sir James Langmuir that in Goa here lies that application of spiritual powers for practical concerns which is what he so ardently seeks. You understand?'

Ned replied eagerly on Alexandra's behalf, 'Yes, yes! We're listening. Meaning comes from shape, like, anyway.'

'You know already, my friends, how many are working against me here. Not only the Jesuits and the Roman Catholic Brahmins who fear so greatly the recognition of their Saint Francis in his true semblance as a great *avatar* in the line of Vishnu. And farther back ...' His voice faded away ito a vague suggestion of primeval secret order. 'But also the Moslems obsessed with their absurd devotion to the principle of a single God. God, gods – what foolish concepts to dispute about. And now our Hindu friends, those who gave me food and lodging at the *ashram* when I first came here, are growing unfriendly towards me. I tell you all this, my friends, not to alarm you, for such threats against ancient wisdoms and ancient powers, such as we are in touch with, are an absurdity; but to inform, to prepare you. They are frightened also because of my powers of healing and extra-sensory knowledge, childish even superfluous powers that always accompany the Inner Wisdom – powers that they themselves, yes, the Christian priests and mullahs and the sadhas and the Buddhist bikkhus possessed for everyday use until they listened to the puerile limitations of reason and its lackey, empirical science. If it was only this what should we care? But these foolish persons are themselves the creatures of Higher Powers than they know, they are being used to an end. And the climax of this great battle which is being waged upon another plane will take place here at Goa as I have already predicted. Now I am sure of it.'

A bearded man in a home-made dressing gown adapted from the Franciscan robe, asked, 'Do these signs accord with those popularly given out as your predictions, Swami?'

'You heard what that fellow said. Yes, the conjunction is there. And it is being used by the powers we know of. But the powers that use *us* will use it also. And they will be stronger. So, while pretending to refuse credence to this calendar conjunction, I gladly encourage talk of it, for by doing so, we bring on the events we need. Only. And I ask you to mark this. *They* seek to turn all into a deathly so-called peace, *we* must bring the forces of destruction and renewal into activity to prevent this plan of our good Himalayan friends.'

'Do you think,' asked an ageing Frenchwoman with the short-cut boyish hair of her existential youth now grey and thinning, 'that *all* the etheric forces of the Himalayan siddhas are concentrated on Goa here, *all* their ray forces? That would be terrible, Swami.'

'It would be terrible if we were not the agents of stronger forces, older powers. I must tell you now that my computations of the linear distances between the Lemurian high places are complete. It has been made clear to me that the old Lemurian name of Madagascar – where indeed we may find the gentle lemurs today – Gondwaland, is not without its magical significant connection with the Gonds here in India. More and more we can see that when the Central Pacific Lemuria was in decline, the Lemurian Occident was a flourishing culture. And here, at Goa, must have been the meeting place where the Lemurian adepts passed on some of their wisdoms to the new Atlantean adepts, both sides using their merchants and such-like as a cloak for their intuitive communications. Now I am afraid that our friends in the Himalayas are attempting to transfer the Atlantean wisdoms to Lemurian realms where they will surely turn to death ... But always remember, please, that the true Atlantean wisdoms, as contained in the mathematical proportions of the columns of Glastonbury and Msûra and Monte Claros, above all, Avebury, are worthy of the highest veneration, the most profound study *in their own Atlantean realms* where they spell life. I want to encourage no vulgar anti-Atlantean prejudice. But, alas, we are not dealing with Atlantis but with the perversion of Atlantean doctrine on Lemurian soil by the Himalayan siddhas who dread the awakening of the Lemurian life essences that will instantly shrivel them into the nothingness that they truly are.'

A soldierly English retired officer of the old school said in a businesslike, casual tone, 'How many Himalayan siddhas do you think there are, Swami? I know Moxon-White estimates eighty. But it's always seemed to me an arbitrary figure.'

'You are right, Major. It is arbitrary and foolish. But then all such numbers must be erroneous. For the siddhas are invisible except to the adepts. Their communications can be received only by adepts. Some may receive one, some another. Not all are speaking to all. And so it is and will be with the older and stronger Lemurian energies that *we* are tapping. But this is only the mystery that lies behind all the mysteries of the Magical Orders. How many of us know all of those who are in our own degree? How many of us know who are the highest masters, if indeed they exist? Much of this secrecy *seems* foolish and trivial. Frankly, and to tell you the truth, I think it is so. But so it is. And all *we* can do as practical men is to perfect our powers of communication. How can we speak to the older forces of Lemurian wisdom? This is what I have tried to teach you under the simple guise of the *īda* and the *pingalā*, the solar and lunar currents. I have enabled you to free those currents and to unite them so that you may open your *cakras*, your psychic centres of the body. Each of you knows the postures. Those postures you will practise all day and every day before this coming crisis. As you also know I reserve to myself the magnetic fluids. But I must warn you that there are many things I do not know. There lie the dangers. But all this will be fought, of course, on the simple plane of legend, of Hindu and Christian and Moslem, of so-called religion, of the chain of avatars who have followed the merry dancing fellow Vishnu's arrow through time – Saint Francis and Akbar and our old magician friend Abbé Faria who I believe may yet give us a sign. But it is on this surface plane that the death-peace schemes that threaten us are most apparent. Have you noticed anything special about Divali this year, about the Festival of Light?'

An elderly Indian lady said, 'I think, Swami, that the spirit of

Divali this year has lasted on and on for more weeks than I ever remember, a spirit of joy and festivity.'

'You are right and you are wrong. It is so that the worshippers of Vishnu have remained restless and will do so, I think, until December 3, the day of the Saint Francis procession. All through the Moslem month of Ramadan in fact. But where have they been worshipping? At the Shri Santadurga. Please note *this*. Once again in the service of this deadening *peace*. Shall I tell this young lady the story of Goa's foundation so that she may show to Sir James how we are combining all aspects of human knowledge here – history, legend, art, and occult science?'

To Alexandra's surprise, there was an excited shout from the devotees of 'Yes, yes,' like some school prize-giving acclaim.

'You must know, my dear, that when the sea-god Varuna gave this beautiful land to Vishnu, like many less divine persons, like little maidens I think, he was capricious. He tried to take back his gift. To do so he enlisted the help of Siva. Siva came as a little, little white ant and tried to gnaw through the bow-thread with which Vishnu was to loose his arrow in order to mark his territory. In the end Vishnu's claims were accepted. But only through the good offices of the goddess Santadurga, she who brings peace. It is she whom our simple friends are worshipping today. It is a good legend. It is true and it is a story. It is a story and it is true. Like everything else. But its time has come to too great fulness. The peace that lies upon us now, the rule of the mother in her aspect of peace, the rule of Our Lady of Fatima who in another guise draws them in increasing numbers to the Cathedral, is being used by dead forces, by the Brahmins who have always hated Siva the disturber and Kali the destroyer, by the Jesuits who withhold the magical body of Saint Francis and affect to despise the Abbé Faria's etheric fluids. And they, of course, the Brahmins and the Jesuits and the Moslem worthies, are only the instruments of the siddhas of the Himalayas who fear the return of Lemurian wisdom. But it *will* return. There are signs – a dugong, that beautiful mermaid creature of the seas, has been seen for the first time on Goan shores. Surely this is the gift of Varuna the sea-god to Siva Pasupatí, lord of the animals. It is time that Siva and his consort Kali came to contest here once more, to contest with Durga, the mother of peace, to bring the destruction that is renewal, to teach that indulgence without desire which kills desire.'

He clapped his hands and from the bungalow there came leaping and swaying a troupe of nearly naked men of varying shades from white to black – some Alexandra thought she recognized as the demure grey-robed attendants, some she could have sworn she had seen as members of the community at Colva Beach. All had great yellow stripes painted across their foreheads and their naked chests and bellies; all had their hair strewn with ashes. One lean, dark figure with thick matted hair carried a trident. They set up the black marble lingam on a stone pedestal and began to wash it with milk and with turmeric, then they hung upon it garlands of marigolds. Now appeared women, unveiled, in garish saris, barefooted, with highly painted faces and hung with ear-rings and bracelets and anklets that clattered and tinkled ... Alexandra tried to find some bathetical image to lower the atmosphere – like a noisy washing-up session. The men and the women ranged themselves in two rows facing one another and began to chant one of those eerie, high-sounding Vedic hymns that always frightened her in their suggestion of total human isolation.

'The men and the women must not mingle yet,' said the Swami gravely, 'for that would produce evil magnetism. But,' he added, with a coy giggle, 'soon the tantric exercises will begin. So, my dear young lady, *you* must leave us. But you will tell Sir James of the powers that we practise here and the plans that we consider. And, my dear friends, all of you, please go to your postures. You, little redbeard, you will stay.'

'Oh, no, Ned. Don't, don't! Oliver will want to see you. Please!'

But Ned took both her hands, put them together and kissed them. Then he took her by the shoulders and turned her towards the bungalow door through which she must go away.

'I think your baby needs you and his father also if you can find him,' the Swami said, with what Alexandra thought was real malice in his laughter, 'not the redbeard fellow.'

Alexandra felt sure that Ned would react angrily at the malice, but he smiled at her gently and lovingly. It suddenly came to Alexandra that perhaps this awful man could harm, perhaps he was already harming her baby. She turned and ran through the bungalow out on to the high road, from which, magically, all the vast morning crowds had vanished. She hitched a ride with a lorry into Panaji and ran to the hotel. Oliver had not caught his head in the rococo balcony ironwork, but he had, for the first time in his life, been sick and sick again. He looked pale and he shivered. Telma swore that it was nothing that she had given him to eat.

'It's that goddamned guru,' she said.

Whatever it was, Alexandra was taking no more chances. She hurried Oliver back to Colva Beach, where once more on the sands they could become part of the gentle, monotonous swell of the ocean, mother and child alike.

Erroll, coming out of the spacious dining-room on to the narrow, intricately railed balcony, paused, dazzle-eyed, for at least two minutes, as the beaded curtain swung behind him. Vertiginous, dilapidated, hardly wider than a ledge, in which the Portuguese nineteenth-century rococo arabesques could now scarcely be told from rust, the balcony was yet a haven of shade above the glaring, noisy, dusty street into which the ferries continually disgorged crowds of underfed, careworn, yet chattering morning workers who swarmed into the baking town. It was not the sun's blaze that stayed Erroll in his breezy, post-breakfast course, but rather the sudden looming towards him of a great sun-like face, a child's drawing of a sun – flushed-cheeked, eyes hidden by huge black glasses, vast crown so totally bald that it had become recontoured by knotty veins that replaced the undulations of the long-lost hair. At one side a tiny golden ear-ring hanging from a huge elephant-ear only served to emphasize the bulk of the human being from which it hung. Out of the cavernous blubbery mouth, opened to reveal gaps intervalled by black decay, came a rich organ-toned voice and the purest of Central European accents, all throaty *r*'s and prolonged *o*'s.

'So, you do not find it possible to convey my messages, however arcane their meaning, to your great-uncle.'

'I'm afraid not. I have no understanding of and little patience with what you call the occult sciences. It would be grossly impertinent for me to act as an intermediary in such matters.'

'Nevertheless, Mr Langmuir, although I do not find in you that renunciation of naïve so-called empirical science that these ridiculous newspapers had led me to believe,' a curiously small, feminine hand, a bare almost immodest arm pointed down at the morning newspaper on the small ornate ironwork table, 'I am not credulous enough, I fear, to accept that your crisis of confidence, based, I am afraid, upon some very sentimental Western notions of the tough-souled Indian peasantry, occurred here, exactly here, in this meeting place of the ancient wisdoms, purely fortuitously. No, no, one would require the childlike faith of the rationalist to accept so simple a view of the universe.'

Hamo lifted his eyes from his unfinished letters on which he had been pointedly intent and got up. To Erroll's further surprise even the Lodger's high willowiness seemed nothing beside the enormous hippopotamus bulk of the extraordinary figure confronting him.

Hamo said, 'I am only sorry that my partially quoted words should have caused confusion to so many people. As I explained to you, a Mr,' and he looked at a card, 'Parthasanathy has already preceded you with the erroneous idea that I was urging a return to primitive husbandry.'

At this, the Thing burst into a falsetto cackle. 'Jana Sangh! Our estimable friends of the Right-wing Congress? Please let me beg you, my friend, my dear friend, not to allow *those* idiots to bore you. I myself am able to pursue my esoteric studies and teaching here by the simple faith of the people in that lovable, dancing fellow Vishnu. You know, I suppose, that in his sixth *avatára* he gave this land here to the Brahmins. Oh, please, remember it, Mr Langmuir, the local people are very proud of the little gift – especially the Brahmins. They call me Swami and I am happy to accept the title. But I have too much respect for Hinduism, for the Mahabharata which contains much of the old wisdoms, and for the Ramayana which does great honour to man's sly powers of invention, to be patient with the travesties that these Jana Sangh people and their kind make of the mysterious and the traditional. Don't bother with them.'

'I am afraid I have far too much to do . . .'

'Good. So. We say good-bye. But allow me first please to give you some advice. And. By the way. Also. Thank you for the excellent brandy. If only the Portuguese had left more brandy behind here and less mumbo-jumbo about the relics of the great magus Francis Xavier. However. Remember what I told you. The ancient Lemurian intuitive sciences survive here very strongly for those who have the powers to inhale them. Or rather, I should say, to arouse and inhale them . . . More powerfully perhaps than in the Pacific itself where the artefacts of those ancient giants survive. More powerfully because it was here that they distilled their wisdoms, here at the meeting place of old and new, of Lemuria and Atlantis. Such rudiments of their wisdom indeed as they taught to the Atlanteans are all that in our present cosmic consciousness we can comprehend.

'This despite all the claims of your compatriot Major Harvey-Whetmore. Ah, that well meaning, credulous British officer! But for especially sensitive people – and I think that you may well be such a man – Goa stimulates forgotten powers, unrecognized fluids. If this should happen, remember the story of the Abbé Faria, whose statue you may see in our town. A great magus, yet destroyed when he went to France. There he sought to use his Lemurian science, or animal magnetism as the foolish savants of that day liked to call it, in Atlantean realms. And what does Chateaubriand tell us? *"L'abbé Faria se vanta de tuer un serin en le magnétisant! le serin fut le plus fort, et l'abbé, hors de lui, fut obligé de quitter la partie, de peur d'être tué par le serin.'"*

Here his cackling laughter startled even the few other occupants of the balcony who, awoken from their snoozing, slowly raised their moribund reptile dry old faces and peered beneath their ancient straw hats to see no doubt if the clamour announced the happy return of the old Portuguese colonial days. A very thin woman who to Erroll looked like the ghost of his favourites, Myrna Loy or Katharine Hepburn, looked up gloomily from a table covered with cigarette ash and stubs.

'Oh God! Not gurus as well as ginger ale!'

Erroll, remembering his beloved stars, gave her a wink.

'Beware then of canaries! The Abbé Faria paid his price by being immortalized not as the considerable magus he was, but in the foolish pages of Dumas' novel. And then in a mere travesty.'

The Swami made for the curtained door, bowing to Erroll. Then he turned. 'In your pursuit of rice, the symbol of marriage and fertility, Mr Langmuir, it is possible that you may go to Portugal where I believe rice is also grown. If so I shall be grateful if you will visit a place called Monte Claros near to Sintra. This escarpment – do you say? *diese Klippe* – formerly joined Atlantis to the present mainland of Europe. I should be glad of some reports on the declivities of the shadows there and their mathematical conjunctions. Especially at the Winter Solstice. I would go myself but so many young people are coming now as my disciples and – also – I have my studies. Now too I await certain astrological conjunctions in the coming week. We attend a climax here. By the way, if you are in Austria, my native land, give my greetings to those rogues the gods of the Valhalla, as from one fraud to another.'

Giggling archly, the Swami left, with his bare shoulder peeping roguishly into view for a moment, after the rest of his mountainous bulk had disappeared.

When Hamo sat down again, Erroll thought he looked for the first time aged, like a moulting old stork. Seeking to lighten the atmosphere, Erroll used the first parody at hand.

'Er ... What was that?' he asked, and added, quickly, ' "said Dougal. 'I think it was a swami,' Florence told him. 'Whatever that may mean,' said Dougall." '

Then, his failed joke gabbled away, he said rather lamely, 'It's the Magic Roundabout' and he went on to another tack. 'Well, whatever you said into camera for Kit, it went over big.'

'I am sorry if I appeared impolite in preferring to give that television interview without your presence. You see I'm new to all those lights and so on.'

Hamo still seemed to be dazed from their impact.

Erroll said, 'That's all right. Anyway Kit's terrifically chuffed. He's marked it as the star interview of the whole Asian series. We'll have "that was the Langmuir, that was" before we're done.'

He had spoken without thought, but Hamo seemed not to notice.

'Oh! I don't know. I tried to be as non-technical as possible as Coates had asked me. So it probably came out rather dogmatically. However, I may not let it be used.'

'What?'

'Much depends on what I finally decide to put into this report. I'll have to make up my mind in the coming week down at this hotel you've found for me.'

'Old Kit knows your intentions? About the interview, I mean?'

'Oh yes. I made it perfectly clear to Coates. He's a sensible man like most technicians. His vulgarity, I think, is mainly the protective clowning of the world he lives in.'

'Ah.'

There was a pause of some minutes. The tall thin woman left her little table and, swaying slightly as she moved, came to the curtained exit where Erroll stood. Close to, her thirties hat, her thirties fur-trimmed coat *were* Myrna Loy or Katharine Hepburn, but her face was grey and older than time. She was barefooted and carrying her shoes. Erroll realized that he must have stared, for she said, 'A woman's loveliest feature is her legs, right? Then I don't want those goddamned pinching shoes to give me crippled birds' claws. Gurus, purple ink, ginger ale, birds' claws. Uugh!' She groaned in his face and went by him.

'Gawd!' said Erroll.

But Hamo was gazing intently at the near bank of the wide Mandovi river that was the prospect before them.

'The man of the second family seems to have some regular business in the town,' he said suddenly, 'but both the boys are without work, I think. She's so modest about suckling that baby. But she gossips a lot with the old woman and with the woman of the big family. Look, they're off to wash their pots now. They always go to the same place. It's the place where that thin-looking boy is always bathing himself after defecating. I think he must have dysentery.'

Erroll said, 'Gawd! How did you work all that lot out?'

'Oh, I can see them from my bedroom window. I haven't slept much these two nights here. And they seem to be restless sleepers, too. They make little fires, you know, and cook over them at all sorts of hours. And the babies are restless. I think they have worms. They keep the women up. They're road labourers, a lot of them. And others sell the shrimps they net there. It's quite a community.'

'Poor bloody untouchables, I shouldn't wonder. But as you say they make a community. There's probably a lot more friendliness and help in time of trouble and all that lark than you'd get in the commuter belt round London.'

'That's what I've tried to tell myself, but there have been some terrible fights. I thought that second man would kill that boy from the first family last night. And the rest just stood watching.' He stared out again.

Erroll said, 'Well, they're better clothed than the Colva hippy community. Kit was filming that lot on that super beach down the coast. There's nothing they don't show. Not that I want the girls to forsake their little hippie ways. There are some luscious blonde dollies down there. I thought I saw your –' he broke off and added, 'but there's a whole Piccadilly Circus of them.'

The silence brought Hamo back. 'Oh! The hippies. I saw something about them in this paper.' He turned over a page. 'Yes. An irate letter. I must say, it sounds deserved.'

He read, 'Sir, recently at Baga I was amazed to observe the number of stark naked hippies on the beach. These foreigners continue to mock us because of our inability to make them follow the minimum laws of decency in any country. They are creating a morality problem among our youth of incalculable proportions. I was appalled to see young boys, ostensibly strolling the beaches or pretending to go for a swim, but really ogling at the stark naked women who evidently enjoyed the attention. Are we Goans so helpless before these people that we tolerate this mockery of our people whom we love, this insult to our traditions of modesty, decency and goodness? Are we still suffering so much, we Goan men and women, from a hangover of white supremacy that we have not the courage to stop this insult?

'How many of the boys who have seen or heard from their friends about scenes of stark naked men and women lying side by side on the beach can resist the attraction of bunking class to have a look at the blatant nudity? How many of our respectable girls will feel safe to walk alone in the streets knowing that there are breadmen and ice-fruit vendors, etc., who have stared at nude women during the day, prowling around?

'I suggest that the Goan fathers and mothers organize their own squad to *gherao* or surround these naked hippies so that they cannot move. If they dare to strike out or resort to violence there will be a law and order situation on hand. Yours etcetera.'

'Gawd! Sounds a bit explosive. I hope that ...' He stopped. 'I've had your cases put in the hall. Your car's due here at 4.30. An hour to Dabolim airport, ferry and all. And half an hour's wait, I'm afraid. I hope you're going to be all right.'

'Don't be absurd. It will do you good to discover how little I need your services. When does Coates's party go?'

'We push off in about ten minutes. Look, Chief. I can still cancel it all. I mean, are you going to be all right? You've got that great long motor journey from Bangalore. And then supposing this hotel isn't all that Kit cracks it up to be?'

'To be without your perpetual chatter will put it in the de luxe category.'

'All right. All right. Anyway, Kit says the food there's international, so you can write your reports without the squits.'

'No barrack-room language, please.' For a moment Hamos' features resumed some of their old satisfactions at so familiar an interchange. 'I shall give myself some luncheon and watch the life from this balcony. With the constant arrival of ferries there is always coming and going. And the fact that its purpose remains mysterious has its soothing side. I've been initiated enough into the ordering of things ... I'm afraid I shan't altogether be able to escape even here. The local authorities continue to be distressed by my cancellation of the visit to the rice fields. They insist on interpreting it as some sort of criticism of their policy, although I've explained again and again that it's just the reverse. I've been led a great deal too far into critical generalities in what I've said already and until I know what my interim report is going to be, I don't want to be involved further. In any case, I've told them that all this examination of the practical results of Magic is purely informative, not to say historical. Our proper work begins from here onward when we start assessing the problems of sorghum culture that we shall be asked to solve. You agree with that, don't you?' He looked up to Erroll with the pathos of a Landseer spaniel.

'I couldn't agree more. Roll on our meeting at Karachi. Roll on East Africa. Roll on the sorghum crops.'

'Yes ... but all the same, make the most of this experience with Coates. You can't go on with laboratory work all your life, you know. The modern world hardly allows for stopping still.' He appeared to have surprised himself by his observation, for he added with weary distaste, 'Meanwhile, since I've refused the Ministry's conducted tour, I'll have to receive this Mr Aires da Braga they're sending along to tell me what they're doing in the rice fields. After all, because it's all over for me doesn't mean it isn't central to their lives. And, in any case, it's intended as a great compliment to my contribution. But I don't intend the gentleman to talk to me for more than half an hour. I seem to get tired so quickly these days, Erroll.'

'I don't intend that he should talk to you at all. And I'm not going to let it happen. Kit looks on you as a gold mine! His personal gold mine ...'

'But da Braga's bringing the local journalists with him. He might lose face. You know ...'

'Journalists! Look, if you see a pack of journalists now, you might just as well put your head in a gas oven. You're not going to do it. I'm not stirring from here if you don't agree ... It's for yourself, Chief. Not just for us. Look. I tell you what: you take those binoculars your niece or whoever she was gave you. We've carted them half across the world, so it's time they came in useful. There's a sandbank up the river here. Through the town, past the statue of that Dracula abbé and his hypnotized victim, and down the esplanade. There's everything there according to Percy of the camera crew. Storks! Pelicans! The lot. A spot of bird watching. That's it. You can't get into trouble that way. Except with the Indian mynahs. No. Take that back. It wasn't funny. And don't get back here until your car's due. Will you promise me? And I'll write a note for da Braga that'll do you proud.'

Hamo was so surprised that he made no protest at this ordering of his life, except to point out severely that Alexandra was not his niece but his goddaughter.

And so, half an hour later, filled with fish soup and kid curry, this storklike figure set off in search of alleged storks. For the most part, determined to see neither poverty nor youths, he saw nothing. There are intervals – and he carefully recalled them – between knowledge and meaning, between intention and pursuit, when the senses pass on to the intelligence, impressions, aural, visual, tactile, so blurred and confused that, not interfering with the process of reason, they still hold it quiescent, below consciousness. He sought deliberately to maintain such a state; and his height and alien appearance helped him to do so, for as he walked down the shady streets flanked by high, regular, peeling stuccoed houses (slums, but gracious havens of cool regularity in the roasting, rank human jungle of India) children at play, scavenging animals, half-starved clerks, barbers'-shop idlers, even a few busy moneymakers scattered before him (spectre of some British visitor from the vanished Raj, haunting his vanished sister – *a ilha illustrissima*). As a result he was aware only of a blur of colour that, thank God, called up no memories.

Then suddenly he was stopped in his tracks by a crowd of men – clerks and shopkeepers passing their siesta, he supposed them, from their sober, Western-style dress – gathered to watch some spectacle. Stork as he was, he needed to crane but little to see, within a small, regular concrete square, various lines of youths, drawn up in two irregular and apparently opposed formations. From moment to moment, and here and there, a youth would break out of his line and seek by swift devious movements to make his way through the opposing ranks. In turn, opposing youths in sudden rapid sweeps would intercept the invaders, touch them and thereby apparently condemn them to return to their ranks, or even to withdraw from the game. But what game? Hamo could find in it only some sort of Grandmother's Steps played with immense skill and agility not by children but by older adolescents, who were nearly young men. It seemed, as he watched, perhaps the more so as among all the many players there was none who approached the Fairest Youth nor yet any who repelled, an intricate rite of delicate sexual overtone, but one, he was relieved, totally without erotic display, totally without exciting violence. A rite, in short, from which he was totally excluded. One of the crowd about him, an ingratiating, soberly dressed office employee of some kind, sought to please him with explanation.

'You do not know our *folliò*, Sir. It is a very old game. It is hard, you see, to reach the other side without being touched. You must be very quick, I think.'

The man's speech had the merit – historical accident no doubt – of being without the absurd dated slang of the former Raj, but it seemed only to exclude British Hamo the more from the youthful ritual. If the man lacked British slang he did not want for Western moralizing, an European heritage, as much Catholic as Protestant it appeared.

'It is like *life*, Sir. Many of these boys will rise to good positions, but first they must fight their way through the ranks of their rivals. It is the rule of life, I think. Oh well done! That boy is through. They are from our finest schools, Sir. Scholars many of them as well as athletes.'

(Oh what a missed opportunity for the uncles!) But as Hamo was not competing he moved away from this eager, onlooking crowd of the middle-aged, of former players, but not before he had seen one youthful spectator as excluded as himself who looked with hungry eagerness into the magic square, and not before he had recognized in him the plain, famished, stone-breaking untouchable youth whom he had seen from his hotel window so often defecating on the river bank and washing his bottom in the river. To his shame, the youth gave him a look of despairing recognition, as though he too, looking up from his public wretchedness on the open riverside, had seen into the luxurious privacy of Hamo's hotel bedroom, watched him, perhaps, when, impatient of the walk to the corridor lavatory, he had peed into the washbasin. Determined to refuse this demand for a shared exclusion, Hamo set off briskly away from the crowd along a broad street that led, according to Erroll's directions, towards the mudbank sanctuary of birds.

Yes, this must be the handsome eighteenth-century secretariat. And indeed, although he had no particular taste for architecture, he welcomed its enlightened symmetry and order in a world where he could find no bearings. But so, it seemed, did the plain youth, for there he was, a little to the side, staring at the building, seeking no doubt to find what it was that drew a tall, rich foreigner to gaze so long at so familiar an object. Nevertheless the parody in his stance was intolerable and Hamo walked on rapidly into the open square, regardless of the sweat that poured down him as he quickened his pace in the blazing sunshine. That, he thought, must be the statue. Against the sudden glare it was like a great vampire bat looming over a crouching bird, until he recognized the soutane of the priest and the clinging garments of the woman. Isolated from the converging street, the extraordinary object stood alone in a square planted with formal flower beds. Or rather, not quite alone, for just in time, Hamo saw the vast, white-gowned figure of the Austrian Swami apparently addressing a group of mainly white disciples, a blur of sandals and beads and beards – probably the hippies, their notorious shameless nudity partly clothed for the town visit. He turned sharply towards the river, and almost collided with the drab, worm-eaten youth, who preceded him in a series of breathtaking and highly embarrassing cartwheels along the esplanade as they descended to the sandy river bank.

In the distance Hamo could see what he thought might be a flock of birds, some swimming, some wading at the river's edge – but nothing of the extravagant dimensions of elongated cranes or swollen pelicans, nothing but what looked like gulls, those very prototypes of indistinguishable 'birds', dull grey and black and white, that had always made the idea of the observation of that zoological class so boring to him. However, he persisted in examining them further, through the binoculars, finding to his annoyance that his attempts at focusing were extremely clumsy. Was he losing all his skills? And then, among the groups of larger or smaller, more or less grey, more or less sharply defined grey gulls, he thought he could discern some crane-like creature with a dull scarlet head and neck. The need to make sure of what he could see pressed upon him. He strode across the firm sunbaked sand until he came to a protruding limestone rock. Up this he climbed, and carefully focusing, found that he could distinguish among the gullish tedium not only – yes, a long blacklegged, grey-winged red-headed crane, its heavy bill grubbing in the mud, but two gloriously iridescent smaller birds with beaks like curved scimitars. He thought – those must be ibises. Then, surprised at his own delight, he wondered if here at last in this occupation was his refuge. Himself alone on this long stretch of river shore, for of worm-eaten youths there were no traces, and these creatures, beautiful enough to delight, strange enough to absorb, yet totally isolated from him, from all human concerns; no union but of time and place.

Yet surely exactly these fairest rarities *might* be threatened. Or, no, why not some rarity, less fair to his unpractised eye, some birds among the gullish crowd, for the hopeless are not only fair, but drab, yes, and foul too? In lands where he had worked no magic, where not even crops could grow to bring men out of the old stone caves, the hunters hunted desperately the disappearing wild. Conservation, preservation – to what final cranky Edens were his new-found weaknesses for the weak leading him? To refuse food to the hungry rather than to create it for them. In a land where food itself ...

And what some food in those lands could do to men came forcefully to him, as close by he heard the familiar sounds; it had happened to *him* in his Asian tour. He saw – hardly to his surprise – the bone-stretched buttocks of the sad lean youth performing their uncontrollable watery task. He felt faintly sick, but it was over, and the youth was racing to the river to wash himself. As the graceful scooping and splashing ablutions were performed, Hamo was observed, standing hesitant, his head turned away, the giant now on a rock. In a minute the youth was back from the river and standing below, whistling for Hamo's attention. Hamo looked down to see the youth holding his cock and smiling suggestively. Hamo leapt down to the other side and moved away fast. But only for a few paces. Then, returning, he signalled to the youth to approach him. His hand went automatically to his wallet – but at the sight of the ill, lean and partly frightened smile of invitation he pushed back the notes he had already begun counting by feel in the concealment of his pocket. Instead, with mimicry worthy of Mungo Park or Livingstone, he persuaded the youth to put the binoculars to his eyes, so large and dark, even splendid in his wasted little pock-marked face. Fright was succeeded by bewilderment, for with Hamo's focus, the youth could see nothing; with clarity came first surprised excitement and then, shortly after, boredom, for what was there to see in these birds however near they came? Then by lucky chance, a ship was steaming by. What ship it was or what was upon its decks, Hamo never knew, to call forth such excitement in the youth that he hardly acknowledged the elaborate Cook mime with which Hamo made clear that the magic glasses were his for his own keeping, a gift in perpetuity. Hamo left him gazing intently through the black matt funnels at the other larger black funnels that were slowly moving down the river.

So cleansing was the act of giving for no reward, indeed for the smallest acknowledgement, that Hamo was already half-way back to the hotel when he thought with worried surprise that he had given away Alexandra's parting present. Yet some vague thought that this was all part of a necessary redemption from his past self kept his usual agonized conscience at bay.

And the image of Alexandra's lost urchin-white little face as he had last seen it blended so easily into the darker, pitted wan little face so eagerly staring at the river, that he was able to forget all in present content – even the note from Mr da Braga which the refreshingly efficient and distant Indo-Portuguese receptionist handed him. Erroll, it was clear, had in his hurry botched his errand, or at any rate the manner of it. Mr da Braga's letter hardly attempted to conceal his anger. Let Mr Langmuir not worry, there would be no report in the Goan newspapers of his stay or departure. Since he had been able to find time neither for a visit to the rice fields nor for a discussion of Goa's outstanding contribution to the Green Revolution, there could be nothing to report, or, at most, a needless increase of the natural resentment that the local farmers had expressed, after they learned of his arrival, at his failure to inspect the technical skill they had lavished upon his hybrid.

He was, as always, upset at the element of discourtesy that had marred his visit, but even this embarrassment rapidly faded into his delight at sinking back into the taxi which, with his luggage already loaded, awaited him at the street corner, outside the hotel. The receptionist came formally to see his departure. So coldly and formally, yet so professionally, that Hamo felt able to give the usual directions for forwarding mail, and to ask that his new address should not, however, be given to strangers. He set off upon the long journey to the airport. His driver, another Indo-Portuguese, maintained the soothing silence so that by the time they drove on to the ferry at Agacaim, Hamo had forgotten Mr da Braga as he had much else. He reflected with a warm satisfaction, which he could feel purring within himself, that at least he had departed from somewhere without any involvement with the manner in which they employed his Magic. The deportment of the Indo-Portuguese had contributed much to this new ease, no doubt; on a journey between two lives one should associate only perhaps with those between two races.

He dragged himself along the ground on his belly. Soundlessly. Digging his fingers into the stony red earth so that he could get himself ready for the next silent heave, but holding all the time feverishly to the precious glasses. Then he would draw up his bare knees and press them into the ground. Finally he would slide himself forward so that his toes fitted into the sockets made by his fingers. Se he moved onward to the top of the cliff from where – or so he had been told – he would look down, not far, perhaps a hundred feet, to where the white girls lay naked, and often, as now at dusk, were mounted and pierced by the naked white men. So near, and with the magic glasses, he would see all – the smooth white breasts, the flat white bellies, the hair curling between the full white thighs. Sometimes, so he had been told, there were curious chains of four or more. All others had seen imperfectly: but he, with the magic glasses, would see everything, close up. But now he must go quietly, not crying out when his body grated against stones, when a bad creature stung his knee, when he cut his leg on glass embedded in the ground, when, in the gathering dusk, he passed by mistake over some thorny plant that left hot needles in his skin. The excitement had brought on the familiar churning in his bowels, but he fiercely constricted his sphincter to defer all such intrusions upon the coming great delight. Imagination and the sliding movements had combined to make his cock erect with desire, but he stopped for a moment and banged it with his hand, so that pain might override lust and put off as long as possible the delicious moments he had looked forward to all the last day.

Above all, he must move silently and as far as possible out of sight. For he knew that behind many bushes and trees there were other boys, boys from the great schools – St Francis Xavier's, the

Fatima, the Bonastarim High – who would resent the presence of a low-caste boy, of a Sudra, who would hate with envy such a boy who had magic glasses that could see forbidden things that were hidden from them. Also there were men, men of all kinds, some very great men from the town who would kill him if they knew he had seen them there. And there was talk of *gherao*, of many joined together to drive these heepis from the beaches, after seeing them, of course. So the more necessary to use the magic glasses now and to use them silently.

At last, forcing back tears because in his eagerness to reach the cliff edge he had dragged through a cruel thorn bush, he looked down. There indeed lay a naked girl, not so beautiful as he had thought, thin, very thin, as thin as himself, but very white and smooth and long with firm breasts like great eggs that he would love to take into his mouth and to suck; there was a dark line between her folded thighs, but who could tell for sure if it was the hair that signalled the entry to paradise? Soon a man would come and enter her. Meanwhile she breathed heavily with desire, her limbs, her arms, her legs moved shamelessly with lustful greed. Her eyes were closed against her own ravishing. His own cock grew thick against his threadbare cotton dhoti, his scrotum tightened with desire. He almost tore his thumb on the rough wheel which brought the woman closer in the magic glasses.

The first pain he felt was sharp and so stinging that he thought it was some bad creature. But then he heard a stone whistling in the air before it caught him on the shoulder blade. And now another cut open the back of his neck. He clambered and groped to his feet. He started to run but a larger stone caught him on the ankle and the pain brought him to the ground. A great rock rolled against his body, pushing him to the very edge of the cliff. And now through the dying light shapes came from behind bushes, trees, boulders – blazered boys, suited men, the whole hidden world of watchers, some peeping Toms, some vigilantes, all avenging citizenry. They came at a run to where he lay, bleeding, moaning, messed with his own void. One gave the little body a kick that rolled it to the edge. Another leaned to take the precious magic glasses from him. But he held tight to them and only rolled further to avoid the theft.

Rolled and fell, fell to the rocks below where, his back broken, blood trickling from his mouth, he lay for more than an hour before he died.

Elinor, advanced in her *prayana*, was called from the other plane by the crashing of the body as it hit the rocks. She heard some shouts and cries from above. Wanted to go to the help of the fallen boy, from whose mouth she saw blood running. But dared not, was too frightened, too unsure of where she was, who she was, why she was in this sudden horror. Knew only a terror that her weakened body would not sustain her in flight. Put all her will into fleeing. And gathering her long towelling bathrobe about her trembling body, fled, faster even than the avenging citizenry running from the blood they had so suddenly shed.

The situation for the local authorities in the following week was enough to daunt even the best-trained bureaucrats. It was all that the British in the days of the Raj had meant by 'out of hand'.

To begin with, the stonebreakers and indeed all the lower castes were roused to a sullenness on the edge of destructive action by the death of the boy. Then the citizenry hid their guilty fear by increasing their demands for expulsion of the hippies. From Old Goa the Catholic community, above all the Jesuit authorities, became increasingly pressing in their demands for the expulsion of the Swami and his growing band of followers as the day of St Francis Xavier's birth approached. The Hindu community, largely Vishnavite, were troubled by rumours of strange Shivite devotees glimpsed in the streets, and by rumours of alien rites, tantric orgies and strange sacrifices to Kali – a whole Dravidian religion from the South and East which defiled the gentler world of Goa.

These rumours also were not unconnected with the Austrian Swami. Yet the Swami had many friends in high places in India as well as among distinguished foreigners. Also many of the authorities themselves were disturbed by his powers and, above all, by his predictions. Few would go near the strange statue of the Abbé Faria at night for it was said that the Swami had announced that some sign would be given at this place. The Moslem community was, as always towards the end of the great fast of Ramadan, in a state of nervous exhaustion and tension. To crown all this, bands of bankrupt peasants, smallholders and unemployed labourers from the rice fields were said to be converging on Panaji in the belief that the great rice magician had come with magic powers to give them again all the lands and yields that had been taken from them since the hybrid Magic had made rich the landowners and driven them into hunger. Nor were there wanting looks over shoulders at this time to ask who was truly loyal to India and who perhaps still yearned for the iron and velvet of Portugal. These were bad days for the authorities, especially as the Congressional elections would soon be approaching.

But an event was to take place that week which was to fill the heavy, humid, storm-bearing air with even more menacing rumours.

Elinor had come to a crisis. She had so perfected the routine of her day since she had advanced through the Swami's classes, a routine of meditation, breathing and posture, that she had felt free for the first time to turn to the proof-reading of her Ph.D. thesis. Up to that time, every intrusion of Crashaw's religious ecstasy, every erotic address he had made to the Virgin, filled her either with anger or with disgust for such hard egocentrism masquerading as mystic experience. It had been such a long pilgrimage, although performed in so few years – from her first awakening to religious feeling, through the Metaphysical Poets, to her present dissolution of self through the Becoming into Being – that it was hard for her to respond without wasteful, hostile emotion to what, she began to see, were the wholly erroneous hard-willed Christian devotions, which had first brought her out of the stew of her mother's semi-Marxist sentimentalism and her father's empty time-serving ethical rhetoric. But now at last she was secure enough in her daily discipline to do so, free enough from all emotions to read Crashaw's burning words without any feeling other than concern for their verbal and schematic structures. If she could do this with Crashaw, to whom she had been so close that she had nearly been received into the Catholic Church, she could do it with all literature, with all life. She was ready to go back into the world, to teach people poetry and prose and drama so that they could teach others who in turn would teach others. It was a discipline of futile life that seemed truly fitting for someone who, with perseverance, would in a few years be rid of will either of body or of mind, of all the chains whether of desire or dislike. She could see what others, still attached to the world, would call the cynicism in this view; but she could only wonder at a dependence which found sentimental words like 'cynicism' to describe the realistic acceptance of everything as indifferent.

She was ready, she had told Thelma, to set off for home as soon as she liked. She could even make little literary jokes to Alexandra and Ned about Henry James and herself as Daisy Miller or the Princess or Chad, for such silly book talk was all that remained of those Moroccan weeks of desire for Ned and hatred of Alexandra. She was free.

And then this awful thing happened. It was only a life in a million lives, a scattering of some vital fluids and energies that would enter into other lives in the eternal process. That it was the life of a poor and ill and probably hungry boy made no difference – that was a legacy from Thelma's sentimental radicalism. She crushed beetles and ants unknowingly under her foot every day, who knew how hungry they were? To wish it had been herself not him was an insidious vanity. She, he, it – it was all the same. Yet she could not relax, meditate, breathe without remembering that however she had denied her body it had brought lust to the boy and, through the lust of others, death to him. She fell back on dismissals that belonged to her more attached days: it was vulgar, she said, it was melodramatic, it was silly. But none of these words were to the point, even if they still had meaning for her any longer. The point was that the boy's death, his death so near her, his pain, her fright, that horrible gurgling of the blood from his mouth that kept on sounding in her ears, all were equal with the most intense pleasures and joys she had ever known, and all were nothing.

Yet she could not feel that. For months now she had lived on increasingly little food and even less sleep, unnoticing, uncaring, and less and less aware of body and self. Now she caught a very heavy cold and felt intensely every moment of the life-cycle of the virus, so sensitive had all her membranes become. Her throat was agony, her eyes itching tear-filled lakes, her chest barred with iron, her lips bound in leather, her head a cavalry charge of horses' hooves. She felt a disgust with every excretion from her body that even in her thoughtless pagan childhood she would have found excessively genteel, prudish, Emily Post. Insomnia became a positive horror to her, the experience of a feverish, sweaty, aching body that would not be dissolved.

Behind it all was the fear that she had walked by chance into a world which was poisoned at source. It was all childish, of course, their secrets and their magic. It was their techniques that concerned her. But she found herself increasingly frightened of where this childishness would end – this boy's death, what more? *It has absolutely nothing to do with me*, she told herself again and again – the obscene, the secret, the furtive were all infantile obsessions that tied the spirit to this illusory world. But still it nagged and nagged. She took to walking by the Mandovi river bank all night in her long blue-grey chiffon gown with her black hair falling about her spectre-white face. People ran from her as they did from Thelma who in her daily walks in her eccentric clothes was avoided as a powerful witch. She visualized herself all too easily, and with bitter laughter that was all too earthly, as a sort of Beardsley drawing at large, Salome, Medusa, a vampire. Sometimes in her confusion she wondered if indeed she was in some way infected with all this childish evil, destined like Kali only finally to assuage her terrible thirst in blood that ran from the mouths of children. They would finish in Greenwich Village or Tenderloin, she and Thelma, two terrible old Gothic horrors.

But all the time her thirst and hunger created other images, so simple and absurd, so un-Gothic that she could hardly bear the silly juxtaposition of images. She dreamed hour after hour of sitting down in a Howard Johnson motel, Holiday Inn, or Regency Hyatt, around her the décor would change from Pompadour and mirrors to Hispanesque and leatherwork to Western and Totem Poles, whispering, haunting muzak would merge from 'La Donna è Mobile', to 'Red Roses for a Blue Lady, Mr Florist take my order please', unalimonied or widowed waitresses dressed in younger and younger aprons and bobby sox would grow older and older, more tired, more matchstick-legged, more desperately lipsticked, but Elinor Tarbett ate and ate on and on in an ecstasy of hunger relieved – spare ribs would vanish in an instant, tossed salads with archipelagos of thousand-island dressings would be engulfed as by earthquakes, filet mignon could never be so tender, while blueberry pie crowned with pecan ice-cream was washed down by gallons of coffee. The haunting obsession, so banal, so ludicrously atavistic, was so strong sometimes that she would run along the riverside over sand and stone, through mud, avoiding now hippie sleepers, now outcast campfires, now the derelict, now the criminal, now the amorous, until she was so exhausted that she fell down and slept where she lay.

But one night – not to lie, assuredly, not to sleep. To be held and stretched and stripped by tearing, violent excited forceful hands, to struggle and fight against the pain, the sheer driving, scraping, tearing wounds of these fierce, animal, exploding entries; to die and die again at the biting of her lips, the breaths of every hot nauseating herb that had assailed her since she first landed at Bombay airport. How many of these men there were she did not know, nor who they were; she could only smell their sweat, feel their bristles, their rags, taste their saliva, know the power of strength twisting her arms, forcing her legs apart. Ask no questions and you'll hear no lies. She had lain for days afterwards in Thelma's hotel room, preferring not to speak, and authority was glad not to hear. It could have been, as many were to say, devotees of Kali, or enraged untouchables, or lustful youths; it could have been, as many were to say, not she at all who had suffered on those caked, sun-split mud flats. So much was delirium at the time, as for example the long-remembered, destructive minutes' joy she had known when, in her hallucination, she had thought she had felt and smelt Ned taking her. But what remained for days was the sheer physical pain. That pain from which at the time she had fainted, which, when she came to alone there on the evil-smelling mud with the roar of the bullfrogs drowning her senses, was so ghastly, so frightening that, twisting her chiffon rags around her, she had crawled on all fours up the embankment, along the street, trailing blood behind her, banishing as she went the shadowy figures of late-night loiterers who feared to be involved.

She had fainted again at the foot of the Faria statue, recumbent like the high-born Brahmin lady; she had come to and seen the enormous figure of the Swami bending over her, arms out-stretched, endowing her probably with that animal magnetic fluid that the metal figure of the Abbé above them was emitting in the eternal thaumaturgy of art to the prostrate Indian lady. But the Swami had not seemed a healer to her at the time, rather the culmination of a long nightmare. She gathered all her strength to save herself from this last mortal violation, all her rags to cover the poor self-induced meagreness of her naked body, and had run through the empty streets to be admitted by an alarmed porter and to lie all night in Thelma's thin, bony but loving arms.

Streets are never quite empty, however; casements never wholly closed. Soon it was known that a woman had been raised from the dead. Some said by the statue itself. Some, by the Abbé returned to life. Most, by the Austrian Swami, who, after all, *was* the Abbé returned, who after all *was* Akbar, who after all *was* St Francis, who after all *was* Parasirama the sixth avatar of Vishnu and the founder of Goa, who after all *was* Vishnu himself. For the followers of the Swami, wanderers, foreigners, Vishnavites, Hindus of all kinds, Catholics, even Moslems, the miracle had happened.

But soon other stories gained ground. A high-born Catholic lady of Brahmin descent coupled with a high Portuguese lineage who, in the proper tradition of both her ancestral lines, seldom stirred from home, had been ravished by evil, magical means. More prosaically, a Hindu Brahmin lady in purdah had been assaulted by a low-caste fisherman. A Moslem lady of high birth in harem had been violated by who knew what? Followers of Kali were abroad, Saktas, practisers of terrible rites. The Swami was in league with foreign witches.

One thing seemed certain to the poor and the hungry, Vishnu had come once more, but this time to bring *them* succour, and those in power were denying him, as the powerful had also sent away the giant rice god, bearer of fertility, who had come to bring fertility to the dispossessed.

There was no end to the rumours which the authorities could ignore or refute equally at their peril.

It was Saturday and the fountains were alight at the Brindavan Garden – up they shot and cascaded down like fireworks without alarms, electric blue, verdigris green, methylated violet, strawberry-ice pink, golden yellow and, above all, blood-red. Behind their dazzling playing could be heard always the background dull roar of the great Krishnaraja Sagar Dam. Along the avenues, between formal beds and the fountain, strolled, in the warm evening air, the wealthy Indian bourgeoisie – the ladies wore saris that equalled, indeed outdared the brilliant colours of the fountains, and their pretty heads of jet-black hair were decorated with hibiscus and frangipani and bobbed a little as they avoided the flying ants lured to the lighted fountains in which they were to burn. The ladies chattered like a flock of birds. The men were in dark suits and club-striped ties, talked gravely of business but with expansive gestures. The little girls in party dresses of pink and blue satin frilled out with many princess petticoats were like so many *jeunes filles en fleurs*. The little boys, all white socks, bare knees and white shirt blouses, were like so many Marcels, all making an infernal din with click-clacks. And, overlooking them, on the terrace of the luxurious hotel, the foreign tourists, eager to get back to the real India of the temples and the mosques, of the rice fields, the bazaars, the city slums or the protected tigers, passed their 'free evening' advertised in the package-tour itinerary, an evening of postcard-writing, bargain-comparing, catching up with the *Herald Tribune* or *Le Figaro*.

Into this lounge of tourist parties, at about a quarter past six one evening, came Hamo to drink a pink gin (Mysore State, thank God, was not dry) before his shower and changing for dinner, to rest a little after a day of report-writing; to make the agonizing decision which reports to send, with what emphasis in priorities, and with what accompanying letter to Sir Alec.

Reclining in a cane chaise longue – long enough for once to accommodate his legs – he found the scene before him so absurd, so pantomimic, so utterly remote from all the horrors that had haunted him increasingly since Tokyo, that he felt that here he would make a balanced, sane decision, would send a balanced, sane report to Sir Alec and his colleagues which would finally efface the unfortunate hysteria of some of his remarks to the Press in the recent weeks. These Indians that he could see now were like children, children at an endless Victorian children's party, they gave reassurance that the little crippled match-sellers and the blind flower-girls were the figments only of a 'temperature', of a feverish chill from which he was at last recuperating. Even the tourist voices around him seemed at first reassuring, for idleness and travel had bred in him a curious new habit of listening to what strangers said, of observing people at random.

Two middle-aged French women were comparing the relative prices of saris in Mysore and in Bangalore. An English lady was telling her uninterested daughter that she felt sure that the resthouse at Trivandrum was the one in which Uncle Derek had killed a cobra all those years ago – 'I quite see that it's very uninteresting,' she said, 'and God knows the old boy told the story until one could scream, but it isn't altogether easy to find subjects that *don't* bore you, Angela, you know.' Some Italians in excessive beach wear and strange little orange jockey-caps were recounting with a great deal of laughter, as far as Hamo could tell from his knowledge of their tongue, how an elephant had screamed when it had been badly wounded in collision with a lorry. A German couple were making earnest note of the delightful package tour that a Swedish couple had taken, a tour which comprised the health-giving proportion of eleven days sunbathing to three of sightseeing instead of their own where the proportions were reversed: 'Ach, so. That is a *real* winter tour, to lay up the good sunshine,' the German wife cried in delight. It was the endless rumbling of a stout, dowdy American matron's voice that finally held him captive. She was holding equally captive a more sophisticated smart-looking couple of her compatriots, or rather the wife only, for as she talked, the husband gave more and more attention to the stock-market columns of the *Herald Tribune*.

'Did you ever teach school?' the rumbling voice said. 'Well, that's the way it is with my villagers. You don't *tell* them. That way they're sure to act contrary. No. You question and suggest. I remember about five years ago. The rains came out of season. I've known it before in the jungle. As the rain poured down day after day – and it rains some here when it rains – I could see what was going to happen. The bunds would burst their banks, the paddy-fields would be flooded, the crops would be ruined. But my villagers sat there in that damned despair that just holds them. And did nothing. Nothing. Not even the old headman and he's a pretty good old fellow. So I would throw out a remark here and a remark there — "Of course, I'm so ignorant, I should start getting scared and start building up that bund against floods. But then *I* know nothing." You know, I played the poor, innocent little ingénue. At my age! But it worked. Three days later the headman and some others came to me. "We're going to build up the bund," they said, "Why! For Lord's sakes!" – my mother was raised in Georgia and it comes back when I am excited – "that sounds a *wonderful* idea." And it was. They worked four nights and days on it and the crop was saved. Yes. Children. That's what they are.'

'And you've given twenty years of your life to working with those people. They certainly must love you.'

'They do and they don't. They're human.'

'But the Indian Government ...'

'Oh, the Government are very suspicious of all we do. We're *American*, you know.'

The other lady sighed. And they remained silent for a while.

The silence roused the husband from his newspaper. He made an effort to be polite.

'*You've* lived here all these years. Can't you explain to them that they ought to get these beggars off the streets? All around and over the automobiles in the villages. That's no good for tourism.'

'But, Harry, it's just this awful poverty that this lady's been explaining ...'

'No, no, the man's right. Anyhow *we're* not so darned rich, are we? But, you see, to those people you come there with the car and the chauffeur like a Rockefeller fallen out of the sky. Many of them are near starving.'

The man said, 'God! Isn't it awful? The eyes of these people looking into the window of the automobile. One poor sick kid. And an old guy. Guess I shan't sleep tonight thinking of those poor goddamned starving folk.'

It could have been that this volte-face was made to put an end to the conversation; but it could have been a real switch of feeling, a sudden overpowering indulgent sentimentalism. As such, it was to Hamo a terrible parody of his own gradual change of emotions during his stay in Asia. I must scrap the whole idea of Report B, he thought; it's the product of an hysteric emotionalism which has no place in scientific work. In which case I shall send letter A with Report A.

He read through the two alternative letters to Sir Alec that he had written to accompany whichever report he finally sent in.

The letter A he would now post read:

Dear Sir Alec,

As you will see from the accompanying report, I have covered in my travels the rice research institutes of Louisiana and California (unfortunately I was not able to visit the rice fields of Arkansas), of Japan, of Northern Australia, and of Los Baños, Philippines. I have noted (Appendix A) a number of techniques in hybridization that I think we might study seriously; I have also outlined some of the techniques in plant physiology and biochemistry that appeared to my unspecialized eye to offer new lines of approach.

I have also inspected in much greater detail the work being done in the South-East Asian and Indian peninsular countries, where the hybrid Magic dominates rice culture. There have been deficiencies in understanding and application which I trust that I have been able to put right (Appendix B). There are also certain local problems, many incidentally with a wider scientific interest, where I think we should offer assistance (Appendix C). I have ventured to list (Appendix D) a number of individuals, mostly assistants or postgraduates, who struck me as having exceptional ability and I have suggested that they could profitably be invited to work for a year or so with our staff. I have also (Appendix E) made recommendations for the providing of certain expensive equipment to laboratories in those areas where I believe that it would materially further the work in hand, and, perhaps more imporant, where, with Watton's expert advice, I estimate that there is a technical staff capable of employing such equipment profitably. My real work, I feel, now lies ahead of me, in Pakistan and Africa where I shall try to assess exactly what is required for the 'crash programme' (I use your expression) that we are to carry out on the adaptability to varying soil conditions and the potential improvement of yield and nutritive qualities of sorghum.

I hope that Lady Jardine is in good health and that you had the usual 'lucky' weather for your family summer holiday on Mull.

Yes, it would do. But he could not bring himself to destroy letter B. Even among these happy childish lights and colours, these tourist trivialities, wan, peaked, beautiful faces pleaded not to be thrown on to the rubbish heap of the hopeless.

The American, looking up from his paper, said, 'Well, that's Goa out of our schedule. See this headline story in the British *Times*? I'm not taking you where there's danger of riot.'

'I should think not. Anyway, what in heaven is Goa?'

The rumbler explained, 'It's a famous ex-Portuguese colony. They were worse than the British. It's all this heritage of colonialism that makes our work here so difficult. There's no trust. I certainly shouldn't go *there*. Well, for heaven's sake, what are they rioting about in Goa?'

'Oh, some crap about a rice god. A giant that was going to bring fertility or something to the crops, who turns out to be, would you believe it, some tall British scientist! And now he's disappeared and the poor bastards think he's being kept from them.'

'Oh, that's so typical. But all the same, I don't think you should go there.'

'Why, make sure of that! Don't take any notice of him – he's just kidding. This Goa thing never was on our itinerary, I'm sure.'

Hamo, in a few short strides, had reached the reception desk. At least, if by his unconsidered, self-indulgent blabbing to the Press he had misled these poor men into believing that he could help, he must have the courage to go there and show them the god that had failed.

As he arranged his air passage to Dabolim for the next morning, a reception clerk handed him a parcel with Indian stamps. Taking it back to the table, he unpacked, to his great surprise, his binoculars in their case. He read, with apprehension, the accompanying letter from that very efficient young Indo-Portuguese lady receptionist at the Panaji Hotel :

Dear Sir,

These binoculars stamped with your name were found by the police in the possession of a youth who was murdered here last Tuesday night. It is presumed that they were stolen from you. If you can inform the police here of any circumstances connected with their loss, your information will be gratefully received since investigation into the murder is proceeding.

There followed a sentence that appeared to come from a shocked heart:

I fear that the murdered boy stole these glasses from you for the purposes of lewd viewing.

We have at all times the pleasure to be your obedient servants ...

Hamo went up to his room. He took out Reports A and B. He destroyed with some difficulty the bulky copies of Report A. He took downstairs the two copies of Report B and attached to one, with a paper clip, letter B, which read:

Dear Sir Alec,

I have now completed, as you will see from the attached report, a survey of all the rice stations which it was agreed that I should visit. My inspection of those in the United States, the Philippines, Japan and North Australia enlightened me greatly. Appendixes A to C concern information about techniques in my own field, and, with the hope that they may be useful to my colleagues, reports from experts in allied fields, also suggestions for equipment which I think we could profitably acquire.

Inevitably my most intense study has been reserved for the many laboratories in the countries of South-East Asia and of the Indian peninsula where the hybrid rice Magic, for the discovery of which our Institute was responsible, now forms the staple of rice agriculture. On the whole, I must state that the assiduity and intelligence with which our findings have been applied have led to results which can only be called revolutionary and with which the Rapson Trust has every reason to be greatly satisfied. There have been misunderstandings, there are special local problems, there are special financial needs, outstanding individual workers could profit by a year or so at the Institute, certain laboratories lack expensive equipment and, more importantly, have staff qualified to use it if they were provided with it. All these I have listed in Appendices D to H.

It would appear then that the first, retrospective phase of my work is over, and that I should now proceed to Pakistan and the African countries where I can assess the problems outstanding in the various improvements of sorghum culture which we have agreed *up to now* should be the next major research project of the Bureau in its programme of assistance to what my experience has now told me are rightly called 'under-developed countries'.

Please note that I write 'up to now', for I wish to make an earnest and serious plea for a change of programme. You told me, with your greater experience of the world, that I should soon find myself involved in the political aspects of the work we carry out. I should like to amend what you said to 'human aspects'. I have rigidly eschewed political involvement. For this reason I have accepted on trust the statement of the authorities that the large growth in yield, the greater nutritive value, the increased annual spread of rice crops brough about by the cultivation of Magic has produced a marked diminution in that urban undernourishment which is the major problem of most of these countries, notably, of course, India (into Burma, as you forecast with your political knowledge, I was unable to obtain entry). I have neither the time nor the competence to check this happy conclusion, therefore I have accepted it. But the process is clearly a slow one. And, whatever may be called its political aspect, one is constantly reminded here that it is a pressing human one.

Meanwhile the success of Magic has brought in its train a number of *rural* difficulties, most of them inherent in the social, political or economic structures of the countries concerned. I refer to matters of land tenure, provision of capital, cooperative systems of storage and maintenance of agricultural machinery, distribution of fertilizers, irrigation and innumerable other allied problems. About these I am incompetent to speak and it would be impertinent of me to do so. Different states have different approaches. I am no politician or social dogmatist to judge them. We can, we may think, do little to help here; and where help is impossible, moral exhortation is rightly resented as impertinence.

There *is*, however, one aspect of this question where, I believe, that we can and should act decisively. I refer to what are often spoken of in these countries as 'hopeless lands' which have been farmed for many decades with very small yields owing to the inherent poverties of the soils. The position of the small-scale cultivators of these soils was always poor; with the advent of the rich yields of Magic to which their soils are unresponsive, it has become indeed 'hopeless'. It is my clear belief that if, over a period of three or four years, we were to concentrate our energies on the production of hybrids particularly fitted for these various soils – stony, marshy, and so on – we could solve their problems. They are, of course, a very small minority in these over-populated lands. Their problems will in the long run be solved by population control or emigration to cities where in time industrialization and the fruits of Magic will have abolished starvation and poverty. But I fear it will be over a *very* very long time. Meanwhile, by acting thus '*irrationally*', we should be emphasizing by *practice* our belief in the supremacy of the human aspect of our work. Such action would avoid, on the one hand, impertinent moral exhortation or, worse, interference in the administration, and on the other, the unchecked supply of finance to governments of dubious efficiency. It would also, however quixotic, be practicable. I remember my great-uncle, Sir James Langmuir, telling me that politics is the art of the practicable. I hope that when my accompanying report reaches him, as no doubt either in its full form or in a digest it will, in his capacity as Chairman of the Rapson Trust, that you and any other colleagues concerned will stress this *very* practical aspect of it.

It is, indeed, a case of first things first, for our work on Magic, revolutionary though it has been, will never be complete until the human, to use a necessary word, the *moral* concerns involved are made clear to the beneficiaries; above all, until that acceptance of 'hopelessness' so endemic in these parts has been clearly and manifestly rejected.

It is hard, indeed, to postpone the sorghum research, but surely we must attempt to complete one task before taking on another.

I do not see who can lose by this change of priorities, unless it be those European and American firms dealing in what I have learned to call by the ugly name 'agro-business'. Increase in export markets our work, it is true, would not assist. But far more important, as I am sure my colleagues will agree, the work will be of great intrinsic scientific interest; and, of course, as with all research, the further experiments to which it may lead are incalculable.

I have suggested in the first place research by six teams consisting of a plant geneticist, a plant physiologist and a biochemist, backed in each team by a full complement of laboratory technicians. It may be that the leaders of two teams should be plant geneticists (I hope that I may qualify for one such position), of two others, plant physiologists (I should strongly suggest Hart for one of these), and for two teams, biochemists (do you think we should be lucky enough to interest Miss Kinlake?). For the whole project I think we should need the attachment of a tropical botanist and a tropical entomologist. A preliminary necessity would be an intensive and extensive soil survey of various so-called 'poverty' areas of South-East Asia, India and Ceylon. I also urge in my report the association with our teams of various promising young scientists in these countries. The detailed analyses of these varous aspects of the report which I trust will be of service to you and my colleagues are contained in Appendixes I to M.

It is my intention now to proceed to New Delhi, there to think over various aspects of the work that will be entailed, until such time as I hear, as I very earnestly hope I shall, that the Rapson Trust accepts my report. I shall then fly home at once to consult with you and my colleagues.

I trust that Lady Jardine is in good health and I hope that you had your usual 'lucky' weather for your family summer holiday on Mull . . .

Hamo placed this report and letter in an envelope addressed to Sir Alec and gave it to the reception clerk for immediate posting to England, and at the same time he handed in an exact copy addressed to himself at his flat in London.

The weather in Goa during December is usually most pleasantly cool. But this year on December 3rd, the anniversary of the death of Saint Francis Xavier, Patron Saint of All Missions, the temperature was excessively – unaccountably – high, the humidity almost unbearable. In old Goa, where a thousand or two of pilgrims had assembled, sleeping in tents or directly in the open air, where the image-mongers, lemonade-sellers and popcorn-vendors were already gathering, though furtively, for the restoration of Jesuit control in the last decades had chastized them severely even from the forecourts of the churches, the mercury topped 28 degrees centigrade; only the nuns walking the cloisters of Saint Monica and the priests officiating in the vast baroque Cathedral were safe from the sun's fury. In the Bom Jesus itself, after the visitor had passed through the West Door in the fine Renaissance façade, the great flaming sun of the baroque altar broke the cool darkness, yet the tomb of the Saint himself, in jasper and chalcedony with its coloured marble scenes of the Saint's earthly progress and the glistering, yet more glacial wrought silver of the sanctified coffin offered some proper repose to the eye. Outside, where stood the ruins of the Inquisitorial Palace, the heat brought to life again the many *autos-da-fé* that the square had once known, so that a fanciful ear might have found in every sound of the waking crowd a horrid crackle or an agonizing scream, an over-wrought eye might have made of the sun's rays flashing against the parked pilgrim motor-coaches the fierce flames that consumed a thousand or more pagans and heretics. Even the statue of Camoens suggested alarm today rather than delight at his beloved *illustrissima ilha*.

In Panaji by the banks of the Mandovi the temperature was perhaps a degree less, but the humidity, with the ocean so near, was even greater. Scrawny Thelma was stripped down to the old-fashioned bra and panties she still wore. Elinor lay ghostlike on the bed in another tulle gown, this time of pale malmaison pink that suggested Bernhardt in the *Dame aux camélias* rather than

Bernhardt in *Salomé*. She had said nothing for the last three days, but she had dutifully taken the cold soups, the crèmes caramels, and the sweet champagne which Thelma had wheedled and bullied out of the hotel staff. Alexandra, in the next room, to which she had come, despite her longing to be one with the sand and the sea, so that she might consult a doctor for Oliver whose diarrhoea had proved persistent, was hardly aware of the heat in her anxious concern to be exact in the programme of administering the medicines and starch foods which had been prescribed for her baby. There was no communication between the two rooms. It would be difficult to say whether Elinor or Oliver felt more deprived by Ned's continuous absence, or Alexandra or Thelma more aggrieved at that deprivation.

Suddenly Elinor hoisted herself up on her bed and looked at her mother with such a mixture of earnestness and impatience that Thelma, recalling some of the Victorian stories forced upon her in her childhood by a pious grandmother, started with terror for a moment at the awful possibility that here was a deathbed. But Elinor only said: 'I want to see Alexandra, Mother, immediately, and alone.'

To Alexandra, summoned and only persuaded with great difficulty to leave Oliver to Thelma's care, Elinor said: 'You know that Mother and I are leaving tomorrow. It's mostly gone wrong for me, you'll be glad to know.'

Alexandra said, 'Oh dear! You *do* dramatize.'

'Yes,' Elinor admitted. 'That's true. It's partly why it's all gone wrong. That and my hubris, my pride. But it doesn't matter. Teaching school will lower *that* soon enough. And then I shall start all over again. But through exercise and meditation only. There mustn't be any of this magic. I thought it didn't matter because either it was accidental, a power that just came with non-involvement, or else it was just charlatanism. Either way it couldn't affect the eventual dissolution of the self. And if it did do some harm it was only in the so-called real world, to people and things that are passing shadowy beings anyway. But I was wrong, Alexandra.'

Something of Alexandra's impatience with all this talk, her wish to return to Oliver, must have communicated itself to Elinor, for she said:

365

'Oh, not that I'd want the sort of false calm you've found, that kind of animal peace, the detachment of the cow concentrating on its udder. But mine wasn't detachment either. I see that now. It couldn't be, while I was getting my disciplines from a corrupt source. Not that I want to blow up the Swami into a devil-figure or something. Part of him's a man who really *has* acquired some strange detachment. But he's let the powers, the incidental powers it's brought with it, go to his head. And part of him's a frightened, shrivelled common fake – like any phoney card trickster at a fair – who's scared out of his wits at what he's got into. But that doesn't matter either. It's only that there's just two kinds of people drawn to magic, and, once the proper discipline gets involved with it, it gets involved with those sorts of people. You know what kind they are?'

Alexandra felt as she had at the Swami's audience, that she was being involved in something threatening. She sought evasion by appearing not to have heard the question.

'Oh, for God's sake, you *are* a cow. You can smell nothing except the cud you chew and that baby's messes. Well, understand this, Alexandra Grant,' and the sharp tone of her voice, the pinched lines round her mouth gave Alexandra a sudden vision of the American schoolmarm that Elinor would become in ten years' time, 'being a vegetable isn't the true peace. Get with child a mandrake root. Perhaps even you will shriek if I tear your roots out of the warm earth of Oliver's potties and nappies. Tell me where all past years are and who cleft the devil's foot? Have a look at his feet. Do that, Alexandra. Have a look at that Swami's feet. Or rub him with garlic in front of a mirror, or whatever. Some involvement with magic, even childish magic, might save you from bovine inanition. But he won't vanish, that's the trouble. He's no devil, alas. He's just a huge mass of flesh with a little tiny, screwy, crooked mind that's tried to be more. Poor bastard.'

She stared suddenly with such contempt that Alexandra found it hard not to smack her face.

'I don't believe you've the guts. Or the intelligence to do it,' Elinor said.

She tried to raise herself from the bed, but she was already panting and sweating with the effort of talking for so long, and now she fell back with a thud against the bedpost that stunned her for a moment. She began to cry.

'Well, God, *I* can't make any move. You can see that. I'm to be a stretcher case even for the aeroplane. What was I saying? Yeah. It's all ballsed up when magic comes into it because it draws two kinds of people. Just my dear daddy the Senator and my dear momma the lush. That's who. The power-hungry and the neurotic. There isn't a person in that crowd around the Swami that doesn't fit into one or other of those categories. Except maybe for Ned. Look! It's for Ned you've got to act. For Ned and a lot of innocent people like that dead boy that are going to get hurt, by chance, when the Swami gets his growing band of loving disciples and screwy Shivites and Saktras, Ned the new recruit along with them, to burst through that procession and expose the body of Francis Xavier, when he calls upon those Lemurian powers of his to break the bondage of the Himalayan siddhas, when he shows himself to the crowd as the avatar of Vishnu. He's going to have a hell of a lot of madmen yelling for him, and a hell of a crowd of angry Catholics, and Hindus and Moslems too, I guess, right on his tracks. In fact all hell is going to break loose right there at old Goa around noon today when the procession starts out from the Bom Jesus to the Cathedral. And if you don't stop it, the authorities can't. And even if you *can't* stop it, you can get Ned away. Well, for God's sake, didn't you *know* all this? You and your baby and its squits! God save us from letting ordinary people have the running of this world or any other.'

Elinor sounded to Alexandra more and more like Thelma, so that she at once felt more at ease with her and also less respectful. She said:

'I think I understand more than you suppose. I think I've sensed more of this than I've allowed myself to know. It just seemed either so silly or so frightening that I thought of other things. But surely, with the insistence of the Church authorities, the police will be there in full force, enough to control it?'

'Hooray for the fuzz!' Elinor laughed maliciously, and in an imitation Oxford accent, she said, 'I do think the Goan police are so splendid. Look, they're going to have a hell of a lot on their hands. The Swami's a poor half-magician but he's a very

shrewd organizer of mischief. Most of this I know under oath so
if the bed goes up in flames with me in it, you'll know. But I
don't think their magic is very strong. Sheep rot is about the
limit of their powers, I think, and I had that as a kid.'

Alexandra was surprised that Elinor was really enjoying this
unusual indulgence in humour. If I ever had lots of money,
Alexandra thought, I'd give her a theatre. She'd be a nice kind of
person if she was an actress.

'Well, here goes of what I shouldn't tell. When Ned last
spoke of it, the Swami was relying on some other troubles –
some agricultural riots or something – to draw off most of the
police. And then he's sure that there'll be Moslem–Hindu troubles
with the end of Ramadan. And he's arranged a little sideshow
with the Shaktras he's brought up from Bengal to cause trouble
with the Vishnavites at that great Hindu temple Shri Mangesh.
No, there'll be plenty enough action. Oh, for pity's sake, it all
seemed unimportant to me before that boy's death and before
what happened that night, and since then I've been trying to
forget it. Hoping I suppose that I could still get back my detachment. But I can't. I don't think my psyche could stand much
more guilt, especially if anything should happen to Ned.'

Alexandra felt so disgusted at such egotism that she turned
away, then she said crossly to conceal her distaste, 'Well, what do
you suppose *I* can do?'

'You can go to where the Swami is. I can tell you where.
They're in two detachments on the swamp scrub on each side of
old Goa. They're to converge. The Swami's on the river side,
where it turns before it reaches old Goa. My guess is that the
Swami's dead scared that at the crisis he won't hear these
Lemurian voices of his. He's frightened that the moment of
truth is near for him, that after this he'll have to live with the
knowledge that he's a charlatan, instead of the half-doubt. That
would be far worse for him than what the world thinks. He'd
take any chance to get out of it. But his followers believe in him
too much. You'll have to help him to get away before they realize
and shame him into going on with it. And if he's too afraid of
them you must use that Sir James. He's relying on that old boy's
millions for his old age.'

'But if he fails here surely his reputation will collapse? Sir

James, you know, is one of those "nothing to do with failure" people.'

'Well, that's your problem. You know this Sir James.'

'I don't. I've never met him.'

'Well, the Swami thinks you're his *éminence grise*. Oh, for Jesus' sake! Lots of people may get killed! You're supposed to be the humanist, not me. Anyway, even if you *do* persuade the Swami to leave, you'll have a problem on your hands smuggling him through old Goa. The Catholics will be out for his blood. If you *can't* get the old buzzard away, you must unfix Ned. Offer him your bub to suck or something of the kind. He wants you for a mother. Surely you know that. The only trouble will be if he's not with the Swami's party.'

Alexandra said, 'I think we needn't talk about Ned. We're neither of us any good to him. Anyway, when you say such silly vulgar things as what you've just said, it's hard to believe that all the rest of this business isn't rubbish.'

'You know it's true!'

'Yes. I think I do. And I must do what I can. But how am I to get there?'

'Like any other person, I suppose. Hire, beg or borrow an automobile.'

'But I don't drive.'

'You don't what? Oh God! The British! We have a problem here. As my awful father says. Not that he's ever solved one. We can't bring a stranger in on this. I don't think I have the answer. Yes, I have too. We must get my mother in here.'

To the summoned Thelma, she said, 'How long since you drove an automobile?'

'I haven't driven in thirty-five years. I drove up from Gijón over the frontier when the Barcelona thing broke. And that Nancy Cunard gave me some sort of cassoulet at Perpignan that wasn't wholesome. When I started on for Montpellier, I commenced to throw up and I landed right into a plane tree and into a hospital. And, honey, when I married that stinking Congressman, he insisted that I had a chauffeur. That's when I never drove an automobile again.'

It didn't sound very promising to Alexandra, but Elinor said, 'Well, it's a calculated risk, but you're going to drive now.'

And she explained all the circumstances. There and then Thelma, in her bra and panties, did a kind of samba.

'So we're finally going to get that guru,' she said.

Alexandra would have expected the sight to be macabre, but in fact it was truly girlish and touching, perhaps because Thelma really hadn't understood the purpose of the expedition at all.

So Thelma climbed into a large picture hat and a kind of three-quarter-length summer frock and all her pearls, and took her travellers' cheque books, and set off to hire a car. Alexandra, with a possible scheme in mind, stuffed some old clothes and shoes into an airline bag which she slung around her neck, and with the greatest reluctance and bravery, left a tearful Oliver with a tearful Elinor. She went downstairs to wait for Thelma's return.

As she came down the staircase, she saw, to her amazement, the giant figure of Hamo almost touching the ceiling of the little entrance hall. He was expostulating with the porter. She had never seen him so wild in his gestures. It was hard to believe that he could be angry. She stood very still on the half-landing. Remembering a remark of the Swami's, and Elinor's recent story of rural disturbances, she saw that somewhere in this absurd but frightening jigsaw, the improbable and comic figure of her godfather fitted in. But he's such a big piece to fit in, she thought. Almost instantly, she added, and such a fine one, as she saw him standing there so tall and English and upright and indignant, at once so good and simple and so ludicrous. She couldn't imagine how he was going to be fitted in, but she knew at once that he was the piece that she had been unconsciously seeking all these months in order to make sense of everything. And yet he remained totally ridiculous. Perhaps it was just because of that. In any case she must remain silently out of his notice until she'd time at least to think of some way of dealing with this sudden overwhelming revelation.

'I think everyone here must have gone mad,' he was saying angrily. 'The difficulties I had at the airport and on the ferry! And police and soldiers everywhere! And when I explain that I have come to *help* the situation, you tell me that nobody is there to make use of me. I have given you six names at the Ministry of Agriculture and three at the Ministry of Tourism and you tell me that not one of them is at his desk. It's hard to say whether this is incompetence or panic. But whichever it is, it doesn't promise very well for Goa. Now you have the impertinence ... No, let me withdraw that, presumably you have your orders. But you tell me that the last incoming telephone call was from some idiot in the police saying that nobody is to be allowed into the streets, because of the dangers of mob action. Then *why* may I ask is an elderly and totally unprotected American lady permitted to endanger her life in contradiction to your orders?'

'No one stops Senhora Tarbett. She carries evil spells. Maybe you do not believe, Sir, but ...'

'I most certainly do not. Irresponsible nonsense.' Hamo banged on the reception desk so fiercely that the inkwell fell to the floor, broke into pieces and splashed navy-blue ink over his immaculate white linen trousers and the porter's beige tunic.

At once Alexandra knew. She ran down the stairs, threw her arms round Hamo's neck, and kissed him on his little moustache. To reach his mouth she had to jump in the air, and, in doing so, she swung the airline bag so that it hit him sharply on the back of the head. It seemed to Alexandra the best of omens.

'Hamo darling!' she cried. 'Do you remember the Meissen figure? And now the inkwell! But it isn't only *you* who are divinely clumsy, you see. All the same, you *are* Myshkin. *I* only did that because your beautiful clumsiness is infectious. Oh! I'm so happy. I know that it's going to be all right. Even if there is this bad time to go through.'

He disengaged himself, but he held her hands in his. 'Alexandra! You oughtn't to be here. The whole situation's out of hand. And it's all my fault.' Looking at her thin white face and the great eyes staring out of mauve, almost transparent eyelids, he was both excited and horrified to feel an urge, a very strong urge to pull her down on to the old sofa in the hallway and begin at once to explore every inch of her wonderful meagre street urchin's body under her clothing. He said sternly, 'I think if I can speak to these people, I can give them hope for the future that will check their desperation at any rate until things are under control. But you mustn't move from your room until you're allowed to. You see,' he said, trying to find simple words, 'it's all been my fault. Magic, that's the rice I hybridized, has put

371

a lot of people out of work and others can't grow it on their poor lands and so they've been ruined. And when I discovered this, it shocked me so much that I said a lot of foolish impulsive things to the journalists. I'm not very good with the Press, I'm afraid. Then the rumour got about that I'd come as a sort of champion of the poor and underprivileged. Actually I *am* determined to start a new programme of research to assist these people. It just isn't good enough to dismiss people as hopeless. But it'll take time. That's what I've got to explain to them. They must wait. And it may not work in the end. It'll be hard for them. But it is the *only* way. Otherwise it'll all end in violence and worse misery for them. But I need an interpreter. And all these idiots at the ministries have panicked and left their desks. It's intolerable.'

She pulled him down on to the couch. *She* held his face in her hands lovingly. At intervals kissing him, she said, 'You *are* Myshkin. Oh, damn! You're probably never even read Dostoevsky. We've got to find some means of communication. You see all this time I've been looking. I mean not only for myself. But for Oliver. That's my baby. You don't even know that. Oh dear! There isn't time for talking now too. Oh, not *just* for him, you idiot. For me especially. You see all those other things – the Birkins and dandies and gurus – just won't do. But you've *never* bullied or cringed. And I need someone so much. I've been waiting for someone. It's you. You've acted with divine idiocy, just simply doing all the mad contradictory things that were right. I want,' she ended, and she began to kiss his eyelids, 'I want you to marry me.'

It was a sensation he had never known, a lust and a sort of bursting through of worship into desire that made his head swim, his ears ring. If only, he thought, there had been girls like this, like boys when he was younger. But, at the same time, he knew it was all wrong. First, because all women married to queers were deceived. Second, because it was a sort of hero-worship on her part and ... He tried to remind himself that she had no cock, but then when had he ever cared whether the youths he fucked had cocks or not? He said, 'Look, Alexandra darling, for you are a darling and that I can say which I never dared say before. This is all make-believe. I don't know what this divine idiocy is, but there's nothing good in what *I've* done. I just went on in my own

selfish way, doing work I liked and pretending that the con-
sequences were not my affair. Then when I saw those conse-
quences I immediately indulged in a lot of emotional guilt and
breast-beating. Now, it's true, I *am* trying to put things right.
But that isn't heroism, it's just muddle. As a matter of fact, I
don't think that there are such things as heroes. The whole idea
does more harm than good.' As he heard himself say it, he wondered if the world would blow up around him – his grandfather
hero of Loos, his father twice hero of Arnhem, his housemaster
hero of Greek ideals, Leslie hero of sexual realism – he had spat
in their faces now, all those who had been the mainstay of his
life. Yes, and where had they got him to? Not that it was their
fault – they hadn't asked to be put on pedestals. 'No, there *are*
no heroes,' he said decisively.

'All right,' she replied, 'If you say so. But I want you. Very,
very badly. And so does Oliver. He needs a father. And there'll
be others for us. And as to your having boys, as if *that* was
important!'

He knew then that it was all no good, that she hadn't really
understood; that he and she too, in their own ways, were among
the hopeless.

She put her arms round him and pulled him to her. But he
disengaged himself and held her at arm's length.

'No,' he said, 'No. It just won't do. It's another muddle. I've
hurt enough people. Above all I'm not going to hurt *you*.'

Yet he hardly knew how to restrain himself from feeling into
every corner of her. At last she broke through his withholding,
and pulled him into her arms. This time he kissed her eagerly,
although he was crying with despair.

'God Almighty! You certainly know how to pick your times!'
Thelma's rasp shattered their union. Hamo stood up, almost
bumping his head. He was crimson in the cheeks. Alexandra
scowled at the interruption; but she too stood up, ready for her
orders.

'This is Hamo Langmuir. He's come here to prevent a riot.
Not the Swami one. But another one about rice.' As she heard
herself speak, she expected Thelma to laugh at her, but it was
quite otherwise.

'So what's stopping him?' she asked. 'Except that there isn't any riot. Not that I could see. Just a hell of a lot of police and soldiers and nobody on the streets. They're expecting a march on the city or something. Peasants on the move. They have real cockeyed revolutions round here. No proletariat, only peasants. Hon, is this the middle ages? And then it seems there's been a violation of that famous temple of theirs, the fancy one at Mangesh or whatever, and old Vishnu's followers are out to get somebody's blood. Let's hope it's that guru's.'

'I don't know anything about that. It's the peasants *I* have come to speak to,' Hamo said. He found Thelma's outré garb and eccentric manner most disconcerting.

'Well, go right ahead. In revolutions, there's only one rule – get your slogans across clearly and your action will follow. I learned that in Barcelona.'

'But I need an interpreter and a motor car. And they won't even let me leave this hotel.'

'What? Arturo here stopped you? Oh, Arturo! you naughty, naughty boy! Look, you kids just don't understand revolution. I *do*. I wasn't in Catalonia at the big bad time for nothing. There's just four things you need in revolutions – exhortation, because people believe, bullying, because people are bad, flattery, because people are human, and a hell of a lot of money, because people are poor. Don't get me wrong, that's not the dialectic of the thing. You'll find *that* in Trotsky. This is just the know-how. It's got me the oldest Peugeot in this town. But it'll get us far enough to tear the guts out of that guru. Let me talk to Arturo. He and I are good friends. Besides he thinks I'm a witch.'

While Thelma took the frightened and yet flattered porter behind the reception desk, Hamo and Alexandra stood, holding hands. They couldn't find any words. Alexandra was using her wishing power that he shouldn't escape her; Hamo was desperately trying to find reasons why he was dogmatic and pig-headed in believing that marriage for him would be a wrong action.

'What do you want to tell these peasants?' Thelma asked, and, interrupting Hamo's lengthy, complicated, stammering answer, she said, 'So, "you're the Magic man and they must go home now, but you'll help them later", right? Well, I hope they like the message. It sounds crypto-fascist to me. Have you got that, Arturo? He's the Magic man. They must go home now. He will help them later. Right. Arturo will take you in the hotel bus. There'll be police and soldiers, but he's a good boy, he'll avoid them where he can. And where he can't I've given him a hell of a lot of money and that means the police and the soldiers will avoid you.'

'But I can't accept money like this . . .'

'Oh, don't let that worry you. It belongs to a skunk called Senator Tarbett. And he's often said to me – in private, mind – that every Asian life lost keeps revolution further away from the great United States. So this is quite his sort of bonanza. Come on, Alexandra, we don't have too much time.'

Alexandra gave Hamo a long kiss before she left, and it was of this that he thought, as he automatiaclly boarded the hotel bus next to Arturo, automatically saw the empty stately eighteenth-century streets pass him by, automatically knew that Arturo had stopped to hand out money to some soldiers. It was only when they drew near to the town gardens, to the crescent-shaped flower beds and the bad heroic statues and the wedding-cake bandstand – the public formality which aped, in tropical guise, Coimbra or Oporto – that loud cries could be heard, shouts, chanting. There'll be two dangerous moments, Hamo thought, when they hear I'm the Magic man, they'll try to mob me as some sort of God; and then, when they're told I can't help them immediately, they'll turn ugly. Then is when calmness and trust must work, or never.

'You know what to say?'

'Sir,' Arturo said, 'My family is Goan. But I was born in Calcutta. I am only recently from Bengal. I do not understand their language very well.'

'Oh.' This was a facer. 'Well. Well, first make absolutely clear to them that I'm the Magic man. Can you do *that*?'

'Yes, Sir.' Arturo was steering the bus rather wildly. Clearly the man was afraid.

But there was no going back now, for the first ranks of the crowd poured into the square. All men, but of every age and kind, mostly in Indian dress, though many in the regulation shop-keeping, drab, European suiting. They appeared to be carrying an idol – perhaps a rice god. Many among them were nearly naked, smeared and strewn with ashes. An overpowering wave of incense and sour butter came from them. A few had cudgels, but not many, Hamo noted, carried sickles or machetes or other farm implements, as he had feared. Perhaps they were too poor to possess even a few such tools.

They came in a mass – many hundreds at least – down the bottleneck of one of the straight, tree-lined avenidas, and debouched like a great wave into the square, scattering all over the gardens. Yet a large number was drawn towards the hotel bus as the only moving thing in sight, although they did not appear to be more than a little curious, a bit obstreperous rather than hostile when they saw its two occupants.

'I think, Sir,' Arturo began, but Hamo said commandingly: 'Now, now, pull yourself together. Tell them who I am. Shout it loudly.'

As though hypnotized with fright, Arturo did exactly that, and, as Hamo had feared, the crowd immediately began to rush towards them. Well, he had no wish to be carried shoulder-high as a god, but still, if he could thus persuade them.

'Sir,' Arturo cried, 'they are very angry.'

He tried to turn the bus round to return to the hotel, but already many of the shouting crowd were behind them. In turning he knocked down an old, long white-haired man. In a second the crowd were upon the bus, rocking it from side to side and shouting, and banging their fists on the body; then a stone hit and shattered the windscreen, though only a few pieces were dislodged.

'Tell them I'm here to help. For God's sake, man, tell them.'

But Arturo was sobbing. And in a minute Hamo was thrown heavily on his side, as the whole bus was turned over.

He was such a long man that it took the crowd many agonizing minutes to pull him through the jagged windscreen. His face, his hands, his ankles were all bleeding from the cruel glass spikes. As his long marionette was tossed across from one part of the crowd to another he saw the bus with Arturo in it burst into flames. The pain of the blows, the agony of the stretching of his limbs as they pulled at him from every angle, emptied his mind of thoughts. Twice he was dropped on to the tarmac and was kicked and trampled on. Yet, even so, he felt the pain of another innocent man dead due to his muddle. Then the agony of his right arm pulled from its socket brought unconsciousness. When he came to, he was being carried and bounced from group to group of the shouting, screaming people towards the river. Once there was some hold-up and he called out for help, but if there were authority, then it had been rolled over, crushed down, made nothing. At last with a great heave they threw him far out into the water. He came to the surface and was hit on the temple by a rock that whizzed at him through the air. His head was bursting out through his ears, filthy water was pouring in to suffocate the breath from his lungs. The river sucked him down, pulled him under. He had only time to think, it would never have done, women's bodies suck you in, I need the hard resistance of a youth. And he was gone.

Thelma, grinding the gears of the old Peugeot and cursing as they rattled along the winding river road to old Goa, caught the sounds of shouting behind them, and said: 'I think there's trouble in the town.'

Alexandra said immediately, 'They've killed Hamo,' then she added, 'no, that's superstitious.'

Thelma said, 'He's a bit old for you, isn't he, hon? And he looks as though he's had a lot of women in his day. Those British officer types. They're pretty wooden, you know. They were the skunks that made Munich.'

Alexandra didn't understand, so she searched for a piece of wood to touch for herself and for Hamo, but there wasn't a scrap, everything was plastic or chromium in these bloody motor cars. They drove by field after field of young bright yellow-green rice.

'God, it's fertile,' Thelma said, looking suddenly young and happy, 'And that fucking Senator thinks I'm gonna cash in my chips!'

But, as they came towards old Goa, the road became more and more choked with pilgrims pouring in towards the Bom Jesus and the Cathedral. Everywhere on the side of the road, gay, pious family parties were making their morning meal like weekend picnickers, before setting off to line the processional route. Everywhere there was the smell of wood smoke and the noseprickling scent of curry cooking.

About two miles from the once great, now almost deserted city, they turned off the road by a jungle track, according to Elinor's vague directions; and now there was no chance of smashing on anything, for the car, under Thelma's random control, jumped and reared like a steer in a comic Western. Alexandra held on tight to the peeling chromium grab-handle, yet even so she wrenched her arm badly and twice hit her head on the roof hard enough to see stars. And suddenly, there, in a clearing in the scrub, sat the Swami, all alone, cross-legged on a small outcrop of rock. He sat so still that Alexandra could see that the lizards were basking and darting round his bare feet. The expression on his solar face was one of absolute and desperate emptiness. He seemed not to hear their approach.

'Stop,' she said to Thelma. 'I must go and speak to him alone.'

'Well, for God's sake! I don't want to go near the brute.'

Thelma braked so suddenly that Alexandra, who had opened the door in her eagerness to try out the scheme that had come to her, fell from the car on to a prickly plant and scratched her knees.

Bleeding she came up to him. 'It's all left you, hasn't it?' she said, praying that this inspiration should prove the right one.

For a moment the Swami looked bewildered by her appearance; then he frowned angrily; then, as suddenly, he nodded.

'The Lemurians have gone beyond our reach,' he said. 'No powers, not even mine, can arrive at them. But I am sure that this is only a temporary division. I need more spiritual energy but my reserves are for the present exhausted. *Später ... aber später ist zu spät*. The crisis is upon us.'

Alexandra sat down by his side. 'You simply must be patient,' she said. 'You must wait until you feel your powers have been renewed, even if it is many weeks. Nothing is ever gained by impulsive action.'

She thought of Hamo's words, but she recognized that she was speaking to the Swami in exactly the words and tone she had always intended to use with Oliver when he grew older. Her only fear now, as she had expected then, was that she might spoil all by laughing.

'But my followers,' the Swami asked, 'they are asking for a

sign. I gave them a sign, or the good Abbé did so by raising the Brahmin woman from the dead, but now there is no more response from the Lemurian sages. Can it be that I have made false measurements, false computations of their high places? What is the distance from Madagascar to Macao? Perhaps you can help me with this.'

He seized Alexandra's arms eagerly. She had difficulty in not shuddering and drawing away at his touch, but controlling herself, she said :

'These things cannot be done in haste, Swami.' Her brain now appeared to be concocting faster than her tongue could follow. She had a strange sensation that all her life she had been preparing for exactly this situation.

'Do you want me to say what I believe?' Something in the old man's panic combined with her sudden appearance gave him trust in her.

'Yes. Yes.'

'Very well. I believe that you have not sufficiently mastered the *Atlantean* sciences in their own realms so that you can oppose the true use of Atlantean knowledge against the false uses made by the Himalayan siddhas.'

'Quite on the contrary. I have studied the Atlantean sciences for many years.'

She followed her own desperation, wondering how soon she would blunder. 'But you have never made your own measurements. You have never described for yourself the conjunctions at Avebury.'

She had tripped up here, for, looking at her cunningly, he said, 'You know nothing of it all, do you?'

'No, but something is speaking through me. Something that frightens me. First you must go to Avebury and Glastonbury.'

For a moment both his panic and his dignified belief in himself seemed to disappear. He was all cheap cunning. 'And you will urge Sir James Langmuir to give me his assistance?'

She said, 'I'll consider it very closely. I'll talk to my godfather, his great-nephew. He's here in Goa.'

The Swami laughed scornfully. 'I know that. *He* can do nothing. Anyway he will be dead soon. They will kill him.'

Alexandra was seized with such a shivering that her teeth

chattered, but luckily the Swami was preoccupied with allowing his belief and his dignity to flow into him again.

'Meanwhile,' he said with a tragic air, 'I must allow this deathful peace of the vile Himalayas to continue? No, I can't do that. It will be to betray my trust. I must try to force these Lemurian rays through myself . . .'

'And if you fail?'

'Then when my followers open the magnus Francis's coffin, there will be nothing but dust. But if my powers are replenished, the body will be there miraculously intact, as it was for two centuries, until the Himalayan siddhas acting through the Jesuits brought it to corruption.'

'But even so, the Jesuits, the Catholic faithful will never forgive you for violating the tomb. They will have you arrested.'

'Have me arrested?' The Swami laughed. 'My dear foolish little person, if I have the Lemurian powers, all the forces of the Roman Catholic Church, all the Moslems, and all the followers of Vishnu, all the soldiers and all the police can *seek* to destroy me – and they will – but they can *do* nothing, nothing.'

'And if, as you suspect, your powers fail and there is nothing but dust?'

'Ah, then! Then I am afraid, for my own followers will turn on me. And you know, most of them are crazy people. Oh, not the little redbeard. Do you know that he is teaching them dances while we wait for the procession? Dances! these crazy people! And some few others are all right. There are young Indian men in the other group waiting on the other side of the old city who are sane. They believe in my powers but with the humour and scepticism that are necessary in all occult matters. Do you understand that?'

'Yes, I think I do. Well, we must rely on *them*.'

'But they are so few. And the rest – Indian, European, American, all alike are absolutely mad. They will tear me in pieces if their hopes are lost – can you say that in English – "hopes are lost"? And in a very cruel way.'

The Swami began to cry hysterically. At the same time Thelma hooted from the Peugeot impatiently. Alexandra made a decision.

She walked over to Thelma who she found drinking out of a

whisky bottle. 'I've got to get that Swami away,' she said, 'But I must see Ned first. Will you look after the Swami while I do that?'

'Will I do what? I'm not sitting with any fucking guru.' Looking at the bottle, Alexandra saw that Thelma had drunk nearly three-quarters in the short time they had been there. After so many weeks' abstinence, the effect was nearly lethal. Thelma was both confused and quarrelsome. 'Phooey to you and your guru! This civil war's a load of crap. How in the hell you dare to bring me into it, I don't know. I was in the Barcelona thing, real stuff.' She began to cry. 'I'm going home to my little baby Elinor.'

Manoeuvring the car with explosive noises and roller-coaster jerks she almost ran over Alexandra, smashed the left headlamp on a tree, and took off at high speed in full rodeo form for the main road.

Alexandra went back to the Swami. Taking out of her airline bag her old beige felt hat with the mauve streamers, and stretching the crown to tearing point, she forced it onto his bald head.

'Stay there until I come back.'

Astonishment seemed likely to cause him to obey. He looked so funny, but she stopped herself from laughing. She knew then that she had brought the right clothes.

The next step proved more difficult. Edging her way through the mangrove swamp she came upon the extraordinary sight of a large body – fifty or so – of the Swami's followers – of every kind from Shivites, American ladies in saris, learned occulists from France and Germany, Indians of various eccentric beliefs in their special eccentric religious get-up, some old-fashioned hippies, an English retired major, an academic maiden lady or two, some red-faced central-European gentlemen of middle age in boy-scout dress – all intent under Ned's leadership in dancing 'Batteries'. Scratch, scratch, crow, crow, strain, strain, they went. Ned was clearly in seventh heaven, and it was not easy to bring him down to earth, especially to detach him without breaking up the dance. When she achieved this, the others danced on hynotically.

Persuading him was less difficult.

'Well, I'm not, like, surprised, y'know. But it seemed worth following. I mean you know like the Seekers in the seventeenth century. I mean we're looking for a sign, aren't we? And who's to know, the Swami *might* have been the vessel. But I'm not surprised that he isn't. Well, are you? Anyway, does it matter if there *are* riots? I mean about this deathful place, that he *is* right about. That we've always agreed about.'

'Yes, but this time, really, truly, lots of people, ordinary, not bad people will be killed. Elinor would say it too. I mean if she could be here.'

'Ordinary people! Then they've asked for it. I mind more about you. All right. I'll keep them dancing.' He smiled suddenly. 'Don't know that I could stop them actually. They're sort of hypotized, I think.'

She loved him so for this that she kissed him. Then she ran back to the Swami.

Getting her old fox and lamb coat on to him was more difficult. There would be no point in splitting it. At last she simply put it round his shoulders, and taking the long mauve chiffon ribbon from the hat she used it as a sash to tie round his waist. He looked something of a bundle. But after all, Toad had had to escape as an old woman, and what was good enough for Toad ... She powdered his face and painted it with Thelma's bright scarlet lipstick until he looked like some semblance of Thelma herself swollen to bursting point in a distorting mirror. Below the coat his white gown hung down, and, below that, his dainty feet were bare. Into his hand she put a forgotten old pair of shoes with diamanté high heels that she had found in Thelma's cupboard.

'There now, you'll do,' she said, 'I'm sure no one's ever worn fox and lamb who was more suited to the combination. Ned's keeping that lot dancing. What about the other group? When will they move in on the procession?'

But there was no answer from the Swami. He just goggled at her through all his paint and powder from under his Ascot hat.

It was all she could do to keep him moving; he was a barrel-like old woman, the kind that rolls when she walks because her thighs are so fat. When they reached the high road there was such a pressure of happy pilgrims that they could not go against the stream back into Panaji, but must flow towards the ruined city.

And there it was: the churches, the towers, the domes, the cool stone, the symmetries and the fantasies of the West still defying, after centuries, the natural disorder, the vegetable greed of the tropical jungle. It was so incredibly beautiful that Alexandra felt ashamed – ashamed that she had never in all these weeks thought to come here, ashamed that she knew so little of the visual arts that for the life of her she could only say that it was all probably baroque, no, that doorway was certainly older – Renaissance, could it be, here in the Indian jungle? – and a tower looked Byzantine which was obviously nonsense. She knew nothing, nothing, had cultivated no visual sense, none of the knowledge that could give what she saw, as she could what she read, a fuller dimension. And for what she read, how much for all her two one in English, did she care? Ten, twenty books, and those all in the English tradition. Her life was running away, being in absurd plots like this Swami's one, and in Oliver. But there must be some centre more than the chance muddle of people.

She tried to be practical. She said aloud, 'I shall have to do publisher's reading. You see I must be at home to work for the next year or two because of Oliver. I don't believe in these crèches.'

The Swami goggled at her.

They must have come to a halt among a band of the most pious of Panaji, for women in bright rainbow saris appeared to recognize the eccentric old American woman. They peered at her with curiosity, some even showed pleasure at seeing her there, but most looked away from her with superstitious fear. A smartly dressed Indian gentleman in European clothes even addressed the supposed Thelma.

'Madam, you are welcome. We had no knowledge that you were a Catholic. You should have been here in 1952. Then the papal legate came here and three archbishops and seventeen bishops. Today I fear there will only be one archbishop and four bishops.'

But Thelma-Swami still only goggled.

'Ah,' said the man, 'they are coming. You hear the Te Deum. My little grandson Paolo is among the two hundred choristers.'

The chanting made Alexandra want to cry. And the beauty of

the procession. The white surplices and the white of the priests' robes against the gaily coloured crowd. The monks, brown, black, white – she didn't even know one from another – Dominicans, Franciscans, Benedictines, and what were Capuchins like? Of black, brown and white races she knew nothing. And all the gold in the banners and in the great mitres and the silver croziers of the two or three, were they bishops or archbishops? And all those in purple, who could they be? Cardinals, perhaps, but then the man would have told of such grandees. Monsignori? But surely they only had purple stockings. Many of the priests had long white beards, and others were so young that they seemed like girls. The older choristers were swinging great silver things from which incense filled the air, joining the savoury smells of the pilgrims' cooking. And all the time singing – high high trebles, and then the deepest bass. Suddenly everyone was on their knees, the Swami, too, and his hand was on her shoulder forcing her down. He was crossing himself and muttering or chanting – it was hard to tell which.

'*Es ist das heilige Sakrament,*' he whispered. '*Wissen sie, ich bin in Salzburg geboren. Ich bin katholisch getauft.*'

And now the procession was reaching its end with more choristers and a long, long line of nuns.

At once from far beyond the crowd on the other side there came shouting and a chant of another kind, a monotone, to Alexandra an eerie note. To Swami-Thelma's ear electric in its effect.

'Shiva,' he whispered, 'and Durga. But they have no power. There will be no renewal as I hoped, only destruction. Now it will only be a foolish blasphemy.'

Once again inspiration engulfed Alexandra. I'm wasting my life, she thought, but I *am* good at plotting, and she spoke loudly to the well-dressed Indian gentleman.

'The American lady must have air, please. She is fainting. Please help me.'

He seemed to enjoy the officious action of clearing a path and when the people saw the vast bizarre, tottering figure that Alexandra with the greatest difficulty supported on her arm, they made a clearing, partly out of natural submission to an authoritative voice, partly from superstitious fear of the witch. As they made their way through, men, women and children alike earnestly crossed themselves.

When they reached the procession, the nuns who were passing at that moment held up their march to let them through. There was more difficulty in making a path through the crowd on the other side, where some alarm had already broken out at the distant Shivite chanting. They were jostled, bruised and scratched. But at last they were free of the crowd. The Swami strode hastily away, past the back of the Cathedral, past an enormous splendid palace. Clambering through scrub and over ruins of vast mansions, they passed under a great arch, and there, by the river bank, was drawn up the Swami's other group.

At first when the Swami spoke, there was such astonishment at his costume that he was greeted with silence, but, as he continued, there was an increasing, swelling, angry roar. The naked yellow-barred Shivites, true and false, began a menacing, swaying movement towards them. A long, thin faced tow-bearded Scandinavian in pince-nez and white linen gown cried: '*This* is not our Swami, this is not Sant Sarada. It is some evil, emanation, some elemental raised by the magic of the Himalayans. Let us say our spells.'

All, Indian and European, began to advance on the Swami, chanting.

Alexandra could feel already the agonies of her coming death – she thought of Oliver, she thought of Hamo. Then suddenly a memory of *Little Dorrit*, of Mr Pancks exposing the old fraud Casby to the tenants of Bleeding Heart Yard by cutting off his patriarchal locks, came back to her. She pulled the beige hat from off the Swami's head, trusting that the absurdity of his appearance would make her laugh and that her laughter would prove infectious. After all, *he* had said that among the young Indian followers were men with humour.

With his great goggling face and bald head, the rouge and lipstick running with sweat, he seemed to her like the pumpkin man. It worked. She began to laugh hysterically.

'You see,' she cried, 'he's just a fraud, a poor old fraud.'

Some of the younger Indian men took up her laughter, and, although there were still angry shouts, the menacing, chanting advance ceased.

'Go on,' she whispered to the Swami, 'get away while you can.'

Raising his skirts to his knees, fox and lamb trussed about him by the mauve ribbon sash, high-heeled shoes still held delicately in one hand, he ran for his life. The last sight of him was his bald head above the water as he swam the river.

Well, she thought, and they say Eng. Lit.'s of no practical use. But before their mood could change, she herself hared over boulders and thickets, following the course of the river. She had to trudge nine miles back to Panaji. Her legs seemed made of iron as an incredible exhaustion came over her mind, her body and her spirit. She thought of the spells that Sauron had put upon Frodo and Sam so that they became too tired to move. And then she said to herself, enough of superstitious imagining. A story is a story is a story, even a good one like *The Lord of the Rings*.

When at last she came in to her hotel room, the day had been so extraordinary that she felt no surprise when she saw Zoe sitting in the one armchair with Oliver on her knee, feeding him with apple purée from a teaspoon.

Zoe said, 'Darling, before I give you a hug, I've got to be angry with you. Very, very angry. You had no right to leave this child with those two American freaks. Oh, I dare say they're amusing enough to be with. But it's an absolute basic rule with babies or children when their imaginations are beginning to work, that they *must* not come into contact with anyone who's in the slightest degree crazy.' She frowned, then added, 'Is it as serious as *The Times* seemed to say it could be?'

The authorities, on the whole, had good reason to be satisfied with the day's events. Some disturbances had taken place at the great temple of Vishnu at Shri Mangesh. Two worshippers had been injured by stones. But for the rest, communal disturbances —Hindu/Catholic, Hindu/Moslem, Moslem/Catholic – had been kept to a minimum. The agrarian rioters, against whom the main force of authority had been levelled, had never come within miles of the confines of the city; and only one death and two severely injured were reported from their confrontation with the police. A plant geneticist, who had shown himself unfriendly to India and uncooperative to Goa in particular, had mysteriously drowned in the Mandovi, killed, it was said, by followers of Vishnu. A hotel porter, a Bengali immigrant, who had disobeyed the curfew, had been burned to death in a bus. The Austrian Swami, long a figure of the greatest controversy, had disappeared from the scene. The larger part of his followers, including many of these offensive hippies, had been expelled – one, the red-bearded young leader of some dangerous mass ritual, had suffered injury on arrest, but he was leaving on an aeroplane with his leg in plaster. The Jesuit Father in charge of the organization of the procession at old Goa had written to the Chief of Police to thank him for his efficiency. There were a number of letters to the paper the next week comparing the sense of order in Panaji with the lawlessness to be seen in so many far richer Indian cities. An account strongly on the credit side.

Epilogue

Alexandra Comes Home

Alexandra could see, as she thought, every olive tree, every vine, every boulder of Cyprus as they passed over that island in a clear, pale, cool sunshine. 'That rings black Cyprus with a lake of fire' – what nonsense bad poetry was. But the Isles of Greece, however Sappho burned, were increasingly streaked and barred by wisps of cloud. When they reached Corfu, the sun blazed down upon them, but below there was nothing but miles and miles of slow-moving, white wool.

It was then that Zoe, who had been so silent though efficient in the days of preparation for departure, began to talk and talk, as though, indeed, she were unwinding the wool below them, as she turned her ear-ring savagely in her ear.

'I think we were right,' she said, 'to cable to Sir James. After all, even if they were never close ... but although he's tough as nails, he's very old ... and one can never tell with shocks ... so that it was the most extraordinary piece of luck your being able to forewarn by telephoning Rodrigo Knight. Not that I mean his being Sir James's secretary isn't an extraordinary thing in itself. I'm only so glad it's working out. Although I shouldn't have thought that any of your friends ... but then there *is* this feeling that the sixties have been rather disastrous, and that we're glad to turn our back on them.

'I think that's what made *Leslie* decide to go all out for money. He felt that all his ideals about teaching were a sort of nonsense, or so he told me. I mean that really a great number of them *are* unteachable. And that anyway there are other ways of living than the narrow literate ones we've tried to impose. Well, he'll tell you if he comes to England. But I don't expect he will, because he works from five in the morning until midnight, or so Perry writes. But apparently the hotel's colossally successful and he's already started a second and plans a whole chain. Of course he makes everything *very* comfortable and Corfu *has* sunshine which is what most people are after. I mean all these executives, who are working themselves to the bone, just want to relax completely for the fortnight or so they allow themselves. They only want sun and comfort and they'll pay anything for them.'

Alexandra forced her way in. 'It was covered in cloud when we passed over it just now.'

'Was it? Oh! was it? Well, I expect it's an off day. But, of course, Leslie's only symptomatic. I do think you *will* find there's a new sense of purpose about when you get back.' She looked distastefully to where Ned was drawing on his plaster-encased leg to amuse Oliver. To her pleasure, Oliver's attention was not long engaged. He was enchanted with his new grandmother and the noise she made. He kept looking at her and saying 'Zoo'. It was his first word.

'Of course, it's not my sort of world, Ally. I shall always be a radical of a kind. But then I've never had to think of money, you see. But there's no doubt it *is* most people's mainspring. And perhaps we'd better face it. I mean, Concepcion, for example ... I don't blame them, but they *did* let me down most appallingly, as soon as this well-paid factory job at Coventry came along.

'Well, you can see it even in Perry – I mean this film, especially with Kit Coates as director, is going to make *three* times what the book brought in – and heaven knows that was enough! So I mean all that about the Corporation and Auntie's high standards in a world of declining taste *did* have to go by the board. It was so marvellous that just when he handed in his resignation, Leslie should have been starting up in Corfu. It was ideal for Perry. *And* he's got a boat there.

'It's brought them together tremendously. They rather needed to gang up because they were faced with this Little Mam problem. She sold up the restaurant quite unexpectedly and said she wanted to see more of her sons. It was the worst moment possible, just when they were starting new lives. They've staved her off somehow, but I'm afraid she *has* been a bit hurt. Of course, it simply isn't an old people's world. Not that she's really old, but all that small-scale business ... Anyhow, she's staying with me for the moment. And I make a fuss of her. She *can* be quite fun.

But she's been too busy bringing them up, you know, to be a real person.

'Now that's something you can't say about Great-grand-mother. You know how they were when you went down there. Well, there's no talk of death now. He's finished the memoirs. And then Sarawak or Borneo or wherever it was he gave the constitution to, had some celebration and they invited him out for it. But he didn't take her. It was terribly selfish and she was very hurt. But I think she ought to have known. After all, she had always been very much a *hostess* for him. That was their generation. Anyhow, I invited her to stay at Number 8. And she's been there ever since. Eighty-eight, and not a thing wrong with her, but rather formidable.

'It's fascinating, of course, the sophistication of her generation. I mean the gaps in it. She *had* to read Perry's novel when it was a best seller everywhere. And she recognized me in Honey. Oh! There, I keep forgetting you've never read it. Well, that's the central woman. But do you know she had *absolutely* no idea that the man Honey had an affair with was a queer. So she couldn't make any sense of the book. Little Mam got it in one. But then she *would*, with Leslie.

'Heaven knows where Perry thought it up. *I* never had any connections with homosexuals. Except poor darling Hamo. Oh the waste of *that*, Ally! But I mustn't talk to *you* about it. You've obviously got so much to digest about *that* which mustn't be interfered with by surface people like me.

'But it was a stroke of genius on Perry's part. Because, of course, Honey's marriage has been taken as a sort of symbol of the fruitlessness of the sixties. You can imagine how Kit Coates will play that up. I only hope he doesn't coarsen it.

'But enough of other people. I want *you* to rest and rest and take your time ...'

And then she repeated it all over again, twice, in slightly different words and order before they reached London airport.

At Cromwell Road air terminal, they put Ned into a taxi for King's Cross and the mysterious North, to Zoe's obvious relief, and to Oliver's total lack of concern. It shocked Alexandra a little that a child should be so unforgiving, just because poor Ned had neglected Oliver when he had stomach trouble, or so it seemed.

Peering out of the taxi window as they came towards Baker Street, Alexandra had to crane on and on before she found, suddenly and meaninglessly, the sky, above an incredibly tall glass and concrete office thing.

'Oh God, Mama, what a boring slab! ... Where are they all? Whole squares and streets have gone. Beautiful ones.' It was the one promise she had made to herself, with her new-found wish to cultivate a visual sense – to enjoy London.

'It's Langmuir House,' Zoe told her, 'a new office block. The largest in London, I believe. Something to do with Sir James.'

Alexandra said violently, startling her mother, 'I'd like to pull every stone of it down.'

Way up on the roof were little black dots. Sir James was mixing well with the workmen for the topping-out ceremony. Rodrigo observed him as usual with admiration for his arrogant bonhomie. His downing of pints of beer seemed to be as much designed to make his fellow (but subordinate) directors appear condescending as to make the building workers feel at ease. Their ease, he clearly took for granted, because they were part of the process of building which was now complete. He was simple and direct with them from foreman downwards, for where his relationships were transitory, he always found a general topic – in this case, the week's League results – and a general mood – in this case, friendly gratitude for work done – and left it at that. Even with the architect, he was straightforward and easy. When Rodrigo had pointed out the gross mediocrity of the design, Sir James had been delighted.

'That's the sort of thing I want you to tell me. Although it hardly needs a modish eye to see it. It was intentional. My choice. Directors of companies looking for premises in the extended West End expect to find what the estate agents call prestige properties, that is, for offices, so-called modern. Characterless but lavish. I saw at once that to get it we needed a bad architect with a well-known name, or, as you more kindly say, a mediocre one. In Rattenbury we found our man.'

But to Rattenbury, whom he need not see again, he was now chatting easily; they talked of mutual friends at Rattenbury's club, and exchanged racing tips. Only with those with whom he was in constant communication did Sir James bother to be tricky, and with them, in varying manner, with Rodrigo himself indeed, he practised his usual game of tenterhooks – every variation of sudden change from friendliness to reserve, from intimacy to withdrawal, from listening attentively to abrupt interruption. It was how he 'was', how they expected him to be, yet he never let them get really used to it.

For Rodrigo it was a constant source of admiration, in particular because it was wedded to real elegance. His suits set the mark by being 'right', yet never to be labelled – somewhere between country gentleman and diplomat, yet also somewhere between the styles of the older generation and the younger, always with a touch of vulgarity to ridicule the conventional, yet essentially correct to reprove the socially uncertain. His face, too, enhanced his manner, wine-flushed yet sun-tanned, grey-haired but with a boyish lock or two, protruding blue eyes staring apoplectically, but with little laughter lines and creases that smoothed the anxious stare into light-heartedness. Two things were totally absent from his face – all pathos and all concern. He moved with a light easiness, hurried without a puff of breath, yet his stocky little body was on the heavy side. Good food and good wine in plenty were in perfect harmony with regular squash, regular swimming and sauna baths. If the dandy were to soil his fingers with money-making – and it seemed increasingly to Rodrigo that any dandy must do so in order to express himself in the modern world – then Sir James had found the answer.

Rodrigo whispered into his ear, 'I think Eliot Wilshaw wants to make a speech.'

Sir James turned abruptly from Rattenbury's account of racing in Sydney. 'We'll go now,' he said to the company in general, 'These ceremonies are delightful. So long as they are not protracted. Good-bye.'

The company, from the youngest building worker to the oldest director, except Eliot Wilshaw, clearly felt absolute conviction of the sentiment.

As they were driven away, Sir James said, 'You were quite right to tell me. We needed American investment to start these office blocks. But we can't have American long-windedness every time a new building's finished. Wouldn't do at all.'

As they neared Number 8, Zoe said suddenly, 'Look, darling, we *must* get on to a better footing than this. Officially, of course, I'm not in Corfu because I jibbed at the Colonels. And that's true as well. But I'd have swallowed even them really, although I know one shouldn't, if Perry had wanted me. But he didn't. He's taken his secretary, a girl with the name of Nipple or something. I think he may want a divorce.'

To Alexandra's worry, she found her hand taken by her mother's and pressed. She returned the pressure.

Zoe said, 'Thank you, darling. It *has* been rather a horrid time for me. You see I love him so much. And the old girls' unspoken sympathy about the house all day isn't the greatest of help.'

Alexandra made a solemn pact with herself to try to reach and to help Zoe; she also made a firm decision to get away from Number 8 as soon as possible.

They walked about among the massive pieces of furniture in the huge, high rooms. For some reason Mrs Edgerton, on hearing of Hamo's death, had shrouded all the furniture in dust covers. These she had half removed in order to show his heiress round the flat. It meant, Alexandra felt, that she had really no idea of what was there and what wasn't. Every chair, every sofa, every table was so impersonal, so heavy, so totally without style. Not vulgar, not pretentious; just lifeless. She saw suddenly, with her new visual sense, that things could be awful, not because they were wrong, but also because they were nothing. It made Hamo's life even sadder for her. A kind of austere, rigid nothingness pervaded the flat – a frightened neatness. No wonder the divine idiot trying to break out had fallen into muddle and disaster. There must surely be some centre, some shabby centre to this apparent emptiness. Something sad and hidden.

She must get rid of Mrs Edgerton. Now. For if there *were* dirty photos or compromising letters or whatever they were called, it would be the most awful thing if this worshipping housekeeper should see them. And she must get rid of her for good, as obviously they wouldn't what was called 'suit one another'.

She had no need to worry. From the start, Mrs Edgerton (Hamo had always said Mrs E. so that Alexandra was surprised to find that it was only an initial) had made her new independent status clear by saying 'Miss Grant' and not, as on those lunch and tea-parties of childhood, 'Miss Alexandra'. As now: 'As you know, Miss Grant, Mr Langmuir has left me an annuity so that, with my savings, I shall be quite independent. My sister wants me to join her in Angmering but I've never cared for the seaside – Piccadilly Circus in the summer and the back of beyond in winter. I shall probably settle near my niece in Leicester. But I shall take my time to look around. I shouldn't bother you with such things – you'll have quite enough with the estate – but sometimes people worry about what happens to what they used to call dependants. So if you'll excuse me, I'll get along. Two women in one house never did.'

Alexandra could have kissed her. But holding on to her new resolve, to try to reach people, to live less in herself, she said, 'I talked to him, you know, the day he died. It was incredible. He knew he was in danger but all he could think of was the desperate poverty of the Indian farm labourers.'

It was a shorthand account; but it was all she cared to or could serve up for the world.

'Ah! I wouldn't understand that, Miss Grant. You see I only knew Mr Langmuir before all this abroad when he was as regular as clockwork in his habits. Like a timetable only a good deal more reliable. One thing he did let himself go with – his bath. Singing and splashing! And then to drown in that river! Well, we mustn't be morbid. Oh, by the way, there's all this unopened mail.'

'Isn't there anything in the flat, any furniture you'd like, Mrs Edgerton? I mean, you know, as that thing you get when people die?'

'Well, furniture's hardly a memento, is it? Besides, it'll be a bit too heavy for my purposes. To be honest, I think it was a bit gloomy for Mr Langmuir. But there, he was a gentleman weighed down by inheritance, money and the rest of it. It never allowed him any real sort of freedom. All this work and fixed habits. But he was the kindest, most courteous gentleman to work for and that's all that concerned me.'

Alexandra saw no way of coping with all this. 'Some *little* thing?'

'Well, if it'd make you feel easier. There was two jars. They're labelled "Cumin" and "Marjoram", but I used them for curry powder, and for cinnamon for his baked custards. They were the only thing he ever bought me for the kitchen. I expect Mrs Grant chose them. But there you are . . .'

Mrs Edgerton had gone, having taken the pots from Alexandra's clumsy hands and made them into a neat, easily portable parcel. Alexandra walked round the huge high rooms; wherever she touched the panelled walls some service lift made its appearance or some cupboard opened before her. What was revealed inside them, however, was always emptiness. They belonged to a vanished glory of the flats in an Edwardian past. They worried Alexandra – either, she thought, bodies will fall out of them like in those detective stories, or clergymen will be standing there in their underpants, like in those farces. Either way, she didn't care to be involved.

In any case, she was merely postponing the nasty moment – the moment when she opened the locker in the centre of his desk, the only locked thing for which there had been a labelled key among all the estate papers in the deed box in the bank. Her apprehension of what personal secrets might be found there had forced her to snub and offend even Zoe by refusing to allow her to come to the flat.

When she took out the drawer from the inner compartment, it contained two packets of letters tied in ribbons – the one very bulky, the other very thin. She felt furious. If they should prove threatening letters, she would go through any police embarrassment to send the man to prison.

The larger bundle was all letters from the war years. Letters, it seemed, from a never-ending series of army camps; stilted letters, with references to platoon football matches, and other company sports, tight-lipped expressions of satisfaction at London's courage in the air raids, delight at Matapan and at the North African landings; inquiries about prep-school cricket-match results and gratification at Hamo's long jump success, a remonstrance about low marks in history, delight at a mathematics prize, an injunction about confirmation. 'I told a chap called Anderson here that you were being confirmed, he said that it could "do you no harm". It made me think that perhaps that's where my generation have messed it all up. By being so negative. Try not to let that sort of spirit catch up on you. I don't go to communion often, but when I do, it makes me, if only for a day or two, a different man. Something good enters into me. I'm afraid this term's weather has been pretty foul. You must have had to cancel a lot of fixtures. English summer ! . . .'

Alexandra felt too embarrassed by the remoteness and the absurdity of it all.

She undid the other bundle. It contained one letter in the same hand. She noted particularly, 'Don't let your grandmother or anyone else speak to you against your mother. It may be many years before you see her, since America is very far away. In years to come, you may wonder how I let it all happen. The answer is that from the start she was always far too full of life, too full of fun, too anxious to get the most out of things for a dull chap like me. So long as I can get up to Perthshire for leaves and just mess around a bit on the estate, I'm happy. But what sort of a life was that for her? And if she joined me at base, the officers' wives' world of bridge and gossip . . . And so I let her drift away . . . You'll understand more of this in later years.' Another letter in a large, sprawling hand, read, 'My darling, darling boy, if you never see me again, do try to think of the fun we had last Christmas. Do you remember how we laughed at Widow Twankey ironing that huge pair of drawers? . . .'

Alexandra tore them both up, and a photograph of a kind of actress person in a sort of Spanish hat and a fringed Spanish cloak with her hand on her hip; she also destroyed the careful friendly letter from the Chaplain telling of Major Langmuir's death at Arnhem and his popularity in the regiment. There was some kind of police information from Montreal about Hamo's mother being found dead in her bed in a hotel bedroom – she destroyed this too.

Alexandra thought of Mrs Edgerton's comments. And now this. Money and mothers. Marx and Freud. The determinism of that generation was too dispiriting! Determinedly she remembered only Hamo's clumsiness and gentleness, his brilliant technical reasoning and his childish worldly knowledge. These were what had made him good and special, all the rest was conventional, psychological or sociological nonsense.

She turned to reading the unopened mail. A Mr Lacey sent back a cheque for a hundred pounds – 'I have to confess complete failure in tracing the young lad who interested you. I'm sorry but not surprised. These landless peasants move about like monkeys. One minute here, the next gone. You will be shocked to hear that the Jonkheer had a stroke some weeks ago. There's talk now of a Japanese president for the Club. Ensworthy's as sick as I am at the thought. We both think of resigning. However, this will hardly interest you . . .'

A Mr Subramanian simply returned his cheque for the same amount, with a short note, saying, 'I was unable to perform the task you asked of me. I herewith return your cheque. I confess that I am happy to be free of such a commission . . .'

A Mr Dissawardene wrote at greater length. His wife, it seemed, had been most active in attempting to trace a certain Muthu. 'We are more zealous than you suppose, Mr Langmuir, in our concern for those who serve us.' His daughter and son-in-law, it appeared, forbade mention of Hamo's name, but his wife often expressed wonder at what Dr Malcolm (whoever that might be) had been after. 'For myself, I am old enough to know that human motives are too complicated and too many for our understanding. A wise old judge from the U.K. used always to tell me this in court, but I did not listen. In those days I thought I could understand everything . . .'

A Mrs Kovalam wrote that it had not been possible to trace the family from which the drowned boy came. Anti-social elements of this kind were seldom stable members of society, frequently they were little better than nomads. In any case the social benefits scheme . . . Meanwhile she returned to him his cheque for £100.

Alexandra destroyed all these letters and all the returned cheques. She thought, his ships come home with a vengeance. She saw him, as Mrs Edgerton had described him, singing and splashing in the bath, surrounded by floating paper ships. And they had all sunk.

But now she came upon a bulky package addressed from India in his own hand. She began to read it laconically. Then she sat down in a chair and tried to puzzle out the accompanying reports. Over an hour later, fortified by coffee she had made for herself, she was still reading them.

Then she telephoned to Sir Alec at the Institute. The telephone conversation didn't at all appease her. She said: 'Very well, if you refuse to take it seriously, I shall have to speak to Sir James Langmuir.'

To Rodrigo she said, 'I'm sorry, Roddy, but if you don't do this for me, I shan't see you again.'

Half an hour later, Sir Alec's secretary telephoned to her to say that he would be glad if she would come to meet him and some of Hamo Langmuir's colleagues. Would Monday afternoon suit her; it appeared to be the only time that Sir James Langmuir could be present? She said that it would.

Entering his little cluttered office – cluttered because he never used it except as a sort of left-luggage office, not because it was worked in – Nelson Hart saw a little, white-faced creature with shoulder-straight hair, in a long expensive-looking fur coat and below it huge wide green trousers. Her eyes stared angrily, her mouth pouted sulkily. A rich hippie! He could hardly think of any kind of girl he could less easily talk to, but from all that had been said since Hamo's death, by Sir Alec, and by inference by the old boy Sir James this morning, this girl who had got the money had been the Lodger's thing in life. He felt awful enough about the man's terrible death, but to have maligned him all those years – though, save for a faint hint of breasts, it really might not have been 'maligned' at all, these girls like boys! – but she was clearly angry, there must have been some bad balls-up somewhere.

He said abruptly, having meant to make any other opening but this: 'The meeting was this morning, I'm afraid. You've missed it.'

She said – and he thought, oh, my God, she's going to cry –

'But they specially asked me to come this afternoon. It was all for me it was fixed. Or, at least, to suit Sir James.'

He said, a little more relaxed, 'That's the trouble, I'm afraid. He changed the time at the last minute. He's a terrific tycoon, you know. Parleying with the Prime Minister, organizing the world's rubber supply in his spare time and all that.' She didn't respond to his facetious tone. 'Please, do sit down. I am sorry, I'm the only one here. Sir Alec cleared off after lunch. Organizing the world's maize supply.' Then realizing that he'd made the same kind of joke twice, he said, 'Sorry.'

She said, 'Oh, it's not your fault. And it's kind of you to receive me.'

He thought, well, it is really, because his prolamin analysis was being interrupted. He must keep it as short as possible. But he said, 'Oh, good heavens! I worked very closely with Hamo Langmuir. He was the most brilliant man we had.'

He thought, I've never really believed that he was *very* good, his limitations were too serious; however, it'll do for shorthand.

She said, 'Yes, I know. You're Nelson Hart, the plant physiologist.'

'He talked to you about his work, then?'

'No, no. We hardly ever saw each other.'

He thought, oh, then, I didn't malign him, but what does it matter; anyway, why the hell's she so upset?

He concentrated on the fact that prolamin analysis was more important than this. He said, 'The meeting was rather technical, you know, although we simplified it to put our views over to Sir James. All the same, I don't think Hamo would have expected you to . . .'

'But it was me who insisted on his report being discussed. I found the copy you see in his papers. And, oh, well, it all fitted in. You see I talked with him just before he went to his death. He felt he'd got in a muddle and he had. But, well, the report wasn't part of the muddle. No, it was the other way – trying to clear it up. I know it was.'

She saw that he could make nothing of all this. She tried again. 'He wanted so urgently that *you* should endorse it. He felt that your part of the work was so vital. I could tell that from his detailed report to you. He must have admired you greatly.'

402

Coming here in the tube she had rehearsed everything carefully; she had felt that she understood the new rice project in detail, but as that gloomy commissionaire had brought her through all those strange rooms with plants growing, great monstrous and beautiful things, some commonplace, some exotic; as she had glimpsed all these complicated machines in endless rooms off endless corridors, she had realized that she had understood nothing. Now, faced with this key man in Hamo's plan, she decided that she could say nothing that would not be silly.

She said, 'Nobody here has taken any notice of what he asked for. That Sir Alec as good as told me that it was all nonsense – "Our programmes are decided on a broad basis, Miss Grant, and after very mature deliberation. Not sudden emotional impulses" – Oh, I can't do Scots, but he was awful. That's why I pulled strings and things to get Sir James here. I wanted to explain about Hamo and what his life had meant and how this was the logical result of it.'

He thought, just as well you weren't here, my dear. He said, 'Oh, I see. Well, look, I think you have no serious reason to worry. To begin with Sir Alec's a sort of front man. Though don't quote me. Admin and so on. He hasn't done any serious scientific work for twenty years, if then. Of course he didn't want any change of programme. It would mean too much hard work and possibly upsetting too many people in the ministries and foundations. But we knew nothing about it. I mean Hamo's colleagues. As soon as we'd all read his report, we found it full of the most exciting possibilities. It's just the very fact of dealing with the socially unpromising that gives it so much potential purely scientific promise. Or so I suspect. It means we're leaving the comfortable old tramlines. Did you ever see a tram? I never did. And so we all said this morning. Every one of us, I think,' he added after a pause, 'you would have been happy to hear how every one of Hamo's colleagues paid tribute to his work.'

He'd got it out at last, he thought, and he relaxed his stomach muscles in relief. She brushed it aside.

'But what's the decision?' she demanded.

'Oh, that'll take a little time. My firm impression was that we shall go ahead with Langmuir's scheme. With possible modifications. Some of them due to the absence of his own very marked personality. But let me say at once that you're the person responsible. You were quite right, I see it, now you've told me. Getting on to Sir James was a master stroke. He was obviously furious that he'd never been told of Hamo's request – "My great-nephew, one of the most brilliant men of our time ..." I'd never seen him before, but he's a formidable old monster. And, of course, Sir Alec crumpled up. He always does when anyone stands up to him. And now it's all in Sir James's hands. He'll put it up to the Rapson and the Ministry and so on. And with every scientist in the place having spoken up for it, I don't see what other decision they can make. No, I'm pretty sure that in a couple of months' time we shall be working on these new rice hybrids.'

She was crying now and blowing her nose and looking simply ghastly, he thought. He said in what he could hear with embarrassment was a hearty voice, 'Well, would you like to see where Hamo worked? There's a lot of his stuff in progress still ...'

But she shook her head. 'I shouldn't understand.' Then she smiled. It was unfair to land him with this. She would make a joke: 'Besides I've got to look at some houses. I've got to live somewhere grand, you know. Now I'm an heiress.'

He thought, oh, my God, a rich bitch in hippie clothes. He said, 'I'll get the commissionaire to show you the way out.' He telephoned and while they waited, he said, 'Let me make a formal apology about the meeting. But I'm sure they tried to let you know. In fact, I thing I heard something about their telephoning to you.'

'Probably. I was out all yesterday looking for houses. I can't possibly go on living at home.' Then realizing that she had obtruded the personal, she returned to her joke, 'Looking for somewhere grand takes so much time. Grand houses are so big to look over.'

At the reception-police-guard-place, another commissionaire approached her: 'Miss Grant? Sir James Langmuir left this letter for you.'

Dear Miss Grant,

I was most disappointed not to have the opportunity of meeting you this morning. Rodrigo Knight telephoned you many times, I believe, to tell you that we had to make a last-minute change of plan for our meeting.

I have to thank you for a number of things. First, for giving me some notification, before I saw the newspapers, of Hamo's death. Secondly, for advising me of this report of his which an inefficient administration at the Institute had apparently mislaid! Above all, for your stalwart part, which I heard about from roundabout sources, in helping Swami Sant Sarada to escape from an undisciplined and deluded mob.

I can't say I'm altogether sorry, apart from the inconvenience to you, that our first meeting should not have taken place at what was really a rather routine technical committee. I want greatly to hear from you about Hamo whom I believe you saw a few hours before he died. We did not see each other often, but like his father, my nephew, he was a thoroughly honourable chap and, without any doubt, a brilliant man in his own field. I only wish you could have heard the tributes paid to him by all the specialist scientists today. I am so very anxious for your impressions of the Swami Sarada – surely one of the most remarkable men of our age. He writes to me that you urged him to concern himself with the *Atlantean* occult sciences. Apparently you are not yourself an adept or even a seeker. One can only suppose that you were being used as a voice. But this in itself, added to all the rest, makes me very anxious to meet you. Why do you not telephone to Rodrigo Knight and let him arrange a quiet luncheon or dinner for the three of us?

By the way, we decided at this morning's' meeting to hold a memorial service for Hamo. There is no doubt that many scientists, and not only from the Institute, would like such a thing. For the first time my office with the somewhat absurd title of Grand Scrivener Extraordinary which I hold in a city company will be of practical use, for it gives me a chance to hold a service in that rather beautiful church Saint Thomas à Becket, Mutton Lane. I shall give the address myself. Cards will be sent, of course, to yourself and your parents. Would you let Rodrigo know of any other names? I shall see you then, and shake hands, but that will only make our luncheon or dinner the more necessary.

Alexandra spent the whole half-hour tube journey reading this letter again and again for signs. On the whole she felt it spoke against Sir James's support of Hamo's scheme, certainly it treated it wtih a monstrous lack of concern. Or, perhaps, that was merely part of the secrecy that all tycoons used for matters under discussion. After all, that Nelson Hart had ... And clearly that Sir Alec had blundered badly ... But then the condescension of the letter was so appalling. She felt sure now that he had changed the meeting time deliberately to avoid any plea from her for the real meaning of Hamo's views. All the calm that she had known since Oliver's birth, or in the months before it, was vanishing rapidly. She was filled with anger. When she got back home, she telephoned at once to Sir James's office, but she asked to speak not to Rodrigo, but to one of Sir James's business secretaries.

She said, 'Will you please tell Sir James that I'm afraid that I can't lunch or dine with him. I'm house-hunting all day, you see, and then I have a young child so I don't go out at night. But will you say that Swami Sant Sarada, he's called the Austrian Swami by the way, is *at least* three-quarters charlatan. Have you got that? *At least* three-quarters charlatan.'

If the secretary's shocked repetition of her words, or was it *surprised* repetition? was a foreshadowing of Sir James's annoyance, then she had given him a scratch that would make him think twice about snubbing her again. He must be made to know that he had someone resolute to deal with.

Roddy rang later that evening. 'Oh, dear,' he said, 'I tried and tried to let you know about the meeting. In the end I had to leave a message with Lady Needham. She seemed so sure of giving it to you.'

Alexandra thought, damn the very old. She said, 'Well never mind all that. What has Sir James decided?'

'Ally, dear, do be reasonable. First he couldn't decide just like that. No doubt he'll influence the other members of the Rapson as he wants. But he'll have to consult them. And they're very important figures in finance and industry themselves.'

'You mean they'll be concerned about whether they'll be backing something that won't give them large-scale customers in Asia. Like Hamo said.'

'I don't know what he said. We haven't all read this famous report, you know. But I can promise you that Sir James and probably the others will see things on a larger scale than immediate commercial interests.'

'Oh. Well, what did *you* think at the meeting?'

'Ally, I'm a *social* secretary. I don't go to meetings like that. I know he was furious with that Sir Alec. He called him a second-rate bureaucrat. He'd be most influenced by what the scientists said. If it looked like a scheme of real formal meaning to them ... He's much more an aesthete than you'd think. Dandies are.'

'But surely he said something about the *social* importance of what Hamo was trying to do. His concern with the hopeless.'

'I don't know about the hopeless. It isn't a word to use here. But, after all, it was Sir James who was one of the chief City figures behind all this revival of Young England Toryism – you know, making England richer and redressing the social balance by helping the hard cases. Disraeli dandyism. Although, of course, he's strictly non-political. So what you told me of Hamo's scheme made *me* immediately sure that he'd be favourable to it. I put it in that light to him and he rang Sir Alec at once and blew him up. One thing he can't stand is people who don't come into the open.'

'Oh, good,' Alexandra said; for the first time she felt a little cheered, though it worried her that Rodrigo talked in such a *stupid* way now he worked for this Sir James. 'Then he'll be pleased that I left that message for him.'

'What message?'

'He wanted to know about the Austrian Swami. He seems to believe he's some sort of genius. But I told him that he's mostly a charlatan.'

'Oh!'

'Well, you said he liked people to give their real opinions.'

'Yes, I'm sure it'll be all right. It's only that all this psychic business ...'

'And you say he's this brilliant man. Look, this scheme of Hamo's is something that's *real* and important ...'

'Oh, I know, Ally. And I feel sure that he'll come out for it. He came back from the meeting in a very good mood. Full of putting bureaucrats in their place. I'm certain it's going to be all right. Only it's a bit disconcerting when anyone starts to talk of his psychic interests. To begin with I just don't understand a word of them, and then, they *do* matter immensely to him. It's some sort of compensation, I think. But it'll be all right. Ally, when can we meet, please?'

At first she was going to say, I can't be fussing with that until we know about Hamo's report. But then she suddenly felt turned off with all this being anxious and this obsessiveness. Impossible though living at Number 8 was, Oliver had a new grandmother, a new great-grandmother, and a new great-great-grandmother, all of whom he seemed to adore as much as they loved him. She was free to leave him for whole days or even nights. She had money. She loved watching Roddy enjoy himself as he did in grand surroundings. She said: 'I want to take you out to dinner. But you choose where. I thought perhaps that place where they gave you those pancakes with caviar and whipped cream.'

She could almost see his tongue flicking out like a cat's to lick the cream from his lips as he purred his pleased acceptance back at her over the telephone. She thought, I must find a real way of *enjoying* life as well as taking it seriously. Meanwhile she would have to acrobat her path along the two wires of fun and of duty.

Church was a new experience to Alexandra. Not that this church seemed very like religion. It was so extremely smart and decorative, almost like a drawing-room of Zoe's, although the blue-painted vault with gold stars was more theatrical and new than would do in the home. But the furnishing, the pews and the carving, especially the pulpit, were 'in the best of taste'. And, truth to tell, with her new cultivation of the eye, they *did* give her pleasure. All the lines of the vaulted ceiling and the pillars and columns, and half pillars on the walls, seemed to work together with the furnishing. Probably what Zoe called 'pulling everything together'. And the tablets with their plump cherub faces blowing little puffs of air, and a recumbent figure of a man in a big wig, some armour and a bare stomach made super ornaments. She wondered if getting money would inevitably force her into 'taste' like Zoe. All the same it didn't look like religion, less in a funny way than the Swami's ghastly villa, but God, if he existed, would prefer these surroundings, she supposed.

The offering to Him was perfunctory but it made speedy way for the handsome Sir James to go up into the handsome pulpit. She *hoped* it was all what Hamo would have wanted. But she *felt* he would have wanted something more conventional, more churchy. On the other hand, he had so admired this great-uncle...

Which was more than she did. She felt a real worry about this old actorish sort of creature – his wavy grey hair, his red flushed face, his popping blue eyes, and what a cruel mouth! But the voice was nice, so easy, smooth and flowing, and, if a little drawling, that seemed only to be poking a little fun at himself ... and at the occasion! Damn him! The whole act was a great deal too charming and condescending – this recital of Hamo's scientific achievements – Glorious Wheat and Magic Rice and the modification of the Mendel–Osborne method. People shouldn't talk about what they don't understand. 'And a brilliant future before him. That sorghum crop upon which Africa depended as much as Asia upon rice.' It took her a few moments to absorb this. Then she had to force herself not to rise and shout, like those Victorian banns scenes, like Mrs Yeobright. She said aloud, 'Damn him, damn him, damn him,' so that Zoe, who knew she was in a state but couldn't understand why, took her hand and held it.

Now she forced herself to listen to him.

'Hamo Langmuir's death at the hands of a mob is for all of us here today who knew him a personal and a scientific tragedy. But it is also something else. It is a manifest representation of the instinctive hatred of the stupid, the unteachable and the weak, for the clever, the educated and the strong. In little – and I make no belittlement of Hamo as a man and as a scientist in using that expression – it represents the danger which civilization faces today.

'Hamo Langmuir was one of the strong of this world. His life was given to discoveries which would increase the number of those who are strong, by increasing the total amount of wealth at the disposal of society, by adding to the number of well-fed whose lot would naturally be cast on the side of a sane, organized, disciplined society. Science is knowledge and knowledge is order. But there are elements within society whom no amount of increased nutrition, no amount of increased social well-being, no amount of increased education can make strong, ordered, controlled and disciplined. These are the naturally unteachable, the naturally hopeless. Years of misguided sentimentalism, of capitulation to these elements, of paying of blackmail to the weak by the strong have brought us to a point where society is deeply threatened, where knowledge and science – the things for which Hamo Langmuir lived – are in real peril. The senseless death of this brilliant scientist should serve as a warning to us all, that we can take no risks, no easy sentimental indulgence in making sure that the unstable, the weak and the diseased strains in the human race as in the rest of the natural world should be eliminated.

'This was the work to which Hamo Langmuir was dedicated in agriculture. It is our job – the job of the administrators and the authorities – to apply the same dogged weeding-out of the weak strains in human society.

'For myself I believe that all our science, our organization, our wise accretion of material wealth, in short what we call civilization or culture, will not suffice to restrain the disruptive forces which misguided and often purely self-flattering sentimentalism has so nearly unleashed. To all of you met here today to remember a brave and brilliant young man – fellow scientists of Hamo Langmuir's whose work in the future will continue to add to the forces of reason and order and strength; administrators who will channel this work wisely; and the makers of wealth who will give it force and practical expression – I shall say something with which none of you will have much sympathy – but I have never, as those of you who know me will attest, judged values by committee consensus. It is my certain belief that this saving of our civilization from the weak, the exploited and the diseased cannot be accomplished by natural science alone. There is a whole further realm of spiritual science, hidden from us for centuries through our own wilful blindness, an occult science, which, harnessed and leashed as it will be, I believe, in the next decade, in the service of civilized order, will allow the great discoveries of natural science, the work of men like Hamo Langmuir, to forge ahead without any threat of such wasteful muddle as his tragic and meaningless death. Weakness means muddle. We simply cannot afford the indulgence of the hopeless in a world on the edge of discoveries both natural and psychic that will eliminate disorder.'

Later he stood at the porch so bland and charming, and perfunctory. His handshake with each departing friend and acquaintance was so firm and so very short-lasting.

She was determined not to let herself make a foolish scene.

She would ask his intentions; if they were hostile, she would rally all her weapons for war, but with a proper campaign in full self-control.

Rodrigo gave her name to Sir James with a look that she knew tried to cover alarm. Sir James said: 'How good of you. When you're so busy with house-hunting.' His smile hovered between charm and a sneer.

She said, 'Does this mean that you've decided to reject Hamo's whole plan for work on rice in the so-called hopeless areas?'

He turned his smile wholly to sneer. 'Oh, yes. I think it was a momentary aberration on his part. The sentimentalism of an overworked man. Quite right of you, though, to bring it to our attention.'

'But Hamo died because he cared about these people.'

'I very much trust not. In any case, the entire planning of the World Food Programme can hardly be overturned for the sudden brainwave of one man, however brilliant.'

'But all his colleagues support him.'

'They're naturally attracted by theoretical considerations of so-called pure science which can only be secondary in such affairs, I'm afraid.'

'So you support this Sir Alec in all his timid, cringing bungling ...'

'Oh, come, Sir Alec acted improperly, and, thanks to you, we know it. But this doesn't invalidate a programme organized over a decade.'

She restrained herself from hitting him by kicking her own ankle. She said, 'So all this order,' and she waved her arm at Wren's elegant form, 'comes down to brutal bullying of the weak, does it? Well, I can promise you you'll have your fill of the neurotic and the weak and the hopeless with your famous Swami.'

She was conscious of Zoe's protesting whisper, of Rodrigo's misery, even of someone attempting physically to edge her out of the scene. She turned to the distinguished people behind, who were forming up to shake Sir James's hand.

'All right,' she said, 'I'm not going to make a scene.'

'Now, that *is* wise,' Sir James said, 'But do let me beg you, my dear young lady, not to let yourself get obsessed with all this.

Obsession is the greatest waste of intelligence and energy. As well as of youth and beauty. And just one word of warning: you seem intent on a planned scheme of slander against Swami Sant Sarada. As a holy man, of course, he is quite outside the range of any such malice. But for myself, as his admirer, and, I hope, his disciple, I should feel forced to take legal proceedings if you continued such a very wrong course of action.'

He looked at her still without any real anger or hatred, only a smile of patronage. In the taxi going home with Zoe, her controlled rage gave way to tears.

Driving rain had kept down the number of purely curious spectators that the considerable newspaper publicity given to the opening of Sir James Langmuir's College of Occult Science at Avebury might otherwise have drawn to that strange massive circle of earthworks and those mysterious concentric circles of stones. Not that the college itself was to be built within that area of strong psychic waves. The Swami had wisely forbidden this – wisely, perhaps, because the Ministry of Works and the National Trust had alike declared their total opposition to such building, even backed by all the influence and money of Sir James.

No, the College was to cover the land at present occupied by the Museum, the rectory, the manor house, and the parish church of St Mary. All these had been built in later centuries, by Christian secular and ecclesiastical persons instinctively and positively avoiding the powerful etheric waves concentrated within the holy places. That the Atlantean adepts had, in fact, exerted strong psychic pressures to prevent any outsider building there, the Swami made clear to Sir James. Indeed the crushed skeleton of a fourteeth-century barber-surgeon showed what happened to Christian profaners of the sacred circles, until in the seventeenth and eighteenth centuries the Atlantean cosmic forces had temporarily weakened. The Swami was deeply drawn to Avebury, however, because the forces were now in the process of ritual renewal.

The truth of this assertion he made evident by the self-mockery with which he admitted that these same etheric forces had directed their current against himself, when for a short while he had played with the idea of setting up the College within the boundaries of the ceremonial sanctuary itself. If more proof were needed of the occult powers at work, the unexpected sudden collapse of the opposition of the Church Commissioners to Sir James's acquirement of St Mary's church for the purpose of demolition seemed to crown it. The negotiations had proved hardly more difficult than the purchase of the many small properties which Langmuir House now so powerfully replaced.

But, driving rain or no, the small village, set improbably and inconveniently by a main road in a right- and left-angle bend, was packed with cameramen, newspaper reporters, spectators apparently idle, motorists immensely frustrated, and police of all kinds. The heights of the earthworks were lined with members of various occult groups, in particular the Southampton Transcendental Meditators and the Ashford Atlanteans. Some few were exerting adverse waves of consciousness against a scheme which they suspected of calling forth malign powers; but most were setting their vibrations in harmony with what would be the start of a new order in which the occult Atlantean sciences would control the more haphazard and generally neophytic natural sciences, that had proved so dangerously inadequate after decades of foolish autarchy. Some groups, who had assembled within the two holy rings, were fighting the Lemurian forces, which it was now feared might seek to put pressure on the Swami in his new adherence to Atlantean wisdom. This, of course, was without the knowledge of the Swami himself, who would have been quick to point out that the older Lemurian wisdoms were inevitably superior within Lemurian realms, but since Lemurian adepts had shown themselves to have passed beyond concern even for those their proper regions, they were hardly likely to bother with the *parvenu* world of Atlantis.

There were also a number of mathematicians, astronomers, professors of engineering, retired colonels and majors of the Sappers, and astrologers who, while not necessarily accepting the spiritual claims of the Swami or even the value of the proposed new college, were interested in any research into Atlantean science, colonial and decadent though the offshoots of Avebury no doubt must prove to be.

To the motorist sightseers, lured by the highly coloured forecasts of the journalists to brave the stinging rain that swept across

the open earthworks and down into the village streets before a
strong south-west gale, and, indeed, to the journalists themselves,
the occult groups in their mackintoshes and plastic pixie hats, in
their wellingtons and their tweed capes, were something of a
disappointment. They looked like the spectators at a point-to-
point, only there were a great many more of them than was usual
at the average meeting.

What, in default of occult interest, and while the arrival of the
Swami and Sir James was impatiently awaited, *did* draw attention were the isolated individuals, a motley collection, who
walked among the crowd handing out leaflets, and crying feebly
'What Sir James won't tell you. Read all about it. What Sir James
won't tell you.'

They were suitably attired to meet the driving rain: Alexandra in a long fur coat and top boots, Lady Needham in a thick
mustard-coloured tweed twin suit, the Little Mam with a silk
scarf over her head, a short fur coat and navy-blue trousers, Zoe
in a camel-hair coat and a petunia head-square, Nelson Hart in a
sports coat, innumerable scarves and top boots over grey flannels,
Erroll in a short coat with a black fur collar and a small black fur
hat, Ned in a complete daffodil yellow old-fashioned cyclists'
outfit borrowed from his dad, and Rodrigo in a long, high-
collared, large-lapelled white patent-leather overcoat.

Each was noble to be there; Lady Needham, because of her
age, but she considered that an eye must be kept on Alexandra
otherwise Oliver would suffer from a cranky and disordered
mother; the Little Mam, because of her sciatica, but she dreaded
Alexandra getting cut off from the normal world and the possible
results of that for Oliver; Zoe, because she was tortured with the
thought of Oliver left with a 'nanny' that Alexandra had hired at
great expense, but she felt that she must sacrifice Oliver for
Alexandra wherever necessary, otherwise she would be punished
for her failure as a mother by some misfortune happening to her
grandson. In any case, all three ladies were attached to the cause
of the neglected, the forgotten and the downtrodden. Nelson
Hart was ashamed to be in such a cranky public display, but he
felt angry at the disregard of his scientific judgement and guilty
because his work at the Institute would be easier without Hamo.
Erroll was worried at being away from Kit's movie-making at

what might be a critical juncture, but he hoped that he might finally expiate his guilt over leaving Hamo in Goa; Ned truly believed that the Occult College was of far greater importance to the 'hopeless' than any scheme of rice improvement, but he could not bear to hurt Alexandra. Rodrigo bravely told himself, with little credence, that Sir James would respect him more for taking such a stand, but he hoped that this bravery might finally win Ally over.

As for Alexandra herself, she stomped about feeling angrily – but not wholly justifiably – that they were all making these sacrifices to please her and not out of any concern for Hamo's proposals. Such a sense of her own power disgusted her. And, as the rain ran down her neck and the bitter wind pierced even the folds of her warm fur coat, she began to wonder what sense there was in urging this scheme at all. After all, you should only act out of conviction and knowledge. The conviction and know-ledge that lay behind Hamo's scheme had come to *him* from *his* Asian experiences – and of these experiences she knew nothing. As her faith dwindled, she shouted more loudly, 'What Sir James won't tell you,' and pressed upon the low-spirited sightseers leaflets of extracts from Hamo's proposals, five thousand copies of which she had had printed at her own expense.

As the silver Bentley drew near to Marlborough, Sir James pressed a further Havana cigar upon his grotesque companion. He had found the Swami's brandy-drinking and cigar-smoking creditable rather than shocking. Only a sentimentalist would have wished that extraordinary psychic powers should prove incompatible with business astuteness and a taste for good living. Sir James was not a sentimentalist; and he admitted to himself a certain satisfaction that his own tastes and passions were reflected in this great man. He did not particularly care for the huge freckled bare shoulder that, as the car occasionally swayed, was pushed near to his gaze; nor would he have chosen to travel next to a mass of scabbed bare leg obtruding cross-kneed from a white cotton gown – but these were the man's stock in trade, they had some traditional Eastern licence, he overlooked them, but was annoyed that they hadn't come by the Daimler which would have given much more room between them both. What did disturb him more was a certain evasiveness in the Swami's replies. He recognized Sir James's psychic gift as genuine, it seemed; thought him a likely candidate for admission to the inner circle of adepts; had no doubt that to have an adept so highly placed in the external world of financial power would accelerate the cosmic revolution to which they were both committed; thought the proposed College a useful means for the harnessing of the cosmic forces so strongly centred in Avebury; saw in their partnership a means af reaching powers and circles that, unleashed, could alter the whole human psychic condition as completely as science was altering the physical universe or medicine the human body. All this was excellent, but, whenever it came to the actual imparting of the Names or the Words, to giving the Cryptic Knowledge as well as the Conditioning Postures and Breathing, the Swami moved off into reminiscence, in which he abounded, or general astral ethical talk which Sir James found very near to sentimental rubbish.

It was all exceedingly irritating. Then, in Marlborough's wide but ancient high street, they came into a traffic jam caused mainly by the diversions resulting from the crowds at Avebury, but partly by the driving rain. The chauffeur was new and inexpert; he braked too often and too suddenly. Rodrigo Knight (he would have to sack him) was absent from duty that morning and Sir James felt unsure of what arrangements had been made for the evening banquet for the Swami. He had drunk and eaten too well with the old man the night before. Without Rodrigo's organization, he had gone late to the sauna bath and his gymnastic exercises seemed to have followed too soon upon that relaxation. He felt irritated, sweaty and a little giddy as he had not done since the days of his first managing-directorships thirty years before. The Swami was in high spirits, giggling and showing his few black tusks, as he outlined his plans for the expenditure of the money Sir James was putting up for the College, or told sly stories of the sexual peccadilloes of other notable gurus.

Suddenly Sir James said, 'Yes, yes, that's enough of all that. Now. Some plain questions. Who are the Himalayan adepts? What powers are you using to counteract their influence? You say that you are harnessing benevolent, Atlantean, psychic impulses. What form of words do you use to condition your mind to reach the plane on which they function? I shall need to know all this before we can hope to use the Atlantean cosmic sciences. We must make such powers our servants not our masters.'

The Swami stopped in his tracks, as he was outlining the ceremonial year as he had seen it in the lives of the cosmic students. He was aghast. He had thought Sir James a somewhat autocratic man, but he had not supposed him a megalomaniac. His mind went back to his youth, to his own great master, Stefan Georg, to the days long before he had learnt of the Eastern or occult wisdoms, when he tramped with other *Wandervögeln* youth from lovely Salzburg up into the Schwarzwälder, reciting the Master's poems. Stefan Georg, too, had taken the Nazis to be harmless followers, useful because of their power in the material world, and then, when they monstrously tried to use him, the old man, the great Master, had withdrawn, out of the Germany he so loved, into the Swiss Alps. So, if this Sir James really was a brutal, insane materialist, the Swami accepted that he too would have to withdraw from all the delightful prospects for his old age of an honoured and comfortable College, where the powers that used him would find their expression among the ancient and sacred places and stones of the Old Wisdom. He could not compromise. He could doubt at times how much he knew, but he always believed that he had these powers in trust.

He said, 'We do not *use* the powers, they use us.'

Sir James knew a sudden access of fury at being so addressed, at having his time wasted. A sense of imperative need for immediate control of this secret power that sat so ridiculously beside him made the blood pound in his ears. He employed the peremptory tone he always adopted with recalcitrant subordinates, but he used it aware that, for once, he had no idea of its effect.

He said, "You will give me the unspoken names and words or you don't get a penny for this College.'

The Swami laughed at him. 'To begin with, my poor Sir James, these names can't be communicated in speech, only telepathically, and you are not endowed to receive them. Secondly, I do as I am instructed. Thirdly, there is much that I do not know. Fourthly, if we are able to work together, it will take many months of trial and error and endurance before I can judge whether you are a worthy vessel or not.'

Once again, he laughed in Sir James's face so that some spittle settled on Sir James's immaculate suit. Sir James took out a handkerchief and very deliberately wiped it away. But his hand shook violently and he had a premonition of failure.

'I order you to tell me,' he said.

The Swami's mocking laugh was wholly genuine. Sir James could not believe his ears.

'Do you understand? I am giving you an *order*.'

At that moment the car came to the end of the high street and the traffic jam. It shot forward with a jolt. Sir James had a sudden, last, calming vision of the elegant formal eighteenth-century college building, then he felt a searing pain in his left arm, and a tearing of his chest, he made a choking sound, and his head fell forward. The chauffeur, with a clear road before him, put on speed. The Swami felt a little disturbed at what had happened, but not surprised; after all, the powers that acted through him were very strong. He removed his thoughts from Sir James. And as West Kennet Long Barrow's great tumulic height came into view he felt forces, warm and powerful, filling him with pride at having proved stronger than this foolish man. But then how could it be otherwise in this countryside where the old wisdoms of which he was an adept had their sway?

As the silver Bentley, waved on by impressed policemen, came to a halt before the Avebury circles, Alexandra looked round for her little group and realized that Rodrigo was no longer there. But there was no time to examine her feelings at the discovery. She led them all – a feeble, helpless little group – in a feeble, helpless little cry, 'Read what Sir James won't tell you. Read the truth.' But Sir James, of course, told them nothing, since he was dead. The Swami regretted that his power had been so strong at so inopportune a moment, but he assumed a look of spiritual playfulness to meet the battery of cameramen.

'To my great-nephew, Hamo Langmuir and in the event of his demise to his heir or heirs.' Sir James had been a lonely man and, save for his megalomania, a conventionally pious one. So Alexandra passed from being a rich young woman to becoming a millionairess. *Paris-Match* did a piece on her; as did *Dimanche-Soir, Die Stern* and *Oggi*. David Frost thought of making a programme round her. Had she gone to New York (but she did not) her reputation as a very rich hippie might have made her the butt of William Buckley Junior's synthetic aristocratic scorn. More devastatingly to herself, she was inundated with appeals and threats from charity, from the helpless, the hopeless, the insane and the socially desperate. These, with the help of Rodrigo (continuing, despite his defection, on the same salary as that paid by Sir James), she sorted out. Mainly – and it was hard to keep to it in the face of all the desperation that poured in upon her – she fended off all these claims until she had decided more fully what her life and her pleasures and her services should be. In this she received, against every pressure, the loyal and constant support of Rodrigo. 'Ally's not to be fussed,' he said one hundred or more times a day. Ned agreed and would have liked to be there saying it, but the whole of this very rich thing was so alarming and unnatural to him that one day, quite suddenly, he disappeared, leaving a note to say that he had returned home north.

Among the pressures upon Alexandra's purse were a few more intimate than others, to which she had to give longer personal consideration. Not much to Leslie's suggestion that she should invest in a company to be formed under his direction, that would provide holidays at super-super prices in various châteaux, palaces, yachts and islands of super-super luxury and isolation. 'I shouldn't think it's an idea that would appeal to you,' Leslie wrote, 'but it appeals *enormously* to me and I am quite certain we'd get fifty per cent or more back on your outlay. But I don't expect you'll be forthcoming.' He was right. She wasn't.

More difficult was the scheme proposed by Perry and Erroll – a combination so completely unexpected that this in itself made it hard for her to reason about it. It seemed that Kit Coates, growing ever more swollen-headed and arbitrary, had come near to ruining Perry's script and was far from appreciating fully Erroll's camera potentiality. What they thought would appeal to Alexandra was the prospect of embarking upon a quite new venture, the forming of a film company, with Erroll as head cameraman, and Perry as script writer, and a very brilliant, *modest*, sympathetic man, whom she would like when she met him, as director, to make – and here was the point – a film, completely new in form, novel-documentary, documentary-fiction, of what Erroll called 'an ordinary chap's waking up to how things really are', of what Perry liked to think might be named, 'the things the sahibs didn't show them', and of what this brilliant, modest, as yet unnamed man said could be a meta-movie; in short, the essence of the life of the Asian 'hopeless', given documentary veracity and cinematic significant form. It would be, they suggested, the most telling way in which – given that they could not, even Alexandra, for all her inherited money, could not, control the programme of the World Food Programme – they could serve Hamo's wonderful vision. At first Alexandra favoured it as some revenge on Kit Coates for scrapping Hamo's television appeal for the Asian hopeless as a dead duck. Then she thought that she could easily quench her disgust by sending them a large cheque and forgetting about it. But as she dwelt upon it, she became more angry. At last she replied that, one, she knew nothing of cinema, two, Hamo's vision was his own and neither hers nor theirs, three, she thought that since Perry had devoted his life (and the lives of others) to being a novelist, he should write another novel, four, if Erroll was a talented cameraman, as she was sure he was, he should stop thinking of himself as an ordinary chap which was a most uncreditable thing to be, five, she had no idea what a meta-movie might be, but if it had anything to do with meta-novels then she didn't wish to have anything to do with it.

Lazing by the poolside of Leslie's chief Corfu hotel, Perry and Erroll, when they received her reply, both called her a bitch. Susan Nebble thought she sounded worse than that, she sounded a prig. But Leslie, though he made little of it, said, 'Good for Ally.' And poor ageing Martin, who was sent each day to the market by Leslie to do the hotel haggling, was delighted when the news eventually trickled down to him.

But what positively was Alexandra to do? Some time she spent in finding a nurse for Oliver and a house for them both. She never found the first, or, at any rate, one who satisfied her for more than a week or two; but, perhaps, this was, in great degree, because three generations of women were always lined up to take on the office, and then she was determined to spend at least three hours a day with her son herself. But the second she did acquire. A large eighteenth-century house with a garden in Highgate village. The furnishing took many months, because, although Zoe was primarily responsible, Lady Needham often interfered, and Little Mam had so many practical suggestions to make; and then, every four days or so, Alexandra would emerge from her ocean of legal documents, balance sheets and business interviews, see what was happening and countermand the whole thing. It was a blazing summer, however, and the eighteenth-century house had a very satisfactory sun roof put in by an actress in the thirties. Here Alexandra would lie naked and oiled for the few hours a day that business allowed her, usually with Oliver, some-times with Rodrigo, but always practising that relaxation of mind and body which the pace and complexity of modern busi-ness necessitate.

For she had found what, for the next few years at any rate, she wished to do. It happened by chance, when the question of the first leases for offices at Langmuir House was put before her. It had never occurred to her that the whole place was not already leased out, even occupied. But, in fact, the office leases were still no more than discussions, verbal promises. From that moment, she had a continuously arduous life : first, to see that the building never should be occupied; second, to see that it should be pulled down; lastly, but the prospect seemed very distant, to build in its place a number of apartment blocks and houses of original modern design and lease them, at however great a loss, to those whose lives and work would normally bring them to that area. And, after that, well, after that, there was no end to the blocks she would seek to acquire, the pleasant dwellings she would seek to create or preserve.

There *would*, of course, be an end, as the innumerable lawyers, stockbrokers, housing officials, building commissioners, G.L.C. Councillors, hardheaded but friendly men, furious associates of Sir Judas's, aspiring young architects, and Roddy, all kept telling her. First, and this soon became apparent, the legal proceedings would outrun all Jarndyce – to put up was hard enough, to pull down what had just been put up was well-nigh impossible. Time was against her. And then the expense – legal, especially, for her many opponents were prepared to take her through every court

– would be formidable. To solve the first difficulty she began by applying herself to all the legal and financial questions involved, but weeks spent poring over books and documents made her realize that she would only qualify herself for the role of Miss Flite, for the overplayed stock English repertory part of the madwoman at law. She began, instead, to sort out the lawyers and the financial advisers that she could trust. She made some bad mistakes, but, in the end, she felt that she had a good team. They, because of their honesty, then urged upon her endlessly point two – when she had acquired for preservation a terrace or a side of a square, or when, say, she had bought five multiple blocks and pulled them down and replaced them by houses and flats at subsidised rents, even old Sir Judas's great fortune would be used up. But London, she said, would be a little nearer to the unique city it could be; and, as for herself, she had no intention of being poor, or that Oliver should be, she had a wealthy mother, she said, and a grandmother with considerable savings, and a great-grandmother with some capital, all of whom when they died would leave her their money. And, in any case, she was young and quite clever and could work.

'And who are going to *live* in your flats and houses?' Rodrigo asked, as they rested after love-making on the roof one afternoon. Well, she was clear who would not.

'And, Roddy, after all, I *have* made it clear to others too. It wasn't easy, you know, to have those squatters turned out of Langmuir House by the police. You wouldn't have liked being called a bloody bitch in five sorts of Marxist jargon. And the police and the organizers were so bloody to the squatters too. And I refused Ned ... Ned of all people when he wanted to move his new mime group in there. Yes, even after he looked like a hurt faithful dog and admitted that he'd intended to take over for good. But I *did* refuse.'

'Who *are* going to live in your houses then?' Rodrigo asked impatiently, 'Unmarried mothers?'

'Bad taste isn't *always* funny. The people who pay for them.'

'But profitable rents will be colossal.'

'Then I shan't charge profitable rents. I shall charge what would have been profitable twelve years ago. And I shan't raise them in the future.'

'You mean,' said Roddy loftily, 'houses for ordinary people.'

'Don't insult my tenants to be,' she said, 'There'll be all kinds of people I suppose. The people who need or want to live in them. I shan't know them, so I can't tell you what kinds. But, at least, I shan't stand away from them and call them ordinary. And they won't be cadgers either. I've seen enough of that on beaches, cadging and violence. But don't you see, Roddy, it's all I can do to fight the Sir Judases, the bullies. Just to use their weapons, their market prices against them and all the other wicked rubbish. I haven't any creative gifts like Hamo, and I don't *want* to create Utopias or chaos, and I can't grasp the helpless of Asia, that's beyond me. But this is where I do have power and I'm going to use it.'

'In private patronage. And you've always contradicted when I said how like your mother you are.'

'No. *Not* private patronage. Private subsidy. Slowly, but I hope effectively, by such little power as I've got, to betray the whole filthy system from inside, to erode it as much as I can.'

'Like Rahab betraying Jericho.'

'You know I don't know the Bible things. Who to, anyway?'

'The children of Israel.'

'Well, surely theirs is always the right side.'

'They thought so.'

'Well, then ...'

'Millionairess! It's such an old gag. James and Shaw and almost everybody else have used it.'

'Yes, I'm quite aware, Roddy, that I'm a fictive device. But I intend to make something real of the enormity.'

'I believe,' said Rodrigo, starting to lick the beads of sweat from the back of her neck, 'that I think your side's right. Only I'm too cowardly for such an endless and continual fight. Look how I deserted you at Avebury.'

'Oh, *that*! You had your job to think of. It was silly and selfish of me to have involved you.'

'But I've liked being involved since. Only it would be much better for us if we were married. We could really plan. And for Oliver.'

'Would it?'

'You think I want to keep my job. To have this soft life. I do, of course. But I *don't* want to trade on you.'

'You don't. You never have. It's quite the other way. If it hadn't been for your organizing in these last months ... But it's got to stop, Roddy. You must start to read for the law like that partner of Sir Judas suggested. Your mother's right. Working with me is gradually alienating all those city men who'd taken to you when you worked for the old bully. Who knows, when you're a barrister you may represent me against some monster corporation that's after the same hideous property block as I'm after? But I shouldn't think so. I think you'll become an M.P. and practise your Tory Democracy. You will set out to give opportunity to able and aggressive young men to become so rich that they can afford to spare something for the hopeless. But I warn you, I shall be fighting you, trying to undo the accretion of great wealth by the bullies, looking after the interests of those who haven't yet fallen upon hopeless days.'

He rolled on top of her, kissing her neck, her cheeks, putting his tongue in her ears, kissing her breasts, and then, excited by her passivity, biting, until, when he had finished and rolled back on his own pad, her right shoulder and ear were bleeding. She lay smiling, staring up at Highgate's hottest sky.

'You see,' he said, 'you like bullies, really.'

She sat up and stared at him. 'No,' she said, 'No, I don't. I know now.'

It was clear she meant both the bites and all else that Rodrigo had to propose.

He took it all as a joke. But it wasn't. He accepted her support while he ate his dinners at Inner Temple. And when again he begged to offer marriage in return, she again refused. What sort of a wife for a leading young P.P.S. would a conventional subverter like her make? He would do better with a recognized bohemian, a jet-set hippie. And it was true, as she became more absorbed in her schemes, more given to taking Zoe and Oliver on holidays round England to see good low-cost housing projects advised by the architectural critic, Prothero Blair, who'd been at school with Roddy; to Denmark, because she wanted to look at the terrace houses of Utzon and Jacobsen, and on to Stockholm to see the Gröndal estate; to Israel, because she hoped to meet

Moshe Safdie; best of all to Italy, where the Olivetti housing was almost an excuse; more ordered in her life under the discipline of the extremely expensive, highly recommended man and wife who ran the house for her, so her figure filled out and her clothes became more costly but less fantastic. Hamo would never have seen in her now the ragged match-selling boy he longed to chum up with. She was every bit the young unmarried matron.

On the evening of the day that the demolition of Langmuir House began, she took the three generations out. They saw a revival of Shaw's *Candida* which touched each of them a little too closely in different ways. But they took the edge off it by a quiet supper at the Savoy Grill. When they got back to Highgate the telephone was ringing. The three older ladies trooped automatically into the big room where Oliver lay asleep. There later, Alexandra joined them.

'It was Ned. He's going to the ashram at Pondicherry. He wanted me to go too. It *was* a temptation. To give up all the money, I mean, for a bit. To try to make myself believe in his mimes. That's how he's going to support himself there. By teaching mime. People in ashrams all want that. And he thinks The Mother may have something for him.'

Zoe laughed. Alexandra turned on her fiercely.

'And so she may have. Just because one Swami was a fraud, and we don't *know* that *he* was, doesn't mean *this,* even pulling down disgusting buildings and putting up good ones, is all there is. I'm sorry,' she added, touching Zoe's arm, 'Anyway, you'll be pleased. I've said I wouldn't go. I can't be everywhere at once.'

'I should hope not indeed with this young man to think of,' Lady Needham said, pointing to Oliver who was sleeping happily with his thumb in his mouth.

'Yes,' the Little Mam chimed in, 'there's where the future of this wretched world lies.'

'I know,' Zoe said meditatively, 'that people don't fuss any longer about thumb-sucking, but it *does* worry me. Psychologically more than anything else. One has to think so far into the future with children.'

Alexandra banged her hand violently on the low bed rail, but Oliver slept too well to be woken.

'Stop it,' she cried, 'all of you! We've had enough of Forster's harvest predictions. Things may have turned sour for all of us, but we must not heap it all on *him*. He needs a father,' she added in a casual tone as though she were making a shopping list. 'If one could only find one that wasn't on the side of either the bullies or the scroungers. Come on, let me give you all a drink before you go home.'

Each of the older ladies looked, in her own way, sad. But they didn't glance at each other. They loved Alexandra, and more still Oliver, too much, to be in conspiracy.

Alexandra led the way out of Oliver's room like a hostess leading the women out at a dinner party. Or, she suddenly thought to herself, Mrs Bennet leading in Jane and Lizzie and her other daughters to the ballroom. These silly, unfair, self-mocking, bookish thoughts that rushed into one's head! She was not a selfish, bossy, foolish woman like Mrs Bennet! Damn English Literature! Damn the past and the future! I have enough to do making something of the present. But neither the past nor the future were escapable. She saw it clearly. 'Abraca-dabra!' she said aloud, so that the older women *did*, at last, exchange worried glances. But she knew that no magic spells could solve her problems.

More about Penguins and Pelicans

V. S. Naipaul in Penguins

The Mimic Men

Winner of the W. H. Smith Book Award for 1968

'We pretended to be real, to be learning, to be preparing ourselves for life, we mimic men of the New World, one unknown corner of it, with all its reminders of the corruption that came so quickly to the new.'

Just forty, Ralph Singh – a disgraced colonial minister exiled from the Caribbean island of his birth – writes his biography in a genteel hotel in a run-down London suburb.

As he writes, he finds that he was born to disorder : even as a boy 'sunk in the taint of fantasy' . . . a fantasy which Singh acts out in real life : as precocious schoolboy, randy London student and property speculator.

Supremely confident, Singh turns to politics – and finds himself caught up in the upheaval of empire, in the turmoil of too-large events which move too fast . . .

And

The Suffrage of Elvira

The Mystic Masseur

A Flag on the Island (*Short Stories*)

Mr Stone and the Knights Companion

A House for Mr Biswas

Non-fiction

An Area of Darkness

The Loss of El Dorado

Not for sale in the U.S.A.

John Updike in Penguins

Couples

Ten couples live in Tarbox, an out-of-the-way New England town. Well-to-do, 35-ish, they form an exclusive, competitive group. Ski-ing, entertaining, playing with word-games . . . and sex. Discreetly, tentatively changing partners, they conduct their rituals under the baleful eye of their self-appointed ringmaster, Freddy Thorne.

But when Piet Hanema and Foxy Whitman have an affair, they reject expediency and caution. For once, the other unshockable couples are deeply shocked . . . and Tarbox claims its first sacrificial victims.

John Updike's searching, poetic treatment of the couples' involvements and aberrations serves to expose the life of a community with astonishing particularity. In every sense, he gives us the anatomy of a generation.

Also available

Bech : A Book

Rabbit, Run

Rabbit Redux

Museums and Women and Other Stories

Pigeon Feathers and Other Stories

Seventy Poems

Not for sale in the U.S.A. or Canada

Also by Angus Wilson

Hemlock and After

Angus Wilson's first novel was the product of a master and placed him directly at the centre of the literary scene. His exact handling of the intimate and conflictive personality lurking behind the public image of a famous novelist cuts sharply into the hypocrisies of middle-class society.

   As John Betjeman wrote: 'He is mercilessly accurate and never dull.'

Not for sale in the U.S.A. or Canada

Anglo-Saxon Attitudes

In a time of often slipshod and ephemeral writing, Angus Wilson maintains a standard of craftsmanship worthy of the Victorian novelists. *Anglo-Saxon Attitudes* raises profound questions of moral and intellectual honesty in a witty, readable story of archaeological faking. The moral seriousness, as V. S. Pritchett noted, of this brilliant and ambitious novel, 'is matched by the comic explosions of our tradition'.

Not for sale in the U.S.A.

Also by Angus Wilson

The Middle Age of Mrs Eliot

Meg Eliot's life as the wife of a successful barrister is as
poised as the fine ceramics collection in her Westminster
home – a round of charity committees and cocktail parties,
all managed with artistry and adroit command. But then
a cruel and seemingly senseless accident destroys this easy
existence . . . and Meg discovers that she knows little of
herself and her friends, and even less about the art of living.

'What makes this novel tower above the fiction of a decade
is the full-length presentation of Mrs Eliot herself . . .
She may be one of fiction's great female creatures, produced,
like Emma Bovary, by a man' – *Daily Telegraph*

And
No Laughing Matter

Not for sale in the U.S.A.